THE OLD WOMAN OF THE SEA

THE OLD WOMAN OF THE SEA

A NOVEL

BY
GAVIN BANTOCK

First Servant Books

First Servant Books

To the memory of

MARGARET MORE BANTOCK

(1904 - 1966)

ACKNOWLEDGEMENTS

The oil painting *House by the Sea* used on the cover was painted by Edward Steel Harper (1878-1951), the author's godfather.

The pastel *Mermaids* used on the back cover is the work of Myrrha Bantock (1906-1995), the author's aunt.

The inset illustration on the back cover is compiled from drawings by Anton Bantock (1933–2015), the author's elder brother.

The poem *Crying Distance* appears in the author's collection *Dragons* (Anvil Press Poetry, 1979, now Carcanet). The author is grateful to Peter Jay of Anvil for allowing him to quote the poem in this novel, and also other material from the author's Anvil collection *A New Thing Breathing* (1969).

The author is grateful to John Wheway for material written by him included in this work.

Special thanks to Masashi Miyahara of Machinami Tsushinsha for publishing the first edition of this work.

AUTHOR'S NOTE

This novel was first written in the summer of 1975 in Japan and was revised and edited thirty-six years later.

CONTENTS

THE OLD WOMAN OF THE SEA

The waves were pounding on the gloomy shore,
Thrashing each mighty crest down with a roar.
The sky was dark, and low it swept,
As from the sea there slowly stepped
A woman, aged and bent,
Whose life was almost spent.
Her flesh and bones all shrunk and sunken in,
She grew upon her back a grisly fin.
Her face half hidden in her tangled hair,
Once glinting eyes could only gape and stare.
Her slimy garment, green and dripping wet,
Hung limply like a festering fishing net.
Then suddenly she shrieked; she screamed and swore,
And stumbled far along the moaning shore.
Thus in the distant mist she disappeared,
Her wasted shape dissolving – twisted, weird;
And she was gone upon her age-long trail,
Leaving a gleaming pathway like a snail.
The sky swept lower and a storm burst out,
Insanely coiling in a water spout;
A streak of lightning flashed out bright,
Its flickering glitter cleaving the murky light.
But still that frail Old Woman of the Sea
Wandered in the distance to eternity.

Poem written by Bruce Dinwiddy at the age of 15,
and published in his school magazine.

PRELUDE

THE MAN AND THE GIRL stood by the edge of the sea. He was in his sixties, she in her middle teens. Both were bareheaded. They stood in the coarse green-yellow marram grass near the top of a sand dune. They faced inland, their backs to the prevailing south-west wind. The wind blew their hair forwards – his fine and grey, hers long and brown like polished antique wood. They stood for several minutes, neither speaking.

With slow and fumbling movements, the father took a dark metal canister from the shabby green zip-bag he was holding. He put the bag on the ground, and holding the canister away from his body, carefully unscrewed the lid. With the same deliberate movements, he tilted the canister. Fine grey ash swept away in the wind, and disappeared into the low undulations of the dunes. He handed the canister to his daughter; she too tilted it, further this time, and another cloud of ashes flew away from them like smoke, disappearing almost instantaneously. The father spoke a few words to the girl; then, rather awkwardly, they both held the canister between them and emptied it completely. The small cloud disintegrated not far from their feet.

Taking his time, the man put the lid back on the canister, which he replaced in the bag; he carefully zipped it up again. The girl's face was lowered; the man put his arm gently round her shoulder. Together they walked inland.

Like a blind deaf-mute trying to master language, the sea moaned endlessly behind them.

2

1. CAMBRIAN COAST EXPRESS

BRUCE DINWIDDY felt like a child. The train was coming. Four consecutive events had told him there were only a few more minutes to wait. A bell had clanked huskily twice somewhere inside the booking office. The level-crossing gates about a hundred yards up the line had been closed to traffic, clearing the line. Bruce saw the enormously fat woman in charge of the gates heaving her weight against the solid white-painted frames, then standing back and letting the gates swing and lock home of their own accord. Then the solitary signal further up the track had suddenly lowered its stocky arm; and lastly, the short, white-haired station master had appeared on the platform scratching his head; he was not in uniform. Bruce knew this sequence almost by heart. It was one the enduring memories of his childhood, and was always associated with the holidays. His mother and himself, with one or two of his brothers or sister, drove over from their home in the Midlands to get the house ready, and on the second or third day they went to meet their father at the station. He never travelled by car if he could help it; he preferred the steady comfort of a railway carriage, lunch in the restaurant car, and time to write letters, read the Daily Telegraph, or sleep – without having to worry about the possibility of an accident. Or maybe he simply did not trust anyone enough to let them drive a car in which he was a passenger; he certainly did not trust any of his children. Bruce was now twenty-three, but he still felt the same excitement, the same tense filling of the heart, although he knew, his mother now three years dead, that those long family holidays belonged irredeemably to the past, and for the first time in his life he sensed the inklings of growing old.

Not far beyond the signal, the line curved and disappeared behind a row of pine trees. Smoke rose from behind these, and Bruce remembered how this had always made him think a dragon would suddenly appear, bronze green and shining, rushing low along the ground. A childish idea, but even now, he thought, as the train came into view, the analogy was remarkably apt – the steam, the cinders falling from the ash-box underneath the engine, the noise of the wheels, rails and brakes. As the locomotive passed the signal box at the end of the platform, the driver leaned out and rapidly and expertly exchanged tokens – large steel flask-shaped hoops, weighted and joined with heavy bolts at their narrow ends – with the signalman, to ensure that there would be no head-on collisions further along the single track. The train shrieked slowly to a standstill and Bruce saw the name proudly printed on boards on the side of each of the coaches – CAMBRIAN COAST EXPRESS.

The Cambrian Coast Express, a splendid fifteen-coach assemblage, one of the finer relics of the long-defunct Great Western Railways, had pulled out of London Paddington at ten-thirty that same morning. During the English part of its journey, that is, passing through Birmingham, Wolverhampton and Shrewsbury, it indeed lived up to the last word in its title, and made very few stops. Reaching the border and passing into Wales, however, it changed its personality, as a carp becomes a dragon on attaining the higher reaches of a mountain river: it ceased to be an express and became entirely Cambrian. In this transformation, it was assisted by the scenery. A famous train is not merely itself; part of it is also the countryside through which it passes. The unrelieved flat of the Midlands, notwithstanding the freak Wrekin near Shrewsbury, gave way to wooded foothills, to hills, and finally to bare mountains. The locomotive took on the nature of a straining animal. Bruce's mother had given it even human qualities. As it struggled up into the Welsh mountains, she said, it seemed to be muttering 'I think I can, I think I can.' At times, it moved so slowly that it was almost possible to lean out of a carriage window and pick flowers from the embankments. The number of stops increased; the names, too, enhanced the Cambrian image. Admittedly, several of these, like Welshpool or Newtown, sounded disappointingly English and contributed nothing; but one felt unmistakably in a foreign country when names, virtually unpronounceable, like Caersws, Llanbrynmair and Machynlleth, appeared on the platform signboards. Somewhere where there were trees and a rushing river the train reached the top of its climb, and picking up speed seemed almost to canter down winding narrow valleys, happily chattering over and over again (so Bruce's mother said) 'I knew I could do it, I knew I could do it.' In mid-afternoon, the train reached a remote station called Dovey Junction. Here it was divided into two, each part having six coaches, the restaurant car and two coaches having been left behind, intentionally of course, at Shrewsbury. It was from Dovey Junction that the train assumed the middle role of its title: it came in sight of the sea. It wound along the northern shore of the Dovey estuary, and travelling west, tried to race its other half taking the southern shore to Aberystwyth, and finally, at Aberdovey, turned north, with the open sea – Cardigan Bay – on its left. Some four or five hours later, hugging the coast all the while in a rugged half-circle leftwards, it arrived at the terminus Pwllheli on the inner side of the Lleyn peninsula – the northern 'arm' of Wales – across the bay. Before that, however, at approximately five-thirty, it crossed another estuary, over the bridge at Barmouth, which offered the most-photographed panorama in the British Isles – the mountains, dominated by the hard-edged dome of Cader Idris, closing together inland towards Dolgelly. At precisely five minutes past six – if it were running on time, and it normally was – the train arrived at one of the last stops before it made its more pronounced left turn round the bay, the bay which in this north-west corner bore the name of Tremadog. It was on the platform of this station – named Harlieg – that Bruce Dinwiddy was now standing.

The train was almost empty. In recent years the roads in Wales had been vastly improved. Many of the narrow, walled and unmetalled lanes had been widened and tarmacked. More and more cars streamed into the mountainous country, and huge caravans caused mile-long hold-ups. Tourists from the Midlands preferred this 'freedom' because they could savour the scenery to their hearts' content and stop whenever they wished for roadside picnics. The trains were running at a loss. Indeed, the Beeching axe had already hovered over the Cambrian line, but local pressure had won a temporary reprieve. Furthermore, it was now mid-September; the holiday season was virtually over. The shopkeepers of Harlieg, dependent on the summer tourist trade for continued solvency, were busy counting up their takings and were getting ready to put their feet up for the long winter months. The Midland families, the screaming children with buckets and spades, had all gone home. Now the only visitors were the elderly retired, staying for the quiet, for long afternoons of golf, or merely to gaze with vacant eyes at the unparallelled view to the north of the mountains of Snowdonia. It was now more than ever that trains like the Cambrian Coast Express seemed almost senile; even the steam locomotives would soon disappear in favour of diesels. Such trains, thought Bruce, belonged to a bygone age. There was something melancholy about the empty carriages; their luxurious fittings had seen better days, and a better style of passenger had passed this way. He did not mean to be snobbish in thinking like this, but coming as he did from what had once been known as the upper middle class, Bruce could not avoid such thoughts. Actually, unknown to him or anyone else prominent in this story, one of the passengers on this particular day was Bertrand Russell, venerable and pipe-smoking under his halo of white hair in a first-class compartment at the front of the train, travelling home to his mansion in Penrhyndeudraeth some five or six miles further down the line. In view of the absence of crowds, therefore, it was no problem at all for Bruce to pick out from the half-dozen passengers who alighted his friend Stephen Pewit.

*

Stephen Pewit looked about him irritably. He had not eaten since eight o'clock that morning. His mother had thrust a plate of fried bread and thick grey bacon before him, complaining in her near-hysterical voice that he was going away again, that he never spent enough time at home, that he didn't care about his mother who slaved for him day after day, that this, that and the other. His father, accustomed to the morning tirade, sat fingering through the Daily Mirror. Stephen rarely spoke to his father, a habit which his father was quite content to echo, by observing a heavy silence in the presence of his son, their only child. Heavy rain in Birmingham and the sullen aspect of almost everyone he encountered had done little to raise Stephen's spirits. He had had an argument with the bus conductor, who refused to change the pound note he had proffered. Prolonging the argument as long as possible with a certain degree of vicious enjoyment, he had managed to stay on the bus until one stop before his destination; then he was firmly put off. He had had a free ride at least, he felt with some satisfaction. He walked the rest of the way to Snow Hill station.

He had bought a single ticket to Harlieg, complaining to the booking clerk of the high cost – four pounds, seventeen – and boarded the train in growing depression. He felt unmitigated hatred for everyone. He tried to find an empty compartment, for the train was fairly crowded during the first half of its journey, but the best he could manage was a non-smoker occupied by a middle-aged couple who argued with quite passionate bursts punctuated by long periods of brooding silence about whether they should change at Wolverhampton or Wellington – all the way to Shrewsbury. Stephen sat opposite them, staring at them with undisguised animosity. By the time they were getting ready to leave the train, his silent attack had begun to take effect: the couple relapsed into an uneasy truce, their eyes reflecting doubt and anxiety as they glanced at Stephen and then at one another. Stephen felt sardonic pleasure at the thought of having driven them from his compartment. He normally enjoyed train journeys, as rare and novel events, but today he was past caring about the freshness of the scenery which gradually took place of the sooty rows of terrace houses with their tiny box-like back gardens and the huge grey anonymous warehouses and derelict factories which spread as far as the eye could see across the rain-soaked landscape of the Black Country. He had never been to Wales before; and even though, as the train rushed down out of the rain shadow towards Aberdovey, sunshine broke out over everything, he still felt no lifting out of the gloom that was, he realized, always with him nowadays. He made no attempt to open any of the books he had brought with him, or to look out of the window: he merely sat, analyzing the pattern of the upholstery, wondering why industrial designers had so little imagination. As it was, he almost missed Harlieg station. Only the voice of the station master, who belonged to the local choir, saved him from travelling perhaps to the end of the line. The voice was more than a mere announcement: it was almost a song of its own, a war song, a battle cry, belonging to some past age of warriors crying across rocky valleys from mountain to mountain and echoing from the screes.

'Harlieg!'

2. HARLIEG

STEPHEN STOOD ON THE PLATFORM feeling he had just woken up from a kind of half-sleep. He felt acutely uncomfortable. His clothes were still damp, not so much from their contact with the rain in the morning, as from a small steam leak in the heating system of the compartment, which, although switched off, persisted in efforts usually reserved for winter. Stephen's stiff beige military-style raincoat acted as an insulator and intensified the clammy warmth of his body; his grey pork-pie hat was heavy with moisture: the entire crown of his head throbbed and ached. In his left hand he held a large paper carrier, in his right a typewriter case.

Bruce looked at him as if he were seeing him for the first time as a stranger might. He saw a short, squat young man who gave the impression of being middle-aged: flat-footed, with something frog-like about him. He had prominent, yellowish eyes, a flat back to his head, and a thick, short neck seemingly unable to turn the head to either side. All this, with the hint of a paunch and large buttocks, suggested a man half way to becoming a Yahoo, an image enhanced by his large, rather wet red-lipped mouth, and nose like a big toe spotted with conspicuous black pores. His complexion was coarse and almost colourless. Like a crater on the surface of the moon was a large chicken-pox scar below his right eye. Bruce's friend: Stephen Pewit, from Birmingham.

By contrast, Bruce was almost spindly. His hair was fine, light brown and rather long; Stephen's was dark, thick and somewhat wild, swept back, deliberately, Bruce knew, like Beethoven, but rather short at the back. Bruce's eyes were grey-green or blue-green, he was never quite sure, and had something elfin about them. His nose was long enough to be thought elegant but slightly turned up at the tip, his mouth not too generous in the lips; his general facial features were not quite regular; his chin might be thought a trifle weak. There was something adolescent, unformed, slight, about the whole of his appearance. He too was a little flat-footed.

Bruce approached Stephen, smiling, almost shyly, with delight. They shook hands. It was always the same – a few short formal shakes which seemed entirely unnatural to both of them; yet they still did it. They did not speak; this also was a custom: they both despised small talk, Stephen because he hardly knew how to make it, Bruce because he felt times like this should be pregnant with significance. Only a grand remark, some deeply philosophical never-to-be-forgotten statement, would suffice. The result was usually highly stilted conversation, until the strangeness of meeting again had worn off.

Taking Stephen's typewriter with his left hand, Bruce pointed upwards beyond the other side of the station. His words, however, were hardly auspicious.
'That's the castle.'

Harlieg was dominated by three what seemed in those surroundings immense buildings – the castle, the College and the Royal Dragon Hotel. The castle stood on a rounded shoulder of rock growing out from the long mountainous edge of Wales. It was difficult to imagine what else could have been there except a castle: the situation was ideal, the outlook commanding the whole of Tremadog Bay, the construction somehow inevitable. The solid grey walls and rounded towers now seemed part of the natural scenery. Bruce had never been able to think of the castle as a man-made structure, nor could he believe it was a natural phenomenon: to him it seemed actually human, almost a real living person, of remarkable age, not unfriendly, sitting there for centuries on end, gazing out to sea. They looked up at it, two or three hundred feet above them. Behind them, the train, blowing its breathy whistle once, moved slowly out of the station; and as the sounds of the grunting engine and wheels diminished, two other sounds came to their ears: to the left of the castle, at the northern end of the town which lay behind it on the steep mountain-side, a thin straggling green-backed waterfall spattered down, falling free some hundred feet to the level on which they were now standing – sea level. The other sound was more erratic – single cries of jackdaws circling round the towers of the castle. Bruce had often tried to find a word or phrase to express the tinny roughness of those cries, but all he could think of was the somehow inappropriate word 'Ensconced! Ensconced!' Something in the second syllable seemed to catch and echo the jackdaws' sound.

They left the station. For a while they walked along the right side of the line towards the level crossing. Before they reached it, Stephen uttered his first words of greeting; again, there was nothing particularly splendid about his utterance.

'I'm sweating like a pig.'

'So am I.'

'How far is it?'

'About a mile.'

'Isn't there a bus?'

'No. There isn't even a proper road. Anyway, it's much better to walk.'

They reached the white gates of the level crossing, now opened for road traffic across the line. Bruce pointed to a bungalow adjacent to the railway track.

'That's where the fattest lady in Wales lives. She opens the gate.'

'Is that why she's fat?'

'I don't know. Her name's Mrs. Rice.'

'What's that got to do with it? It doesn't sound like a Welsh name.'

'Her husband was English.'

The road continued close under the castle rock. Here there was a half-ruined outer wall of the castle precincts. A round-arched gateway with steps behind it had once given access to the castle above. It was now sealed up with barbed wire and a tangle of brambles. After about a hundred yards the road split. The left fork rose steeply up into the town, the edge of which they could now see above them – a neat jumble of grey stone walls, with doors of bright pastel shades and window frames mainly painted white, and slate roofs. The right fork continued straight on before them along the flat. In the cleft of the fork stood a three-storey stone building, with a raised semicircular stone terrace in front of it. The ground floor was a general food shop bearing the name Blenheim House.

'That's where we used to get our food. It's going bankrupt. It's too old-fashioned.'

'Stupid name for a Welsh shop.' Stephen's irritation was increased by Bruce's cold-hearted dismissal. Bruce was so often like that, he felt. Stephen's father was in the retail trade, and even though Stephen hated to acknowledge that, Bruce's unfeeling remarks gave him a slight twinge of pain.

'They speak Welsh in there. It has a lovely sound.'

'Do we have to go up that hill?'

'No.'

They continued along the flat to the right of the shop. Stephen glanced in at a side-window as they passed. A nervous-looking grey-haired woman was in there tidying up before closing for the day. Stephen saw her open one of the big jars of sweets standing in two rows on the counter, take out a wine gum and pop it into her mouth. Even while this momentary glimpse filled him with a kind of sadness, a humorous thought sprang into his mind. That's why the shop's going bankrupt: she eats all her own stock.

Bruce was pointing to their right. Stephen could see what he thought was the clubhouse of a golf course, beyond it the links. He could see a black and white pole with a yellow flag fluttering at the top of it, and beyond it, about half a mile distant, sand dunes.

'The sea's over there. You can't see it yet.'

'I saw it from the train.' Even though Stephen had made no attempt to look out of the window, it had been impossible for him not to be aware of the sea. It was something he had seen only a few times in his life. Already, Bruce's enthusiasm was beginning to grate on his ears.

'Three hundred years ago the sea came right up to the castle. Ships came in just where we're standing now. It's going back every year, receding. I can remember...there's already a new line of sandhills beginning just below our house.'

He pointed in the opposite direction to a house built of rather pale grey stones half way up the cliff. Stephen frowned. He looked disappointed.

'Is that your house? I thought you said it was by the sea.'

'No. That's where my mother was born. You see that window with double panes, different from the others? She was born in that room. It's a kind of guesthouse now. My mother's father founded the golf course, you know. He used to be Crown Agent for North Wales. They lived there. It's called Crown Grange.'

Stephen did not enquire what a Crown Agent was. He was tired of all these English names. From Bruce's previous descriptions of the town, he had expected something more remote, more exotic, alien. It seemed now as if Wales was nothing but an English colony. They went on walking. A few minutes later, the road split again; the left fork again led upwards, into the southern fringes of the town, but the gradient was much more gentle than that of the first hill.

'This is a much newer road than the other one. It was made as a kind of by-pass. There's too much traffic through the town at the top. Most of it comes this way now. There's an awful lot in the summer when the trippers come.' Stephen did not like the tone of Bruce's voice when he uttered the word 'trippers'. His mother, father and himself, if they ever had the chance to take a holiday at the seaside, would be among such trippers, he thought; and Bruce would probably look down on them. Again Bruce was pointing, this time straight ahead between the two roads.

'That's the College.'

Stephen hardly heard him. Something was changing in the gloom of his mind. It was if clouds were clearing, as if sun were trying to break through into a world of long twilight. He forgot all about Bruce and the twitter of his running commentary. He simply looked about him; his sense of bewilderment and dissatisfaction was beginning to leave him. He breathed deeply. The air was utterly different from the smoky haze of Birmingham. Stephen had lived in the city almost all his life, and ever since his childhood had suffered from recurrent bouts of asthma. Now, the clarity of this air, the tang of what he recognized must be the smell of the sea, was something quite new to him, even at his age of nineteen. The smell of factories, car paint and fish markets became for him for the first time a memory – not as something past to be forgotten, but as a new experience; something, he felt, not to be cast off with loathing, but to be cherished.

They were still walking along the flat parallel to the railway line. They had reached the pines visible from the station; they grew to the right, between them and the line. Stephen noticed a few broken, dark dry-looking branches and fir-cones scattered on the ground beneath them. Stephen now looked up to his left. A long, dignified and obviously thoughtfully designed stone building dominated the cliffside there, something like a German castle or gothic mansion. It was Harlieg College. Bruce's voice came back to him.

'It used to be a private mansion. Built by a millionaire who made his money in the slate mines up in the mountains. He used to have tremendous parties – brilliant, artistic affairs. Harlieg used to be a real cultural mecca, a colony of artists lived here. They held magnificent concerts, festivals and recitals. My mother used to go there; she played the piano there once. I think that's where she met my father for the first time. When the millionaire died, the house became a college for deprived adults—'

He stopped suddenly as a short explosion of harsh laughter burst from Stephen.

'Depraved adults? Was your father one of them?'

'Probably.' Bruce laughed too. 'I mean, the College is for adults who couldn't have a normal education—'

Another explosion from Stephen.

'That'd suit me fine. I didn't have a normal education. Could I enrol there?'

'I expect so. Just tell them you're a depraved adult who couldn't stick a normal education, and they'll accept you like a shot.' Bruce laughed but stopped when he saw Stephen was frowning. 'You see these pines? They were planted to stop the train smoke from blackening the stonework.'

'Rather futile. They seem to be entirely ineffectual. The stone looks as dark and dirty as Birmingham Town Hall before it was cleaned.'

'Yes, they don't seem to make much difference. I used to collect fir-cones here when I was a boy.'

'What did you do with them. Stick them up your arse?'

'I'm not as depraved as all that.'

'I didn't say you were. But if your mother had tried to stop you doing that with them you'd have felt deprived, wouldn't you?'

'Perhaps.' They both laughed. This was more like the kind of conversation they enjoyed.

They continued walking. On their left, immediately below the College, were three long, grey barrack-like wooden buildings. Stephen guessed they were dormitories. He looked with interest at the towels and swimming things hanging from some of the window-sills. As they reached the last of the pines, he noticed that they had left the town behind them. There were fewer houses on the cliffside. The sand dunes to their right were much nearer. One more outsize building, however, disfigured the view almost directly ahead. This too was on the cliff, at a slightly higher level than the College, about two hundred yards further to the south; it was situated on a part of the cliff that jutted out further than the rest. Stephen frowned again. He had been enjoying the solid masonry of the Welsh buildings. Now he encountered the concrete monstrosity of the Royal Dragon Hotel. It was a plain rectangular block, topped by a dozen or so wide chimneys, each with six chimney pots – reminiscent of a pottery factory or thick, insensitive robot-like hands sticking up in derision without thumbs. Two or three hundred windows faced the sea, one or two of them open; a towel was hanging from one window-sill. The end facing Stephen and Bruce had very few windows and most of them were small – toilets or bathrooms; and there was a smaller building made of the same dull concrete attached to the main block at this point.

'That's the kitchen's this end. The chef hanged himself in the boiler room about five years ago.'

Stephen looked sharply at Bruce.

'Why?'

'Autumn depression. It was about this time of the year.'

It was beginning to get darker. A few lights were on inside the hotel. A low mist was rising over the golf links. The sun would not set for another hour or so, but clouds obliterated large areas of the western sky. It felt colder. Bruce laughed.

'It's funny.'

'What's funny?'

'That pork-pie hat of yours.'

'What's the matter with it?'

'Nothing. I was just thinking. It used to belong to my father.'

'Does he want it back?'

'Of course not.'

'Does it look funny?'

'No. It suits you.'

'Well, it's better than yours.'

Bruce was wearing a black woollen slightly peaked Indian skull-cap. The black cotton thigh-length tunic he was wearing, also from India, matched it. He also had on a pair of black jeans. Both of them customarily wore eccentric clothes. They took pride in it. Stephen made no attempt to hide the fact; but Bruce liked to imagine that he was not aware of any peculiarity in his own mode of dress. He wanted people to think he was some kind of genius who could not be bothered with such mundane matters as dress and respectability. Both of them were stared at wherever they went. They both enjoyed this attention.

The road, by now rough surfaced and pot-holed, came to an end. Another pair of level-crossing gates painted black led the road over to the other side of the line. There it became a simple grass track strengthened in places with slate chippings.

'That's the way we go by car. There's a track through the sandhills. We used to call it the Bumps.'

'A girl I used to know used that word to describe her monthly periods.'

16

'Subjects of that kind are usually beyond my range of
conversation. Anyway, we don't have to go that way. We stay on
this side of the line.'

'Your remarks are ambiguous. What are you talking about?'

'Not about girls or their monthly bumps.'

The road before them narrowed to a broad pathway
continuing along below the hotel. As they passed the level-crossing
gate, Stephen saw some words painted in white on one of the
black-tarred cross-beams: GO HOME FILTHY ENGLISH.

'Who wrote that?'

'Hooligans. Village morons.'

Stephen felt his feelings of the morning returning. There was
no getting away from it: people were the same everywhere.
Nevertheless, he felt disposed to make light of it.

'I don't believe you. I think you painted it yourself. For my
benefit.'

'Are you one of the filthy English then?'

'Oh, yes, undoubtedly. Entirely. Among the very filthiest.'

'I agree.' They both laughed again, and Bruce pointed to a small
black triangle showing above the dunes about half a mile further on.
'That's the house.'

They walked on. The three vast buildings – the castle, the
College and the hotel – passed behind them. They were no longer
part of the landscape, but the image of them loomed large in
Stephen's mind. Suddenly he stopped walking.

'What's that?'

'What's what?'

'That sound.'

'I can't hear anything.'

Bruce walked on. Stephen stood listening for a while, his head
bowed and tilted slightly to one side, his arms held closely at his
sides. Bruce stopped again and waited for his friend. A little further
on they came to a pair of black ladder-stiles made of old tarred
railway sleepers standing astride the wire fences on either side of

the railway track. The path ended in a T-junction; to the left it led steeply up the cliff. They turned right and crossed the line, Stephen having some difficulty climbing up and down the steep steps of the stiles. The path, now a barely visible track of short, worn-out grass, led upwards into low dunes covered with sharp-pointed marram grass and dark shadows of stunted thorn bushes. The whole of Stephen's body was tensed; he felt an inexplicable wave of fear filling his mind. It seemed to be taking the form of a kind of agoraphobia, but whatever it was he was unable to identify it clearly. He stepped forward hesitantly, his head still bent and twisted to one side. He felt as if a great wall of windless air were pressing against his ribs and skull, trying to hinder his progress. Not only was it people who were constantly antagonistic, he thought. Nature too was standing in opposition against him.

He could hear the sea.

3. HOUSE BY THE SEA

THE HOUSE WAS SUDDENLY before them, slightly to their left. There was one light on, in an upstair window. Bruce, who had arranged this on purpose, was especially pleased with the effect now obtained. The clouded sunset to the west and the sea below it behind the house emphasized the sharp angle of the roof – a striking silhouette, broken only by the single rectangle of dim light. A haunted house by the sea. Even Bruce himself, who had wanted to present the house to his friend as dramatically as possible, was struck by the ghostliness of the scene. Smoke, faint against the fading light, rose almost straight up from one of the three pots of the single red-brick chimney. There was only the slightest breath of wind, hardly more than a cool pressure of air against their faces warm with walking. As they reached the top of the sandhills from the railway line, the whole bay came into view, and at the same time the quiet susurration of the waves came more loudly to their ears. The tide was right in. The sea was flat and glittering golden white, with large areas shadowed over by the clouds. Stephen once again stood still. He could distinguish only the general curve of the shore, black mountains to the north, and the long dark line of the Lleyn peninsula across the bay to the west. Lights of a few villages twinkled over there. But it was the house itself which held his attention.

At this point, the footpath joined the grassy car track (the 'Bumps') that wound its way through the sandhills from the level-crossing gate and led towards the house. As they approached, Stephen noticed that the steeply canted roof was not black as it had first appeared but covered with small red tiles; and that the outer walls consisted of dark horizontal boards. The house was bigger than he had expected; he had not imagined there would be two storeys. They reached a level area on the north and west sides. It was covered with smooth, tough grass, something of a lawn. There was no other 'garden' as far as he could see.

There was a verandah set in the west front of the house facing the sea, and the green front door, facing north and well-protected from the weather, tucked as it was under the eaves, led out into it. Bruce had left in unlocked. They went in, Stephen's leather shoes sounding loud on the wooden floor of the small hallway inside. Bruce switched on the light.
'Welcome to Tremarfon.'
'What do you mean?'
'That's the name of the house. It means "View of Caernarvon". It's a silly name really. We can't see Caernarvon from here. It's on the other side of the peninsula. Over there.' Bruce pointed to the north-west, where dark clouds were merged with the hills.

They took off their hats, and Stephen struggled out of his unwieldy raincoat, which hissed and knocked against the wooden walls of the narrow passage leading from the hall. They went into the living-room, a square room with large windows overlooking the sea and sandhills on the west and north sides. Against the east wall, the back of the house, stood an old Welsh dresser with a copper kettle on top of it. On the south side was a narrow open fireplace with a surround of small brick-like red tiles; the coals had burned low. Next to it, by the door, was an upright piano. In the centre stood a large oval gate-legged table. The west window looked out into the verandah, and the north window was a bay containing a padded window seat covered with faded green linen.

'Are you hungry?'

'Not specially.'

Stephen's whole body seemed numb. He had no sensations of hunger now. He felt neither hot nor cold nor particularly tired or energetic. The sound of the train still seemed to be reverberating in his ears. He felt disorientated. The occasion and the place were somehow too big to absorb into the turmoil of cold fog in his mind. He sat down at the piano.

'Wait a moment. I'll make some tea.'

While Bruce was putting the kettle on in the kitchen, he heard piano chords from the living-room; even in the kitchen, which led off the passage from the hall, they sounded loud, carried throughout the house in the wooden boards of the walls. Bruce felt an immediate flurry of anger rising from a deeper-seated fear. So far he had been in control of the situation; now there was a danger of losing it. He hadn't wanted it to be like this. He hoped they would both sit at the piano together, and improvise one of their duets. It was a kind of ritual with them. For three years now they had performed it whenever they met where there was a piano, ever since Stephen had first come to Bruce's house in the suburbs of Birmingham. They would sit down at the piano – Stephen at the bass, Bruce at the treble – and would begin to hammer out Beethoven sagas, Bach-like fugues, floating preludes, percussive toccatas, romances. No key, no fixed time-signature; and yet, more often than not, their extemporizations had corresponded – sometimes in harshly satisfying conflict, sometimes with intense rhythmic energy, or with the most tender of melodic lines which they took up from each other in perfect harmony. They rarely talked about it or discussed what to play. They just sat down and began. It was something they did together, one of the strong threads of their friendship.

Bruce went back to the living-room. Stephen was bent low over the keyboard, his head to one side, the whites of his eyes showing, reminiscent somehow, Bruce felt, of a mad cow. His thick, wide hands thrust out slow ugly chords at irregular intervals. He seemed oblivious of Bruce. Bruce fetched a chair.

'Move down.'

Stephen appeared not to hear him; he went on playing.

'Move down, Stephen.'

Stephen came out of his trance, and in one abrupt movement shifted the piano stool to the left. Bruce placed his chair beside it and sat down. Stephen broke out into a crashing march, very fast. Bruce waited for a moment to join in. He watched Stephen's fingers: his thumb repeatedly returned to F sharp. Bruce struck the F sharp two octaves above middle C. Stephen immediately changed his recurrent chord and struck F natural. Bruce tried to follow him, trying to find a footing in Stephen's torrent of sound, but his interpolating notes jangled like a barrel-organ playing in front of a symphony orchestra. He tried again and again to merge his sounds with Stephen's relentless playing. His chair was lower than the piano stool and this increased his sense of inferiority. He tried invading the walls of Stephen's impregnable fortress with rapid clashing discords, but Stephen threw them off like toy soldiers made of tin. Bruce began a piercing half-tone trill and held it, but it sounded like a pixie laughing nervously at an ogre. It was no use: he couldn't get in.

'Not so fast.'

Stephen stopped playing. Bruce played a simple melodic phrase. Stephen took it up in the bass. Bruce repeated it. Stephen inverted it and doubled the tempo. Bruce stuck to his phrase, an octave higher. The music developed into a steady fugue; at least, it sounded like a fugue, but a musical expert would probably have laughed. The improvisation grew more complex. It was going well. They continued for about ten minutes. Bruce felt more at ease. He was there with his friend. They were together at the piano; their hands were communicating through the agency of their ears and eyes. An inner understanding was binding them together. Bruce felt a certain satisfaction; but he knew that the pleasure for him lay not so much in the music itself as in the knowledge that they were playing together. For Stephen, he knew, the pleasure was in the music alone; and not only that, the pleasure was in his own music rather than in the duet. With his vastly superior technique, he knew he was master of the occasion. They stopped. They always knew when to stop. It happened by instinct. Bruce smiled.

'Not bad.'

'Tolerable.' Stephen froze. 'Is that a train?'

A distant continuous shriek came to their ears.

'No. The kettle's boiling.'

Bruce went out. Stephen began playing again, the same slow irregular chords as before. Bruce knew that their duet had been a mere interlude for Stephen, not serious music. He made the tea and returned to the living-room. Stephen turned round.

'The piano needs tuning.'

'It's very old. Tenants mess about with it when we're not here. We let the place between Easter and summer. They just mess about on it – honky-tonk, tinkle-tinkle.'

'That's all we do.'

'No, there's something more to ours. Don't you think so?'

Stephen did not answer. He was gazing at the brass candle-holders fixed on swivels to the front of the piano. The bowl of one of them was missing.

'Who broke that off?'

'You did.'

'Don't be absurd.'

They sat at a smaller table by the west window. Bruce poured out the tea.

'You've put milk in it.'

'You always have it with milk and sugar, don't you?'

'I don't now.'

'Sorry. Shall I pour it out?'

'If you don't mind.'

Bruce took the cup to the kitchen. Stephen was always so unpredictable. He was never the same ten days running. But at the same time Bruce knew that it was precisely this unpredictability which made Stephen such an exciting person to be with.

When he came back into the room, Stephen was staring out of the window down at the shore. Bruce made up the fire.

'Do you want to see round the house? I'll show you your room.'

'There are some people down there. A man and a girl.'

'Taking a stroll, I expect.'

'They're not taking a stroll.'

'What are they doing?'

'Bending down.'

'Collecting firewood.' Bruce came to the window.

'They've been there for several minutes.'

'Must have found something interesting. Lots of marvellous things get washed up. Where are they?'

Bruce peered down to where Stephen was pointing. He could not see anyone. With the light on in the room, it was too dark outside to see anything clearly.

'I can't see anything.'

'They've gone now.'

'Ghosts.' Bruce laughed softly. He always liked to dramatize things whenever there was a chance. He knew it was false, mere sensationalism; but he also knew how susceptible Stephen was to anything of that kind. As for Stephen himself, he never needed to dramatize. Everything he did was already charged with drama; his life was one long string of dramatic incidents – real blood and thunder. He had the capacity for becoming involved in the most extraordinary affairs; even the simplest things turned into major crises. Bruce had often listened to his friend's accounts of his past – how he had almost been a child-prodigy pianist, goaded on by his proud parents; how he had screamed and boiled through day-long tantrums; how he had lifted the lid of his grandmother's coffin four days after she had died, when he was only twelve; his sordid encounters with ageing pederasts. Bruce was alternately fascinated and disgusted, almost envious of the variety and intensity of Stephen's experiences. By comparison, Bruce had experienced nothing: he had been too well protected. All the drama of his life was in the mind – dreams, delusions of grandeur, romanticizing, feigned. Often when he was with Stephen, Bruce felt like a fraud. His childhood had been too easy, it seemed, the events nondescript, pale, petty, pathetic.

They turned from the window.

'Shall I show you round the house now?'

Stephen nodded. He followed Bruce into the hall. The stairs wound up to the left into the heart of the house. Apart from the living-room and the kitchen, the ground floor consisted of a bedroom, a tiny bathroom, an even tinier lavatory, a box-like larder and a store-room. Bruce showed Stephen everything, proudly as if they were all his own. All of the rooms, except for the living-room and kitchen, were walled with vertical boards stained olive-green. There was a large notice, white letters on red, on the wall of the passage-way, supplied by an insurance firm in Liverpool: IT IS DANGEROUS TO DROP LIGHTED MATCHES. In some of the rooms pieces of paper were pinned to the wall with typewritten warnings on them: AS THESE PREMISES ARE CONSTRUCTED OF WOOD, YOU ARE EARNESTLY REQUESTED TO EXERCISE SPECIAL CARE IN THE USE OF MATCHES, CIGARETTES, ETC. In the downstair bedroom, Stephen read one of these out in a loud, pompous, mocking voice, exploding into laughter before he could reach the end.

'Who on earth concocted that great mouthful of shit?'

Bruce was stung by his friend's note of derision.

'That was typed by my mother.' There was a hint of a tremor in Bruce's voice.

'Did she make up the words too?'

'No. My father did.' Bruce's voice now had a cold edge.

'You are earnestly requested to replace each sheet of toilet paper after use.' Again Stephen dissolved into laughter, and tears shone in his eyes. Bruce also laughed, unable to help himself. Stephen continued his recitation.

'As these premises are constructed of paper, you are earnestly desired to exercise extreme caution when passing water. That would be more to the point.'

'In your case anyway. You always leave steaming puddles on the floor. You've got no sense of direction.'

Stephen looked sharply at Bruce.

'There's more in your remark than you imagine, especially the last sentence.'

They went up to the first floor, their footsteps on the uncarpeted treads sounding hollow in the wooden house. There were three rooms upstairs – a large bedroom to the north corresponding to the living-room below, a very small east-facing room with a dormer window set in the slope of the roof, and another middle-sized bedroom to the south set half over the kitchen and half over the downstair bedroom. They stopped in the south room.

'Is this all right for you? I'm in the big room. I always sleep there, unless we have visitors.'

Stephen made no comment. If he were not a visitor, what was he? His resentment rose again, but almost as quickly evaporated. Bruce had always been his superior in such matters. He always had the best chair, the biggest portion of food, the last cigarette. Bruce belonged to a different class altogether; Stephen had to defer to him. He had no choice. He was not a snob, but he loved to visit Bruce's family home outside Birmingham – its big rooms filled with curios, oils and statues, the long white portrait gallery, the grand piano in the music room, the dark passages. It was a world quite new to him – a world of dignity and grace, and mystery, to which he had long aspired. Ever since the time, when out with school friends of his, he had encountered his father drunk one night, he had been ashamed of his background. It was bad enough to have a father whose highest ambition was to run a stall selling cheap china seconds in the Bull Ring Market Hall; but seeing his father drooling and singing on the bus that night had been the last straw. Ever since then – he had been thirteen at the time – he had attempted to disassociate himself from his working-class background. He had even trained himself to speak middle-class Queen's English, something everyone else in his family dismissed in derision as highbrow la-di-da nonsense; and he had achieved a certain measure of success. Bruce had never detected that his friend's language was not, as it were, his own. Stephen often felt as if he were speaking a kind of foreign language when he was with Bruce and Bruce's friends; and the strain was sometimes exhausting. One slip, Stephen felt, and Bruce would reject him as a snob and a fraud. He wished he had been born into a world like Bruce's – with reasonable wealth, a background distinguished by artistic achievement – Bruce's grandfather had been a well-known poet in his time – living in a house with an aura of genius about it. But he was realist enough to appreciate what he had already obtained – companionship with Bruce, a step up and acceptance into a better world. Bruce introduced him to people Stephen longed to emulate, to a society from which the circumstances of his birth had excluded him. Offered now this lesser room, he was content, or at least, had he been in a normal state of mind he would have been content. He looked at the dull green walls, the upper sections sloping inwards to accommodate the outside roof, the two single divan-beds at either side under the slopes, the table and chair under the window. There was something simple and garret-like about the room that Stephen found attractive.

'Fine.'

'We'll bring your things up soon.'

Bruce was enjoying showing Stephen round. Of all the places he knew in the world, and he had travelled widely, this house by the sea was the place he loved best. Although he had been born in the Midlands, his family had moved to Harlieg in the first months of the war, to escape the bombing. The first three years of Bruce's life had been spent here by the sea. It was in his bones – the sea, the wind, the mountains. Wales was in his blood. He was a Celt in spirit, he thought. He cherished, he loved the idea. There was nothing romantic in this. All his earliest memories went back to this same house and its immediate surroundings – the gorse bushes where he had thrown his little red and white horse, found, faded and damp, two years later; the beach where he ran into the wind, wheeling in half circles and falling into his mother's arms, crying 'Too windy! Too windy!' He could even remember his sister's christening party. He was hardly three then; he had sat in the same living-room downstairs at a table which had one leg too short; he remembered rocking it to and fro as he and one of his brothers sat there for tea. Now for the first time in his life, his father was letting him stay there unsupervised, with Stephen his friend, and no one else to disturb them.

'You wouldn't believe this place can sleep fourteen people, would you? There are four annexes outside – two on the east side, one on the south, and one down in front of the house.' He went to the window. 'You can see the south one down here.' Stephen stood by him. He could see the large square tiles, arranged diamond-wise, of a small annexe just below the window. 'That was my mother's room; my sister was born in there. We don't use it now.'

They went downstairs and into the living-room.

'The other annexe is down there.' He pointed out of the front window. 'You can hardly see it now. My father sleeps there when he's here. He's built a turf bank almost all the way round it to keep the wind out.'

'This is a much larger place than I imagined.' Stephen immediately felt this remark of his was somehow artificial. He wished he had some natural small talk. It was so difficult to be casual. Bruce also sensed Stephen's awkwardness. It was typical of Stephen to have used the word 'larger' rather than the more homely 'bigger' that Bruce himself would have used.

'Let's get some supper. You like sausages, don't you?'

'I'll help you.'

In the kitchen, Bruce laid out the beef sausages for grilling, pronging each with a fork. Stephen cut potatoes chips, after scrubbing but not peeling them, taking care not to cut his fingers on the sharp steel bone-handled kitchen-knife Bruce had given him. Bruce opened a tin of processed peas.

'I'll hope this will do. I'm not much of a cook.'

'Have you got any newspaper?'

'What for?'

'To drain the fat off the chips when they're done.'

'Is that how you do it?' Bruce had never used newspaper for cooking before; he thought the only place you could find that was in a fish and chip shop.

'We always do it that way.'

'I see. There's some in the back room there, behind the back door.'

It was quite dark now outside. Looking out of the kitchen window, Bruce could see a few lights in the houses up on the cliff. A bus – a creeping row of lights – made its way along the road.

'The ground seems to be trembling. What's happening?' Stephen came wide-eyed out of the back room, clutching some old newspapers. Bruce laughed.

'It is a train this time. The house is built on sand. Everything down here on the flat's built on sand. The sea used to go right up to—'

'You told me.'

Stephen always stopped Bruce when he was about to repeat himself, something he often did, a habit acquired from his mother. They fell silent as the train rumbled past, a dull background to the chortling fat in the chip pan and the occasional spit of the sausages under the grill. Bruce caught sight of the moving snake of lights low down in the sandhills under the cliff, some two hundred yards from the house. It always reminded him of his father, who used to arrive by one of the evening trains, and they all had to go out and wave to him from the bank a little way from the house, with hell to pay if they did not get there in time. His father never waved his hand as they did; he would hold his handkerchief fluttering from the train window and simply lift it up and down in the slipstream. Such things were in the past now. They were not children any more. Bruce felt an unexpected pluck of sentimentality – his father waving his handkerchief in the dusk and no line of children on the bank ever again. Stephen's voice interrupted his sad reverie.

'Are there many trains?'

'Not so many these days. They're going to close the line soon. And there aren't any trains on Sundays. I think that one was the last today.'

'Strange place this. I thought it was an earthquake or something.'

'There are stranger things than that.' Bruce caught Stephen's eye but offered no further explanation. They concentrated on the supper preparations, working in perfect accord. When it was ready they carried the things through into the living-room. They had made another pot of tea to go with it.

The curtains were drawn back still. The glaring darkness outside was almost overpowering, like thick gleaming oil pressing hard against the window panes. Bruce drew the curtains.

'Aren't there any other houses near here?'

'None. Are you frightened? I am sometimes.'

'Of course not.' Again they caught each other's glances.

'My mother said it was terrible during the war. No lights anywhere. Complete black-out. Of course, I was too young to remember, but my mother told me there was such a shortage of blackout cloth that they had to make blinds out of brown paper, several layers. There was a rumour that the Germans were going to invade from Ireland – just here, in fact. It was on the wireless. The same night, my mother was going round to her annexe when a man with a gun appeared on the bank over there, a black silhouette; he was coming up from the beach, an enemy from the sea. My mother was very brave. She called out, "Who's there?"—'

'She should have said "Friend or foe?"'

'Don't spoil my story. She thought the invasion had already begun; but a voice came back out of the darkness: "Don't you be worrying yourself, Mrs. Dinwiddy. It is only I, Bob Evans, getting a rabbit." It was the local poacher!'

'What did she do, ask him in for a cup of tea?'

'I don't know. Quite probably. She was very friendly with all the locals. After all, she was born—'

'You told me.'

Bruce laughed. During supper, he told Stephen a number of other 'local' stories. Stephen was a good listener, and never seemed to mind how much Bruce talked as long as he did not repeat himself. Towards the end of the meal, the subject came round again to the solitariness of the house.

'I don't much like going round to the annexes at night. I used to sleep round in the east annexe. It's very dark. There's no outside light round that way. Shall we go outside now?'

'Yes.'

They stood on the lawn in front of the house. Bruce had not switched the verandah light on, and they could see that the sky was completely clear, the stars exceptionally bright. There was a hint of autumn in the cold air.

'We can't see stars like that in Birmingham, can we?'

Stephen was not looking at the sky. He was peering down again into the darkness of the shore.

'I think those people are still there. They haven't moved.'

The sea sounded very loud in the absence of wind. The tide had gone back quite a way by now. A long strip of beach gleamed faintly beyond the edge of the sandhills.

'What do you mean? You said that before. Where are they?'

Stephen pointed. Bruce strained his eyes, but as far as he could see there was nothing but the empty beach.

'It's just your imagination.' He suddenly felt cold and shuddered. 'Let's go back in.'

Back in the bright light of the living-room with its cheerful orange flickers from the fireplace, Bruce felt the tension in the air evaporate.

'Do you want to take your things upstairs? You can leave your typewriter down here if you like. You can work here in the daytime.'

'I haven't brought my typewriter.'

'What's in there then?' Bruce pointed at the black typewriter case standing primly near the door.

'Books.'

'I thought you were coming here to write.'

Stephen shook his head.

'What did you come here for then?'

Again Stephen shook his head, more faintly this time.

'I can't tell you now.'

4. MORNING

BRUCE STOOD with his arms folded on top of the chest of drawers in front of his bedroom window. It was shortly after seven o'clock and the sun had not yet risen. He let his gaze wander slowly, almost lovingly, across the landscape he knew almost by heart. The view north before him was one he never tired of, and he knew that as long as he lived he would never be able to forget it. It was permanently engraved in his brain, like a pale blue salt stain across the white sail of his mind.

To the right, the cliff lay in dark shadow, its height delaying the sunrise. Half a mile away, the Royal Dragon Hotel, the College and the castle seemed to be hunched together – foreshortened by the angle from which he was looking at them. The last of these, the castle, was the highest, dominating the extreme left end of the skyline of the cliff before it turned further inland beyond the town. Ten miles beyond, stretching right across the horizon from east to west lay the mountains of Snowdonia, pale in the morning light, yet perfectly clear. First, the smooth shoulder of Moelwyn Mawr, which seemed almost to grow out of the left-hand tower of the castle, in spite of the vast distance between them; next, the knife-edge of Cnicht. The sun on it now emphasized its serrated edge. Then a group of lower hills gradually prepared the way for the right-hand flanks of Snowdon itself – the precipitous Llwyd ridge and beyond it, just visible, the grisly red-brown fins of Crib Goch, the most dangerous ridge in the British Isles, though Bruce had scaled it at the age of six. Further beyond, he could just see the savage tops of the Glyders, so harmless from here, but in fact ruthless outcrops of rock where not a few mountaineers had met their ends. Then Snowdon itself, the queen of the range – a precise tilted right-angle its pinnacle, delicate blue yet immovable – one of the oldest mountains in the world, once a volcano, and twice submerged beneath the sea millions of years before the Ice Ages. The left-hand slope of Snowdon, called the Saddleback, where you could sometimes see the smoke of the mountain train, led gently down to where it met the two humps of Moel Ddu, leading to the steep right side of Moel Hebog, with its absolutely flat top a quarter of a mile wide. Then came the long western incline of Hebog it was possible to drive a car up. From there the mountains lost something of their drama, dissolving away west and south in the long curve of the Lleyn peninsula. Prominent among these was the last challenge in the range – knobbly Bwylch Mawr, and immediately below, the black trapezium of Moel-y-Gwyst, not really a mountain, being less than a thousand feet high, but perilous because of the huge slate quarry on its far side.

Between Bruce and the mountains lay the vast triangle of the Traeth – land left behind by the sea – consisting of golf links to the right and centre, and sand dunes reaching far out to the point on the left. Behind these lay the 'Tortoise' Mountain, a long low gorse-covered hill with a 'head' to its left, which in former days must have formed two separate islands. Mist lay over the golf links now, the same as had risen the evening before.

To the left, the beach and the sea. Once again the tide was full, almost up to the sand dunes. Bruce could never for long keep his eyes away from the sea. It was the only thing in the landscape constantly moving, and yet it never seemed to move. Now a dark shadow was slowly rushing across it, diminishing as it went. The sun was rising above the cliff to the right of the house. As the spreading wall of light hit first the sea and then the sandhills, Bruce was aware that he was actually witnessing the turning of the world, could sense the exact speed of its motion. The rising and the setting of the sun were a myth for children; the revolution of the earth now was a reality he could see with his own eyes. It gave him a sense of power to be able to comprehend motion so much greater than he himself – a young poet gazing out of a window at the pristine world.

He felt aware of his lower body pressing against the chest of drawers. He would swim now. He changed out of his cotton pyjamas into swimming shorts of the same material. Bruce almost had a fetish for the cool simplicity of cotton, especially when it was clean and white. All his underwear was cotton; he abhorred nylon and other synthetic fabrics. They stuck to his skin, they soon stank of perspiration. Cotton shirts, cotton slacks, cotton sheets on his bed. He felt the smooth firmness of the shorts against his skin. It felt good. He felt good this morning. Bruce imagined himself chaste, not in the sense of being virgin or celibate, both of which, however, he was, but in the fact that as a rule he abstained from self-gratification. At a younger age he had been unable to avoid the habit, and even now he sometimes allowed himself the pleasure. For the most part, however, he allowed nature to take its course – relishing nevertheless the immense feelings of strength it gave him to withhold himself from what he had been taught was a sin. Nature, however, compensated. No matter how long he refrained, the involuntary behaviour of his body always brought pleasure and relief, the longer the abstention the greater the pleasure. At times, the restraint exerted tremendous pressure on his will. He found himself at times thinking almost continually about his body; but for two years now he had remained almost entirely pure in this respect.

To be pure was the mainstay of his existence. He had slept with none but himself, neither woman, boy or man, and he intended it to remain that way. Sex repelled him as much as it fascinated him. He still found it hard to reconcile himself to the moral paradox of abstention and pleasure. He had kissed a girl on the lips on only one occasion, at a party, and since he had not loved her, the experience had left him cold, even disappointed. Besides, he had been half drunk at the time, and the absence of excitement and pleasure on that occasion had perhaps turned him forever from the normal ways of the flesh. A woman, a girl, for him, was not someone to be touched, merely adored from the distance. In this, he was amazingly immature for his age and quite out of touch with the moral climate of the time, but as yet he was totally unaware of this as a shortcoming. He would be an ascetic, a saint, a man like Gandhi, like Christ – above all physical sordidness. Only at the back of his mind did he feel some unease or sense of inconsistency: the pleasure was always there.

He sensed the heady tenderness of his body as he went down the creaking stairs. There was no sound from Stephen's room. He went into the living-room. The curtains were already drawn back: it was his custom to do that before going to bed. The room seemed so much fresher in the morning; but even as he looked at the table, he saw it was scattered with cigarette ash, and grey circles where the milk-bottle had stood the evening before. The fireplace was piled high with the ash he had shovelled over the coals the night before, to keep the fire in till the next morning. He could see a faint glow of cinders through the pale grey screes of this miniature volcano. He took the poker, shook down the ash, swept the hearth clean, and put fresh coal on the rapidly reddening fire. The gassy coal hissed and spat with energy, matching his own freshness.

He opened the heavy front door, which he never locked at night, and went outside. It was cold in the shadow on the west side of the house. The grass was grey with dew, but as soon as he walked down the path towards the beach he felt the sun on his back, warm, invigorating. He began to run. The sand was almost icy cold as he ran down and then up onto the new adolescent line of sandhills, and down again onto the rocks.

His family had always called them the rocks; but they were really only rounded stones, some of them as big as human skulls – all of them smooth and pale blue, with occasional white lines of strata in them. He leapt over them lightly, sure of foot from long experience. Where he crossed it, the line of rocks was about twenty feet wide. Along to the left, the line widened and formed, with the addition of huge brown quarry-cut mountain boulders, a buttress against the railway embankment which at that south end of the beach crept round under the final flanks of the cliff, a crumbling, grassy promontory about a hundred feet high. The shore there was a maze of pools between barnacled rocks sunk deep into the sand, where they could catch shrimps when the tide was out. To his right, the line of blue stones continued, diminishing into the sand about half a mile further along the shore. In the winter more stones would be uncovered; in the summer, sand, blown there by the endless south-west winds, hid many of them.

The narrow strip of beach left by the tide was cold, smooth and dark with moisture. The sea was a bare thirty yards away. There was no wind, and the waves were small and slow. They fell in long low lines – a single clap, a hiss as the water ran back, and silence; then another single clap. He ran straight into the sea, kicking out and diving down into the water barely up to his knees beyond the narrow surf line. He did this almost every morning. It was part of his purity, an exercise in Spartan discipline. He wished he had the strength to stay in longer, but the cold was too intense. The courageous gesture lasted exactly thirty seconds, which he counted out, holding his breath.

He charged noisily out of the water straight into the sun. He picked up the towel he had brought down with him and dried himself. Momentarily he was exhausted. He wished he didn't smoke. There was a weakness he would have to master. His chest felt tight, and his ears ached. He walked heavily up to the house, feeling better every moment. By the time he reached the lawn, he was all a man of the morning – warm, brilliant, glistening, indomitable.

He went into the little bathroom and washed his face, thinking how insipid the soft Welsh water was after his plunge in the horny sea, then went upstairs to dress. There was still no sound from Stephen's room. He decided not wake him yet; he would prepare breakfast first. He went downstairs again, hung his swimming shorts and towel on the clothes rack in the kitchen, and put the kettle on. He also switched the electric cooker on to get the heating plates hot before putting the pans on. He went outside again.

A short way south-west of the house, on a little grassy hillock, Stephen was standing, motionless, gazing at the sea. Once again, Bruce felt a pucker of irritation. The view – the beach, the sea, the mountains – was his view; it was his privilege alone to show it to his friend. As with the piano the evening before, Stephen had helped himself. Bruce tried to dismiss the unreasonableness of his feelings; the day was too beautiful to harbour such thoughts – but he found it difficult. Things were not going quite the way he had ordained. He walked over and stood by Stephen. Neither of them spoke for a while. In spite of his immediate feelings, Bruce respected Stephen's silence. Stephen had a way of looking and listening which Bruce envied. He didn't have the same depths of concentration, the staying power; meditation bored him. He preferred action. Stephen was at such times totally absorbed, as if nothing could disturb him. At such times Bruce tried to see what Stephen was looking at, tried to hear what he was listening to; but always after a few minutes he felt rising impatience. He felt it now.

'I've just been for a swim.'
'I saw you.'
'I didn't see you. Where were you?'
'Here. You didn't stay in long.'
'It was too cold. When did you get up?'
'Just after you.'
'What do you think of the view?'

Stephen said nothing. Bruce had an irresistible desire to repeat Stephen's mocking recitation of the previous evening – 'You are earnestly requested to exercise special care in the use of question marks' – but he held it back, fearing his friend's disapproval.

'I've climbed nearly all the mountains you can see from here.'

Stephen almost said 'So what?' but thought better of it. He remained silent. Bruce pointed across to the Lleyn peninsula. There were three mild mountains there, the middle one higher than the other two.

'Those three mountains are called the Rivals.'

Stephen threw a glance at Bruce. The whites of his eyes were slightly but noticeably redder than usual. There was something yellow about his eyes, too.

'Is there any significance in that remark?'

Bruce had not intended so, but the moment the words were in his mouth he had realized their dramatic possibilities. As a result, his voice had carried special emphasis.

'Nothing special. That really is what they're called. Anyway, there are three mountains, not two.'

'That could be significant.'

'We're not rivals either.'

Stephen stretched his arm towards the beach.

'That's where they were.'

'Who?'

'Those people last night. They were looking at something down there.'

'Tide's been in since then. There won't be anything there now.'

'I'm going down to the beach.'

'Let's have breakfast first.'

'If you insist.'

They went back to the house. Bruce was troubled. Stephen was not usually so short with him. There was something repressed, almost surly, about him. Bruce wondered what he had done to offend his friend. But Stephen, he thought by way of self-justification, had been like that ever since he had arrived at Harlieg. There was something on his mind.

There was something on Stephen's mind – more, much more, than he could explain to Bruce. Before coming to Wales, he had made a resolution; but he had not expected Harlieg to be like this. His concept of the sea had been merely that of a seaside, a place for holiday-makers – a pier, bathing huts, a crowded front, penny-in-the-slot machines, fish and chips. This desolation, this openness, this wide, wild, gentle bay was an utterly new experience for him. His mind, confused, embittered, soiled, was now freshly knocked awry, shocked by the calmness of the morning. The very dimensions of the landscape confounded him. He was unable to take in the vastness, the silence, the agelessness centuries old.

They made breakfast. Bruce never as a rule took any breakfast, except for a cup of coffee; but he thought Stephen would like all the usual things – cornflakes, bacon, toast, marmalade. But not eggs. Stephen detested eggs. Once when he was a boy he had opened a bad one at breakfast. The very sight of an egg now revolted him. Bruce knew this, and with a deliberate perverseness always offered one to Stephen.

'How about a fresh, brown, new-laid, boiled egg? Or would you rather have it scrambled in thick oil?'

'Fuck off.'

'I thought you loved them, especially underdone, runny – and brown.'

'It's not funny.'

'I said "runny".'

'Why do you always get at me?'

'I am earnestly requested to exercise specially care with the addles of—'

'I said fuck off!'

Bruce fucked off, or rather, he did not labour the joke, as his father might have done. Enough was enough.

Stephen wanted cornflakes and coffee. He couldn't face the prospect of bacon. Bruce switched off the cooker, screwing up his nose at the smell of the overheated plates. In the living-room, he watched Stephen crunching his cereal. The last flakes in the dish always reminded him of autumn leaves on the ground after rain. It had originally been the leaves themselves that suggested the analogy. Thoughts of autumn always softened his mind. He was still at an age when autumn moved him most of all the seasons – the colours, the mists, the silently smoking bonfires, the harsh laughs of jays in the larches, the sadness everywhere. Bruce sat at the head of the table, his back to the dresser. From that position he could see out of both windows. It was the best place. Like his father, he now took it as a matter of course. Stephen sat to his right, facing the fire. He was not aware of Bruce's sense of superiority. He was looking at the flames in the hearth.

'Why do they burn green?'

'It's the salt in the coal. It's sea-coal.'

'Rubbish. Sea-coal comes from Newcastle in ships.'

'The wood burns like that, too; I mean driftwood from the beach. It's the salt.'

Bruce did not directly contradict Stephen. Stephen was too often better informed. Besides, Bruce wanted to avoid argument. Too often before they had quarrelled about such trivial matters. They washed up the breakfast things together and stood by the front window of the living-room smoking. Bruce was trying to think of a way to lighten the atmosphere.

'Shall we go down to the beach?'

'I'd rather go by myself, if you don't mind.'

'Let me come the first time. I want to show you.'

'If you insist.'

They threw their cigarettes into the fire and went out. The sand on the pathway down to the beach was softer now the dew had evaporated. Stephen stepped on it like the first man touching the moon, testing it with his weight, like a cat, like an inexperienced mountaineer in the snow. Bruce was slightly amused. His amusement increased when they came to the rocks. Stephen crossed them like a swan out of water, slipping and lurching like a lady in high-heel shoes crossing a cobbled street. At one point he almost fell right over, one hand touching the stones. Bruce caught his arm. Stephen stopped, in his bent posture, feeling his friend's strong grip. He stood up straight.

'I can manage, thank you.'

'It's always difficult the first time.'

'Said the bishop to the nun.'

Bruce laughed, almost unnaturally loudly. It was the first trace of humour Stephen had shown that morning. He tried a variation on the old theme.

'You are earnestly requested to construct your premises on moral grounds.'

'That's better.'

'That's better. Can you think of another one?'

They often did this, taking up a phrase or sentence that caught their fancy, inventing endless absurd convolutions, till they both almost collapsed in hysterics. Bruce started a new chain.

'You are earnestly requested to bugger off.'

'Said the novice to the bishop.'

'Choirboy would be better. And bugger me.'

'Ah, you've got something there!'

'Said the nun to the pope.'

They staggered laughing off the rocks, and stood on the beach. Stephen walked in a straight line carefully to the sea, now further out. He stopped. Bruce looked at him – a town-dweller at the edge of the sea – and realized how out of his element, how ridiculous his friend looked.

Stephen was wearing shiny black walking shoes, new ones his mother had bought him the week before. He was dressed in a green khaki-coloured suit, slightly shiny in places from frequent pressing, made of some synthetic fabric. His long-sleeved shirt was bright pink, and the cuffs protruded a few inches from his jacket sleeves. He was wearing black and gold cuff-links. Bruce gazed at them almost incredulously. Cuff-links on Harlieg beach! Surely no one had ever appeared before in formal cuff-links on that wild shoreline. What a travesty! Such were Bruce's thoughts as he eyed the egg-yellow cravat folded neatly inside the open collar of Stephen's shirt.

Bruce was wearing fawn cotton slacks and a white shirt. He was barefoot. He never wore shoes in or around the Harlieg house: they always got full of sand.

Stephen moved a few paces to the right. He stopped and looked at Bruce, his finger pointing at the ground. Bruce frowned slightly.
'What's the matter?'
'This was the place.'

5. THE BEACH

FOR BRUCE there were few things more fascinating than walking along the tideline on Harlieg beach. It always took him back in mind and spirit to his childhood, the passing of which, its happy innocence, its untroubled freedom, he regretted so much. Time and time again, he felt a loathing for maturity, for all the ungainly embroilments of being an adult — examinations, employment, the trivia of everyday life, responsibility, sex. With nostalgia, shabbily romantic he almost knew, he looked back on those glorious days, knowing though in his heart of hearts that there had been nothing really glorious, free or innocent about them. His childhood, he realized, had in many ways been a period of unrelieved mediocrity; he had missed so much; there were so many things he would like to have done. The tideline, however, was always a journey of discovery, a hinterland full of promise and astonishment; and it was never the same. At home, his room was full of treasures he had found there — a spherical green fisherman's float, an outsize cowrie, a piece of bleached, smooth wood like a squat snake with an eye, a scallop shell he used as an ashtray.

He had ignored Stephen's remark, not wanting to spoil the pleasure of this forage along the shore. They were walking along only a few yards from the line of rocks, and had almost reached the point where they faded away into the sand. They walked with their eyes on the sand before them. The actual line of the tide was dominated by huge damp rolls of brown seaweed. Shifting one of these with a stick, Stephen was surprised by the sudden myriad activity of nearly-transparent sand-hoppers he had found beneath it. At first he recoiled, but then he bent down and picked one up, examining it carefully. Once again, Bruce found himself envying his friend's fine attention to detail. It had never occurred to Bruce to pick up and actually look at a sand-hopper. They were merely there; they had always been there ever since he could remember. He had never looked at one with adult eyes. The pleasure of accompanying his friend along the beach, a new experience for Stephen, was slightly clouded by Stephen's strange preoccupation with the people he said he had seen on the beach the evening before. Stephen had stopped for several minutes at the point where he thought he had seen them, and Bruce could not understand why it should seem so important. It was faintly disturbing since, on both occasions in the darkness the previous evening, he had been quite certain there had been no one at all on the beach; and it was not Stephen's custom to manufacture mystery and drama where there were none; his life was full enough without the need for that. Bruce felt a momentary flutter of fear: it was uncanny when Stephen seemed to be doing seriously what he did as a matter of habit – fabricating suspense – as more of a joke really than anything. Perhaps Stephen was really aware of something he himself could not sense. Had Stephen sensed the existence of certain phantom beings down there on the beach? Or more disturbing, did Stephen have friends down there, friends who had secretly arrived on the same train and were waiting for Stephen on the sand? Stephen's mysterious attitude irritated him. Why bother about other people when they two were alone together in that house by the sea?

Stephen bent down and picked up a shell.
'What do you call this?'
'It's a mermaid's pencil.'
'Mermaid's penis?'
'Pencil.' They looked at each other, a faint smile hovering between them. 'Pity it isn't a perfect one. The point's broken off. I'll find you another one.'
'I've never seen one of these before. I wonder what the mermaids write.'

'Dirges of the sea.'

'Where do they write them?'

'On the sand. "One day I wrote her name upon the strand, But came the waves and washéd it away." Spenser. The most beautiful lines in the English language.'

'Except yours, I suppose.'

'Of course. Look, there's another one.' He picked up a pink mermaid's pencil. 'It's perfect, too.' He offered it to Stephen.

'I'd rather keep this one.'

'This one's much better.'

'It wasn't the first.'

Faintly irritated, Bruce dropped his shell to the sand; then he crushed it with his heel, viciously.

'Was that necessary?'

'I'm helping Nature make sand.'

'Don't make ridiculous excuses. You enjoyed smashing that.'

'Does Nature enjoy it?'

They went on along the line. Suddenly Bruce stopped.

'God! I almost put my foot on it!'

It was a dead bird. It had been dead at least a week. Its flesh had dried, or been eaten, or washed away by the salt sea. It was now a tangle of white and grey feathers and bones.

'It's a kittiwake, a kind of gull.'

'It was.'

A couple of black flies – they were no more obnoxious than common house-flies – rose up from the carcase and alighted on the sand a few yards away, waiting. Stephen bent over the wreckage.

'The bones look as if they're made of plastic.'

'Nijinsky had bones like that, in his feet, hollow ones. That's why he could fly.' Bruce leant forward in an ugly arabesque, flapping his arms. Stephen stared at the bird.

Half a dozen people in their late teens ran out of the sand dunes a quarter of a mile ahead of them. They were shouting, and throwing about a large red-and-yellow beach ball. Stephen watched them, smiling faintly. These were the kind of people he had expected to see at the seaside. Bruce frowned.

'Trippers. Let's go back. What a pity! They spoil everything.'

Stephen was not of the same opinion, but in this instance, as he often did, he deferred to Bruce. They turned back. Bruce picked up a long white salt-bleached stick; a piece of dried black seaweed was caught in one of its forks. Holding the stick behind him, its point touching the ground, Bruce started to run.

'Follow me! I'll make a line. You must follow it.' It was a game he had often played in his childhood. He waved the stick from side to side keeping its end on the ground, making curves and loops in the sand. At first Stephen good-naturedly followed the line, but he soon grew tired of it. There were so many things to look at on the sand – tiny pink shells like babies' toenails, empty sea-eggs, black dried sea-slugs with their two pairs of parallel 'feelers', the wedge-shaped bones of cuttle fish, razor shells, small pebbles with single strands of seaweed or worm-like barnacles fixed to their surfaces. All of them were new to him; he knew the names of none of them, but he stored each image in his mind. In this respect, he was like a child – not childish like Bruce – but like a real child, serious, full of wonder, learning pictures, making names. It was an endearing quality. Bruce had sometimes noticed it; it went with Stephen's total absorption when looking and listening; and whenever he noticed it, Bruce felt not so much the childlike simplicity of his friend, but rather the age-old wisdom of the very young.

A single seagull flew along low over the sea from the south, calling. The sound, for Bruce, was always unforgettable. It was one of the voices of the sea – inconsolably melancholy, solitary beyond human loneliness. It was the saddest sound he knew, and one of the most beautiful. The gull seemed to be looking about; he could see it moving its head from side to side, the smooth white undersides of its wings flexing strongly.

Stephen had stopped again. He too was listening. His face was the same as when he and Bruce listened to records together – strained, tremulous, sensitive to every nuance of the music. Bruce stared at him, fascinated.

'There's no sound like that in all the world.'

Stephen did not answer. He went on listening, his mouth working, his hands trembling. The gull had long since merged into the haze north along the shore. Bruce could not prevent himself from speaking again.

'A seagull's cry is like the voice after the end of the world.'

'I wasn't listening to that.'

*

They sat on the sand in the warm sun. It was almost noon. In his childhood holidays, this hour was always for Bruce the best of the day. He and his brothers and sister would spend the whole morning on the beach, and then, at just this hour, their mother, clad in a black skirted swimming costume, looking almost scrawny with her thin legs and arms, rough grey hair and the insides of her thighs dappled and dimpled with child-bearing, would appear above the rocks where the path came down from the house. Her arms would be heaped with towels and swimming things. They would change on the beach, and then all together rush into the sea. His mother had given him sixpence, when, her hand under his chin, he had swum, choking with salt and half-blind with blue and green and sunshine, his first three strokes. Today was such a day; now was the hour – but no one came down the path from the house. Bruce stood up.

'I'm going to swim.'

Bruce had never seen Stephen in anything except the type of clothes he was now wearing. To him, the idea of Stephen's body virtually naked was in no way fascinating except as an object for mockery. He visualized white hairless legs, a flabby stomach and back, nipples almost blue with cold, and gooseflesh all over.

'Why don't you come in too?'

'I haven't got any swimming things.'

'You can swim in your underpants.'

'They're not presentable.'

'Why don't you like swimming?'

'I can't swim. I've never been in the sea before.'

'Not even to paddle.'

'No.'

'Not even to piddle?'

'I don't do things like that.'

'Why don't you try now?'
'I don't have to do everything the same as you, do I?'
'You're a weakling.'
'No, I'm not.'
'Anyway, I'm going up to get changed.'
'I'll wait here.'

Bruce leapt up over the rocks to the path. He changed swiftly in the downstair bedroom and once again enjoyed the feel of soft clean cotton against his skin, feeling a momentary pulse or two of pleasure. Forcing his mind away from temptation, he ran out into the sunshine, his towel stiff with salt wrapped round his neck. When he got back to the beach, he found Stephen removing his second sock with some difficulty. The black shiny shoes stood, something like an epilogue to The Walrus and the Carpenter, side by side on the sand, or like two baby grand pianos in a desert. Stephen began to roll up his trouser legs. Bruce ran into the sea, plunging down like a young brown-mottled swan landing. Stephen followed him slowly to the edge of the sea. Bruce stood up, glistening with water, and watched Stephen. Stephen made no sudden starts or little chortles as might be expected at one's first encounter with the coldness of the sea. He merely stood there, and watched the dying waves wash round his ankles. He stared in amazement as his feet sank into the sand at each return of the water. His feet disappeared. In a sudden panic he tried to turn round, and his feet, at first unable to follow the swing of his body, stuck and then came out suddenly. He sat down. Bruce laughed and kicked the shallow water where he was standing. Stephen got to his feet, looking angry. The back flap of his jacket and the seat of his trousers were dark with water.

'Take them off!' Bruce's laughter changed into a derisive jeer.
'Fuck off!'
'Piss off yourself. It looks as if you have already. Stephen Pee-wit!'
'Shut up, will you!'
Rather than angry now, Stephen looked dismayed. His face reddened. He walked away from the sea, sat down by the rocks

and began to put his socks and shoes back on. Bruce swam in the sea.

Bruce always felt a little uneasy swimming in the sea. Although he never stayed in long as he soon became cold, he enjoyed the stinging saltiness of the water. Especially when the sea was rough and shouting, he loved to throw himself head first into the huge waves or buffet them with his back. But somehow when he was in the sea he always felt a certain sense of sacrilege. The sea was not mere water: it had a life of its own, like the castle, almost a human life; it had a soul. When he had been in the sea as a child, he had sometimes urinated, enjoying the warmth of his own water as it met the cold. He never told others when he did that, and afterwards swam from the spot. Once or twice, soon after puberty, he had pulled down his swimming trunks and brought himself to orgasm under the water, looking with guilty interest at the stringy white lumps drifting away like infant ghosts. Nowadays, however, he never did such things. He had come to recognize the sea, as those who know it well do, as a kind of mother, a kind of guardian – even the chief source of all his energy. He noticed how people always become excited when they catch sight of the sea suddenly, from a train or a car, or even when they see a lake or river; as if they feel the primeval womb of their ancestors, and sense the joy, the mystery of returning home. To Bruce, as a poet, the sea was now the single inspiration of all his work. He had come to rely on it as a reservoir, an eternal spring of music, images and emotional forces. The voice of his poetry was almost always the voice of the sea. The sea was a priestess, or the deity a priestess worshipped – visible as a vast, moving sky, as unseen as the spirit of the wind. Somehow, to behave as a seaside holiday-maker, to swim and play in the water, were unclean things, an insult to the godliness, a spiritually punishable offence. He himself felt little of man's one-ness with the ocean; his communication was entirely of the mind, a romantic leaning, a dream-like exchange. Had he been able to feel how natural it was to commune, naked, with the surf, he would never now have felt this strange discomfort when he went for a swim in the sea.

He looked up at the sun. The sky behind it was not blue, but, suddenly it seemed, hideously black – as astronauts see it. It filled him with a momentary surge of terror. He ran out of the water.

Stephen was sitting on the sand, his hands joined round his drawn-up knees. Bruce saw that the fingers were white, yellow in fact, like dead flesh. Stephen's face was resting on his knees, his eyes boring into the sand. He seemed to be enduring some private mental agony.

He was; but he didn't know how to explain it clearly, even to himself. He was not sure, indeed, what he felt. He had been trying to find a moment to speak of it to Bruce – his bitterness, his utter disgust with himself, with people, the world, with everything. Nor could he understand what it was he felt here at this house by the sea, what he had seen, or heard, or sensed ever since he had arrived. His mind was a black sand-storm. It had been for months – flying glass, shrapnel, burning coals, icicles. All of them seemed to be colliding in his brain, grinding themselves to bits, freezing into a cold ball which burst again, exploding minute splinters at the inside of his skull. And the dust never seemed to settle. He seethed, not with anger at Bruce's mocking remarks, not with his family's moronic bullying, nor with the injustice of the world, but with non-comprehension, forces – snatches of music, brilliant metaphors, cutting fragments of philosophy, booming accusations from the Devil – which he knew no way to control. He stared at the sand, millions of shattered rocks, pulverized shells, whole dynasties of species, representing aeons of patient, ruthless disintegration – all of it emerging, entire, unified, perfect, in this glistening, pastel-gentle, wide, wildly still sweep of the beach in the serene curve of Tremadog Bay.

6. THE ZIG-ZAG

AFTER A LIGHT LUNCH of beans on toast, apples and tea, they went to fetch the milk. Fetching the milk was a daily ritual at Tremarfon. Since the house was isolated from the rest of the town, matters like the delivery of goods or disposal of rubbish were quite a problem. Many of the authorities concerned simply refused to venture so far out of their ordinary rounds. There was also the fact that the house was owned not by Welsh people but by English foreigners. As a result, the milk had to be fetched from a pick-up point on the roadside half way up the cliff.

At first Stephen had refused to go. He had been silent since their slight altercation on the beach, not refraining from speech entirely, but keeping conversation to an absolute minimum. Bruce, not realizing how much to blame he had been for the immediate present situation, although of course he was not to blame for Stephen's deep mental turmoil, felt irritated that his friend was marring what should have been a magnificent holiday; he was even further irritated by the fact that, although he had already washed all the apples, Stephen chose to peel his with a knife. Bruce was often impatient with other people's way of doing things when they did not coincide with his own. He always ate an apple directly, peel included, holding it in his hand. He felt there was something effeminate or unnecessarily finicky about peeling it, cutting it into four sections, and removing the segments of core. The vitamins, he told Stephen, were mainly in the peel. Stephen was equally irritated by Bruce's housewife mentality. The subject was soon dropped, however, after Bruce had asked for and been given Stephen's peel to eat – an eccentricity of which Stephen somewhat to his surprise found himself heartily approving. Bruce explained about the milk, and Stephen, not accustomed to walking any considerable distance, had not taken to the idea.

'All the way up there?'

'It doesn't take long.'

'I'll get asthma.'

'You only get asthma if you stay in a stuffy room.'

'What do you know about it?'

'My sister used to get it.'

'Well, you've never had it, have you?'

There was a pause.

'I don't want to go by myself.' There was a faint note of self-pity in Bruce's voice.

'We don't have to do everything together. We're not little girls.'

'I want to show you the view.'

Stephen had never in his life climbed a mountain, let alone a mere hill. He had no idea what it meant, either physically or mentally, to achieve height by effort and earn a view. It was the promise of a new experience which finally decided him.

'All right, I'll come.'

They took the same path to the railway line, and crossed over. As he stepped over the brown rails of the line with their shining silver top surfaces, Stephen was surprised by their size. The wheels, he thought, must be almost as tall he was. Bruce was thinking of his childhood again.

'We used to put pennies on the line.'

'What for?'

'And watch the trains go over them. They used to get flattened out – as big as this.' He made a circle with his fingers. 'Some stupid boys used to play a game called "Last Over". One of them was nearly killed once.'

'Were you one of the stupid boys?'

Bruce looked at Stephen with annoyance. He had a high opinion of his own goodness and common sense, and when Stephen stuck a pin into his self-respect – as he did now, seeming to enjoy it – Bruce was always irritated. He hated to be thought in the wrong. They crossed the second stile. Stephen, who had managed the first one without difficulty, slipped and hit his knee on one of the steps, feeling a surge of anger as he saw Bruce at the top of the stile looking down on him with a superior smile. On the other side, the footpath to the station stretched away to the left, parallel to the line. The path they had to take led straight up to the foot of the cliff, where it became a zig-zag. In speaking of the cliff, it should be pointed out that it was not a cliff in the sense of a precipice, although parts of it were quite inaccessible. It was merely the edge of Wales; in former days it had been the shore itself, inclining steeply into the sea. Now it was simply like the fairly steep side of a mountain. Above them, it rose to some eight or nine hundred feet, although they could not see from where they were standing the upper slopes, which curved over into the heart of

Wales. Stretching north beyond the town, it kept approximately the same height all the way to the Snowdon mountains; to the south it petered out, and beyond the point where the railway line went round the corner barely a mile away, there was hardly any cliff at all. The main road from the south into Harlieg traversed the slope of the cliff, about half way up it. There were some twenty houses below or above the road, dotted along the part of the route visible from Tremarfon. Above the road, the cliff gradually rounded off and beyond its ridge-like summit, descended again 'over the back', where it gradually merged with bigger mountains inland.

As they walked towards the foot of the cliff, Stephen noticed the sandy turf giving way to pale brown soil mixed with bits of granite and slate. A heavy sweet scent reached his nostrils: to his right was a dark mass of gorse, some of it in brilliant yellow flower. Stephen had not often smelt flowers like this – real, growing ones. Most of the flowers he had seen were cut ones, in shops or in the Birmingham Market.

They began to climb. At first there were fifteen rough-hewn stone steps, with thick stone walls either side. The rough-hewn stones had shifted slightly, partly because of the loose weight of the cliff made unstable by rain, and partly because of an overgrowth of ivy. To Stephen's eyes, the ivy, in its dark green, black and grey coils, seemed extraordinarily old, and twisted with evil. He was to see much of it in Wales. Although it was almost the hottest hour of the day, the sun, still in the south, had not yet had time to face the cliff directly, and there was still a heavy dampness everywhere. At the top of the steps, the path turned sharply right, leading steeply upwards – the first angle of the zig-zag. The overhanging bank on the left was a heavy fringe of brambles, bracken and wild flowers – ragged robin, foxgloves, briar roses, small clumps of gorse, and many others the names of which were unknown even to Bruce. Initially, the combined scent of these, sweet and moist, was delightful to Stephen, but by the time they had reached the second elbow of the zig-zag, hardly three or four minutes' effort, he had begun to sweat and wheeze, so that the heady dampness was a harassment rather than a pleasure. He inwardly cursed the sluggish weakness of his body. A mottled brown horsefly settled on his hand and before he was aware of it had punctured the skin sharply. Stephen flung it off with an exclamation, rubbing the back of his hand. He was breathing noisily. The flowers and greenery around him lost their fragrance. Suddenly they seemed to Stephen virulent and sickly. The colours of the flowers were engendered in the warm darkness of mouldering earth. The delicate ferns were veils hiding the face of a hideous woman. There was nothing beautiful, anywhere. It was all a lie. His bitterness returned. Bruce, aware of Stephen's condition and enjoying his own healthy strength, deliberately kept up his pace, walking on his toes in his sandals and swinging the leather milk bag he had taken down from inside the back door of the house. The empty bottles in it clinked.

'Don't go so fast.'

'Come on. It's easy. Are you tired?' Bruce stopped and smiled down at Stephen, who was suddenly aware of his friend's tremendous power. Bruce had always been the stronger, never more so than now. Stephen felt almost like crying.

'Can't you see? I told you this would happen. Don't go so fast.'

'We'll soon be at the top.'

'There's no need to hurry.'

Bruce knew there was no need to hurry, but whenever he had to exert himself, he liked to get it over as soon as possible. For this reason, whenever he had unpleasant tasks to perform, he often did them badly. His father on many occasions had forced him to do again things he had been given to do, and Bruce, angry and impatient, felt his hatred for his father at such times increase tenfold. He despised his father, not in the way Stephen disrespected his, but because his father was so hard, so slow and so heavy-handed. He destroyed all the spontaneity of living that Bruce had so much admired in his mother; he killed the simplest of pleasures by overplanning, too much anticipation. For his father, the next was always better than the now; for his mother, the now had been all; for her, the future had been a darkening roadway, the past a treasure-house of memories. Bruce took after his mother rather than his father. Quickness was the thing.

He waited for Stephen to catch up with him, but as soon as Stephen came panting to a standstill at Bruce's side, Bruce at once began to walk again, not giving his friend any time to catch his breath, a form of deliberate cruelty which almost drove Stephen to despair. After a little while, however, Bruce himself began to feel tired and slowed his pace. Stephen looked up to his right. An ugly white box-like house, quite un-Welsh, like something out of the suburbs of a Midland town, stood there on the cliff. Almost all the windows were small and mean. The woodwork, gutters and drainpipes were painted a brilliant impossible green. Bruce had always been strongly aware of the branch of pipes leading out of the wall from the bathroom, right in the middle of the front wall facing the sea – thin ones from basin and bath, a thicker one for the lavatory. What poor artistic sense, Bruce always thought, what lack of imagination! The anatomy of the house was almost transparent.

'You see that house? It's slipping down the cliff. Excavation wasn't deep enough. One day we'll wake up in the morning and find it at the bottom. That's what my mother always used to say. Look, you can see cracks in the wall.'

It was true; and as they drew level with it, Stephen could see that the terrace in front of the house was not horizontal, and crevices in it had been cemented over. The idea of a slowly descending house intrigued him.

'How long has it been there?'

'About forty years, I think. It belongs to a spinster. She watches us with binoculars. She's always fussing and complaining.'

'Like you. You're a spinster.' Stephen knew about Bruce's apparent lack of interest in the opposite sex except as something upon which Bruce could pour scorn and ridicule. He suspected that Bruce's chasteness was a cover for something less seemly. Fear, lack of success with girls, he thought, were the real reasons for Bruce's antipathy. He forgot for a moment that he himself was in much the same predicament.

'Speak for yourself. You're not only a spinster; you're a turd as well.'

'It takes turd to make a quarrel.' Now that they were gaining height, Stephen was beginning to recover something of his composure. They went on climbing. The zig-zag became narrower, the alternate slopes shorter. A few minutes later they were at the top. There was a stone wall with a gate in it. A car rushed past; it seemed to be moving at an abnormal speed, perhaps because they were both standing a little lower than the level of the road and there was no pavement the other side of the wall. Stephen was feeling much better now. The first exhaustion had worn off. He was in his second wind, and as is usual at such times he felt more energetic than ever, even proud of his achievement at getting as high as this without collapsing. He looked at the view.

Because of some pines to the right and because the two friends were on the cliff itself, they could no longer see the hotel, college or castle; some of the mountains were out of sight too. Apart from the house below, at the extreme outer edge of the sandhills, the main view was of the sea, the beach, now almost completely uncovered by the receding tide, and the Traeth. It was, to Stephen's eyes, magnificent.

He had never before seen such stretches of water and sand. The faint agoraphobia he had sensed the evening before had now become wonder and bewilderment. Looking down on the landscape now, he found it hard to believe it was real. The sea was too flat, too still to be a moving liquid substance; the sandhills were too unfamiliar to his eyes, too strange to belong to the world as he knew it. He followed with his eyes the line of the shore to the right. What appeared from the level of the house to be a point at the end of the long low range of sandhills was not a point at all. In the corner of the bay, he could now see, the dunes turned inland again and swept round in a great curve contrary to that of the bay as a whole, towards the Tortoise hill. Beyond, between the dunes and the mountains, an estuary stretched far inland to the right and out of sight. The beach near the opening of the estuary was immensely wide. There the sandhills had faded away. It was like a desert, a huge expanse of sand and patches of green and yellow vegetation. The far boundaries of the golf links seemed comparatively near; beyond them in the desert was space enough for three or four golf courses more.

'That's the Traeth.' Bruce was exchanging the bottles in the bag for two full ones from a box set in the bank below the wall.

Stephen said nothing. His eyes were fixed on the wilderness at the far end of the beach.

'Have you ever been right over there?'

'I once went round by bicycle. There's a swamp there. I went round the back of it behind that Tortoise mountain you can see down there and came back by the road.'

'What's it like over there? The flat part.'

'Terrifying.'

Stephen looked at him. Bruce continued.

'They used to use it for gunnery practice. During the War. It's littered with rusty shell-cases and rotting corrugated iron, like a forgotten battlefield; forsaken. They used to put a flag up. White for safety, yellow for danger. If there was a red flag up, we weren't allowed even to go down to the beach near the house. There are some mines there, too. Old ones. Washed up from the estuary – unexploded ones. Once they burned one on the beach. We watched it through my father's telescope. Some bomb-disposal people were down there. It's funny. It didn't explode.'

'There are some people down there now.'

Bruce looked where Stephen was pointing. It was true. There were four or five figures there in the distance, like ants, scarcely moving. Or was it ten? Or was it a hundred?

A goods train rattled slowly past below, just like a toy that had developed a life of its own. Smoke rose up between them and the Traeth, then cleared.

'I can't see them now.'

Bruce looked again. Stephen was right. The people seemed to have disappeared. Stephen's eyes were open very wide.

'I'd like to walk along there. Is it far?'

'You wouldn't be able to stand it.'

'Why not?'

'It'd drive you mad.'

'Why? How?' Stephen's eyes were round with fear.

'Along there, even in the middle of the day, even when the weather's fine and sunny, you can hear them.'

'Hear what?'

Bruce slowly turned and stared at Stephen. Stephen could see nothing but the strange light burning in Bruce's eyes.

'You can hear the mermaids singing.'

7. THE VERANDAH

THE VERANDAH on the west side of the house was always, when the weather was fine, a pleasant place to sit in the afternoon. The sun, in the south-west, was not yet low enough to shine directly into the eyes of anyone sitting there, but it warmed their bodies and feet; and there was always the expanse of the sea to calm the mind. Bruce and Stephen sat back in the long grey teakwood seat drinking tea and enjoying the very gentle breeze which came in from the west across the bay. The mountains to the north and the Lleyn peninsula were almost invisible in haze. The seat was one of those often seen in front of golf clubhouses, on seafronts or terraces, or in public shelters and parks, the kind that sometimes have metal plaques on them bearing the names of the donors. Such seats were designed to withstand the most inclement of weathers, and the one in the verandah showed its age: its smooth surface had the texture of stone worn by recurrent gales and the constant working of the tides. A table of the same material stood to their right with the tea things on it, the most colourful item being an old tea-stained patchwork quilted cosy. Just in front of the table, hanging from the eaves where the roof came low over the verandah, was a long brown strand of seaweed, swinging lightly in the breeze. Bruce had brought it up before lunch, shining and soft with sea-water, to serve as a kind of weather indicator. They had done that for years in the family. If the seaweed stayed moist, it would rain; if it dried, as it almost had now, swinging stiffly, fine weather was in the offing. Bruce, not scientifically minded, often wondered how it worked. To him it seemed that when the weather was dry the seaweed was dry; when it rained, the seaweed was wet – not so much an indicator as a measure. But he still brought up the seaweed out of habit. As far as the weather was concerned, it was a perfect day.

They had not talked a great deal. Stephen had little inclination to be sociable. He seemed totally absorbed in the scenery, mostly watching the sea, now coming in again. Bruce did not know how to penetrate Stephen's grey wall of moroseness. They just sat, mostly thinking. Bruce was wearing his swimming shorts and shirt; Stephen was in the same unyielding suit, socks and shoes.

They had known each other for just over three years. Bruce, visiting a friend of his, had listened to a tape-recording of someone trying to read a poem; the reader was having excessive difficulty controlling himself and repeatedly burst out in long whistling whinnies of laughter. Something childlike in the voice had fascinated Bruce. He had asked his friend to introduce him to the reader. A meeting had been arranged.

Bruce first met Stephen, therefore, in the coffee lounge of the Chesterton Hotel in Birmingham. At first, he had been disappointed with Stephen's appearance, having expected someone younger, more boyish, more elf-like. He found nothing to attract him in Stephen's peculiarly artificial clothes, his ugly snub-nosed face, his squat figure, the flat back of his head; and he had always been suspicious, irrationally he realized, of people who allowed their hair to grow over their ears the way Stephen did while keeping it short at the back. He had soon become impressed, however, with Stephen's logical mind and his way of refusing to accept conventions or concepts without first examining them thoroughly. Stephen's truculent attitude to established ideas and entrenched authority was a refreshing experience for Bruce, who would have held the same attitudes had he not lacked the courage and conviction. Stephen was always experimental, radical, uncomfortably original. They had on that first occasion talked for hours, and then on later occasions for days on end.

Stephen was not sure why he liked Bruce. He was not even sure whether he liked him at all. It may have been Bruce's stability that attracted him, and the inflexibility of his views; or conversely, his romantic leanings, his aspirations towards human nobility. They had not seemed false or empty then. Or it may have been something in Bruce's face. Stephen's life had been a mess. A chronic asthmatic in childhood, often bedridden, he had shown early talents in music, and was consequently encouraged, almost hysterically, by his mother and her relatives − all of them hungry for fame or reflected glory − to master the piano. Early success and subsequent over-praise had led him to complacency and relaxation of effort. He had believed, and had been made to believe, that he was a child prodigy, whereas he was nothing of the kind. He soon became frustrated and unmanageable. School was a constant torture, and he had just given up regular attendance, then aged fifteen, just before his first meeting with Bruce, who had then been almost nineteen.

Bruce had listened to Stephen's history with growing compassion and anger. He had long imagined himself superior to others in moral strength and had set out to reform Stephen according to his own fixed rules and maxims. He at once recognized Stephen's originality of thought, his interest in music, philosophy and literature, and felt it a profound pity that Stephen had no self-discipline or external control in the form of sensible parents, teachers or friends to help him exercise or express his talents. Stephen had shown him a short prose extract he had written; Bruce had at once seen its potential and encouraged Stephen to forget about the piano and devote himself to writing poetry and novels. Stephen, hypnotized by Bruce's strength and encouragement, both of which things he needed, had thrown himself with energy into composition. In addition, Bruce had more or less forced Stephen to enrol in a course of further education at a technical college in Birmingham, and all seemed to augur well.

A few months after their first meeting, Bruce had gone away to university. Returning to Birmingham after his first term, he had found Stephen back where he had been when they had first met. Stephen had thrown up his studies, stopped writing, and got involved with a group of ageing homosexuals, whose communications base was the barber's shop Stephen went to. Once again, Bruce tried to rescue his new-found friend. Stephen, however, could never endure long in one endeavour. Like a wild horse he kicked the traces. A long struggle ensued – Bruce becoming more dictatorial, moralistic and pitying, Stephen more demoralized, confused and hysterical. There were, however, a few constants: they talked often; they listened to music, Stephen teaching Bruce for the first time in his life how to listen properly – pointing out to him the elegant brilliance of classical music, whereas before Bruce had favoured only the purple grandeur of the late romantics. And Stephen had gradually developed an infatuation for Bruce.

It was a kind of love. It had reached a crisis when Stephen had felt one day an irresistible need to hold Bruce's hand. He did not dare to mention his longing to Bruce directly and tried to express his feelings in a letter which he had handed to him. Bruce, unable even to consider any kind of physical contact apart from the normal shaking of hands, had coldly rejected him, sermonizing grimly. Stephen, shattered, had found comfort once again among his pederast companions, and Bruce had watched him from a distance, half disgusted, and almost with feelings of alarm, half fascinated. At the same time, perhaps through Stephen's influence or perhaps because they were already latent, he had begun to realize that he himself was developing similar tendencies. There was nothing bestial, he thought, in his case, and he never once entertained ideas of sleeping with anyone: the old and ugly had no fascination for him. Stephen attracted him physically not at all. It was to the purity, the freshness, to the unsuspecting beauty of young boys that Bruce turned his eyes. He knew, or rather he felt in a hazily romantic way, that to touch was to kill. Stephen, already touched and soiled, was either unable to understand this, or profoundly envious of Bruce's inviolability. Stephen had steadily deteriorated, but they had still met, fascinated with each other's minds. Bruce remained chaste, severe, a thousand miles tall, looking down on Stephen with the same pity, the same disapproval. Stephen had taken a succession of menial jobs, constantly afraid of becoming, as he had once confided to Bruce, like a tramp they often saw sleeping or shuffling about in the Birmingham Art Gallery.

Now Bruce had graduated from university and was going into teaching. At the present time he was waiting to join the staff of a new school for foreigners which was being established in a Victorian mansion in Berkshire. The term was to start late in September, or early October, it was not certain when. Using this opportunity to spend a few weeks by the sea, writing, reading and talking, Bruce had invited Stephen to stay with him at Harlieg.

Suddenly Stephen sat forwards and shook his head rapidly.
'I loved you once.'
'I killed it.'
'Did you?'
'You never mentioned it again.'
'Can I have a cigarette?'
'We smoke too much.'

They lit cigarettes, Bruce not minding now as Stephen briefly touched his hand while lighting his for him. Bruce never minded Stephen smoking his cigarettes, eating out as his expense, allowing him to pay for things. It gave him a sense of control over his friend. He never mentioned this, however. He knew that if he once complained of Stephen's readiness to accept and his lack of gratitude, Stephen would get up in a temper and go. Bruce had no wish to lose his friend. Troublesome though he was, erratic, hysterical, a constant disappointment in his moral weakness, Stephen was always an inspiration, an unfailingly stimulating companion. What did it matter, finally, who paid?

'Aren't you going to do any writing here?'
'I told you, I didn't bring my typewriter.'
'I can lend you a pen, and paper.'
'I don't have any ideas. Anyway, writing's a waste of time, futile.'
'Why? You never said so before.'
'Things are different now. Art's just an excuse. All art's a false compensation for failure in life. Artists are liars.'
'Am I a liar? What do you mean?'
'Are you an artist?'
'Of course.'
'Are you? You're going to be a teacher. You're going to have a salary. You're going to work for Society with a capital S. Inside. You're safe. You're comfortable. You always have been. You don't have to worry. Artists, real artists, aren't like that. They've got to be honest. They've got to live raw. They've got to suffer.'
'My God, haven't I suffered?'

'You don't know what it means.'

Bruce knew there was much truth in this. Compared with the gale-force winds of Stephen's life, his own so far had been a mere breeze. He thought he had suffered agonies of love and rejection. He thought he had known pain and loneliness. But it was Stephen who really knew these things, who had really been tortured. Stephen had written about such things in his early attempts at writing novels: there they were perhaps too intense, too real to be considered true art – and the novels had never been finished. Bruce's poems were full of lovely words, of singing pain, of suffering raised to god-like proportions – monuments of endurance, heroic, titanic, hollow.

'You think I'm just a fake.'
'That's what you are. It's not what I think.'
'Don't my poems mean anything then?'
'They sound good.'
'Aren't they real?'
'I'm not sure.'
'I thought you liked them.'
'I admire your use of language.'
'What about the thoughts? That's what matters.'
'You're not a thinker.'
'What am I then?'
'A moralist. Your ideas are not your own.'
'What are you then?'
'I'm not sure.'
'I think you're a great writer. Or you could be. If only you'd finish something. You're always starting, but you never finish anything.'
'I'm going to finish something while I'm here.' Stephen's eyes glittered as he stared out at the sea.
'But you didn't bring your typewriter.'
'You don't understand what I mean.'
'Why can't you say what you mean?'
'I will if you want me to.'

They looked at each other. The strand of seaweed rustled as a faint strengthening of the breeze caused it to touch the end pillar of the verandah. It was like the cast-off skin of a snake, the shrivelled garment, no longer needed, forgotten, of some half-human creature out of the sea. Stephen opened his mouth to speak. He seemed to be hesitating. He clenched his fists and looked at the ground. Then he muttered, almost growled out in a low undertone, the thought that had been on his mind for so long now.

'I came here to kill myself.'

8. SUNSET

THE SUN HAD BEGUN its long near-vertical drop towards the Lleyn peninsula. Now visible just below the overhanging roof of the verandah, it shone, not powerfully, directly into their eyes. Bruce, his eyes burning with fear, stared at Stephen.

'Why, Stephen?'

He knew his friend was unstable and unpredictable; he knew he was prone to sudden reverses, sudden fits of destructive energy; he knew Stephen had on several occasions had psychiatric treatment. But he thought his friend had too much pride, too much stubborn resistance ever to think of anything so radical as self-destruction. Now he understood why Stephen had seemed so often morose and silent ever since he had come to Harlieg. He felt a sudden flash of anger at Stephen's blind stupidity – to throw away his talents, to throw away all Bruce's efforts on his behalf, even to be thinking of such things.

'You're not such a fool.'
'It's been going on too long.'
'Things are not so bad as they seem.' Bruce felt the futility of his words, that there was no comfort in them.
'You don't know anything about it.'

'There's always a way out.' Again Bruce inwardly cursed at his moral inadequacy. In real emergencies like this all his high-flown maxims and attitudinizing seemed meaningless. He felt powerless now to help his friend.

'This is one of them. This is the only way out.'

'I don't mean that. You're being dramatic.'

'You don't know what it's been like. You don't realize at all.'

There was a tremor in his voice, a hint of tears.

'People laugh at me. They point at me. Wherever I go I feel a stranger, someone to be mocked at. Last week near my home a group of boys threw stones at me and bits of broken bottles. For no reason at all. Everybody stares at me. It's not just a recent thing. It's been going on for years. It was just the same at school. And they always made fun of my name. I can't get away from it. How would you feel with a name like mine? Pewit. Should be Pyooit, but they always call me Pee-wit. Pee-wee. Pee-wee, they shouted, Mr. Pee-wee. Even you do it.'

'I'm sorry. I should have known better.'

'It's easy to be sorry now, ridiculous; it's just words anyway. Nobody can be sorry now. It's gone on too long. Nobody understands. I'm just being laughed at. Even my mother doesn't care about what really matters – music, books. She and my father dismiss it all as highbrow nonsense. And sometimes even I think it is. Other people just use me. Sometimes I wake up in the morning and find I'm in bed with some filthy middle-aged man stinking of sweat. They slobber all over me, and rub me up, grunting and jerking at my body. It's foul. They make me drunk in the evening. I don't know how to get away.'

'Why do you go to those places?'

'Where else can I go? I can't stay at home, and nobody accepts me anywhere else.'

'That's stupid. Anyway, you've got away now. You're here.'

'It's not stupid. You don't live where I live. You don't know anything about the sort of environment I have to put up with. All they care about is alcohol, drugs, money and sex. They don't talk about anything else.'

'Not everybody's like that.'

'I suppose you think you and your friends are better. That's rubbish. They're all false. They think they understand about art; they talk rubbish. It's all empty crap. Dropping names, dropping big words to impress each other and others who might overhear them.'

'That's what you do.'

'I use words. I mean what I say when I say something. I don't mess about. You're all just playing.'

'Look, I tried to help you.'

'Tried to educate me. Tried to make me go straight. Some idiotic course. Even the teachers couldn't understand what they were teaching. They just read out of books. They were incompetent.'

'You like music, don't you?'

'What good's that? I used to have a piano, but when we moved into the flat, we had to give it away.'

'You can go to concerts in the Town Hall.'

'They're going to stop them soon. The orchestra's going to close down. They're going to have a brass band instead and just do pop classics. Who wants rubbish like that?'

'You should have more strength. More discipline.'

'Don't try that moral stuff on me. I don't like it. And it doesn't do me the slightest good. Nobody can do anything now.'

'I tried to help.'

'Why? It was a waste of time, wasn't it?'

'No, it wasn't a waste of time. It isn't. You've got talent, Stephen. You can write. I was one of the first to recognize it.'

'Talent. Talent. You've got to be a genius to get anywhere these days. I don't want to be mediocre.'

'That's just what you're not.'

'That's just what I am. Second-rate. You know very well my writing's no good. You just stuff me up with pep-talk and cushy encouragement. Just to salve your conscience. So you can be the saviour, the good stinking Samaritan. I know what you're up to. You've never done anything for me. For me, for me. Don't you realize who I am? You've never helped me, Bruce. You set me up with some course of action, and then walk away, patting yourself on the back and saying "I've done my good deed; I'm happy". It makes me sick. You're so complacent. Just a smug old maid. Just now you said you were the first to recognize my talent. That's what's more important to you, that you were the first; what happens to the talent is bugger all.'

'No, Stephen. You don't understand me.'

Bruce felt tears warm at the brims of his eyes. He felt rejected. What Stephen was saying might well be true, but he Bruce had never thought of it like that; he had never realized how shallow he had seemed. It was true, but he did believe he had tried to be truly benevolent.

'I haven't always done things the right way. But I thought I was sincere.'

'You've never done things the right way, and you don't know what sincere means. You don't have any feelings. Everything you say's just trumped up verbiage. Grand gestures. Histrionics. Your heart's just a cold block like the moon. Most sentimental people are like that.'

'No.'

Bruce knew now that what Stephen was saying was not true. Maybe his way of saying things, his way of doing things, was grandiloquent and pompous, but he was fired by something deeper than that. He knew it was not all false. There was something genuine deep down. He looked out over the sea. It was brilliant with golden light. It glittered, alive with electric movement. It filled him now with power, and it was a power he was determined to use, consciously, perhaps for the first time. Stephen had to be smashed completely. He had to be shattered like the light on the sea, like a pane of glass glaring with reflected sunlight. He had to be ground down like sand, scorched, melted, and hammered into solid rock. Then, if there was anything left after that, he could begin again; he could climb up and find his feet in a new world. He could be re-created with the purity of a glass flask, with the strong brilliance of a crystal chandelier. Bruce brought the flat of his hand sharply down on the broad wooden arm of the seat. Stephen started, turning his eyes almost fearfully towards him.

'Right. You've said enough; you've said all I want hear. Now I'm going to say something. I'm tired of your self-pity. I'm tired of your soft, flabby attitudes. I'm sick of your petty weaknesses. You've got no guts. I've spent bloody hours trying to help you, and all you do is throw it back in my face, and I'm not going to tolerate it any longer. O.K. All right. Go away and kill yourself. Run into the sea and drown. Cut your throat and bleed into the sand. Go and do the dramatic thing, but don't do it here in a beautiful place like this. I don't want this house and shore to be cluttered up with morbid memories of your selfish immaturity. Go and do it somewhere else. But I don't believe for one moment you've got the courage to do it. You'd just make a mess of it, like everything else you've done; it'd just be a half-hearted affair to get you sympathy and comfort. Well, you won't get any from me. It's an old, old story. I've heard it all before, and you ought to know better than to try it out on me. You think I'm just a poseur, trying to do good to others for my own self-satisfaction. You're wrong; you've never been more wrong in your life. You don't know me at all. Why should I waste time with a strutting little cocksure fool like you prancing about in funny clothes and silly hats? You think you're so special. You're just a plain third-rate schoolboy. Why do you think people laugh at you? Why do they throw stones at you? Because you're objectionable. You make them do it. Because it makes you feel special. You want them to do it. You want to be different from others, more important. But you're not. I'm telling now quite plainly that you're not: you're just a fake, ten times more fake than I am. At least I know I'm grandiose. I laugh at myself. You've never done that. You're too proud, too full of your own self-dramatization to laugh at yourself. You think I can't feel anything. You don't know what you're talking about.'

Bruce pointed to the sea, then swept his hand dramatically across over the dunes. His voice suddenly became quiet.

'I saw my mother dying. You don't know about that. You met her once or twice, but you don't know anything about pain. She died of cancer. You know that. But you don't know how she died. Getting thinner and thinner. Years and years before I had nightmares about my mother. Somehow I knew she'd die like that. I don't know how I knew, but that's how she did die. You never saw her in hospital. Once I put some scent-spray on her hair, but it went into her eyes, and she cried out "My eyes! My eyes!" in such a thin and terrible voice. I can still hear it often. Even when she was dying I couldn't make her comfortable, I could only hurt her eyes. But she had tremendous courage. She never told us she knew she was dying. She must have known. One week she was drinking tea out of a cup, the next week she couldn't even hold the cup. One day she found an article about cancer in a magazine; there were lots of coloured photographs. She showed them to us, saying how interesting they were, and all the time staring at us directly in the eyes, with a kind of intense searching gaze, trying to make us betray ourselves into blurting out the truth. She sometimes looked at her face in a hand mirror. She must have seen how thin she was becoming. We almost wanted to take the mirror away, but that would have made it all the more obvious what we were trying to hide. She never said anything directly. But she knew. She smiled, and joked about coming home soon. She laughed as if there were nothing the matter. But her body was one long constant tremor of pain – even though she was heavily drugged. She had tubes coming out of her intestines. The day before she died it was all just a mess of diarrhoea and blood. And she was such a dignified person, so full of life and energy and decency. And she had to die – like that. I saw it, Stephen. I saw everything. And you say I don't know anything, don't feel anything. You say I'm not sincere. You don't know what you're talking about. You don't know anything about it. And now you come here to this beautiful place and want to ruin it forever with your puerile idea of killing yourself. You don't deserve to be here at all. You don't have the right to say anything at all. I've never met such an ungrateful person.'

Bruce felt the tears again and could not prevent them from spilling out of his eyes. He heard Stephen beside him; Stephen was sobbing. Even at that moment, Bruce felt a flash of humour. If anyone could have seen them like that, he wondered, weeping like a couple of sentimental old spinsters, what would they have thought? Stephen sniffed and fell silent. The only sound was the distant sea, moving nearer with the tide minute by minute. The slight wind had dropped. The mountains in the north were becoming dark, almost human as they brooded there, settled in their half-reclining postures like dying titans – enduring the motionless agony of earthly existence. In his mind, Bruce could hear the sun falling, the sun shrieking with searing pain, never able to know the meaning of coolness or darkness. Its flames were not light shooting out into space: they were pure sound – a hideous ululation, one endless scream hitting the sea, singeing their eyes.

Stephen looked at the sea. His head turned slowly as his gaze moved across the beach to the sand dunes, then to the mountains beyond.

'This place—' He did not finish his sentence. He bit his lower lip, as if to hold back another wave of grief.

'My mother's ashes are scattered down there below the house in the sandhills. That's where she is now. I can sometimes hear her crying.'

Stephen scarcely heard him. The dust was settling in his skull. He sat there staring at the sea and the round sun. The colour of the sun was changing. It was no longer impossible to look at. It was no longer a glaring black ball with rings of blinding white light constantly moving round it. It was turning an almost transparent orange colour. But it was not the sun that held his attention; it was not the sweep of the bay. It was Bruce's eyes. There was a greater light in Bruce's eyes; something finer than the glare of the fanatic, something beyond the soft warmth of compassion; something stronger than the hero's glance. There was more power, more pain, more love, it seemed to Stephen, than there could ever be in the eyes of God. He realized, suddenly, with absolute conviction and with a wonderful stirring of his heart, as if an enchanted island were rising out of the ocean, that what he could sense in Bruce's eyes was nothing other, with all its magnificent simplicity, than the sea itself. He heard Bruce's voice.

'That sun. Can you believe it'll come up behind us in the morning?'

It was not a profound utterance, and Bruce had spoken the words without the thought of their having any significance. He was merely full of a kind of wonder that only children have; but he knew that what he had said, even though tritely expressed and as a question, contained a beautiful truth. It would happen, and they could believe it. He heard Stephen's voice.

'I'll write a novel. And it will be here, in this setting.'

A jet-fighter, its engines whining faintly, crossed the bay from the north, low down over the sea, lower, it seemed, than the level of the house, gliding down, a slender silhouette, towards the airfield at Llandanwg round the headland to the south.

Bruce stood up, watching its long slow descent.

'It's radio-controlled. There's no one in it. There's an aeronautical research base over there somewhere.'

Stephen joined him. Together they stood looking at the sea.

9. THE ANNEXE

'HAVE YOU GOT a lamp?'

Stephen came into the living room where Bruce was writing a letter. The fire was blazing noisily. Although it was by no means cold enough to have a fire at all, Bruce kept it going, he explained, to save electricity. There was a boiler behind it which was part of the hot-water system; as long as the fire was in, they did not have to switch on the immersion heater in the kitchen. Bruce was expected to pay for heating and lighting while staying at the house. It was quite dark outside, except for a streak of dark red sky over the long black snake of Lleyn across the bay. They had prepared supper together with unwonted joviality. It was as if they desired to erase the memory of their strong words out in the verandah earlier. There was something artificial about their cheerfulness at first, but after an hour or so, the atmosphere, charged with fresh energy and humour, was genuine enough. Bruce found himself

68

whistling as he laid the table for their meal. When relations were good with Stephen, they were very good. It was possible to feel, and to know, something they could call happiness. All Stephen's stern gloom had evaporated. There was even some colour in his complexion, something Bruce had never seen before. He rejoiced at it. This was how he had wanted it to be when Stephen came to Harlieg – a real benefit to his friend's health and mind. The hope, it seemed, was now to be fulfilled. Things were going his way. Somewhere at the back of his mind, however, like the jet-plane whining across the beauty of the bay, Bruce felt a hard nugget of fear. He wondered how long Stephen's new-found euphoria would continue. None of Stephen's moods, he knew, lasted long. He was too temperamental; he swerved from enthusiasm to deep dejection as unpredictably as an unreined horse. Bruce knew their struggle that afternoon was only a temporary victory for him. There would be more to come. Now, however, he must make the most of the situation. Perhaps this was a real, hopefully a permanent, turning point for Stephen. They would have to see. At the meal they had talked brightly about plans for the coming days. They would work in the mornings and go for walks in the afternoons – not only on the beach, but up the cliff and over the back, or to the town; there were many places to see, many things to do. They would visit the castle, perhaps go to a concert in the town hall, have a drink at the hotel. Stephen was full of interest and animation, and asked many questions, a thing he was very good at when he put his mind to it. He had never, it seemed to Bruce now, been so pleasant, never so humble and eager for information. After the meal, they had sat down at the piano and improvised twelve preludes, some of them simple melodic inventions cantabile style in which their joint endeavour was entirely harmonious, some of them syncopated fugue-like affairs; one of them was a splendid march. At all times, Stephen went out of his way to accommodate Bruce's lesser skills at the keyboard; and then he said 'Enough', and they had stood with their backs to the fire comparing paunches. Stephen pulled up his shirt and exposed a firm roll of excess flesh, inviting Bruce to touch it, which he did, pinching it slightly and laughing. He himself could not yet boast of such signs of physical maturity, although his family had a tendency towards overweight. Then they had fallen silent, smoking in armchairs either side of the fireplace. Stephen was thinking about the novel he was going to write. How would it begin? Where would it begin? What kind of man would the hero be? A young sculptor meeting his friend after a long parting, in the Birmingham Art Gallery, tears streaming from their eyes; a retired gardener and his wife strolling along the shore and finding...finding, what would it be? A dead man? A crate? The cockpit of a crashed jet-fighter? Ideas came rushing into his mind, filling him with excitement and impatience – a tearful farewell, thundering trains disappearing across vast plains and whistling in the distance, laughter in the sea. Fragments, whole episodes, sprang up in his imagination. How to organize, how to fit them together, to make a story. It would be a great novel. His finest work. Stephen Pewit, teenage novelist. Discovered, interviewed, acclaimed. His friend Bruce Dinwiddy, silent with his great eyes, in the background – his inspiration, his guru, his genius. He suddenly recognized the resurgence of his old love for Bruce. It had regenerated, but it was no longer an uncontrollable blazing passion, a mad infatuation, a longing to touch. It was now something more like a form of worship, a magnificent desire to follow, to serve, to gaze at, and gain fire from, those irresistible eyes. Stephen had asked Bruce for some paper; Bruce had given him a whole box full of typing sheets, a pen, ink, and some pencils. Stephen had announced his intention of going upstairs to his room, to make notes, drafts, beginnings. Bruce had urged him on. Half an hour later Stephen had come downstairs again, asking for a lamp.

'The light's in the wrong place. My shadow gets in the way.'
'Do you find it painful to write on the shadow of your head? Does it hurt?' They both laughed.
'I could move the table of course; but I thought I'd ask if there was a lamp I could use.'
'Hm...I never thought of that. Let me see.' Bruce thought for a moment. There was one in his own room, which he was not using at present, but not for a moment did he consider letting Stephen have it. That would not be convenient. He liked to have a lamp beside his bed; then he did not have to get out of bed to turn the light off at night. There was no lamp in the other, small room

upstairs, nor in the downstair bedroom. Maybe in one of the annexes.

'Yes, there's one in my mother's...in the south annexe, the one under your window. I'll go and fetch it.'

He got up and picking up a bunch of keys from a small table behind the front door went outside. It was colder than the previous evening. A very light but keen breeze came from the north, from the mountains which were now part of the darkness. The stars and the lights across the bay were clearer, almost piercing. The red streak in the west had almost disappeared; a dull russet glow was all that remained of the sunset.

He turned left and walked along the side of the house to the south end, feeling for the key he needed. This was the only room that had a Yale lock; he suddenly wondered why. He was glad of it now for it was easy to single out the key in the darkness. He stepped up onto the small verandah let into the outer corner of the annexe, and as he was fumbling for the lock, he noticed the window to the right of the door. The curtains were drawn back and the inside of the room seemed terrifying to him. This was no self-induced drama. He felt an irrational terror grip him like a wolf from behind. He needed light. He must get the door open and put the light on quickly. The lock was stiff. The annexe had not been used since his mother's death, almost two years before. The key turned suddenly. The door at first would not yield to pressure. The doorframe had warped slightly because of the persistent rain blowing in from the sea a good part of the year; but to Bruce it seemed as if someone were pushing at the door from the inside, trying to prevent him from entering a forbidden sanctuary. He was gasping now. He threw his weight against the door and it swung inwards suddenly, straining back on its hinges with a hideous sound, like the single last howl of a traveller sinking rapidly in a desert quicksand at night. He switched on the light.

The room was just as he had remembered it. Only the air was different. There was usually a faint odour from the wash-basin in the left corner, he remembered, but now the room smelt of dampness dried out and renewed many times. It smelt of trapped sunlight dying of starvation. The closed-in space had retained the heat of the day. The air was alive with death – not his mother's death, but the death that comes from disuse, neglect. There were a few dead flies on the leathercloth-covered table under the south window. He saw something else there, too – a folder he had made some years before for his mother. The front of it was a sheet of glass attached to the cardboard cover with black passe-partout tape. Under the glass were the pressed autumn leaves from a copper beech. When he had brought them from their Midland home, they had been a rich red and orange, but now they were dull brown and had curled slightly under the glass. Bruce felt he was looking at it for the first time. He realized he had not often been in that room. Everything was faded and old, but curiously new to his eyes.

He took in the details one by one. The oblong soft-toned dulcitone under the east window with its old-fashioned string-and-wood pedals – he remembered its gentle, deep, plangent notes as his mother tried out her compositions far into the night. The low, wicker-backed nursery chair; the large old-fashioned sagging bed, now with its mattress stained and naked, blankets folded on top; the green-painted chest of drawers – he remembered his mother painting it herself; the curtain wardrobe, its curtain suspended from the spring wire attached to either side. Some of the stitching had rotted and the top of the curtain hung in small loops with rusting rings isolated above them on the wire. The wash-basin in its corner behind the door the taps of which so unwillingly, coughing and spitting, brought water, sometimes brown with rust, through from the house. The old striped Moroccan carpet; many a time it had been scattered with sand from children's feet. The walls were not the same as those in the house. They were made of white plaster-board. The south wall was blotched with great cloud-like patches, like stains much enlarged on a bed-sheet, where the driving south-west gales had forced rain in under the window. He glanced upwards. There was no ceiling as such, the boards of the roof sloping steeply up to the central ridge were varnished brown. He remembered he and his sister as very young children lying in their mother's bed and pointing to the knots in the boards: they could see the shapes of animals formed there – a rabbit, a duck, an owl, a horse. The curtains in the windows, once white and imprinted with large blue realistic flowers with brown stalks, seemed strangely still. They too were stained with the rain; parts of their silk-like linings were hanging down, rotting with excess of sunlight.

There was one picture on the wall over the bed. It was a pastel drawing in dark blues and greens; one of his aunts had done it as a gift. It was a picture of mermaids, hardly mermaids, more like sea-sprites or Nereids, swimming upwards towards the light, their long, grey-streaked locks streaming out behind them. It was a scene from his mother's opera *The Little Mermaid* – the sad Hans Andersen story of the mermaid who fell in love with a shipwrecked prince and sold her tongue and power of speech to an undersea witch in return for a pair of feet with which to follow the prince on land, only to find that he was already married to a beautiful princess. The opera had been performed in Birmingham about fifteen years before his mother's death.

Suddenly Bruce heard the sea; not the quiet waves in the darkness outside down on the shore, but the massive and perpetual thunder of huge ocean breakers. Perhaps it was seeing the signs of rain on the walls and curtains, the memory of gales; perhaps it was the picture. He felt as if he had been down there with the mermaids and had suddenly surfaced into a seething storm amid the wild white horses of the sea. It was a sound he knew well. It was never far from his mind; it was a constant undertone, a background to the unrest in his heart. He heard it in railway stations, in packed theatres, in shopping centres, anywhere where there were many people together. He heard it in the silence of his room, not only here at Harlieg, but in all places, wherever he went, wherever he happened to be. Sometimes a dull, steady roar as if it were far off across sands shining with rain; sometimes a raised, despair-laden crying, many voices, a chorus in and out of unison, with single shouts and shrieks from time to time; sometimes a low and inimitable moan, like cries on the other side of death, like the uttered pain of the war-wounded who lie without hope, without limbs in hospital wards; altogether a sound purely fascinating, like sirens without sexuality, like human beings without body, like voices coined in the turnings of the wind – a dirge of terror, terror without horror in it – mad, white-haired children, smiling, singing, beautiful.

Bruce stood there unable to move. Then suddenly there was silence in his mind – only a ringing and whistling in his ears, the blood spinning through the capillaries round his brain. Then a total silence. Then he heard it. The mermaids were singing. The chorus of his mother's opera – 'Come away, come away, on the lift of a wave'. Not only the music he knew so well, but with it, behind it, the terror-laden music of the sea. Music such as no one knows how to compose, record or emulate. No one can catch it. None of the great sea-music comes anywhere near it, not the *Sea Drift* of Delius, not Debussy's *La Mer*, not the *Sea Symphony* of Vaughan-Williams – not any of the famous attempts in art. This was music beyond music, not the abstract music of the spheres, but music of the earth, irrecoverably tragic, of the ocean, the origin of all living things, and the death of all, of the sea itself, diseased and corrupted by its offspring, sickening and dying.

It stopped. Trembling, Bruce reached for the red wooden lamp on the bedside table and turned towards the door. He was afraid to open it. Once again the thunder of breakers stunned him. He felt that if he opened the door, a wall of water, swirling grey and green-muscled, would be rushing past outside. The whole annexe seemed to be under the sea, like a galleon sinking in a storm; yet at the same time he could hear recurrent bursts of wind buffeting at and whistling through the coarse grasses of the sandhills. It was all in his mind. When at last he opened the door, the darkness outside was hollow and still, the lights were shining across the bay.

If he could have thought calmly, he would have known that he was afraid, more frightened now than he had ever been in his life before. Even then he might not have been able to explain it. Only one immediate cause might have entered his mind – Stephen's threat of suicide. He suddenly realized how much his friend had shocked him. In the daytime, it had seemed almost too easy to dissuade him. But now it was night, and he felt, as if to match the shadow that had fallen over the world, an uncontrollable darkening of the mind. The rhetoric of the afternoon now seemed fragile: Stephen could so easily change his mind. Even now, his enthusiasm disrupted by even such a triviality as this need for a lamp, he might be contemplating ways to terminate his life. Bruce imagined returning to the house – to find Stephen dull-eyed and pulsing weakly on the floor of the living room, the whole room sprayed with blood, a knife in his neck. The night was upon them. If Bruce himself was suggestible, terror-stricken like this, Stephen might be a hundred times more so. Perhaps he was dead already, his request for a lamp merely a ruse to get Bruce out of the way. Bruce felt the overwhelming urgency of returning to the house, but between him and the house was the black wall of the night.

He switched off the annexe light and stepped out onto the little verandah. Everything was still. He could hear, and just distinguish with his eyes, the sea in the darkness. The lamp with its trailing flex was useless in his hands; the keys dangled from his wrist. He slammed the door behind him.

What was it out there? In his mind, the face of his mother rose up, not weeping but somehow unbearably sad. Somewhere out there her ashes were mingled with the grass and sand. He tried to reason. They were only ashes, incinerated fragments of her body, each grain, each splinter, was blown different ways in the wind. They would never again come together. Therefore, and here his reason gave way once more to a swell of fear, there was no place in the sandhills, on the beach, in the sea, where she was not. Anywhere there, everywhere, there was some part of her. No. Her spirit – he tried to control his mind – her spirit had melted away in the dust of the Birmingham hospital where she had died. There was nothing here. Or had after all the spirit come home to its birthplace here overlooking the Traeth, or come home to its real primeval birthplace the sea? The spirit dwells in the flesh, the brain and the bones, and it was the ashes of these that were here. Why should he think that the spirit had left them? Bruce hurried along the concrete path at the side of the house. The coldness was not only the cold of the slow wind from the mountains. It was the coldness of the shore, the heartless grinding of the waves, no matter how subdued they were now, that he could feel. There was no one there, no one who cared about anyone; not even his mother could call from there. Then, above all, hideous black pity crawled at him from the darkness, like a shining black-skinned creature with red tear-worn eyes. His mother was out there, blown from hill to hill of sand, scattered, lost, uncared for, alone. Sentimentality is the coldest kind of pain. Beyond it there is no hope; it is the last headland of human fragility. When a man stands there, a step further leads to mental collapse; tears that come then cannot ever be stopped, even when the eyes dry out. The weeping goes on in the mind.

But Bruce did not and could not weep. He knew he was strong. A mad impulse to rush down and throw himself into the sea was killed almost before it became a thought. He was strong; he had to be. If he were not, he could do nothing for Stephen. And Stephen must be rescued – for the sake of his art if for nothing else; and Bruce knew there were elements of genius in his friend. Stephen must not be allowed to throw away his life. Stephen might not have the will to continue; but Bruce, he himself knew, had. He must use it for Stephen. The novel had to be written, this and many others, and it would be he, Bruce, who would make it possible.

Bruce reached the main verandah. Turning right and opening the heavy front door, he stepped into the yellow warmth of the house; and the whole house was bellowing with triumphant chords from the piano.

10. CREOSOTE

BRUCE WAS AWAKENED the next morning by the sound of the front door closing – a hollow thud spreading up through the wooden walls of the house. He looked at his watch. It was six-thirty. He got up and changed into his swimming things, again with comfortable sensations of purity and growing fullness. He remembered he had locked his door before going to bed the night before. His fear had not left him; he still could not be sure what Stephen might do. Even though he had continued working in his room quite late, using the lamp Bruce had fetched for him, Stephen might well have turned back on himself, and not content with killing merely himself, might include Bruce also — in a kind of ritual of destruction. It was the kind of thing he might well do. This morning, however, such thoughts seemed to Bruce unreasonable, almost insane. Stephen was still alive. He had just gone out. Stephen had left the door of his room open, and seeing the notes on the table, Bruce was tempted to peep; but to do so, he felt, might upset the delicate balance of affairs as they were now. He knew he would never be able to conceal successfully from Stephen that he had seen what he had been writing; guilt would somehow shine through. Better to leave things as they were. He went downstairs and made up the fire in the living room. He looked out of the window. Stephen was on the beach walking rapidly northwards, his head bowed, his hands clenched together behind his back. Once again Bruce was reminded of Beethoven: he too had often taken early-morning walks. There was something deliberate, purposeful about Stephen's way of walking. He seemed to be deep in thought.

Bruce ran down to the shore and plunged into the sea. Drying himself a few minutes later, he felt all his sense of well-being return. He looked along the beach. Stephen was coming back. At that moment, a group of people ran out from the sand dunes in swimming things. Stephen stopped to greet them. They waved and ran into the sea, shouting and screaming. Stephen watched them for a while, then came on to where Bruce was standing, shivering now, for the sun was not yet up.

'Who were those people?'
'College students, I think.'
'What did they say?'
'Nothing. Just greetings. What's the matter?'
'It's going to be a fine day again. Did you find anything interesting?'

Stephen showed him a piece of glass. It was pale green and misty. The sea and the sand had worked at it, removing all the sharp edges.

'I found this green stone.'

'It's a bit of glass.'

'Oh, really? I thought it was a kind of stone. Anyway, I'm going to keep it. There's something I like about it. It's magic. Do you think if I rub it a genie or something will appear?'

'No, but if I rub you up a bit a genius will appear.' Bruce laughed, then stopped. He thought for a moment that he had said too much, but then Stephen laughed and Bruce joined him.

'You idiot!' There was something healthy and unrestrained about his laughter that pleased Bruce. 'Now that is funny. I saw a jelly fish. It smelt like geranium leaves. My mother keeps geraniums in pots.'

'You didn't touch it, did you? They sting sometimes.'

'I wanted to rub its sting to see if a jelly genie would appear and ask me what I'd like for tea.'

'What would you have answered?'

'Jelly. What else?' They both laughed again.

'They can be dangerous sometimes. I was once stung in a most awkward place.'

'Ah, that explains a lot of things.'

Bruce looked down at his swimming shorts.

'What do you mean?'

'Nothing. The jelly fish was dead anyway.'

They went up over the rocks, Stephen slipping about as before, but trying not to show it.

'Why don't you take your shoes and socks off?'

'I might later.'

'You'll soon get used to it.'

After breakfast they got down to work. Bruce suggested Stephen do his writing in the living room.

'It's more spacious down here. And you've got two views.'

Stephen agreed.

'What about you?'

'I'll have to put off writing for a day or two. I've some creosoting to do.'

Since Tremarfon was made of wood, the outside walls had to be creosoted once every few years. In the past, it had been a regular family ritual, at first exciting, but later a tedious chore. It had been neglected since their mother's death. The family as such rarely came to Harlieg now. One of the conditions of Bruce's being allowed to stay in the house on this occasion was that he creosoted as much of the house as possible. His father, always one to emphasize gratitude and repayment of debts, had insisted on it. Bruce was by no means unwilling; he had even thought of it as a gesture before being asked, but he had been just too late to make the offer. His father rarely gave people time to make gestures: everything was rights and duties. Simple kindness was something he seemed not to understand. Other people's spontaneous efforts were weighed down with moral strictures supplied by him. Even if Bruce had had the chance to make the offer, his father, rather than being grateful, would have stressed that nothing less was expected; it was right and proper for Bruce to do it. Since he was paying no rent, a job like that would help redress the balance. And Bruce was not to forget to read the electricity metre and pay for what he had used.

As he went round to the small shed in a dip behind the house, Bruce continued to think about his father. Ever since he could remember, he had felt a kind of resentment against him; and this, he had realized more and more, was because of his hard attitude to Bruce's mother. Even when she had first become ill, his father had refused to regard her as an invalid. He had constantly criticized her as idle, as not interested in family life or household affairs, as one who thought only about her music and smoking. He would not acknowledge that she was ill, until it was too late. But Bruce's resentment went further back than that. His father had always wanted a daughter, and Bruce, the youngest of the sons, had often felt neglected when his father favoured and showered attention on his younger sister. Bruce never felt in any way antagonistic towards his sister; they had always got on well together. He felt his father was at fault; his sister always shared what she had with Bruce.

The little green shed, now stained brown where rust had attacked the corrugated iron, had once been a sand toilet; but it now smelt strongly of paint and turpentine. Bruce brought out a treacle-stained drum of creosote and set it down on the grass. He brought out brushes and a battered paint-pot. While transforming creosote from the drum to the pot, he spilled some onto the grass. Later the grass would turn yellow. His father was so ill-tempered. Once Bruce's eldest brother had spilled a full pot of creosote onto the floor of one of the annexes. His father had shouted and scolded without remorse. Only when Bruce himself, aged only ten at the time, and he felt somehow proud of it now, had suggested that they make the best of the situation and creosote the entire floor had his father quietened down. He had even laughed, as they all had, at this wonderfully simple solution. He wondered if his father ever thought of that episode now. Perhaps it was too trivial, or perhaps, more significantly, it did not reveal him in a favourable light and so he chose not to remember.

Bruce went back up to the house. From that side, one could appreciate what a wonderfully sited house it was – alone there at the edge of the sea. His father had done well to acquire it. It had once belonged to a doctor, whom his father had persuaded that money was more attractive than property; and property was cheap at that time. Then the whole Snowdonia area had become a National Park. No more houses could be built in the sandhills. The house was a treasure not to be lost; it was unique. Sometimes, however, people living in the houses on the cliff had complained about Tremarfon. It was an eyesore, they said. There were too many unsightly outhouses and sheds. The whole property ruined the view. It should all be demolished. His father had stuck to his rights. The property was freehold. It was his. No one could take it away from him – unless it were burned down by a fire caused by sparks from the trains or by careless tenants, or unless the sea, suddenly reversing its slow recession westwards, should come thundering up over the dunes and swallow it up in a great swirl of grey and white. Bruce remembered the picture over the mantelpiece in the living-room. It had been painted by an old artist friend of the family as a joke. He had been told that Tremarfon was a little house with a red roof by the sea, and had been sent a photograph, and had then painted his own version. The oil painting he later gave them showed the house on the beach with grey, windswept breakers just behind it about to sweep it away. Bruce smiled. Perhaps such a thing would actually happen one day.

He decided to start on the east wall above the kitchen window and back door. He fetched the step-ladder from the back room. This, like the old boiler-suit he had brought up from the paint-shed to wear, was stained with great solidified splashes of creosote. His father was not entirely evil. After all, he had got all his sons into university; he had taken them on wonderful holidays abroad, Bruce no less than the others. He had made real and energetic efforts to educate his children. It was only his oft-displayed moral superiority that galled them all. He was always right; it was impossible to prove him wrong, even when everybody, including himself, knew that he was wrong. When they tried to explain something they had done that had displeased him, their father always accused them of making excuses; but when it appeared that he was wrong, and he himself explained, oh, no, he was not making excuses, he was giving them reasons. He was never wrong. Bruce did not yet realize how much of his father's personality he was inheriting.

It was rather satisfying to see the creosote soak into the dark boards. Creosote was so clean, medicinal – not only for the house, but also for the human body. The boards were steeped with it. He remembered the old wooden stave churches in Norway. Treated thus, some of them had remained strong and free of decay for over a thousand years. He wondered how long Tremarfon would survive. Perhaps it would rot from inside: there were already signs of deeply-entrenched woodworm; perhaps it would be burned down. It would burn like a torch with all that creosote in the wood. When the weather was dry, as it was now, sparks from the smokestacks of the trains quite often set the grass in the sand dunes alight. They had to hurry with spades and beat the fires out.

Once, such a fire had almost entirely surrounded the house, but it had been controlled just in time. There was always a danger of such a thing happening again.

He wondered how Stephen was getting on with his novel. The house was strangely silent. Bruce himself had never written a novel. His longest works, none of them published, were epic poems or verse dramas. He had practically no understanding of how to write good prose, not realizing that his poetry would have been much better if he had. He could hardly imagine how Stephen would set about it. Did one think of the story first or the characters? Did one conceive the whole, or only parts? Did one make it up as one went along? As for his own vast attempts, language, images, inversions, inventions, kennings, coinings were of paramount importance; and his created language was always of an elevated kind – bardic, not to be merely read or spoken, but to be intoned in the noble manner. A poet for Bruce was not a man who merely observed things about him, recording his prosaic impressions, as so much modern poetry seemed to him to be doing. A poet was a maker, a shaper of things, a man who moulded myths, modern ones, a man inspired by worthy motives. He had to be a craftsman, not a mere versifier. Too many poets, he felt, were mere line writers; there was no art, no loftiness of spirit, no real making in any of their work. There was too much that was trivial, and too few poets subjected themselves to any form of conscious training. They had no sense of 'ear'. They thought that merely arranging their thoughts in lines of suitable length constituted a poem. Bruce was serious about this, and had trained himself to write in many traditional forms, sonnets, triolets, ballades, blank verse, rhymed pentameters, knowing that most of these attempts were mere exercises, leading towards something greater. In spite of his immense output, he was not yet satisfied with what he had done. Something great was in the offing, he felt. One day, he knew, he would produce his masterpiece and recite it some great public arena. Bruce could not appreciate the strength of the commonplace, the power of simple language, the value of honest statement. Yet, in spite of his lofty ideals, his attitudinizing and self-elevation, Bruce did feel that he was a real poet. He did not merely see things, he looked at them; he did not merely hear, he listened. Stephen had done much to teach him that. Now, when Bruce saw a stone, he thought of the inside of it, the part that no man had ever set eyes on, and he thought of the people who might have seen that stone or handled it, not knowing of that great mystery of its interior. He looked at the grass as one of the greatest lords of the earth – covering all the works of man. When he heard the sea, he did not hear the mere falling of waves, he listened to its voices. He had yet to learn that a stone was a stone, the grass a simple plant, the sea mere water, often dirty.

The sound of the piano reached his ears. He was at once reminded of his mother. She had never for long been far from a piano. Her music had had a delightful melodic freshness, a strong masculinity. It was never soft or nostalgic. Night after night, she would hammer out her 'Sarabande for Icicles', her 'Druids' Chorus', her 'Song of the Open Road', the last of which she had never finished. Now all her compositions were forgotten, tied up in bundles in a cupboard at home. He remembered how she used to play for him and his brothers and sister, sight-reading any score they placed before her. Sometimes she improvised endless Beethoven endings, or imitated an aunt of hers with a drooping eye, playing ghastly romances with mock rubato, deliberately ending them in the wrong key. Now it was Stephen playing. Bruce frowned with irritation. His friend never seemed to be able to settle down to anything for long. He was already obviously tired of writing his novel. The solemn chords echoed through the sound-box of the house, as Bruce dipped his broad brush into the pot and spread the pungent, treacle-like creosote onto the almost black oil-saturated boards of the house.

*

Stephen was stuck. It was not as easy as he had imagined to write a novel. He had very little idea of what a novel actually was. It sounded grand to speak of writing 'my novel'. It gave him a sense of self-importance and intellectual superiority; but when it came down to the actual hard work he was at a loss. His previous attempts had hardly been more than mere long stories. He had almost no sense of structure. He had no idea how any of his stories would end. The fragments, each of them full of fascinating images, would not fit themselves into a unified whole. He had no conception of the art of narrative; he had little ability to see into the minds of others. His work was always centred round himself, even if he wrote in the third person. He had the ability to describe, in lucid prose, but he could not make the story move. He could make his main character think; a stream of consciousness was easy. But somehow his sense of logic failed him when it came to writing. When he talked, to Bruce for example, he could control the flow of conversation with admirable dexterity, but not on the written page. Writing itself bored him. There was no drama in it. Typing was better – one could at least get a better idea of what the finished product would look like published – but even then, putting a new sheet of paper into the machine often disturbed his continuity of thought. He disliked protracted effort. He had made many random notes. That was always enjoyable. To jot down an idea or a beautiful phrase seemed satisfactorily professional. He had then sat down to begin his masterpiece, but it would not materialize. He sat, staring out of the window. The constant moving of the sea fascinated, disturbed him. From time to time he wrote a sentence, but when he re-read it a moment or two later it seemed flat and lifeless, just a sentence, grammatically correct, no more. His mind was so full of possible directions; but there was no exit to his mind. He went to the piano. If only writing were like playing the piano! Here there was no difficulty. To hammer out random chords, to change from key to key with complete freedom, to generate tremendous rhythmic energy – these things were easy, and always relieved his mind. It was only afterwards that he felt the uselessness of such forms of expression. Nothing remained, only a fading memory of the transient joy. It was if his creative talents, like liquid gold, had been poured out carelessly from a goblet, to soak irretrievably into the ground. Even when he captured his extemporizations on a tape-recorder, hearing them through afterwards was never as inspiring as the moments of actual creation. He often secretly thought that they sounded banal.

*

Bruce found himself repeating phrases over and over in his mind. This always happened when he was engaged in tedious activity of the repetitive kind. He disliked this kind of work, but at least there was something to show for it – fresh boards dark with fragrant creosote. Where the boards had been replaced with newer ones, the creosote brought out the grain of the wood. The irregular, continuous lines and whorls of knots reminded Bruce of the sea; the knots, shining because the creosote would not readily sink into them, were like islands in oriental waves. There was something reminiscent of ancient Japanese woodblock prints. Bruce's grandfather had collected a few, and now he was reminded of their antique mellowness and fine detail. Things like washing-up, sweeping the floor – things which had to be done again and again with no apparent effect – he detested. He was glad he was not a woman, bound to the repetitive chores of the household, or a civil servant in some office, endlessly stamping documents no one cared about or would ever look at again. How his mother had suffered! Life is a long prune. Life is a long prune. The phrase, appearing suddenly in his mind, would not go away. It was like a maladjusted gramophone reciting a poem by a maladjusted poet. Life is a long prune. There was a stack of firewood against the wall to the right of the kitchen window. He wondered whether to bother to remove it or not. His father would have done so, but Bruce was not as thorough as his father; but it would be just such a place that his ever-suspicious father would think of checking, and if on some later occasion he found an unpainted section of the wall there would be hell to pay. Not what appears, but what is. Not what appears, but what is. A new phrase came into his mind, and then another. The actual not the apparent. The actual not the apparent. A train went by under the cliff. The rhythm of the phrase matched the rhythm of the wheels on the rails. He shifted enough of the firewood to expose a couple of feet of wall and sloshed creosote down in the space, much of it soaking into the firewood. It'll burn better because of the creosote. It'll burn better because of the creosote. Life is a long prune... After a while, he realized the rhythm of his repeated phrases coincided with the beating of his heart. It suddenly amazed him how many years a heart could beat like that, day after day. A friend is parted from another for twenty years, and they meet again, and in the interim their hearts have been beating like that, non-stop, with varying speeds but faithfully pumping blood round and through the dark, throbbing labyrinth of their bodies. Miraculous machines. But they did not continue for ever. There are so many banal thoughts. A waste of time, a waste of intelligence. Life is a long prune.

He finished the east wall and went into the kitchen by the back door. The sound of the piano had stopped. He switched on the kettle and went through into the living-room.

'Would you like some coffee? I've put the kettle on.'

'A delightful idea.'

'How are you getting on?'

Stephen was standing by the table, one hand, fingertips down, placed on its surface. Before him, arranged neatly in rows, were numerous sheets of notes. He wore a studied, thoughtful expression. Bruce felt this artistic pose had been specially prepared for his entrance.

'Not too bad. I'm getting the feel of it.'

'I thought I heard the piano. Was it you?'

'No. An old lady with seaweed hair came up from the beach and started playing, without my permission, with her feet.' There was a twinkle in Stephen's eye.

'Don't be an idiot. It was you, wasn't it?'

'Who else could it have been?' Stephen felt a note of accusation in Bruce's voice. 'It was to help me to get into the atmosphere. There's going to be a lot about music in the novel.'

'Why don't you include the old lady playing the piano with her feet?'

'With her breasts would be more spectacular. I'm considering it.'

'How much have you done?'

Stephen did not want to admit to having achieved almost nothing. He nodded knowingly.

'Quite a bit. I'm having a little trouble getting the theme together. It takes time, you know. I have to do a lot of thinking.'

He tried hard to keep the note of apology out of his voice, but Bruce detected it. He smiled encouragement.

'Anyway, keep going.'

'Of course. How's the creosote?'

'All over the ground and my hands and clothes.'

'Right through to your underpants?'

'Probably. I haven't looked. I'm becoming addicted to the smell.'

'Of your underpants?'

'Yes, I love it.' They both laughed. Bruce held out his stained hands. 'Smell.' Stephen sniffed and smiled.

'I can think of other more exciting smells on one's hands. But it's got something, I admit.' The kettle began to shriek in the kitchen.

'I'll make the coffee.'

'Essence of coffee and creosote.'

'It's good for the throat.'

They took their coffee sitting in the verandah. Stephen looked across the bay.

'What shall we do after lunch?'

'Anything you like. Don't you want to go on writing?'

'Not specially.'

'It's better to keep at it at first, isn't it? Until it takes hold.'

'You don't understand about writing novels. A lot has to be thought out. I can do that while we take a walk.' Stephen knew he was making excuses; he wondered if Bruce knew it. 'Anyway, we decided to work in the mornings, and relax in the afternoons.'

Bruce felt faintly disappointed, even a little angry. Stephen seemed almost feeble. Bruce's incipient anger, although he did not realize it then, was founded upon his fear. Thoughts of what might happen if the novel failed to materialize lurked at the back of Bruce's mind, not as clear ideas, but as a sense of irritation.

'Let's go to the castle then.'

Stephen looked interested. He had never seen, let alone been in, a castle like the one at Harlieg.

'Can we go up the towers?'

'Of course.'

'This is a magnificent place, Bruce. I really must thank you for asking me here.'

Bruce's irritation immediately faded away. He felt a glow of warmth. It was good to feel that his efforts were appreciated. Stephen was improving. Perhaps things would turn out well after all. Bruce could not prevent himself from making a moral observation.

'I'm glad you like it. I hope you'll be able to make the best use of it. You probably don't realize how lucky you are.'

They returned to their tasks.

11. THE CASTLE

DURING LUNCH they made a shopping list. This was a matter of some embarrassment for Stephen since he was extremely short of money. Whatever they bought would depend on Bruce. Stephen did not like to suggest items of food he favoured for fear of seeming unduly greedy; yet Bruce repeatedly urged him to suggest things. Bruce's generosity was hard to refuse, and Stephen did not know how to cope with it. In the end he gave in to Bruce's constant demands and suggested all sorts of things at random – aubergines, whalemeat in aspic, prunes in double syrup, caviar, liver paté, lychees – to such a preposterous extent that they were both reduced to helpless laughter. The list grew longer and longer and more and more outlandish – glacé cherries, almond essence, tinned turkey (Bruce said 'turby' by mistake, which Stephen altered to 'turpy' with another great explosion of laughter), crystallized ginger, jellied squid – and then suddenly, as often when a joke exhausts itself, they stopped laughing, wiping their eyes and feeling depressingly deflated. When Stephen laughed as he had now, it almost developed into an apoplectic crisis. His face became bright red; veins stood out on his forehead; the long whistling wheezing shrieks, on the humorous side of hysteria, became longer and longer and more and more demented, until his asthmatic condition rendered breathing almost impossible. Indeed, the redness of his face made it seem that he was holding his breath and was near physical collapse. Bruce was reminded of the first time he had ever heard Stephen's voice, on his friend's tape-recorder. This is what he must have looked like while trying to read that poem. He wished he had had a tape-recorder now to catch the frenzy of this insane cataloguing. It was the kind of thing that revealed them at their best, as they both lost themselves in the orgy of almost contrapuntal verbiage, forgetting their own existence.

As silence fell in the room, Bruce happened to glance up at the curtain rod of the west window. Near the centre, where the curtains met when drawn, he could see a short strand of red wool tied to the rod. He instantly remembered that his mother had tied it there when he was hardly five. The memory opened up: she had made some kind of crane for him; he had hauled things up and down – wooden bricks, dinky cars; it was a sort of cable car with a primitive pulley system. He remembered how sad he had been, even at that tender age, when, trying to haul up a load that was too heavy, the wool had snapped. The sadness was not that the wool had snapped but that his mother's efforts had ended in failure. He wanted to cry now, as a wave of nostalgia swept over him; and the memory passed into another. He remembered standing at the same window on a different occasion, a few years later perhaps, looking at the sea. The tide was full, and he had wanted to go down to play on the beach and his mother had said: 'You can go down when the tide's gone out; it's going out now.' Bruce had stood there watching the waves. He could not understand how the tide could be going out: the waves were always rolling forwards. He expected them to turn round and roll the other way, but they never changed direction. How could the tide be going out? He supposed, now he remembered, that that had been his first awareness of the sea as a force of nature – the notion of tides, the curious workings of the waves. The sea had not changed. He had grown up, but the sea had remained the same. Even as he looked at it now, the tide (he knew) was going out, the waves edging back little by little, unwilling, it seemed, to admit defeat. Was there pride in the sea? And if there was pride, was there love? His mother was out there. Was it all an empty gesture – to scatter ashes in the wind as his father and sister had done not many months ago? Was all symbolism empty, meaningless? Bruce could not believe there was no meaning in it. Why did the sea move him so much? Why did he always come back there to the house on the Traeth, full of longing, full of emotions he was unable to understand? There was something there. There was something immense, miraculously controlled, terrifying.

Stephen, almost recovered from his maelstrom of mirth, interrupted his thoughts.

'What are you looking at?'

'The sea. The sea, Stephen.' Bruce turned to his friend, his eyes wide and round and shining intensely with that burning, liquid light that Stephen could never escape from. 'The sea. The sea!'

*

'This is the Bluebell Path.'

'Why is it called the Bluebell Path?'

'Because it's the only place in Harlieg where there aren't any bluebells. I've never seen any here.'

They were half way up the cliff, much more irregular here and less steeply inclined, somewhere between the College and the castle. The Golf Club was below them, but most of the view was obscured by trees that covered that part of the cliff. Just below them, almost hidden by foliage, Bruce could see the roof of the house where his mother had been born, but he didn't bother to point this out to Stephen. He had begun to realize that such details bored him.

'There's a cave here somewhere.'

They soon found it, square-cut, man-made, half full of dark green water. Rusty tins and scraps of newspaper used as toilet paper lay scattered about inside the entrance. There was a heavy, damp smell of decay. One or two large black flies occasionally alighted on their hands and faces, and irritating midges danced in front of their noses.

'How revolting!' Stephen turned away, covering his face. Bruce also felt disgusted. This was a part of Harlieg he had rather not have shown to his friend. It had not been like that in his childhood.

The cave had been dry and clean; they had even gone right inside it. It was only about fifty feet deep; and large blackberries had grown thickly all round the entrance, which they had picked and eaten with relish. Bruce felt angry with the people of the town for letting things go like this; but he knew that so many other places in Britain were being desecrated in the .same way. Didn't anyone care?

They went on up the path, which soon emerged from the trees, and a little while later the two friends were standing on an outcrop of granite known as Harlieg Rock. Stephen, not nearly as exhausted as he had been after their climb up the zig-zag the previous day, took in the view with satisfaction. Not far to the north, at about the same level as they were, stood the castle. Between them and its grey walls lay the town – solid stone houses with slate-blue roofs, built wherever the steep slopes and irregularities of the cliff permitted; the few streets were steep, narrow and winding. Occasional car-horns and the grinding of low gears told their own story. There were few people about. The castle seemed to be deserted. Beyond it to the left Stephen gazed down onto the vast expanse of the Traeth. It seemed remote now, cut off from civilization; and the mountains, visible behind the castle, also seemed to belong to another world, sleeping there in the distance, dreaming of other times and other places.

They walked along the main street of the town; it remained almost on one level curving round with the contours of the hill. Some of the shops were closed, and this created a feeling that the town was half blind, as if it could not see, or did not want to see anyone who walked in the streets, especially strangers like these. They passed a church on a slope above them to the right.

'My parents were married there. All the town came out to watch. We've got a funny old film of it, everybody walking about with quick, tight steps, like wooden puppets suffering from constipation.'

Stephen hardly gave it a glance. Churches meant nothing to him. He had only once been in one, at his grandmother's funeral, and this one in Harlieg seemed in no way different to him. All churches were stale with convention, dying of faith, hope and charity. People who went there were failures. Stephen pursed his lips as if there were a sour taste in his mouth.

'My mother's parents are buried behind the church. Not so many years ago she used to go there with my uncle to cut the grass round the graves. A funny thing happened once.'

'In the graveyard?' Stephen's face brightened with interest. If a church could provide something to laugh about, that was a different matter.

'They were cutting the grass with shears, and suddenly my mother caught my uncle's shoe between the blades. They started laughing. They sat there on the gravestones, laughing and laughing.'

'Is that the end of the story?'

'I suppose so. Don't you think it's funny – laughing like that in a graveyard?'

'I don't imagine the residents of the town would think it so amusing.'

'Actually, my mother hates the idea of burial. Putting the body to rot in a box underground. She thought there was something dirty, primitive and crude about it. She always liked the cleanness of cremation. That's why we scattered her ashes down in the sandhills.'

'You told me.'

They walked along the sober, chapel-conscious street. The sandhills seemed very far away.

*

They bought some food at one of the shops in the centre of the town, as they were not planning to go down the Castle Hill to the Blenheim House store at the bottom. They went into a double-fronted establishment emblazoned boldly with gold letters on green: EMLYN HUGHES – FAMILY GROCER, its windows packed with bottles, jars, tins and packets. Stephen's face reddened as Bruce reminded him of their fantastic list. In the event, they bought wisely, almost frugally. Bruce did not pay: everything was charged to the family account. He hoped his father would not notice; he sometimes paid bills without checking them. It would be better not to buy anything too conspicuous. Emlyn Hughes, in a pale green linen working-coat, was a short, rather tubby Welshman with black hair sleeked back over his head and a pencil behind his ear. He attended to their needs with slick efficiency born of habit. To Bruce he seemed more like a machine than a human being. He watched the shopman's brisk actions with a faint sneer of contempt. Stephen on the contrary was fascinated by the speed at which the goods they ordered piled up on the counter.

'Do we have to carry all this stuff back to the house?'

'No, they'll be sent down. You'll be able to manage that, won't you, Mr. Hughes?'

'No problem at all, Mr. Dinwiddy. This very afternoon we'll be right down with them. Your father's a fine customer, Mr. Dinwiddy. Easy to oblige.'

Out in the street again, they met an old lady in a blue coat and black hat like a shiny basket.

'You one of Lizzie Pym's boys?' Pym was his mother's maiden name.

'Yes, that's right.'

'Which one are you then? You're not Martin, are you?'

'No, I'm Bruce, the youngest boy.'

'I thought so. You look a bit like your mother, now. How's your father then?'

'Very well, thanks. You're Mrs. Edwards, aren't you? You used to be the cook's help.'

'That's right. In Captain Pym's kitchen down in Crown Grange. Oh, she was a lovely lady, now, your mother was. Pity she went like that. Sad, it was. Untimely, you know. We miss her a lot. She was such a life in Harlieg. Mr. Edwards, now, was very shocked. We both were. Couldn't believe it. You down at Tremarfon?'

'That's right.'

Bruce found himself wanting to imitate the old lady's way of speaking. Stephen was fascinated by the short clipped sentences, marvelling at the warmth in the woman's voice. This, with the quick businesslike jargon of Mr. Hughes the Grocer, was his first experience of Welsh English.

'Well, nice to have met you.'

'Yes, and you. Best wishes to Mr. Edwards.'

'Thanks, indeed. And remember me to your father too. Have a fine stay. Hope the weather holds good for you.' The old lady trotted off and disappeared inside a drab-looking drapery shop on the corner a little way back. Bruce heard the single dull clang of the old-fashioned warning bell above the door.

He felt strangely comfortable. So many people in the town remembered his mother, even now after two years; most of them belonged to the older generation. The younger inhabitants hardly knew her at all. After all, perhaps it was not so extraordinary. His mother had spent most of her unmarried years in Harlieg, except for the eighteen months she had been at music college in London, cut short when her own mother had fallen ill and died. For a moment, Bruce could feel the real sense of loss the older townspeople seemed to have felt after his mother's death. She had been truly one of them, in spite of her being English; she had even been able to speak a little Welsh. He himself had hardly thought of it like that. Now his mother was dead, it did not seem to him that she was absent. Somehow she had become more than ever part of him; it was as if he himself was his mother. He carried her in his mind – all her joys, her music, energy, sorrows, and gift of making witty remarks. She could never be lost. She was always with him. But seeing it now from the point of view of the people who had known her here in the town long before he had been born, he felt it was wrong that his mother was not buried in the churchyard. These simple, kind-hearted people did not understand cremation. They could not appreciate the symbolism of scattered ashes. For them, the wind was the wind that blew and brought rain in from the sea, rotting the timbers of their roof-beams and window-frames. The mountains were mountains. Rock was rock. And the sea was a faraway grey stranger they had lived with all their lives, a distant haze of movement beyond the Traeth. The sea held nothing of mystery for them. The proprietress of the shoe-shop, Bruce remembered, had not been down to the beach, she said, for twenty-six years. The shore had little meaning for them. They lived too much with it; it was commonplace; it was there – something for the English invaders to enjoy on holiday, something to attract them to this grey town in the summer months and make them spend their money here. That was what mattered most. It would have been better if his mother had been buried alongside her parents in the precincts of the town far from the isolation down there by the sea. His mother was not a great spirit of the elements, nor even a part of one. She had been a homely, gentle, kindly person, like these people who remembered her. It was a mistake to have abandoned her down there; but now it was too late. The ashes could never be gathered together again. Bruce's momentary sense of comfort passed, leaving only a dull pain.

*

They stood in Harlieg Square behind the castle. 'Behind' was not quite the proper word. Bruce always thought of the castle as facing the sea; but to the townspeople the east or inner side was the front.

The structure of the castle was fairly simple. There was one main square with round towers, Edward I style, at each corner. A smaller square with four more smaller towers, the inner ones higher than all the others, straddled as it were the east wall. This was the main building, the living quarters of the occupants in former days. A causeway led from the town square to the outer wall and arched entrance let into the side of this main block. The upper extremities of the castle, the turrets and battlements, had long since fallen into ruin. It seemed as old as the hills, bare, jagged, exposed to the weather, an empty shell like an extinct volcano, not unlike, it seemed to Bruce, a man-made echo of the Cambrian mountain Snowdon herself, also an extinct volcano, pale and blue in heat-haze to the north.

What had once served as a kind of moat was now a grassy half-circle under the castle walls. A real moat was impracticable, since the rock on which the castle was built was not cut off from the town right down to sea-level; it was just a projection of the cliff. It had thus been impossible to surround the whole structure with water, either fresh or salt. They walked down to the turnstile and ticket office at the near end of the causeway.

'I'm a resident of Harlieg.'

This was untrue, but Bruce had heard his mother use the same words on previous visits, and the castle warden had let them through the gate free of charge. Bruce enjoyed the sense of superiority it gave him to make such an announcement especially now in the presence of Stephen. This time, however, he experienced an abrupt reverse.

'What was that, mister?' The warden was old and bad-tempered looking, as if he were underpaid and thoroughly bored with the job.

'I'm a resident, so I don't have to pay.'

'Everyone pays now.' The warden looked at Bruce with undisguised distaste.

'I'm Bruce Dinwiddy. You know, one of Lizzie Pym's sons.'

'Never heard of anyone with names like that. Never seen you before, either now.' He tore off two tickets from the large dull-green roll on his counter.

Bruce had to pay for the two of them. He was too hot and flustered to be aware of Stephen's faint smile. Inside a ticket office was a small shop selling postcards, guidebooks and pamphlets.

'Shall we get one of these?' Bruce picked up a slim illustrated volume.

'If you dirty that you'll have to pay for it.' Bruce hurriedly replaced the booklet, and they went out quickly onto the causeway. Bruce looked indignant.

'What a thoroughly unpleasant man!'

'He probably thinks the same about you.'

'What harm is there is looking at one of those pamphlets? How does he expect anyone to buy them?'

'A lot of people are like that.'

'I wanted you to have one of those. It tells all the history.'

'It doesn't matter. I don't need one.'

They crossed the causeway, mounted a flight of wooden steps and walked straight through into the open courtyard of the larger square. The castle seemed much smaller from inside, almost homely. Bruce felt he had known it all his life; it was as familiar as a parent. More than that, he felt he had known it longer than his lifetime. He discovered he was looking at it with his mother's eyes. Years ago she had conducted a concert in the same courtyard during a Harlieg pageant attended by then Prime Minister Lloyd George. She had let go of her baton during a dramatic flourish and it had gone shooting into the depths of the orchestra to perforate the second bassoonist's knee. She had always laughed when she told that story. There was another story she often told about the castle. A Welshman sitting on the outer wall of the 'moat' had fallen off down to the grass a few yards below. As he fell, he had cried out, in that almost inimitable Welsh English: 'Hey, boys, where I am?' – his grammar all haywire in the confusion. Bruce gazed at the rows of holes in the stonework of the walls inside the castle walls which at one time had accommodated roof-beams for the banqueting hall and kitchen quarters; and again he felt himself moving back in time: he had once been one of the occupants, sitting down to a great feast while the sunset flamed in gently through the west windows and a bard sang in the musicians' gallery above. He was the bard, singing lays and legends long lost in the hills of Wales. Stephen's voice brought him back to the heat and quiet of the afternoon.

'Let's go up one of the towers.' He was looking up at the walls. They seemed to fascinate him, not, as with Bruce, because of their antiquity or because real soldiers had once patrolled their lengths, but because of their immediate presence as a new place to stand, to obtain a view, to look down, to feel power perhaps. They entered the arched entrance at the foot of one of the towers and made their way up the spiral staircase. To his disappointment, Stephen found it was made of concrete; parts of it were wooden too. He had expected stone, original unaltered stone. They came out onto the south wall.

'Walk in the middle. The parapet's very low.' Bruce always felt nervous on the castle walls. He had no head for heights, although on mountains or precipices he had no such qualms. The wall was hardly three yards wide, the parapet's height less than a foot. He started to walk along the middle towards the south-west tower. He reached it quickly and leaned his back against the smooth curving stonework. Stephen, still at the other end of the wall, was standing at the extreme outer edge, looking over.

'Be careful! You'll fall off!'

Stephen looked at Bruce, and then back at the drop sixty feet below. He felt no giddiness; but the architecture of the castle intrigued him, its solidity, its strangely inevitable simplicity, the way it seemed to grow directly from the rock on which it stood – a miracle of sturdy logic; order triumphant over the vagaries of stone.

Bruce was terrified. He was almost certain Stephen was contemplating jumping over the edge. The plan to kill himself, he was sure, was once more uppermost in his friend's mind. This was the place he had thought of – to leap off the castle walls into oblivion; far more dramatic and sensational than sinking away slowly into the depths of the sea. Bruce was almost sick with apprehension, and yet he could not bring himself to move. He could do nothing but wait, with a strangely unfamiliar sense of anticipation, almost eagerness, for his friend to launch himself forwards. If Stephen was going to take this irrevocable step, let him take it now, quickly, and get it over and done with. Anything was better than this awful tension. Then Stephen, with one last look at the masonry below him, turned and walked towards him, still at the outer edge of the wall, both his arms outstretched like aeroplane wings. He flapped them slightly, exaggerating efforts to keep balance. There was a strange half-smile on his face. He almost seemed to be enjoying the sight of Bruce's mask of horror. He stopped near Bruce, who grabbed his arms as he once again leaned over the edge looking down. Stephen shook himself free.

'You needn't be so old-maidish. I'm not going to jump off.'

'I thought you might fall off. People do.'

'I wouldn't be the first then. If I want to do something dramatic, it must be original. I don't like imitating others.'

'Christ! But you shocked me.'

'You are earnestly entreated to exercise extreme caution while stooping on stone walls.'

Bruce laughed gaily, his voice high with relief. They edged round the inner curve of the tower above the corner of the courtyard and walked slowly along the 'front' west wall. Below they could see the full stretch of the golf links, a few houses, the neat eyesore of a caravan site, the sand dunes, and the sea, white in the sunshine beyond. Immediately below them, like a child's model, was the railway station. A train had just left the platform; its smoke rose up and drifted away below the castle walls. The sounds of the engine and the rattle of the wheels were clear and tiny. The 'fattest lady' came waddling out of her cottage and very slowly opened the two long white gates to the road traffic. The few cars waiting there, one of them a red post-office van, started to move, also like dinky toys, and Bruce noticed how pleasant their body-designs were seen from above. He felt as though he were in the basket of a balloon. He felt light-headed and unstable, the stones of the wall beneath his feet seemed to swaying slightly, floating in clear air.

They reached the north wall. Now they could see all the mountains in their full glory, many more than could be seen from the house. Along to the right spread the splendid long edge of Wales, hill after hill, leading in serried lines to the delicate pinnacle of Snowdon, the old mother of Cambria. Stephen lost all sense of distance, all conception of time. Writing novels seemed less significant than an ant crawling across a desert; all his sordid past seemed petty and mean. He breathed in deeply, and coughed; but for the first time in his life coughing seemed to him to be a chaste action, a cleansing of the whole body before this wild throne of the gods. Grandiose as they seemed, those very words entered his mind, not as an expression of tawdry art, but as genuine truth, something he had never until now been able to believe in. Now, if ever, was the time to leap down from the walls – not to go crashing down to the rocks below, but to rise up like a bird and sail away into the mountains. He felt that such a thing were actually possible, that he had the power now to fly. If only he had faith enough to put it to the test. He looked down again at the great rock below the castle. Sheep were grazing there, nibbling a little, looking up, their mouths constantly working, taking a few steps, and nibbling again – quite oblivious of the two young men gazing down upon them from those ancient heights. Stephen wished he could have been one of those sheep – untroubled with the offal of memories, free of the sordidness of thought and everyday existence, grazing there peacefully with mindless brains.

'Why do they all face the same way?'

'I think it's something to do with the direction of the wind. It's funny, isn't it?' Bruce touched Stephen's arm. 'By the way, this is the Prison Tower.'

Even as he heard his friend's words, Stephen knew there was no escape. Living was a prison, and yet he had no courage to leave it, no will to try. Only a genius can commit suicide, only a genius or madman; and Stephen knew he was neither. He was immeasurably ordinary, more ordinary and aimless than those innocent sheep, and probably more stupid. His mind was too tangled with twisted thoughts, like oil, seaweed and rusty chains knotted in hopeless confusion, even to live now with normal human instincts. There was no way to escape from the putrid slime of the past, the ugly turmoil of the present.

They went down into the tower. Halfway down, the spiral staircase came to an end and led to a wooden bridge across the inside of the tower. Below them was a dark pit. Again with a sense of disappointment, Stephen saw that it was not bottomless. At the same time, he marvelled at the perfect roundness of the tower. He looked down into the pit and for a moment saw a sea of white, soiled, despairing faces all gazing up at him, beseeching him with silent, gasping mouths to save them from their horrible predicament. Streaks of red entered the vision. Their hands, arms and faces were bleeding, and they struggled towards the light, trampling each other down and screaming wordlessly for water and air. It was like the hellish nest of some prehistoric vulture, brutal, bestial, utterly devoid of humanity. He suddenly saw his own face down there among them, and his own clawing arms clutching at a dirty rope someone had hung down into the pit. He felt himself looking up from those hopeless depths and saw that it was Bruce, a cruelly smiling guard in medieval garments, who was holding the rope, which laughing he dropped upon them in the pit. Stephen came back to himself and crossed the bridge. He knelt in a deep sloping stone recess and stared out of the narrow slit window let into the wall there. Again he forgot who and where he was, and thought only of the people who had lived in the castle hundreds of years before. He did not, like a child, imagine that he was an archer repelling a siege. He thought of the craftsmen and labourers who had once assembled there to cut and lay the stones in their allotted places. Someone had designed and shaped that very window, a forgotten villager or an old soldier retired from remote mountain campaigns. Nobody would ever be able to know now, but Stephen, as he fingered the smooth edges of the coping stones, wanted for a moment to remember the hundreds, perhaps thousands, of men whose actual hands had hauled and bludgeoned those huge stones into position, and others whose delicate eyes and fingers had ascertained the exact lines and curves of the walls and towers. Lords had lived in those dark rooms too, and real ladies with tall conical hats with veils attached. Fires had burned in the hearths, some of which he had seen inset in the tower walls, strangely stranded there without floors now that the timbers had all rotted away. Huge banquets had been served in the great hall; people had played music or read old books in those gloomy rooms; prisoners had starved in that very pit below the bridge. These were not just things to be read about in children's fairy-tales. Here they assumed a reality, and Stephen wished he himself could have lived in that reality, instead of the world of endless dull pain that he knew now. Someone, someone that Stephen so much wanted to know and meet, had knelt there in that same window, had looked through and seen the sea below, and had felt safe there, secure and happy. The other place was always happier; the other times were always more full of joy, fascinating mystery, delightful horror. Even pain was bearable, almost lovely, in those places and in those times. Stephen had always felt the same whenever he walked through a museum, staring into glass cases. Who had fashioned that bowl? Who had eaten from that dish, drunk from that goblet? Perhaps Alexander had handled that jewelled box, given it to some admirer long forgotten. The whole museum, any museum, was alive and humming with thousands of people of the past. It was the only way he could bear the loneliness, sadness and boredom of museums, feelings which arose from the fact that he and the other young people wandering from room to room were absolute nonentities gazing at relics from a world of ungraspable splendour. He was not like a visitor to the zoo, staring at animals in cages. Rather he himself was a dumb animal, a goldfish in a bowl, gazing inanely out, while all round him these people of other ages went about their business, each of them with a purpose, a plan, a dream for a happy future.

'How old is this castle?'

'About seven hundred years. I'm not sure exactly.'

'How did they make the towers so round?'

'God knows.'

'Then the builders in those days must have been gods.'

'All builders are gods.' Bruce liked the idea. 'And all gods are builders.'

'Don't be preposterous. Why do you always make such grand statements?'

'You started it.'

'It was only a figure of speech. This castle was built with men's hands. One of my ancestors might have a been a master-craftsman.'

'In that case he hasn't handed much down.'

Stephen laughed in spite of himself, his voice echoing slightly in the heavy grey light. Bruce had a way of mixing bitter truths and humorous remarks that was somehow attractive. He looked at him now; the twinkle was just fading from his eyes.

'You know, most of us know nothing at all about our ancestors. My grandfather was quite famous in his time, but what do I know about his father or mother, or their parents? Nothing. We exist in such narrow spheres of time.'

'Your great-great-grandfather was probably a lavatory attendant on Paddington Station.' Stephen knew he was on dangerous ground now. He watched Bruce thinking of what to say next.

'Your great-aunt's second cousin twice removed might have been a descendant of one of Beethoven's brothers.'

Stephen had not expected Bruce to take this line. He smiled. Sometimes Bruce was amazingly tactful. He knew how Stephen felt about his father, and obviously wanted to avoid the subject.

'Perhaps we'll both be fathers of world-famous children.'

'You know, Stephen, I once had a dream that I was the father of a newly resurrected Jesus Christ.'

'You must have been dazzled by reflected glory.'

'Yes, it was so bright that I woke up. I found I'd fallen asleep with the light on.'

More cheerful now, they continued their descent and came out into the courtyard. Near them, on the grass below the wall and set in a square of low walls, was a heavy, black-painted, iron grill.

'That's the well.'

'How deep is it?'

'Nobody knows.'

'Not even God?'

'There's a story about a girl who drowned there about a hundred years ago.'

'Did she fall or jump?'

They looked at each other, Bruce slightly anxious, Stephen smiling. Then Bruce smiled faintly, and his friend's face became serious. The ghost of suicide had not yet faded into the background of their minds; but for Stephen it was no longer a thinkable idea. His self-dramatization had withered away into the hills of Snowdonia; there was no longer any self to kill.

'It's not sure. Anyway, a few months later they found her body.'

'How could she fall into the well with this grill over it? And how did they find her? Did her rotten head come up in the bucket?'

'There was no grill then, I suppose. This is quite recent. Look, you can see how fresh the cement is. They didn't find her body in this well, anyway.'

'Where was it then? In the sea?'

'No. Miles away, over in the mountains.' Bruce pointed to the hills behind the town. 'That way. There's a lake there. It's called the Lily Lake. She was found there. It's haunted now.'

'It must have been another girl.'

'No, it was the same one. My mother told me about it. One of the locals told her.'

'Is it far from here?'

'About three miles.'

'Did you say it was haunted? I'd like to go there.'

Once again they looked at each other. There was a silence in the castle courtyard. They were alone within those huge, still, grey walls. Bruce looked up. The walls seemed so much higher than he remembered them. Their thoughts and conversation always seemed to return to death and decay, and it was as if Stephen deliberately tried to intensify the atmosphere. Stephen laughed, and they heard, like an echo, the cry of a jackdaw, ensconced somewhere in one of the ruined towers.

As they walked back through the village and along the main road to collect the milk from the top of the zig-zag, Stephen felt as if he were still wandering inside the walls of the castle unable to find a way out. For Bruce too the castle seemed to stay as a great weight in his mind, as if its thick grey walls were the actual bones of his skull. They both felt overwhelmed by its age and vastness, at the absolute inevitability and genius of its position and design. Their own attempts at art seemed paltry, weak-spirited by comparison. Nothing they could do would ever match the splendour, ruinous as it now was, of that brilliantly structured pile of stones. It somehow made them equals in insignificance. Stephen longed to escape from the great grey gloom of his own world which took the form now of this imperishable castle. Bruce wanted to have been, wanted to be now, the man who had masterminded its construction. He wanted to be able announce to vast audiences: 'This castle is mine; I made it. Behold! – there it stands.' The castle had never made him feel like that before. Seeing it now with new eyes in the presence of Stephen, perhaps with Stephen's eyes, had made him feel what a great disadvantage it was to be young and unknown. He could now feel himself actually growing older, as if lines were about to creep across his brow or appear at the corners of his eyes, as if somewhere inside his skull the roots of his hair were beginning to understand that one day they would emerge into the light fine and grey and later glistening white; and then he felt, perhaps for the first time, that human life is short, that there was no time to waste, he must get on, make greater efforts to bring his masterpiece shining into the world. As for Stephen, the castle did not inspire him; rather it depressed him. All human effort was futile; all the great works of the titans were doomed, like this castle, to decay and destruction. Nothing endured. What was the point, he wondered, of trying to live a useful life, to get up each morning, breathing in and out, breath after breath, eating, defecating, writhing in sexual frenzy, getting old, and finally dying? And yet, he felt, life was not all crumbling grey walls, grey skies and perpetual rain. Somewhere behind it all, the sun was forever burning in the heavens. As they slithered and jolted down the zig-zag, the full milk bottles clacking dully in Bruce's bag, Stephen glanced at his friend. How was it that his eyes always seemed to shine so brightly, as if they themselves were as eternal as the sun? Stephen had loved those eyes; he loved them still. Because of that love, he would somehow continue stumbling along among the grey stones of the road. The castle around him was changing its shape, lengthening out into a broad highway walled on either side with those same stones, much lower now, and at the end in the distance, what was it he could see there? A strange, weary, aged, woman's face seemed to be slowly turning there, speaking without words, half hidden in swirls of mist and spray; and beyond it, he could see a vast stretch of grey ocean, moving, swaying, changing endlessly, restless in pale sunlight and totally without sound. Harlieg, it seemed to him, was one of those eerie places at the edge of fairyland, where a chance step could lead him into an enchanted world; but Stephen knew in his bones that he would never be one of those lucky people who found their way into that magic country, brilliant and fascinating with adventure that never harmed anyone, to come back and tell stories of the marvels there, and forever afterwards live in a kind of dream. Life for him held no such promise. He too felt the weight of age, but not age that held the dignity of wisdom and achievement; nothing so noble as that, nothing but careworn weariness, an endless dullness of mediocre middle age, and he a derelict man in a grey raincoat wandering about in suburban parks staring in misery and envy at happy, young people all around him, laughing and light of heart, gazing at the bright futures that shone from their eager eyes. Fitting exactly now into that despondency of Stephen's mind, Bruce's laughing, light-toned voice came to his ears.

'I've just remembered something funny.'

'Another earnestly requested to exercise special desire?'

'No, about the castle. Two years ago we had a university friend of mine to stay here. He had a car. One evening we went up into the town and removed some of the signs outside people's houses – "Rooms to Let", "Bed and Breakfast", "Accommodation", about five or six we got.'

'What did you do with them? Set them up on the beach?'

'No, we climbed down into the moat of the castle and arranged them below the outer wall, wondering what people would think when they saw them there next morning from the castle square.'

'Didn't you get caught?'

'No. It was raining. There was no one about.' Bruce's eyes gleamed with mischief. 'The next evening we went up to the castle to see what had happened to the signs.'

'What did you find? A whole platoon of uniformed policemen waiting to arrest you?'

'No.' Again Bruce's eyes sparkled with wicked merriment. 'The whole castle was ablaze with lights. Every window shone with lamps, candles and chandeliers. We could see people inside the rooms, eating and drinking and dancing. Music from lutes, recorders and trumpets poured out into the night. Couples in brilliant clothes were strolling along the walls accompanied by torch-bearers, and servants with lanterns were hurrying around in the darkness. We heard a superb tenor singing in one of the towers.'

'You're a liar.'

'No, I'm not. I never tell lies.' Bruce laughed. 'But it's a lovely idea, isn't it?'

Stephen wished he had thought of it. They reached the bottom of the zig-zag and just before the first stile, Stephen stopped.

'What's the matter?'

'Would you mind if I used that?'

'Used what?'

'That idea. The castle all alive like that. It's marvellous. I'd like to use it in my novel.'

'You're a thief!' Bruce stepped onto the stile and turned to look down on Stephen. 'You're like one of those jackdaws in the castle. You like stealing glittering things. Go ahead! But don't forget to put a proper acknowledgement in the footnotes!'

Laughing, Bruce leapt over the stile and skipped towards the railway line. Stephen followed him in silence.

12. BARD

WHEN THEY GOT BACK to the house, Stephen decided to take a stroll along the beach. At first Bruce, not eager to let his friend out of his sight, or out of his control, wanted to go with him, but Stephen insisted on going alone. He wanted to think about his novel; he wanted to work out how to use that image of the castle, illuminated, bustling with people. Bruce, relieved that his friend was in a creative frame of mind, gave in and agreed to stay behind.
    'How long will you be?'
    'About an hour, I expect.'
    'We'll have supper when you get back.'

Stephen went down to the shore, Bruce into the house. It was very silent in the living room. Not many years ago in the summer holidays it would have been full of people at this time of day – the family, cousins, friends – all having tea together and talking noisily of the
the day's exploits.

Bruce sat down at the piano and began to improvise. A train straining up a mountain line, lonely hills, buzzards hovering overhead. For Bruce, music was still essentially a matter of pictures; there was always some programme behind the sounds. With Stephen, music was always pure – mathematics expressed in chords and rhythms. After a few minutes, Bruce realized once again that alone he had practically no skill at the piano at all. He needed the basic rhythms and continuity supplied by Stephen in the bass.

Without him his own efforts were futile – mere disconnected chords; melodies would not develop further than a bar or two; the music would not flow. And without Stephen, Bruce's deliberate discords seemed merely ugly; when Stephen forged them with his thick stubby hands, they were always exciting. Stephen always intensified things. Those who were with him found they had sharper eyes, keener ears; everyday events were charged with drama; water became heady wine. When Stephen was absent, Bruce felt the flatness of life; and yet, when he was present, the atmosphere soon became overcharged with tension. He wanted Stephen to be stable, to be comfortable as a friend. But it seemed he would never settle down.

Bruce got up from the piano and wandered out into the verandah to see if he could catch sight of Stephen, but the beach was deserted. Stephen was probably too close under the line of sandhills to be seen from the house, or perhaps he had gone the other way towards the railway line. Bruce slid his hand down his thigh and gently cupped it round his genital area. In spite of a general feeling of malaise, he sensed the promise of a delight to come; but he would have to wait. Not yet. Now was not the time. The longer he held back, the greater the surging pleasure would be. He felt the stirrings of tender nerves.

Suddenly he heard a voice half behind him on the lawn.
'I've brought the things down for you.'
Bruce turned, almost guiltily. A boy was standing there with a large carton of groceries. He was about fourteen, slender, with sandy red hair and a freckled face. Something about him immediately attracted Bruce. He smiled.
'Oh, thank you. Would you put it there?' He pointed to the seat in the verandah. The boy put the carton down with a sigh, and turned round with a smile.
'That was a bit heavy.'
'Sorry you've had the bother of bringing it all the way down here. Did you walk all the way?'
'No. Left my bike over by the stiles. It's got a big frame on the front for deliveries. No trouble at all, only this last bit.'

Bruce felt a warmth blossoming in his heart. The sound of the boy's voice enchanted him. It was low-toned and clear, near to breaking perhaps but showing no signs of it. His eyes were a kind of blue-green and merry and bright; and yet there was an overall seriousness, almost sadness, about him. He was a boy on the threshold of puberty, at the age that Bruce found most fascinating of all. Here was a perfect boy, a total little man at the peak of childhood, like a peach in its one hour of perfection. Bruce felt his heart give a lurch of regret. Why did such human beauty have to be destroyed? Why did nature and time push us forwards into the shock and sordidness of sexual maturity? Why did we have to grow up?

'I haven't seen you before. Do you live in Harlieg?'

'That's right. Wanted to earn a bit of money. It's my first holiday job.' Bruce loved the Welsh lilt of his voice. 'Never been down here before. It's a nice place, isn't it?'

'Lovely. Why don't you come down for a swim one day?' Bruce's mind raced as he wondered how he could fit this into his daily life with Stephen.

'No time, I expect. Have to go back to school next week.'

Bruce wondered how to prolong the conversation. He could have stayed there forever talking with this paragon child.

'Would you like a cup of tea? I'll go and put the kettle on.'

'No, thanks. No time. Got to get back up to the shop.'

'Well, wait a minute. I've got something for you.' Bruce went into the house, ran upstairs and rummaged among some loose change scattered on his table. He picked out a two-shilling piece. At least he could tip the boy. His mother had always done such things. He felt a glow of generosity flush his face, or was it a flame of guilt?

The boy was fingering the seaweed hanging in the verandah.

'What's this for then?'

'It's a kind of weather-vane, to tell us if it's going to be wet or dry. It's not much use really. Just a habit.'

'Never seen one of these before.'

Bruce once again sensed how the town people seemed to live apart from the sea that was so near them.

'Don't you ever come down to the beach then?'

'Once in a while. Not much to do down here. I like soccer. We've got a nice field behind the school – over there on the flat.' The boy pointed north beyond the castle. 'You like soccer?'

'Not really. I like watching it, but I've almost never played it. What position do you play in?'

'Right half.' The boy smiled again, and looked at his watch. 'Well, must be off now.'

Bruce handed him the silver coin.

'Here's a little something. It's a long way to come down all the way here.'

The boy looked surprised, then pleased.

'Oh, thanks. Never say no.' He gave a short laugh, and turned to leave. 'Goodbye.'

'Goodbye. See you again sometime.'

'Maybe.' The boy tossed up the coin, caught it and put it in his pocket. Bruce watched him walk across the lawn, look at his watch again and break into a run. He disappeared behind a sandhill.

Bruce found he was trembling with, he immediately recognized, a kind of disappointment. Why hadn't he shaken hands with the boy? Even to touch him like that would have been something. Or why hadn't he thrown caution to the winds and grasped the boy in his arms and kissed him? Then he felt a warm glow of satisfaction. No, he hadn't touched the boy. He had done nothing to harm him, to contaminate his purity. It was better that way, better to be good. He was going to be a teacher. It might be all right to love those he taught, but let it be just love like this. He thrust down a wave of regret. It was always like this. He never dared, as Stephen did. He was always afraid of what might happen. He was afraid of the shame, the cold rejection. Why was it that boys of this age were so cold in their purity? Did they have no feelings in their hearts? He had said nothing to encourage further communication with Bruce, only one question about football. He was wrapped up in his own world. Children always were. They could not understand the feelings of others. This boy had had no inkling whatever of the thoughts in Bruce's mind. Well – Bruce sighed – perhaps it was better this way. His thoughts might not be clean, but he had done nothing anyone could call wrong. And another thing: Bruce felt a kind of righteous pride in realizing that though he would like to have kissed the boy, there was nothing overtly sexual in his feelings for him. Love was one thing, sex another. In his young mind, the two were separate entities, never, he felt, to be reconciled. There was a kind of joy in knowing that. As he carried the carton into the kitchen and began to unpack the groceries, Bruce found he was whistling, tunelessly yet merrily, like a bird singing in a tree.

Stephen walked along the beach looking at the sand. The idea of writing a novel, even though he found Bruce's castle image delightful in itself, already seemed tedious; but to stop now, before he had hardly made a beginning, would invite immediate criticism and scorn from Bruce. Bruce was so exacting, so well organized; everything had its place and time and manner. Not that his friend was dull or complacent, but that he was so strong. Stephen felt weak without his friend, yet often irritated when he was with him. Bruce always tried to soften the hard edges of experience; he seemed to shy away from reality. He lived in a world of his own, but in that world he had invincible integrity. Stephen realized he was taking a stroll not to think about his novel but to get away for a while from his friend. He felt he owed Bruce too much; he did not know how to reciprocate the kindness his friend constantly forced upon him. Bruce had bought some notebooks in the town, a new pen; he had given them all to Stephen, and Stephen did not know how to thank him. He was not even sure if he wanted them, but to refuse them would seem ungrateful, and Stephen was not so unfeeling as to wish to hurt his friend. Yet even at that time, Stephen had felt that Bruce's motives were not entirely altruistic; Bruce had wanted rather to appear to be kind, to be seen to be kind, or perhaps he wanted to exercise a kind of power or just wanted to feel needed. It even occurred to Stephen that there was an element of meanness in Bruce's gesture, as if he had bought the books and pen, perhaps, in order to retrieve the ones he had lent to Stephen the previous evening. Bruce never gave anything, never lent anything that he treasured, or even anything that might be of some use to himself. Once in Bruce's room at home, Stephen had found two different volumes of Shakespeare's complete works;

Bruce had seen him take one of them from the shelf and turn the pages, savouring the sweet smell of old paper.

'I'll give you one of those if you like.'

'Will you really? I've never had the complete works.'

Bruce picked up the two books, one a large and bound in pale brown cloth, a rather cheap edition, the other small, leather bound with gilt on the spine and cover, the pages edged with gold. He hesitated, weighing them in his hands, wondering which to give away. Then he had started to make excuses. The big one he needed to make notes in; the small one was too good to mark. On the other hand, the small one was convenient for carrying in the pocket. Well, actually he needed both. Finally, he gave Stephen neither; but promised that if he came across another he would keep it for his friend. On subsequent visits, Stephen noticed that the two books were always in their place on the shelf, gradually collecting dust. It was occasions like these which made Stephen doubt his friend's sincerity. Sometimes he longed to get away.

*

Bruce, feeling slightly out of sorts after the delivery boy had gone, decided to prepare a surprise for Stephen. A few months previously, his grandmother, Rowena Helga Dinwiddy, in an almost senile wave of generosity, had allowed Bruce to wander through her house, a little way up the road from the Dinwiddy home, peering in cupboards, browsing through the numerous white-painted bookshelves – to choose for himself some of the possessions of his grandfather, who had died fifteen years previously. Bryan Dinwiddy had, at the beginning of the century, been a man of some distinction – a poet and critic who often gave public readings and lectures, and whose articles and works often appeared in the many magazines of the day. Later in his life, however, his circle of admirers had dwindled to a small and ageing coterie of failed eccentrics, whose literary output had been quite unable to keep up with the times. They were all confirmed latter-day romantics, like faded replicas of Tennyson or William Morris, writing enormously long verse romances based on hazy Celtic mythologies. The public no longer had time for such self-indulgent products. Bryan Dinwiddy had died a sad and disappointed man.

He had been a great collector – not, however, a collector of any distinction or speciality. The house was full of nondescript statues and busts of persons, ancient and modern, who had not quite reached the top of the tree, cracked and rusting gongs, blurred and sentimental oil-paintings of maidens in forest settings, and thousands of books, many of them the works of his cronies and his own, printed with costly bindings at their authors' expense and doomed to decay unread, even with most of the pages uncut, in second-hand bookshops or houses such as this. Some of the books, however, were quite rare editions of classics, and Bruce had chosen about a hundred, many of them reeking with the lilac perfume favoured by his grandmother. Bruce's father had not allowed some of the books to fall into his son's hands and ordered him to return these. Two other items, which passed his father's censorship and which were now among Bruce's most treasured possessions, were a white plaster death-mask of Beethoven and his grandfather's bardic robes.

Bryan Dinwiddy had been a member of the Welsh Eisteddfod – which met annually in Llangollen to recite poetry and award prizes for promising works and oral renderings. The judges and grand masters were all attired in druid-like robes, which they wore over their ordinary everyday clothes. The robes consisted of a long gown reaching to the ground, fastened at the side with wooden buttons; the upper part was a kind of attached over-mantle wrapped round the shoulders and falling in a V-shape over the breast. There was a flowing hood, something like the headdress Chaucer wears in all his portraits. The entire garment was of fine sea-blue linen, not dark, not light, but fresh and satisfying to the eye.

Bruce loved it. He often donned the robes and stood in front of a mirror chanting his poems, sometimes by candlelight. At such times, he felt like a real poet, a splendid maker of lofty verse. All he needed was a harp, a great wooden hall with hammer beams and a band of thanes, and his sense of creativity and power would be perfect. He had not yet shown the garments to Stephen, but meaning to do so had brought them to Harlieg. If there were any place where such attire would be fitting, it was here by the sea.

He went upstairs to his room, unpacked the robes from the old flat carton they had been kept in and put them on. They were fastened in some places by small domestic metal clips instead of buttons. He was a little irritated by these: real bards would never have had such clips. Deep down, but unwilling to admit it, Bruce knew that the whole attire was nothing more than a theatrical guise, a mere stage costume. It even had the faint musty smell of a theatre wardrobe room.

He went downstairs and stood in the verandah, looking along the beach for Stephen.

*

Stephen was beginning to feel tired. They had done a great deal of walking that day, and he was not accustomed to it. Abundance of fresh air and the spaciousness of the surroundings had loosened his limbs and made him use muscles which in a few more years of city life would have begun to atrophy. He had already walked over a mile, he reckoned. He decided to turn back.

At that moment, he heard voices, and the same group of people they had met that morning came out of the sandhills onto the beach only a few yards from where he had come to a standstill. There were six people, three boys and three girls, all of student age. They were carrying baskets, rugs, some cooking pots and a kettle. They were laughing, and two of the couples were holding hands. They put down the things they were carrying in a heap, split up and began to collect driftwood. One of the boys came near Stephen.

'Didn't we see you this morning?'

'That's right. You went for a swim, didn't you?'

'We're going in again soon. Want to join us?'

'I haven't got my swimming things.'

'We're not going to wear any. It'll be dark soon. The sea stays warm a long time, you know.'

He laughed, but Stephen did not feel like smiling. The group seemed so happy and carefree. He wished he could live like that – normal, cheerful, acceptable.

'Are you from the College?'

'That's right. Smashing place here, isn't it?'

'Wonderful.'

'We're going to have a camp fire.'

Stephen wished he could join them. Not for one moment would he have considered swimming in the nude. He had a particular reason for that, but he did not intend to tell anyone. But to make a fire on the beach, cook a meal, and belong to this cheerful group – these were things he would love to have shared.

'Why don't you eat with us?'

'I've got to go back. I'm staying in that house along there. My friend's expecting me back.'

'Oh, that house?' The boy laughed. 'The people in the College call it the House-with-lights-on-all-night.'

'How curious! Why?'

'That family – Dimwitty, isn't it? – seem to stay up all night. It's got a kind of reputation. What do they do all night? Have orgies? Are they all there now?'

'No, only one. He's my friend.'

Stephen suddenly wondered what that really meant. Friend. Was Bruce his friend? Was anyone his friend? He smiled at the boy's 'Dimwitty'. He must remember to use that on Bruce one day.

'Yes, the lights haven't been on so much these days. What are you doing there?'

'Writing a novel. We're both writers.' Stephen enjoyed making this announcement. It sounded impressive. He did not stop to wonder whether it was true or not.

'Wow! Writers, are you? You should come and meet some of the weirdies up at the College.'

'I'd love to. How long have you been there?'

'This is my second year. We're all in the same class.'

'What do you study?'

'Nothing special. It's a sort of general course. We missed regular schooling, see. Illness, family trouble, living abroad – that sort of thing. It's a nice place. Plenty going on.'

Stephen remembered his conversation with Bruce about 'depraved children' and almost smiled. The College sounded attractive, the kind of place he himself was in need of. There was nothing depraved about this boy, nor did he strike Stephen as deprived in any way. He seemed perfectly normal. He was touched by his natural warmth, by the way he had accepted Stephen without hesitation. No strange looks here, no frowns or gradual edging away. Perhaps all the students were people like himself, so this boy could not feel anything different.

'I'm awfully sorry I can't stay down here with you. I have to be getting back. Do you often come down here?'

'Most days. Not if it's raining. We'll probably meet again.'

'I hope so.' Stephen meant it. He felt he was among his own kind with these people, even though this was a new feeling. He walked slowly back towards the house, the shouts and laughter continuing behind him. There was something pleasant in the sound, and Stephen longed to turn back and fall in with them. These were not shouts of derision. They were entirely friendly. Or were they? He stopped for a moment, thinking, then he put the idea out of his mind, remembering the sincerity in the boy's eyes. He would certainly contrive to meet them again. He might even enrol at the College. Just think of it – days of study, friendship, acceptance – all in this unforgettable setting. And how pleased Bruce would be, if Stephen were to settle down into some steady course of instruction, even more pleased because it would arise from having invited Stephen to Harlieg in the first place. He thought of Bruce, his stern master, waiting in the house. Bruce might after all be able to guide him towards something worthwhile, but perhaps Bruce was not himself the kind of friend he needed.

*

Bruce had seen Stephen's encounter with the students, and immediately felt a rising sense of insecurity. Why did Stephen always want to talk with such people? They were all inferior people at the College, failed people, people who had gone wrong somewhere, had had trouble in the past. Such people could only unsettle his friend. His friend. Stephen was his friend; he had invited him here. Bruce felt faint resentment. It was ungrateful of Stephen to stay away so long, hobnobbing with those awful people from the College. It was getting dark. Bruce looked at the western sky, thinking. Stephen had been away well over an hour. Bruce was waiting impatiently to spring his surprise.

He walked down the path to the beach. Before he got to the rocks, however, he turned left and climbed up a grassy sandhill standing between the house and the shore. There was a sandy hollow at the top of it, gouged out by the wind, and Bruce, draped in his blue robes, crouched down in this, waiting.

Stephen looked up at the house. The light was on in the living room. In spite of his thoughts, Stephen felt there was something warm and inviting about it. The red roof seemed a strange neutral colour in the failing light. As he moved nearer, the reflection of the sun was caught in some of the windows, and made the house look as if it were on fire, burning from within. The idea excited him – the house on the shore; a pyromaniac; a blazing pyre of crackling wood and exploding glass; fire by the sea. Something for his novel perhaps.

He started to cross the rocks. He twice fell over, supporting himself with his hands. He was glad Bruce was not there to see him. He cursed the ineptness of his body; it was not geared for life in the open air. He would have to train, take up running, do exercises every morning. Perhaps he would have to learn to swim.

He reached the upper edge of the rocks and started up the path to the house. The fires had gone out in the windows. Only the light in the living-room showed, the cliff darkening behind it. Something attracted his attention to his right, at the top of the sandhill there. He turned his head.

A huge, towering figure was standing there, a black silhouette against the golden sky; a figure in long robes, swaying slightly, its hooded head facing the sea. It raised one arm, and then a great voice boomed out over the sand dunes — half-singing, chanting, crying out a kind of despairing dirge along the shore.

'I dread death,
not in Cambria, nor on sea,
for these eternals are to me.
Die I in Snowdon's mists or in the grey
and foaming of some Hebridean bay,
I dread death not.

'I dread death
not as ending, nor as change;
for I shall soul that oldest range,
ending not in Snowdon's ribs, nor in the air
of Cambrian regions dreaming. Die I there,
I dread death not.'

The voice was vast, round, thundering in the stillness of the evening. The syllables carried far on the air, and seemed to fade into the soft turning of the waves. Stephen stood motionless, held in a kind of spell. He had no time to think, to analyze. The figure, high above him, or so it seemed, was too tall to be human; it seemed to be part of the sandhill; the robe seemed to merge with the long grasses there, to be growing out of them. The apparition was like some genius of the shore. Stephen tried to run, but as in a nightmare he was unable to move. The house seemed to be drifting far, far away, a tiny square of light receding into the distance. He reached out blindly and fell over. The spiky yellow grasses rose round him like a forest whose trees were curving spears; some of them pricked his face, his hands, and one of them caught him in the eye, temporarily blinding him. When he opened his eyes again, they were watering and nothing was distinct. The sandhills round him had become mountains, black and inaccessible; not rocks, but great inclines of black sand stretching up into a blinding goldness of sky. He was lying in the middle of a desert. The dark sand was warm against his arms. The voice went on. He could feel it vibrating up through the ground and thudding through his flesh and bones. He tried to cover his ears with his hands, to keep out those ringing cries, the snare of sea-mad enchantment. He was petrified beyond all reason.

> 'I dread death!
> Not to die in Celtic wind
> is my unfascinating end.
> O let me die to songs of sea,
> and if this joy is joined in me,
> I dread death not.'

The voice stopped, but there was thunder in the sea. Stephen felt as if the sea, stirred into madness and fury, were cheering on the heroic exploits of some mighty god. A magnificent chorus roared all about him, on and on; as if there were no breath in the voices, only endless energy direct from the pounding floods of the bloodstream, like a brilliant organ chord held forever; and the pipes of the organ were grasses and mountain crags, the bellows the huge womb of the mother earth below him.

The roaring continued. Then it was no longer endless thunder. It was Bruce, laughing from the sandhill above him. The shock of recognition was even greater than the shock of terror which had first struck him. Stephen felt a sudden surge of blind fury. He got up, dusting his clothes.

'You fucking idiot! What the bloody-hell do you think you're doing?'

'Reciting a poem. Do you like my robes?' Bruce came bounding down the sandhill like a study-in-blue of Lawrence of Arabia.

'No, I bloody well don't. God, what do you want to go and do a stupid thing like that for? You know I can't stand things like that. My nervous system can't take it.'

'I wanted to show you my bardic attire.'

'You stupid...cunt! What a bloody clever way to amuse yourself! Do you know what things like that do to me?'

'Inspire you.'

'No, they fucking well don't! They make me go mad. You've destroyed everything. I was beginning to like this place. I was beginning to get calmed down. Now you've messed me all up again. You've undone months of efforts towards some sort of recovery. You've ruined everything. Oh, you idiot, idiot!'

Bruce was dismayed. He had never expected this outburst. His performance had been far more effective than he had imagined. He never once thought Stephen would have been so shocked. He had thought his friend would have laughed, would have loved the idea, the wonderful sight of the bard on the hilltop, chanting to the sea. At the same time, he felt triumphant. He possessed the power to terrify. Stephen was standing, both hands over his temples, shaking his head from side to side. Bruce laughed.

'It was only a joke.'

'If that's what you call a joke – Christ!'

'I'm sorry, Stephen. I never meant to—'

'You never think!'

'These are my grandfather's Eisteddfod robes. He used to wear them for recitations.'

'I don't care a bloody shit about your grandfather's recitations.'

'I wanted to show you.'

'Not like that. You've got no imagination. You never think. You don't understand.'

Putting his hand on his friend's shoulder, Bruce began to lead the way up to the house.

'Look, Stephen. I really am sorry.'

'You...it's easy to say that. This has put me right back.'

'I didn't mean it to be like that.'

'No, of course you didn't. You're so full of self-aggrandisement, you never think about what other people feel.'

'Let's go in and have supper.'

'I'm not hungry. Do you think I can eat after that?'

'Oh, come on, Stephen. Don't exaggerate. You're being self-dramatic, too. It was only a joke.'

Stephen fell silent. They walked slowly towards the house. Bruce tried to change the subject.

'You met those people again, didn't you?'

'Do you mind? They're extremely pleasant people. They wanted me to have supper with them on the beach. I wish I had now.'

'Are they students?'

'Yes, and bloody normal, too. No posing about them. They were kind, naturally kind. We're going to meet again.'

Bruce's anxiety rose up again like a demon. He had not wanted things to develop this way. The last thing he wanted to do was alienate his friend, but that was just what he seemed to be doing. He pulled off his blue hood, and spoke gently.

'Look, Stephen. I really am sorry. I realize I shouldn't have done a thing like that.'

'You shouldn't have done it at all.'

'I was wrong.'

'You're often wrong. You don't like to be wrong, do you?'

'No. But in this case I am wrong. I shouldn't have done it. I'll be more careful next time.'

'Next time? What do you mean?'

'I want you to have a good time here, Stephen—'

'A good time!'

'That's why I asked you. I wanted you to share this wonderful place with me. I wanted us to have a really peaceful time, and talk, and write, and make music, go for walks.'

'On your terms.'

'Yes, I see that. I don't consider your feelings enough.'

Looking subdued, Bruce started to unclip the robes. He felt foolish in them now. He draped them over his arm as they reached the verandah.

Stephen was calming down. The shock was passing. He saw the episode now as a mere phantasm, a silly whim of Bruce's, best forgotten. Bruce was so childish. Yet...the apparition had had such power; as though Bruce were quite another being – god-like, awe-inspiring. There had been something real, convincing, in the way he stood there crying to the sea. It was if the sea had done something to him, made the child into a magician, almost a seer. Although it had only been an act, it had been much more than that. Bruce had been possessed. The voice had not been his own; it couldn't have been. Someone, something much greater and older than either of them could comprehend, had been speaking, violently, through him; something which dwelled, huge, terrifying, ungovernable, in the depths of the sea.

They went into the house.

*

The sun had gone down. Mist had risen over the Traeth, low, not moving. They had had supper and were now standing in the verandah. Peace between them had been restored. Bruce had been forgiven. Stephen could laugh now. Everything was going to be all right.

A fire was burning on the beach. Figures occasionally moved across, momentarily blotting out the pinpoint glare of the flames. The darkness round the spot was intense. They could hear faint shouts, screams, fragments of laughter. Once again Stephen wished he were with them.

Suddenly Bruce pointed north towards the sandhills in the far distance, well to the right of the fire on the beach. A faint light, soft, glowing like a candle-flame seen through gauze, was drifting slowly across the Traeth towards the sea. It faded out. Another followed, on the same low, drifting trajectory. And yet another. Stephen tensed.

'What are they?'

'Will o' the wisp.'

'What do you mean?'

'Marsh gas. It comes up out of the swamp over there.'

'Really? What causes it to burn like that?'

'I'm not sure. It's something to do with warm air meeting cool air, I think. I've only seen it once before.'

They stood watching the eerie, slow-moving lights. There was no need to make dramatic or mysterious statements. It was all too easy to imagine a slow procession of tall, dark figures below the lights, holding lanterns aloft, a line of exiled bards moving towards the sea. The fire on the beach seemed now to be part of the strange ritualistic movement. It seemed to be moving at the same speed in the opposite direction; perhaps it was even a sacrificial altar waiting to receive its victims. Suddenly the two friends felt cold. Bruce touched Stephen's arm.

'Let's go in.'

They went into the house; but the lights went on moving across Stephen's mind — a creeping traffic of unearthly beings. Everything, it seemed, was drawn towards the sea; and in return the sea uttered its endless voices and left strange objects on the sand — a secret, incomprehensible exchange. And above it all, in Stephen's mind, a tall figure in dark blue robes, chanting across the waves, crying out to some vast spirit under the sea, lost perhaps, or perhaps part of it, perhaps its very essence; and the sea cried back to the land.

And for Bruce the lights had another meaning. Sea-elves, mermen, shore-gnomes in garments of seaweed were searching the sand dunes; they were searching in the sand and dust for the million fragments of his mother's ashes, and finding them they gathered them together, and took them, in single handfuls, to some more permanent resting place, far down in the depths of the sea.

13. CIGARETTES

THAT NIGHT Bruce decided to stop smoking. Had he been asked why, he would not have been able to explain his reasons clearly. Like Stephen, he was often impulsive, but he differed from his friend in certain respects. Stephen's impulsiveness more often than not led him into dangerous situations. Bruce's took two forms: on the one hand, there were his sudden childish whims, like his unhappy attempt to surprise Stephen with the bardic robes, but usually quite harmless; on the other, there were almost masochistic attempts at restraint and self-discipline. Neither lasted long. In this case there was something of both. It was quite unnecessary for him to stop smoking. Bruce was not a heavy smoker and he rarely inhaled; he was often surprised, almost embarrassed, when he always seemed to produce more smoke than those confirmed in the habit. Perhaps on this occasion he felt the need to compensate for his thoughtless performance, which had so upset his friend. Perhaps he felt a sense of inferiority in having to admit that he had been in the wrong. He needed a boost to restore his self-confidence. Whatever happened, he must remain stronger than Stephen.

Stephen rarely had any cigarettes of his own, partly through lack of money, partly out of habit. He almost always smoked other people's. For the past two days he had been smoking Bruce's. As they sat in the living-room after coming in from watching the lights from the swamp, Bruce noticed that there were three cigarettes in the packet on the table. They each smoked one as they talked. Stephen never worried about such trivial things as cigarettes – as long as there was a steady supply. Bruce always seemed to be well provided in such matters; he always appeared to have a plentiful stock.

A little while later, Bruce, as was normal in the case of it being a choice between Stephen and himself, took the last cigarette from the packet.

'This is my last cigarette.'

'We'll have to get some more tomorrow.'

'I didn't mean that. I meant I'm going to stop smoking. This is my last.' He lit it with a flourish, flicking the match into the fireplace. Stephen glanced at his friend, but for the moment thought no more about it. He was mildly surprised at Bruce's rather grand announcement, but he was used to his friend's sudden self-impositions. Sometimes such gestures irritated him, mainly because he knew that he himself would normally not think of making such efforts, and he was a little envious of Bruce's strength of will.

Bruce sat in his chair beside the fire, smoking slowly and deliberately, watching the smoke curl up, bluish at the lighted end, but brown and poisonous-looking as it seeped from the filtered tip. He was aware of Stephen's gaze and returned it in silence. Then, when the cigarette was only half smoked, he stood up conscious of the dramatic possibilities of the moment. Stephen interrupted him.

'If you're not going to finish that, let me have it.' He reached out his hand.

Bruce lifted the cigarette high in the air slowly and made as if it to fling it into the fire, staring at Stephen all the time. Then he smiled, brought his arm down in a quick movement and handed him the cigarette.

'I hope you enjoy the taste.'

'I love your saliva.'

'I'll give you some more if you like.' He made as if to spit.

'No, thank you, there's enough here.' Stephen drew deeply on the cigarette.

'The last part's always a bit sour, I feel.'

'Said the wet-nurse to the baby.'

They laughed. Stephen had deflated what might have become an unpleasant confrontation. He finished the cigarette and threw it into the fire. It missed and fell into the hearth.

'You are earnestly requested—'

'To exercise your Freudian symbols with undue abandon.' Laughing wheezily, Stephen bent down and put the cigarette carefully onto the glowing coals.

'Are you going to exercise yours in bed tonight?'

'Probably. How about you?'

Bruce laughed, a little primly it seemed to Stephen.

'I don't do things like that.'

Stephen raised his eyebrows.

'Never?'

'Not now anyway.'

Stephen stared hard at his friend. He could never tell when Bruce was lying unless what he said was obviously preposterous. There was no trace of humour in Bruce's face now. Stephen almost believed him, staring at him with a kind of wonder, with a kind of questioning gaze; but he could not fathom those burning, liquid eyes. Bruce was not a saint, yet Stephen despaired of ever knowing what went on in his friend's mind. Could one ever know? He tried to imagine Bruce in bed, Bruce naked, Bruce's face at the moment of orgasm; but somehow the images would not take shape, as if sex were something totally alien to Bruce, as if it were something quite outside the world he lived in, far below his level of existence, something he looked down on with a kind of scorn and disgust. And yet...no one could live without it entirely unless he were mentally or physically diseased. Bruce showed no sign of either. How did he manage then? Stephen was not emotionally involved in such a question; he was not burning with curiosity or desire. But now that the subject had arisen the whole question of Bruce's sexuality took on the nature of a purely intellectual problem, and Stephen's analytical mind was baffled by it. There was so much about his friend he did not know. Perhaps it was all just another pose and Bruce was no better than himself, but chose to hide behind a mask of prudery. He thought of asking Bruce 'What do you do then?' – but thought it wiser to go no further. Better to leave it alone. Stephen yawned.

'I think I'll go up to bed.'

'Me too. Have a good jiggle.'

'Jiggle yourself.'

Bruce merely smiled, removed the fender, and began to bank up the fire with ashes for the night. Stephen went up to his room.

*

The following day the weather continued fine. They were up early, Bruce for his quick swim, Stephen for his short walk. This time they saw no one on the beach. They had breakfast, and Bruce went out to continue his creosoting; Stephen stayed in the living-room to work on his novel. A few hours passed by.

Bruce was gradually working round to the north end of the house. Soon he was coating the boards immediately below the bay window of the living room. He could see Stephen inside, sometimes seated at the table, often getting up and pacing about. Once or twice they exchanged smiles.

Stephen did not seem to be writing much. He sat at the table, staring out of the west window at the sea. Then he wrote a few sentences, laboriously in a slow hand, as if it were an unnatural, recently-acquired skill; then sat back again, a rather self-conscious 'inspired' look on his face. The writer at work. Then he stood up again, one hand to his forehead, walking round the table. Bruce felt he was watching a performance – a scene from a rather nondescript film. Stephen irritated him. When would he ever settle down and get on with some really hard work?

Stephen wanted a cigarette. Like many young people, he had started smoking as an adjunct to adulthood. He told people it 'soothed his nerves'. He felt comfortable holding a cigarette between his fingers, inhaling deeply, watching the coils of vapour, and as he talked gesturing with his little smoking wand. Thus it had become a habit with him, something he had not been aware of until there were no cigarettes, as now, to smoke. He had seen personalities on television – critics, writers, vague intellectuals – and they always seemed to be wielding cigarettes in the same way, almost like miniature weapons or instruments of defence. It was part of their image. Stephen emulated such people.

Normally, when he was engrossed in something, he smoked less, or smoked automatically without thinking about it; but this morning he once again found himself at a loss. His novel would not come. Whenever he tried to write, he found that images of the immediate past juxtaposed themselves between his line of fiction and himself – images of shells, dead birds, mountains in the distance, the castle, vast stretches of sand, the bard on the sandhill, the marsh lights, the turning of the waves. All these things were too real, too near, to write about. They had not been absorbed, had not passed through the furnace of his mind. They were mere autobiography, not true art. It was too early to write about the sea. It was not in his blood. He tried to think about his past life in Birmingham and write about that, but that he had already tried before – in the same way – too soon. He felt he was destroying the freshness of his experiences by trying to cram them into a novel. He realized that what he had said to Bruce about the need for much thought was far truer than he had imagined at the time; not only the need to think, but a need merely to experience all that was going on around him, just letting it flow over him, some of it sinking in. He must not draw on this account until it had accrued more interest.

To add to his growing frustration, Bruce was slapping creosote on the wall just below the window. In spite of strenuous efforts to be reasonable about it, Stephen felt that Bruce was watching him, checking him, almost spying on him – to make sure he was sticking to his writing; almost laughing at him for being so slow and ill at ease and unproductive. Perhaps he had even chosen that part of the wall with the express intention of keeping an eye on his friend. It was impossible to write, even to think, under such conditions. He felt he was being forced into a role that was ill suited to his temperament. He felt as if he were being set to work with Bruce as his task-master. And Stephen felt naturally antagonistic to any form of authority. Bruce, however, was not the same as a schoolmaster, a judge, a probation officer. Stephen knew only too well the staid admonitions of such 'dried-up people', as he called them. Bruce had eyes. Whenever they exchanged glances through the window, it was not Bruce's smile that he noticed. As always, it was his eyes, his great blue-green staring eyes. They seemed to be firing him with an energy he could not understand, but they inspired him always — urged him, warned him, scolded, laughed, gazed sadly or fondly. There was never any one emotion shining out from those eyes; all of them burned together. Mesmer might have had such eyes, Stephen felt, or Svengali. It was impossible not to be affected; he must go on trying. But now he wanted a cigarette. He went outside and round the end of the house. Bruce was stooping low painting the bottom board. Stephen could see the creosote was grainy with sand.

'Have you got any cigarettes?'

Bruce stood up straight. The navy-blue boiler-suit was several sizes too big for him. He looked comical and extraordinarily young. There was creosote on his hands and face, in his hair.

'Aren't there any left?'

'We smoked the last one last night.' It was almost an accusation. 'Have you got any more?'

'I've stopped smoking.'

'I haven't stopped smoking. I can't concentrate. Haven't you got any more?'

'No.'

Stephen was nonplussed. It was not pleasant to ask his friend for anything. He hated to emphasize his dependence on Bruce.

'Shall we go to the town?'

'We went yesterday.'

Stephen did not pursue the subject. The thought of walking up to the town again exhausted him. Although he wanted to smoke, he was unwilling to make the effort to go all that way to buy some cigarettes. Besides, he did not want to deplete his already meagre supply of money. Bruce, on the other hand, did not want Stephen to go to the town by himself. He might get involved with other people. Stephen changed in the company of others and often as a result behaved coldly to his friend, or so it seemed to Bruce. The real problem was Bruce's sense of jealousy, his possessiveness. He wanted the exclusive companionship of Stephen; other people were enemies. Bruce wanted Stephen for his own. Stephen would never improve or settle down under the influence of strangers. Bruce wiped his brush on the edge of his creosote tin and laid it carefully across the top. Stephen noticed that the receptacle was not a professional paint-pot but an old enamelled child's chamber pot. Bruce wiped his hands down the sides of his boiler-suit.

'Let's have some coffee.'

They went into the house, made coffee and came out again to sit in the verandah.

'I wish I had a cigarette.'

'Can't you manage without?'

Bruce himself felt he would like to smoke, but did not say so. His restraint changed from lofty self-discipline into unwillingness to admit the shame of defeat.

'Don't you want to smoke?'

'Of course not. I've given up. It's easy.'

'I don't believe you. Anyway, why should I give up?'

'I'm not asking you to. But it'd probably do you a lot of good. It's a dirty habit.'

Stephen said nothing. Bruce gestured into the living room.

'How's the novel going?' There was a note of mockery in his voice.

'I'm making progress.'

'How much have you written?'

'Quite a lot.'

'Can I read it?'

'It's not ready yet.'

'You haven't written much, have you?'

'It's more difficult than you think.'

'I don't think you set about it in the right way.'

'What do you mean?'

'You're too self-conscious. You make it too much of a ritual.'

'What do you know about it?'

'You spend most of your time laying out and rearranging papers on the table; walking up and down pretending to think; making notes, drafts, titles, lists. That's not writing. It's just ceremony. Artists don't work like that.'

'How are they supposed to work then?'

'They just do it. They don't think about how to do it. They just write. They don't think about being writers, being artists. They just sit down and get on with it. They can't help doing it. It just comes. They're driven by some inner force. Compelled. There's no such thing as Inspiration with a capital I either. You can't wait for it. You must make it.'

'That's a contradiction.'

'No, it's not. Art's ninety-nine per cent hard work. You know the proverb. It's not a glamorous occupation, soulful eyes, dream-like expressions. It's just bloody hard work. You don't know what that means. You have to keep at it, hour after hour, day after day. It's a matter of discipline, regular hours of hard work, persistence. A writer has to produce thousands of lines of rubbish in order to create one beautiful sentence. You just write. I know what I'm talking about because I've done it. I sit down and write. Of course, I make notes too and drafts and things, but mainly I just force myself to write, and write lines and lines, most of it terrible, shoddy stuff. The effort generates more. The more you write, the more you have to write.'

'That's not art; that's just facile gush, prolific rubbish. You're nothing but a hack.'

'Quite. And when you've done that, when you've got through to the end, that's when you start to make art. It's the best part, the most enjoyable, the most creative part. You've got the shape, you've got something to work on. The anxiety of forgetting something, the fear of breaking down, the passion – it's all left you. You've got to the end. Then you really get to work – finely shaping, chiselling here and there, adding a sentence here, changing a word there, polishing, perfecting. That's the real art. A sculptor can't rest till he's got his piece of rock out of the mountain and hammered out the basic shape. That's the rubbish part, if you like. You've got to get to the end of something, reach a certain stage. Then you can start. You're still messing about on the side of the mountain wondering what kind of rock to use; just picking up pebbles here and there and arranging them in pretty patterns. You've got no will to get really down to the job, no staying power, not enough broad sweep or dare. You're just playing about like a child on the shore, afraid to plunge into the cold waves. You just relish the idea of being a writer. You're so weak!'

Stephen's fists were clenched on his knees. His arms were trembling. His face was tensed. He was not angry. He somehow felt ashamed, not shattered. Almost against his will he was impressed. And he could not get away from those eyes. He knew what Bruce was saying was sense. He was ashamed of his own weakness; and he was unable to resist the power of his friend. He nodded slowly.

'Sometimes I get a good idea and write a few pages, but then it seems to fade out; and when I try to start again I just can't get going.'

'I know what you mean. I'll tell you what I do. When I think I'm writing something good and know how I'm going to continue the next bit, that's when I stop. If you stop when it's going well, it's easy to continue when you come back to it. The energy in knowing that you can go ahead gives you new energy to go much further than you planned and you go right on to the next wave of creativity. Yes, it's just like waves, rising up and falling and rising again. You have to stop just when the next wave is beginning to rise. Don't stop at the low points, stop on the way up. That's what I do. It never fails.'

Stephen's face seemed to brighten a little.

'I think I might try that.'

'At least you can try. It may not work. But try it and see what happens.'

Bruce knew he had won another victory, another, temporary, triumph. This was how he would have to do it — constantly hammering at Stephen, moulding him to the shape he was convinced Stephen should take, forcing him to follow the only path that led to success. Stephen stood up.

'I'm going back in.'

'I'll go for a swim. If you want to write, I'll get the lunch. We can have it outside, then you needn't disturb your papers.'

*

Stephen sat at the table. It was early afternoon. He had covered twenty-three pages since lunch, and seven before that. It was coming. He was writing without thinking about writing. The style, he knew, was execrable, but a line was forming; narrative was taking shape. He no longer tried to perfect each sentence as he had before. He wrote whatever came into his head, following the basic pattern of his story, and swept straight on. It began to take hold. He found, just as Bruce had said, that it was like waves of the sea, surges of energy rising, breaking, falling and rising again. He put to test Bruce's idea of stopping just before the crest was reached – deliberately, as a disciplined decision. He knew what he was going to write next; right, hold it for a while. He stood up and went to the window, staring down at the sea. Now, he found, his mind was full of a rich turmoil of ideas, the power of which enabled him to look further ahead and plan beyond the next section. Bruce was right: it worked. Bruce did not write prose, he was not a novelist, but he could certainly teach him something about the art of writing. He sat down again and wrote on swiftly, feeling a wonderful new sense of power in his hands, as if direct lines of electrical energy were streaming out from his brain down the nerves of his arms and into his very fingertips.

Bruce had just gone out to fetch the milk. Stephen reached another place in his story where he could pause for a while and regenerate. He stretched his legs under the table. If only he had a cigarette. He had not dared to ask Bruce again. He could see some people on the beach. He wondered if they were the students he had met before. The sound of the tide, as gentle as ever, came faintly to his ears through the open window. He must have a cigarette.

It did not occur to him to go upstairs and search in Bruce's room. Stephen was honest. No matter how much he might depend on others for his day-to-day needs, he was not a thief. He never pilfered. He was never sly. He stood up, looking round the room in case there was an odd cigarette or half-empty packet lying about. There was nothing. There were about fifty cigarette ends in the cheap tin waste-paper basket, a few more in the hearth. Pity he didn't have a pipe. He had seen tramps smoke old cigarette butts in a pipe. He picked out some of the largest cigarette ends and made them into a little heap on the table. He began to move the filters and pull out the remaining strands of tobacco, dark-stained with tar and singed where they had stopped burning. He soon had a little pile. He went to the lavatory, tore off a few sheets of toilet paper. Fortunately it was of the cheaper kind, thin, single-ply and slightly glossy. He went back to the living-room and began to fashion some peculiar-looking cigarettes. Their thickness varied, and tufts of tobacco stuck out at each end. He licked the edges of the paper and they seemed to stick together. He carefully placed one of the shaggy objects in his mouth and lit a match.

The taste was foul. After a few puffs he began to feel strange. It was not so much the taste itself; perhaps it was the fact that he had not smoked since the night before. He began to feel someone was watching him and looked up, but there was no one outside. He drew once more on his home-made cigarette. The smoke was thick and evil looking. He threw it into the fire in disgust. He went to the bay window, knelt on the window seat and looked out of the narrow side window. Bruce was halfway up the zig-zag walking slowly. Stephen looked at the lawn outside. The weather had been dry for some weeks; the grass was pale, almost yellow.

He went outside. In front of the house, the grass was the same – dried, dying. He picked up a few loose strands lying on the surface. He might be able to smoke this. He collected a handful and took it into the house. Some people smoked herbal cigarettes. What were they made of? He put the grass on the table and began to single out the driest pieces. He was slow with his hands, but he soon had enough for one cigarette. It smelt fresh, almost sweet. Stephen, being a city-dweller, had never smelt a hayfield where the grass has been lying long in the sun. This smell, though by no means as heady as hay, was new to him. He took trouble with this cigarette. He fetched the sharp knife from the kitchen and carefully trimmed the loose 'tobacco' at each end. He tapped the cigarette on the table to pack the contents down. It looked almost like a real cigarette. He lit a match.

It tasted quite different from tobacco. There was not so much flavour and it did not satisfy. But it was not unpleasant. He tried to inhale, but it made him cough. Then it went out. To keep it going he had to light it several times. It was like his writing; he must light it again before it began to go out. He sat at the table looking out of the west window. Before he was aware of what was happening, his head began to swim. The sea seemed to be lop-sided. Some black objects seemed to be jumping out of the water. They seemed to have fins. They must be sharks. No, they couldn't be sharks; there weren't any sharks in British waters. Then one jumped right of the water in a graceful arc. They were dolphins! Stephen stared in fascination. There were so many new things to see at this seaside house. He had never seen dolphins before. He had heard about them, seen pictures in books. There had been a television serial about dolphins and children, too. The sea was full of strange things. He started to count the dolphins.

A slight movement to his right attracted his attention. He turned his head; the cigarette fell out of his hand and rolled on the floor. Bruce was at the window, grinning. He laughed and came round into the house. He picked up the cigarette from the floor.

'You're an addict. You must be. Grass. Toilet paper!' He laughed again. 'Have you mixed in some rabbit droppings, too?'

'I was experimenting.' Stephen was laughing too, relieved that Bruce was not angry or scornful.

'How many pages have you done?'

'Forty-seven.' Stephen flicked through a sheaf of papers showing them to Bruce. He felt proud and satisfied, though a little nauseous from his smoking. 'I thought I'd have a break. I was getting to a crest.'

'Looks good.'

'The style's awful.'

'It's bound to be. It doesn't matter. The great thing is to have got something done.'

Stephen almost glowed. To please Bruce, he found, was a pleasure in itself. It was a thing he had not been able to do often.

'I'm getting the feel of it.'

'I thought you would. Just a minute.'

Bruce went out of the room. Stephen heard him running upstairs. A moment later he returned.

'I had these in my bedroom. Have one.'

He threw something across to Stephen, who failed to catch it. It landed on the table, standing up on its side.

It was a packet of cigarettes.

14. SLOB

'I SAW SOME DOLPHINS.'

Stephen's first reaction of anger, not expressed, at Bruce's meanness about the cigarettes — his keeping them hidden away all that time — had quickly evaporated. He still smarted when he remembered his immediate surge of fury. It had been as if Bruce were paying him for his forty-seven pages, rewarding him for his effort, throwing a sop to his obedient pet, rather than relieving him in a dire need; but as soon as he had lit a cigarette and inhaled deeply, he felt his resentment melting away. He was even able to see the funny side of his abortive attempts at cigarette manufacture. Deeper down in his subconsciousness, however, the episode would be remembered. It was yet another example of Bruce's exercise of power.

'You couldn't have done. There aren't any dolphins in this part of the world. It's too cold. You must have been seeing things.'

'Yes, I saw things. In the sea. I saw them with my own eyes. Eight or nine of them. Just before you came back. One of them jumped right out of the water. Just there.' He pointed.

'They were porpoises.'

'What's the difference?'

'They're smaller. Same family though. Same as whales. They're mammals. That's good. Porpoises are a sign of good weather.' They both looked at the sea. 'Which way were they swimming?'

Stephen gestured to the right. Bruce looked to the north along the shore, screwing up his eyes.

'Yes. There they are again. You were right.' Faint black specks could be seen in the water now and again. 'It's a whole school.'

'School?'

'A school of porpoises. A shoal of whales. It's the same word. One's Norse, with the hard consonant, the other's Anglo-Saxon. Like skirt and shirt – used to be one word.'

'That's just the kind of knowledge you would store up. No fucking use to anyone.'

'Well, you didn't understand me, did you?'

Stephen laughed. His writing and the new cigarette had given him strength. He felt a sense of achievement. Maybe the quality was not what he hoped for, but it was all there, all forty-seven pages of it. No one could take it away from him.

'It must be awfully difficult to be a painter.'

'Why do you say that?'

'I'm just thinking. What you've painted isn't flexible. Once you've done it, it's fixed. If you paint any more on the same canvas, you may destroy what you've done. And you can't go back. Writing's different. You can always keep your first version.'

'A good painter doesn't depend on such chances. He knows how to get his effects. If he paints over them, he can always create them again. It's a matter of training. He does hundreds of sketches, exercises. Writing should be the same.'

'But it's easier to be a writer.'

'Therefore it's more difficult to be a good writer. Let's go and do some slob.'

'Slob?'

'That's another word you don't know. But don't worry, I won't go into etymological detail this time. It's a home-made word. You won't find it in a dictionary.'

'I've seen it. I know what a slob is. You're one.'

'No, I'm not. You don't know what I mean when I use that word.'

'One of your funny ones, I suppose.'

Bruce had quite a supply of these. For example, he used the word 'knickerbocker' when he meant 'flick with the finger', or 'ach-a-biddy' instead of 'nasty'; both were heirlooms from his childhood. He had had trouble with them in his Grammar School days. Most of the boys there came from the working classes and had often laughed at Bruce's polite or unconventional language. Once he had been to tea with one of his classmates, and leaving the house had said to the boy's mother: 'Thank you for having me.' The mother and her son had screamed with laughter at this, Bruce had never been able to understand why. It was not surprising that when Bruce used his 'funny' words, as Stephen called them, his schoolmates thought him peculiar, and put him in a 'special' category – allotting him to the isolation of a higher existence – someone who could be fun at times, but needed watching; someone not entirely to be trusted. Bruce had often suffered at school from this sense of being apart, which also, however, had helped to develop his artistic temperament, something which he was rather proud of.

'Slob actually means, in Ireland anyway, "muddy land". But in our family it means "wet sand".'

'What do you do with it? Slobber on it?'

'No. We build cities.'

'Out of sand?'

'Yes. Not on sand – well, it is on sand actually – but out of sand. It's like concrete. You scoop it out of a hole in the beach, all running with water. You hold it in place like cement, your hands acting as moulds. The water soaks back into the beach, and you're left with a block of hard sand. Then you smooth it. I'll show you.'

'Do you mean sandcastles? Do we use buckets and spades? Is this another of your childish fancies?'

'It's not childish at all. It's got nothing to do with children's seaside games. It's an art.'

'It sounds suspect to me. Slob!' Stephen gave a short laugh and his face turned red.

'You wait and see. As far as I know, our family's the only one in the world who have ever made this kind of thing. I've never seen anything as good as ours anywhere else. We don't make bucket-shaped domes with flags and shell decorations. Nothing sham like that. Our buildings are hollow. They have real rooms. Windows and doors, and chimneys. Let's go down now. I'll show you.'

'I was going to write.'

'Leave that now. You don't want to get tired. You've done enough for one day.'

Stephen was astounded. After urging him so earnestly to get down to his writing, now Bruce was telling him he had done enough. It was an extraordinary contradiction. Stephen began to feel that Bruce was merely manipulating him for his own convenience. Write now because I tell you. Let's go for a walk now. Come down to the beach: I want to show you how well I can build sandcastles. Stephen was nothing but a slave to his friend's whims. Bruce was just using him. In spite of these feelings, however, Stephen was intrigued. Hollow buildings made of sand? Bruce spoke with such eagerness and vigour. And besides, there were his glittering eyes. Perhaps it was true; perhaps he had done enough writing for one day. He glanced at the table and sensed a comfortable opening bud of satisfaction and achievement. Yes, he had done something. Perhaps he could take a break. He felt himself weakening, turning like a ship at sea without a rudder, willy-nilly at the sway of the wind.

'I'll come and watch you.'

'You can't come like that. You'll get your trousers wet. Haven't you got any shorts?'

'I never wear shorts.'

'I tell you what: there's an old pair of trousers in the creosote shed. My brother used to use them for painting. I'll cut the legs off. Wait a minute.'

Before Stephen could protest, Bruce rushed off outside and round the house. Stephen never wore shorts. Didn't Bruce realize that? He never listened to what people said. He just forged ahead on his own fixed course. Stephen heard his friend come back in through the back door. After a while he came in from the kitchen and held up a pair of dark grey worsted trousers. They were stained not only with creosote but with patches of hardened green paint. The legs had been cut off above the knees, one a little higher than the other.

'Put these on.'

'I told you: I never wear shorts.'

'But you must. You can't wear your best trousers. You'll spoil them. And you ought to take your shirt off, too. I'm going to change. Come on, I won't laugh at you. You'll feel much more comfortable.'

'I said I was only going to watch you.'

'You'll still get wet. Come on, Stephen. We must start as soon as possible while the tide's out.'

Stephen stared at his friend's eager face. There was no stopping Bruce when he was fired with enthusiasm like this. They went upstairs, Bruce two at a time, Stephen miserably. Bruce was forcing him into an impossibly ridiculous situation. Stupid, cut-off trousers. In his room, he tried them on. They were rather large, but at least they came almost down to his knees. He took his shirt off. As he did so he felt a sudden surge of liberation. Perhaps it would be better to take everything off and go rolling in the sand dunes, then run naked into the sea — like those people from the college.

He heard Bruce going downstairs telling him to hurry up, and he followed slowly. In the verandah, Bruce in his shorts and a light shirt inspected Stephen.

'Now what's the matter with those? They look a bit funny, but there's nobody down there to see you, and you'll be much cooler. You'd better take your shoes and socks off.'

Stephen did so. Bruce noticed that his friend's legs were much darker and more hairy than he had expected, much more sturdy-looking. His vest was of flannel, with long sleeves.

'Those long sleeves are a good idea. You won't get sunburn.'

They fetched two garden spades from behind the house. They were used — Bruce explained when Stephen had showed surprise at seeing two such incongruous objects in these shore surroundings — for cutting turf to put on the track when it got too sandy; there was no garden at Tremarfon. They went down to the beach. In bare feet, Stephen found it much easier to cross the rocks. The sand near the rocks was fine and dry. Stephen slid his feet through it, enjoying its delicious warmth and listening with curiosity to the faint whistling sound it made as he did so. They moved onto the harder sand nearer the sea, now almost at low tide, and the beach there was cooler to their feet. About half way to the sea, Bruce stopped abruptly.

'We'll do it here.'

'Said the Walrus to the Carpenter's wife.' Stephen's irritation had once again evaporated. In spite of himself and his feeling of being conspicuous and ridiculous in the cut-off trousers, he found something pleasant in the touch of the sand on the soles of his feet. Bruce drew a circle about six feet in diameter with the edge of his spade.

'This is for the island. We must dig outside this circle, a trench all round, and make a mound in the middle.'

'Sounds like hard work. Why do we have to do that?'

'If we try to build at beach level the slob won't set properly. The beach's too wet.'

He started to dig. Not understanding what Bruce meant, Stephen copied him, but he had never used a spade before and was unable to get a proper purchase in the sand because his strokes were too shallow. Bruce watched him out of the corner of his eyes. Stephen was hopeless where practical matters were concerned. Bruce had been brought up to be scornful of those who could not make proper use of their hands and feet. His mother, intensely practical herself, had drilled this into him, using it as a lever to heap ridicule on her husband, Bruce's father, who was also hopeless with his hands, and only dug with a spade when it suited him – as, for example, when he had made the turf bank round his annexe, or to make a show of exercise and usefulness about the house when his wife nagged at him too long. Such people, Bruce felt, were weak, only half developed as human beings. He was extremely proud of his strong, supple, not-too-long hands and his practical ability. Stephen leant on his spade.

'I can't get this thing to work. How do you do it?'

'Like this.' Bruce thrust the blade of his spade into the sand. 'Now let it sink down of its own accord as the water rises. You see?' The blade sank in deeply. 'Then tip it back, like this. You can get a real shovelful then.' He sent the square wet block of sand flying into the centre of the island.

Stephen dug into the sand the way Bruce had shown him. It was easier than he expected. He tilted the spade backwards slowly, liking the sucking noise as air was drawn into the vacuum formed beneath it. He lifted out the sand and swung his spade towards the mound. The sand slid off it and fell onto the beach with a soft thud. Bruce laughed.

'Turd. Try again.'

Stephen was looking at the hole he had made. Water was rising at the bottom of it. He was amazed at the speed at which it filled up. Where was the water coming from? Wherever you dug in the sand, water came up; it was the same where Bruce was digging, making a moat round the island. He bent and dipped his finger in the water and tasted it. It was salt. The beach was saturated with salt water. Under the entire shore, right round the bay, the sea was waiting. Not content with covering two thirds of the earth's surface, it must also lie low, holding sway under the land. How far inland did it reach? And if you dug down somewhere far from the sea, did water come up? Yes, wells in the desert, water diviners. But that water was not salt. He looked down at the sand. Sea was under him. He was standing on a vast quicksand, stable at the moment; but it could without warning suddenly lose its sanity, give up its uneasy détente with the earth's gravity, start heaving from side to side, and ruthlessly draw him down. Under him was the sea, and under that — rock, fire, an impenetrable centre, fire, rock, and the sea again, and beyond that, far below him — the endless blackness of space. Space, stars, below him. The round world was so small, so fragile.

He looked at the sea. From where he was standing it seemed to be higher than the land. And what happened to the sand under the sea? Did it go gently sloping down, or did it come to a sudden end at the top of an underwater precipice? There were so many things Stephen wanted to know, so much that fascinated him about the sea. It was all new to him. Perhaps it was not real; perhaps this is what death was — another way of life, no hideous traumatic change, a mere switching of images on the screen of the brain. Perhaps he had already killed himself; and here he was, digging sand, digging a grave perhaps, at the edge of the sea. He gazed across to the Lleyn peninsula. Something was terribly wrong over there. It had broken up. The long arm of land had turned into a string of islands; but not sea islands. They were cigar shaped, their undersides were not flat, did not follow the line of the sea. He moved his head from side to side. Two of the islands seemed to join together again, linked by a thin thread of land.

'What's happening over there?'

'Where?'

'The land over there seems to be floating. It's like a mirage or something.'

'It's gone down over the horizon. We're very low down here. It goes back to normal when we look at it from the house.'

Stephen looked again across the bay. Now the sky itself seemed to be under the land. It made him feel as if he were standing at one of the entrances of fairyland – half in surroundings he could understand, half in another world.

They dug sand steadily. Soon they had raised a fairly large mound about two feet high. Bruce swung his spade above his head, bringing the flat of the blade repeatedly down, levelling the top of the island. Stephen did the same round the sides. Bruce threw down his spade and knelt down beside one of the pools. Stephen noticed that these were now naturalizing themselves. The marks of the spade cuts at their edges were gradually disappearing; small underwater avalanches constantly changed the contours of the pools, widening them little by little. Bruce thrust both hands deep down into the soft sand under the water. They came up loaded with a streaming conglobation.

'This is...slob.'

He swung rapidly towards the island, and laid both hands down on its flat top near the edge. Bruce vibrated his hands without lifting them and the 'slob' quickly set, its gleaming surface fading as the water drained away beneath it. He removed his hands, then, flattening them, chafed and smoothed the sides but not the top or ends of the block of sea-cement.

'I've laid the foundation stone. The construction of our city has begun.'

'What are you going to build first?'

'A tower.'

He repeated the process, moulding the 'blocks' together into a circle about a foot in diameter; the centre, about five inches across, he left hollow. The tower slowly rose up. When it was about a foot high, Bruce scratched at the outside near the base with two fingers, gouging out the hardened sand. He was making a door. Using one finger, he made two windows higher up, opposite each other. He continued to build. Soon the tower was over two feet high.

'Now I'll make the roof. It's easy because the space in the middle's so small.'

He placed another load of slob lightly over the aperture at the top of the tower, holding three fingers of one hand under it until it set. He added more, and soon there was only a tiny hole at the top. Taking half a handful of slob, Bruce let most of the water run out while it was still in his hands, then he placed it on the top and smoothed it down. He added more to flatten the top of the tower, and using one hand only, formed dollop-like battlements round the rim of the tower, smoothing them flush with the sides. He sat back on his heels.

'Why don't you try?'

'How do you do it?'

Stephen knelt down on the sand. It was cold and uncomfortable. The salt was already affecting his white feet. He dipped his hands in the water, surprised to find the sand at the bottom so soft. He drew up a double handful. He laid it on the island, and took away his hands. The slob melted flat like candle-wax.

'Don't take your hands away so soon; and jiggle them a bit like this first.'

'I don't like jiggling my hands.'

'You like jiggling with your hands.'

'So do you.'

'That's not the point. Look, I'll show you how to do this properly.'

He demonstrated, beginning a new wall. Stephen tried again. Some of the slob ran down onto his ridiculous shorts. He laid the sand on the mound. The same thing happened. He tried again; the same again. In spite of Bruce's encouragement, Stephen began to feel miserable. Why should he have to do such asinine things? Playing with wet sand like a kid from kindergarten. It was like diarrhoea. And wearing such terrible shorts.

Bruce was very patient. He was now making a hall next to the tower, a much larger, square structure. He kept advising Stephen, who began to grow tired of the rather high-pitched stream of instructions.

'Don't smooth the top, only the sides. The next lot doesn't stick if you do that. Don't let so much water escape as you lift it across. That's right. That's good. You're getting it. It's difficult at first, but you're getting the knack. No, no, no, not there. Make it round. If you make it too big, you'll never be able to roof it. No, that's too much!'

Stephen had placed a heavy dollop on the top of his tower, now about a foot high. The whole side of it collapsed. In spite of this setback, he was actually beginning to enjoy it. He could do it. Bruce's enthusiasm was catching. It was almost satisfying – to construct, to build, even on this childish scale. But as he stood back and looked at what they were doing, it gradually dawned on Stephen that what they were doing wasn't so childish after all. A design was taking visible shape and he was a giant looking down on it. He set to work again and completed his tower. He started another structure. This too collapsed after a while. With an exclamation, he knocked it all down with his fists.

'Don't do that. You can repair it. You must be patient.'

Stephen watched Bruce's busy, sensitive hands. This was hardly a human action. Bruce was like a god, building a world for his pastime. Stephen sensed the feverish creative power of his friend, this god-like child, this childlike god, lifting the handfuls of cold liquid rock from the gleaming craters and leaving trails of cool brown lava up the sides of the mound; and all the while working, working with nervous intensity, with a kind of mad, wild passion, with those huge blazing eyes flickering and burning over the task.

The master-architect and his wayward apprentice toiled on though the afternoon.

144

15. CATACLYSM

THEY STOOD LOOKING DOWN on the city. It was nothing less.
There were not many buildings, it was true – hardly a dozen – but
viewed from a short distance away, the island of carved sand rose
like an ancient town on its mound, like some Arab oasis on a hill
solitary in a vast stretch of desert, an oasis without trees,
apparently without life. The buildings – domed, turreted, or
pinnacled with dried trickles of wet sand – had something eastern
about them, like the adobe buildings of a primitive race that had
reached the summit of all development possible in its isolation,
reached the peak of its cultural expression, and then declined, the
people dying of mental starvation and the extinction of vegetation.
They looked down on its narrow streets, its steps, its dark
doorways and unglazed windows, its battlemented walls, its
stagnant, lifeless moat. Bruce saw it like that – a dead city that had
once been peopled. Stephen saw it in a different light. To him, the
supreme irony of it all was that here before him was the perfect
world for a child's imagination to work on. A child would have no
difficulty in filling the streets with life, the houses with families with
names; yet at the same time, no child could have the skill, patience
or will to build a combination of objects of such simple beauty. The
slob city was undoubtedly a work of art. The child's pastime had
transcended itself to become a brilliant and complex game for
adults. For the buildings, at least those made by Bruce, Stephen was
honest enough to realize, were not such simple structures as they
appeared to be. Some of them had as many as three storeys, with
real staircases inside. The ceilings of the largest rooms were
reinforced, in a way similar to concrete, with smooth straight
pieces of driftwood. There were corridors, terraces, towers with
spiral staircases, a church with a twisted spire. There were
archways, chimneys, a harbour for ships that would never come – a
walled city that had no enemies to attack it save the sterility within.
It was a miracle of ordered sand. Stephen was amazed at the
strength of the walls and roofs, fascinated by the shapes and
patterns it was possible to create – all with the twenty fingers of
four hands. Even his hands, short and ugly as they were, could help
lift the beach from its level flatness, and carve and smooth it into

these strange and wonderful forms. Thus it is in the world, Stephen realized. All masterpieces of art, all machines, all the works of the giants − are the creations of men's hands, even the incredibly complex and durable marvels of engineering which shot man-made satellites, at long last, into outer space.

They stood on the south side of the city, the sea to their left, and the sound of voices made them turn. Three people were approaching from the narrow bouldered south end of the beach under the railway embankment. One of them, a girl of about ten, was throwing a piece of driftwood to a half-grown Dalmatian which circled madly round them with the wood in its mouth. Dropping it obediently, the dog waited tense with excitement until the girl picked it up and again threw it ahead of her, and then pranced away insanely leaping, raising its front paws together then its back paws in rapid alternation, abandoned in pure mindless happiness. The other two people were obviously the girl's father and mother, a cheerful looking couple in their mid thirties. The man had a camera slung round his neck and the woman carried a leather bag with a thermos flask sticking out of the top of it. The dog, suddenly seeing the two friends and the inviting mound of sand, abruptly changed tactics, dropping the wood, running directly towards them and coming to a suspicious standstill a few yards away. Bruce instantly felt nervous, almost afraid. People again, always people had to disturb them. They could never get any peace. And this violent dog would go and jump all over their beautiful creation and ruin their afternoon's work. Stephen also felt nervous and afraid, but for quite other reasons. He was terrified of dogs of all kinds, especially violently active ones like the one now staring at them. He also felt a kind a dismay, knowing that the dog was going to destroy their city of sand, and to give him credit, he even felt sympathy for Bruce should that happen. After the frozen moment melted, that is exactly what appeared to be about to happen. The dog took a few leaps towards the city wall, stepped into a street and put its foot through the roof of one of Stephen's single-storey buildings. Surprised by this, the dog struggled back knocking down some of the outer wall.

'Rupert! Come here!' The girl's voice was shrill and imperious, and the dog instantly obeyed, sidling up to her, its ears flattened, and its tail and entire rear end wagging with affection. 'Oh, dear, has he broken your sandcastle?'

Bruce, hardly able to suppress his irritation at the damage done and having his beautiful city dubbed with the childish title of sandcastle, smiled politely.

'Oh, it doesn't matter at all. We can easily repair it.'

By now the family of three had reached the two friends, and the woman, suddenly realizing the extent and quality of their work, let out an exclamation.

'My, now this is a beautiful piece of work! Did you make it yourselves?'

'Yes. Rather childish really.' Bruce let out a little laugh. 'We just thought we'd like to spend the afternoon playing like children.'

The woman glanced at the faces of the two friends as if to guess their ages, then again gazed at the panorama below.

'But this is not childish at all. Look, Fred, they've got real doors and windows. Are they hollow inside?'

'Yes, we use wet sand and let it dry.'

'Like cement.' It was the first time the man had spoken. He too was peering into the buildings with great curiosity. The woman was amazed.

'But how do you make the roofs stay up like that?'

It was Stephen who answered. Seeing that the girl was now holding the dog's collar and that after all the dog seemed quite friendly and safe, almost apologetic even, he felt a little easier.

'It's a kind of art.'

Bruce liked this and smiled at the man and woman.

'I'll show you how we do it.'

He quickly repaired the roof of the broken building and rebuilt the outer wall of the city. The girl and her parents were fascinated and stood close to Bruce watching. The dog was forgotten, and Stephen's anxiety returned. He watched the dog sniff its way round behind the others and circle slowly round the city. One of the spades had been stuck in the sand on the far side, and Stephen's fear turned to a kind of gloating fascination as he saw the dog lift its leg against the shaft of the spade. There was something satisfyingly frank and bold at the way the dog exposed its bald genitals and jetted its pale green urine in several copious spurts against the wood and blade. The girl saw what was happening and again split the air with her piercing voice.

'Rupert! How dare you do that there?'

'I'm afraid our dog has very bad manners.' The woman smiled with embarrassment. 'I'm so sorry.'

Bruce laughed.

'Don't worry. The poor animal has to do it somewhere.'

The man and the woman did not quite know to take this and looked at each other. Stephen saved the situation by bursting out with one of his great bellows of laughter, and so they all laughed. The girl caught the dog and put its lead on, greatly relieving Stephen. The coincidence of the slob construction and the urination episode suddenly reminded Bruce of a time in his childhood when he and one of his brothers had been trying to construct a slob toilet. They had almost finished the bowl and the U-bend when a prim elderly couple approached and asked them what they were making. The two brothers had looked at each other wondering what to answer. Bruce considered whether he could dare to tell the truth and was about to utter the more polite term 'water closet' when his brother came to his rescue and said it was a 'reservoir'. At that age Bruce didn't quite know what a reservoir was, but the elderly couple seemed quite satisfied and went on their way, a little put out, however, by the explosions of laughter from the two boys behind them and muttering about the manners of the 'young generation'.

The man started to fumble with his camera.

'May I take a photo? I've never seen anything quite like this. Quite an achievement, I would say.'

'Please do.' Bruce was flattered by their interest. 'I should think this would be the best angle, with the sun behind you.'

The man took several photographs. His wife nudged him.

'Take one with the two young men as well.' She laughed, but there was admiration in her voice. 'You two might be famous one day. We've never seen anything like this before, as my husband says. You ought to enter it for a competition.'

'A bit difficult to move.' Bruce laughed, and he and Stephen stood at one side of their creation and the man took a picture.

'I'd like another – a close-up of the two of you at work, if you don't mind.' Bruce and Stephen, the latter slightly amused, took up huge handfuls of streaming slob, and the man snapped them. Bruce caught Stephen's eye, his own eyes gleaming with humour, and murmured under his breath.

'World Famous Slob Artists.' And Stephen almost choked with a new paroxysm of held-in mirth.

'Well, we'd best be getting along.' The man snapped his camera cover shut. 'It's quite a way back to the town.' Stephen smiled at them.

'Do you live here?'

'No, we come from Shrewsbury. Just having a little holiday before the kid goes back to school.' His wife took over.

'It's a lovely place, Harlieg. We come here every year. It's got a kind of magic of its own, hasn't it? We've had such a lovely walk this afternoon – right along the top road, then down that zig-zag back there which comes down onto the line.' This was not the one above Tremarfon, but some way further to the south, where the railway line crept close under the cliff. 'And now back along the beach, and through the sandhills. How about you? Do you live here?'

'We're staying in that house.' He pointed to the red roof. 'It belongs to my father.'

'Lucky you.' Her husband was looking at his watch. 'So long, then. It's been nice meeting you, and you've done a marvellous bit of work here.'

'I'm glad you like it.' Bruce noticed the dog straining at its lead and sniffing at Stephen's bare legs. His friend was suddenly acutely aware of the torn-off trousers he was wearing, and his feeling of being utterly ridiculous came upon him with a new wave of loathing. 'If you don't mind, could you send us some prints of the photos you've taken?'

'Glad to oblige.' The man felt in his pocket for a tiny brown diary. 'Who shall we send to them to?'

'Bruce Dinwiddy, care of Tremarfon, Harlieg. If we're not here, they'll be forwarded. How much shall we pay for the prints?' A slight frown crossed Stephen's face. Typical of Bruce to mention the cost.

'Never mind about that. It's a pleasure.' The man put his diary away, and the family of three took their leave, once again apologizing about the dog. Bruce and Stephen watched them for a while, and then turned back to their city. Each felt a pleasant sense of satisfaction that ordinary people should have taken such an interest in their work. Somehow they both felt like real artists, and they stared down on their buildings with a new conviction of achievement.

It was beginning to get dark. Lines of cloud were forming across the western sky. There too were worlds – gold-tinged islands, long estuaries and promontories – places, Stephen thought, where it would be so wonderful to be. There were always these other places. One was never satisfied with the surroundings one dwelled in. One was always yearning to exist in other regions, other times. Even the magnificent scenery around him was not enough. Those lands in the sky promised a more peaceful life than here on earth. Paradise was never here, nor anywhere before or after death. We could see it, know it with our eyes while we were living. That was why it was so hard to live, and so hard to die. Hope was despair. But despair was never hope...His thoughts were interrupted. Bruce, somewhat mysteriously, said he was going up to the house, and he ran up over the rocks leaving Stephen alone on that vast shore.

Stephen suddenly felt terrified. Something strange was happening to the beach. It was becoming cooler. It seemed to be less firm beneath his feet. The sea seemed to be creeping nearer, but not only the sea. The rocks too were closer, and the sand dunes. The mountains, darkening to the north, were huddling round and staring down, a great distance away, but unmistakably staring down at Stephen. The cliff to the east, like a great broad brow, was frowning. Many of the houses up there had brilliant golden eyes, as the slowly descending sun was caught in their window-panes. And the tide was coming in. Stephen felt its approach as an actual function of nature, an enormous power, slow and relentless, devouring the expanse of sand. The beach was coming alive. The pools round the city were slowly filling from within. The water in them was rising, the patches of grey foam in them slowly revolving, changing their shapes. Sand was flaking from their sides and falling into the water with quiet noises. The tide was coming in, not so much with the steady advance of the gentle, ruthless waves. It was coming in upwards, from deep down under the sand, creeping closer, like a softening of the brain, insidious, evil. Stephen felt he was standing on a totally unstable world, as if the entire planet was dissolving beneath his feet, and once again as in a nightmare he felt the thudding horror of being unable to move his feet. He might perhaps have tried to cry out in his terror, but he heard the light steps of Bruce behind him, and turned to see with amazement that his friend was carrying a bundle of newspapers. Bruce put the bundle down and began to shred a copy of The Daily Telegraph.

'What are you doing?'

'Preparing for the conflagration of Troy.'

He took some pieces of lightly screwed-up paper and fed them carefully into the doors and windows of the buildings, gradually filling the rooms, but not packing the paper in too tightly.

'I'm the master-craftsman turning into a pyromaniac.'

'What are you going to do?'

'Burn the city to the ground before the sea gets it. Man, too, has the power to destroy. And in a way it's much more satisfying than building.'

Sunlight gleamed in Bruce's eyes as he worked with the bits of paper. Stephen watched in fascination. This was a new element. Bruce was so much the builder, the maker, the creator. It was rare for him to destroy. Stephen was surprised at the feverishness of his friend's activity. Bruce looked up.

'How far's the sea?'

Stephen looked, but as he did so he felt all sense of scale and proportion melting away. He seemed to be in an aeroplane high in the air looking down on this lonely town in the desert, with the vast ocean with massive slow tidal waves gradually approaching, waves not of the human world but such as might exist in a land of giants. What was the real size of the human world? What was real? Was he himself a giant? This loss of bearings, this dissolution of reality in natural surroundings, was something new to Stephen, and yet again he experienced that rising sense of panic at not being in control, of losing his identity. Then he saw the spade sticking up out of the sand, its lower shaft and blade still dark with the dog's urine, and he came back to himself and once again tried to measure the distance between the sea and himself.

'I'm not sure. I'm hopeless at this kind of thing. About...a hundred yards, I should think.'

Bruce stood up and confirmed Stephen's uncertain statement.

'Yes, about that.' He looked at the sun. 'We've got about half an hour. There's time.'

The timing was important. It must be dark enough to appreciate the flames, but not too dark to conceal the final assault of the sea. The sun still had an hour of life in it, and the clouds helped. It would be dark enough, and perhaps just before the sun went down behind the horizon, there would be, as there often was, a brilliant blaze – the splendid song before death, its last offering to the world day it had created, the gift before the murder. They stood for a while watching those great movements – the sun gradually sinking and the sea slowly approaching, and both in their different ways could not help feeling the existence of some highly ordered system in the universe, of which these vast workings of sea and sun were but an infinitesimal part.

Then, showing he had made a decision by a sharp nod of his head, Bruce took a box of matches from his shirt pocket, struck a light and held it to the paper in one of the rooms of the largest building in the centre of the town. He had laid 'fuses' of paper from one house to another, so that the fire would spread through the streets. The sand inside the building had dampened the paper a little, so it burned slowly. Bruce started fires in one or two other places near the city walls. Soon smoke poured from the windows, and, to their delight, from one of the chimneys.

'Now let's walk away a bit. It looks better from the distance.'

They walked away, the sea sweeping closer to their left. The beach sloped a little, helping the tide. A stone's throw from the city they stopped and turned.

The city was burning. Blue smoke rose from the walls and drifted away towards the rocks. Flames could be seen inside some of the windows. Bruce seemed excited.

'Marvellous, isn't it?'

'Pity those people aren't here with their camera.'

'Too dark probably.' Bruce stared at the burning town. 'It's so real!'

Stephen looked at him. Bruce's face was glowing with pleasure, like a child's. He was extraordinarily animated, talking rapidly – explaining what was happening inside the buildings.

'They don't always collapse. The walls and roofs are sometimes too thick. There isn't enough paper to do much damage. The sand dries inside and trickles down. It sometimes puts the fire out, or makes it burn more slowly. Sand's very good at putting fires out. Did you see the bucket of sand behind the front door up in the house? That's why we have it—'

'You are earnestly entreated to trickle down into the bucket—

Bruce didn't laugh. He was staring at the fires.

'I wonder if the reinforcements will burn. Sometimes the wood in the ceilings catches and then they fall in; but it's usually too damp. Look, the smoke's coming out of that chimney too! Good: the tide's coming much closer. It'll be just right. Let's go nearer.'

None of the buildings had collapsed. Some of the roofs had whitened a little. The edges of some of the windows were blackened by the flames. Again Stephen looked at Bruce's face. It was no longer the face of a child. The fire from the city made deep shadows round his eyes and mouth. He had fallen silent, gazing at the flames – absorbed, obsessed. Stephen was reminded of a wooden carving of a Chinese devil he had seen in Bruce's home. There was something cunning, voluptuous in Bruce's eyes, in the curl of his lips which seemed to be moist as if anticipating something. The architect had sabotaged his own masterpiece. It was no longer a game.

For Bruce, the city had suddenly come alive. People were running in the streets, women were screaming from windows. Terrified priests in flaming robes jumped from the tops of towers. The siren of an ambulance wailed. Panic reigned. It was if a new and totally unprophesied terror had taken hold of the city, creating its own people to witness the conflagration. Great blazes always attract people: here they were fashioned out of nothing merely to suffer the horror of their own destruction. They carried bundles on their backs, or trundled carts piled high with household goods. They held burned and wounded children in their arms. Dogs barked; horses shrieked from stables, their manes ablaze. It was the end of the world — a second end, a sudden dramatic, utterly unprecedented day of judgement, as abrupt as the first death had been slow and agonizing. And a third end was on its way.

Bruce smiled. It was not the destruction he savoured, it was the chasteness of the fire. Fire did not putrefy; fire did not kill. Fire purified. Cities, even dead cities, were full of sickness. Bodies carried within them diseases of all kinds; rats ran in the sewers. In the minds of the people, too, there were twisted thoughts and lascivious desires. Fire was chaste. And Bruce the perpetrator was chaste also. It was he who had done this. Not to destroy, but to cleanse the city. This was the true meaning of power. To do good. The single advantage of power is that it enables he who holds it to do more good. Bruce was the god who had created the city, and the same god had now come to save the city by destroying it.

The fires died down. The city was still standing. Small holes had appeared in one or two of the roofs. The wall between two windows had fallen in. The streets had fallen silent again. Everyone had been driven out of the walls. They were gathered mute and round-eyed at the edges of the grey swirling full moat.

And then it was the turn of the sea. The first thin final spread of a wave had reached the outer edges of the moat. The water was pouring in. The moat for the first time had become truly part of the ocean, as if, Bruce suddenly thought, the sea had risen up round Harlieg Castle and joined its open-ended moat, so that the castle was now really isolated on its rock. And now this city of sand was being drawn back into the sea. The voices could be heard again. Tidal waves were coming. The third doomsday. First the slow starvation and evaporation of all green and red-blooded life. Second the fire. And now the ocean was closing in upon them; and what the sea did was the most final of all. Earthquakes came and went; hurricanes raged; plagues had their day; wars were tiny ripples — the people always somehow recovered. But there was no power more terrible, more constant, more total in its destruction than the power of the sea. All horror was in the sea. Just as the sea was also mother of all life. If there were real gods, they dwelt in the sea. And there were gods, was god, in the sea. Or else why did it come like this? Why did it cry always, near or far-off? Why did it always fascinate, hypnotize, terrify? Why did all things, all people, turn their eyes with longing to the waves, from where after all they had come in the first place? And why did everyone and everything in the end go down to the edges of the sea and disappear there?

Bruce felt like a pagan deity, a minor idol standing abandoned in the desert, as if he and Stephen were those two seated monolithic gods in the Valley of the Kings — as the water began to wash round their ankles. Thus it was with all gods conceived in the minds of men, though this god, the sea, was conceived elsewhere. All man's gods had to die; they too were witnesses of something greater. Christ was a terror-stricken man; God the Father a doddering old uncle; Buddha dreamed and was drowned; Ra turned his back on the world. Chastity was a human failing, murder a trivial lapse of manners. Love was a helpless spasm of the limbs. Death itself was nothing final. Life was always there — a huge, swelling, green-grey muscled, singing, crying, ruthlessly heaving cold-hearted dragon, without eyes, without ears, without sensation. It had no fire, teeth, claws. Body was not there. It was all mouth — ravenous, swallowing, regurgitating, groaning, roaring, singing and sighing sometimes; but always there, never dying. All death, all life, eddied to and from within it. It was not bound down by time or place. The sea was not merely the five oceans of earth. All space and universe were sea – the same numb, senseless grey-green dragon, drinking, spewing, sperm-oozing, mother and son, an endless coition without a name, neither creative nor destructive, but horribly – in a kind of grey death with wide-open glaring liquid eyes – invulnerably alive.

The city was doomed. The moat filled up and overflowed. Fissures appeared between the outer walls and the road circling the island. The walls fell outwards, but there was no sound of crashing stones. They fell with a single flop or slid silently into the water and dissolved. Cracks appeared in one of the towers. It collapsed without a sound. The sea was eating the city without biting. The sea was melting the stone with cold fire, like acid that did not burn. A wall fell outwards, exposing the hollow interior of one of the buildings. Blackened paper shone dully within, partly burned. Bits of driftwood, darkened by fire, projected high up in the rubble, like beams in a burnt-out house, shattered by shells. The island was growing smaller. The sun was revolving deliriously in a crimson agony, its yellow rim not constantly concentric – like tears round a grief-stricken eye. The church spire fell headlong, its bell clanging and suddenly silent. A long scream rose up from the ruins, but it was not the voice of people. The sand was screaming. The sand fashioned into noble forms was losing that nobility. Proud of its moment of glory and honour – to have been chosen to stand in splendour high above the kindred beach – it was unwilling to surrender. A single wall was left, untouched by the sea. Bruce and Stephen watched, knowing the inevitable would come. There was no elation now, no sense of the heroic. The city had no way, no will to fight on. It had to go down. The sea would be triumphant.

The fragment of ruined wall sank away; the last rough-textured pinnacle of the island softened and melted into smoothness. There was nothing left but a gentle swelling on the beach, a breast without a nipple, a subsiding bruise in the sand.

But the sea was not entirely without mind. How else could it do what it was doing now? The fragments of newspaper, the lengths of driftwood, did not stay with the ruin they had shared. The sea, almost gently it seemed, lifted them up and carried them, their duty done, further inland. In the morning, strangers might walk along the tideline and find them, but they would never know the history of the city that had stood there in the desert, millions of years before.

Subdued, shaken, the two friends picked up their spades. They had both felt it, they had both sensed the sinew-rending strains of power. Stephen had found the beauty of creating, the power of forming magnificent shapes out of nothing; he had experienced the futility of destruction. With unfamiliar emotions of dismay, he had seen the steady decay of the island. All things had to decay, but in spite of that man still persevered. There were moments of splendid grandeur even, not to be dismissed. The city had stood, serene and proud, until Bruce had put the match to the paper. But it had stood there surely, and they had made it. Bruce himself was accustomed to making things. All his life he had fashioned things with his hands. But the firing of the city had inspired him. It filled him with unfamiliar joy. Somehow, because of the presence of his friend, he had seen the fire with new eyes. He had often done this burning before, but for the first time he had taken special delight in destroying. It was easy to create. But destroying was more enduring, more satisfying. What had creating meant to him before this? Building model houses, out of bricks, sand; making things out of wood – shelves, boxes, carts, a theatre for puppets, houses in trees. All things for children, and all of them ultimately destroyed. And what of his poems? Would they too share the same fate, within a longer timescale? His bardic pretensions were merely a matter of dressing up – again a game for children. His poetry had the same hollow texture – grand gestures concealing unrealistic ideas; none of them, he now saw, had any true bearing on real, modern life. It was all empty romantic flow; it was all a pose. There was nothing romantic in destroying. Demolition workers' business was far more permanent than that of builders. All great works of art were eventually destroyed. The Mona Lisa was losing its colour already; its paint was cracked and flaking off. No amount of restoration would save it in the end. People would forget how to play Beethoven. Shakespeare's plays would become extinct. Actors would be a lost race. Bruce longed for a place in history. His vast, little works would get him nowhere. He would never be able to make his name in that field. To destroy was a greater art. Maybe Hitler, at first a benevolent despot, a great road builder, had discovered the same. Assassins he could now understand. And now he could begin to understand Stephen. Stephen was not by nature a creator; Bruce had tried to make him one. That's why both of them had so often failed. Stephen had more sense. Stephen, he thought, did not indulge in empty, noble dreams. There were no halls, no harps, no bards, no heroes in his world, nor any left anywhere else in the world. It was no use trying to become one. It was better to be honest, see the world as it was, as Stephen did – instead of trying to set up moral roadways, high-sounding maxims. Good deeds were the pathetic attempts of those who knew they had failed. That was why Christ had committed suicide. There was no going to heaven. Christ had lied in his final hours. The world would never be saved. It was not saved; two thousand years later, it was still in utter confusion. No one could bring salvation now. Better to follow the example of the sea, mindlessly chafing at shore rocks, eating them away, or gradually moving back, leaving empty wildernesses of sand to shriek in the ruthless wind.

They walked up to the house, Stephen with new strength, Bruce with a bitterness of spirit he had never before known, or thought he could know, through every tunnel in the labyrinth of his mind. Stephen would finish his novel this time. Even though no one might read it, it could, it would be written. It would be created. It would exist, complete and perfect. Even then, if he threw it on the fire in a fit of anger or despondency, it would still have had its hour. To fight against the forces of destruction – there was joy in that; and Stephen knew what it meant to fight. He had been fighting all his life – against his parents, teachers, friends, against the carefully established structures of society – laws, religion, civilized art. He had been fighting against himself. But he had never yet fought against the all-obliterating forces of destruction. The sea was his mentor, not to be followed, but to be challenged. Not insanely, like

Canute: there was no changing its ways. But he would meet the waves head on, sacrifice what he had made, and if necessary offer himself and drown. But before that he would fight, and he would relish the joy in setting his wits and strength against this greatest and most fascinating of all powers, the sea.

Behind them, below them, the tide came in, moving quietly in the darkness.

16. GANNET

THE FINE WEATHER HELD. The next morning as usual Bruce went down for his swim. The beach was deserted. Bruce felt exhilarated, filled with a wonderful sense of abandon. It was not that he had given up smoking for he had started again as soon as he had thrown Stephen the packet of cigarettes, nor was it that he enjoyed any special benefits of health. In any case, the sea air never made his cheeks rosy like a child's and the sun never gave him much of a tan. The secret of his wellbeing now lay in his sense of achievement at having exercised self-restraint for so long. He had not touched his body for a little over three weeks, nor had nature yet taken its wonted course. He felt like an adolescent a few days or hours, or even a few minutes, before the sudden self-awareness of puberty – the thrilling shock of the first fully-conscious wet orgasm; but his sense of physical wholesomeness was spiced with the pre-knowledge of what was about to happen. Instead of running down the path to the beach as he usually did, he walked slowly, luxuriating in the sensation of ripeness that tingled from the one centre spreading throughout his body and returning to that deep-rooted centre always. He felt goodwill towards the entire world, perfectly at ease and at one with nature. He felt as pure and fresh as a new pink rose just about to open completely, or like a young animal in a glade of a virgin forest somewhere in a temperate climate. He was happy, he was lovely, he was full. He stood there just above the rocks, under the new line of sandhills, invisible from the house, aware now of a slow rising, throbbing excitement. The cool air stimulated the smooth surfaces of his body. He was alone.

Quite naturally and without thinking, he did something he had never done before in such a time or place. He took his cotton shorts off. No one could see him. He knew what was happening. There was nothing he had to do but stand there and wait for the slowly rising and then suddenly brilliant long surge of joy. His body would always reward him, if only he held off like this. Here was nothing sinful. What he was doing now – or was he doing anything? – was entirely chaste. Where was the crime? Whom was he offending? He was not offending himself; he was not even touching himself. To do so, to induce self-relief, he had been taught, was something to be avoided at all costs, although more recently he had begun to wonder why. He was not exposing himself indecently. There was nobody to see him, no one to be shocked or corrupted or excited but himself. He was wholly a child of nature, alone with the sea and the sky. He stretched his arms above his head, and arched his back a little, holding his right thumb in his left hand. Then he relaxed and looked down. A fresh, healthy-looking, new mushroom was blossoming in his groin. He stretched back again and gazed upwards concentrating on the sky, and the sky was blue, pale, pale blue, almost white. He was free as a hyacinth on a dewy morning. He felt tiny but somehow huge liquid movements within the tops of his thighs, behind the gleaming tower and domes of his flesh, an intense tightness and hardness of all those vital cells, and then, almost blinded with mounting ecstasy, all conscious thought left him. There was nothing but sensation. He became totally blind and deaf. He would have been dumb but his slow full breaths carried in them faint cries or whispers like the distant sea. Then everything in the universe shot to one place. The bed of the ocean had collapsed. All the seas were rushing down. And up. And out. A billion generations of all possible species had passed the point of no return and were pushing their way out of darkness into light. Here, now, at once. Out. Out of the darkness into the light. Out of darkness into light. Out of darkness. Out. Into the light. Into light. In the light they would die. There was nowhere in the inhospitable world for them to blossom into flowers. The seeds would decay in the sand.

He lowered his arms. His body felt hot all over. He felt exhausted and trembled from head to foot. He felt as if he had been running, or flying against a gale. His breath came quickly. His shining flesh was falling down, thickly wettened and whitened. He was a collapsed god. He was Bruce Dinwiddy standing naked on the shore – weak, empty, vile. Elysium had passed away. There had been triumph and glory, but there was no glory or triumph now. Only the large drops and globules of his defilement in the sand, and sliding down and tangled with his wrinkling body, which was now an object of disgust, exciting but not exciting. The body was filthy. It was always secreting juices, some of them vile-smelling but not this juice. The body was a mass of holes that always needed cleaning. It got tired. It was an object of utter and endless contempt.

There were eyes everywhere. He knelt down in the sand and drew cool handfuls of it up between his thighs cleaning away his hot shame which still continued a little. Then he heaped sand over all the wetness around him and tried to hide all signs of what had happened there, but the smell of it stuck in his nostrils. Hastily pulling on his shorts up against his sandy flesh, he crossed the rocks and ran down into the sea. He felt a dull pain of excess where before there had been wildly throbbing joy. Once in the freezing water he used his hands to clean away the clinging sand. He ran out of the sea. He felt colder than ever he had remembered. He ran along the sand. The sea was watching him, but there was no eye there, no voice. Its terrible indifference was far more menacing than any sermon could ever be. It knew. The sea despised him, and therefore the sea had nothing to say. He wheeled round and ran back over the rocks and looked down again at the place where his purity had turned into guilt.

He had polluted what he loved best. The sand could not punish him. The sand was the child of the sea. He had offended the mother. Another shock struck him. Somewhere, all round him, even where he was standing perhaps, were his mother's ashes. What if they were now mingled with his beastliness? What was holy in the last ritual of death if he could behave like that in this sacred resting-place? Was this another kind of destruction? If so, let it be.

But to Bruce now it seemed like a kind of incest – the mother and the son, the ashes, the seed and the sea, the end and the beginning, the conjunction of the dead and the living. What ghastly creature would arise from this unspeakable union? Oedipus had done nothing so hideous. Bruce felt himself the victim of some dreadful unnamed complex. Perhaps there was some deep Freudian tangle in his subconscious personality. What would Freud have made of this? Was this a manifestation of some virulent obsession for his dead mother, a regeneration of a hidden love he had harboured while she had been alive? Bruce had never loved his mother with such passion. Perhaps that was the crime. He felt in need of someone to explain to him the workings of the mind, the complexities of the world. It was all too confusing. He was still a child. Perhaps man always was a child, carrying in his mind always the child he had been, that never left him. He was sure that the butterfly had no inkling of the caterpillar world; but the man could never forget the child. He needed a friend to explain to him, someone to love him and guide him through the forest of the dark adult world.

*

Stephen was standing on the low grass mound near the verandah, notebook in hand.

'You look red.'

'I've been running.' Bruce averted his eyes from Stephen's stare. He went straight into the house and upstairs. The dreadful possibility that Stephen had seen all now occurred to him. But, no, it was impossible to see anyone so close under the sandhills, not from the house. Or was it? Had Stephen been spying on him from somewhere near? He had looked at Bruce strangely. Was it only his imagination? Bruce could never be sure; the uncertainty would always be there – unless he asked Stephen, and they did not have that kind of intimacy. He pulled off his sea-wet shorts, looking to see if there were any traces of his emission. All had been washed clean. His flesh was hard and small, compressed by the sea and the cold. It seemed to be like a small dull-blue animal with a clean little mouth pouting very slightly, that had just returned from a most delightful adventure in sensation, as if it were a rabbit that had undergone a bout of myxomatosis that was not a disease but a great joyful purple swelling of the head. It looked satisfied, almost complacent, though Bruce could feel a dull pain in his groin. He dressed, feeling a resurgence of wellbeing, and went downstairs. Stephen was still outside, gazing at the sea. Bruce spoke lightly.

'When did you get up?'

'Just after you. I heard you going down.'

'What have you been doing?'

'Making notes. What have you been doing?'

'Swimming as usual. Did you go for a walk?'

'No, I've been here all the time. I saw you in the sea.'

'Lovely morning again.'

It was not a lovely morning. In spite of having recovered slightly, Bruce felt irritated. It was always like this – intense elation followed by bleak depression. It took time for him to restore his self-respect. However much he followed the laws of nature, nature always had a way of making him feel guilty whenever his body had given him that blaze of supreme relief. But he knew that it was only a half-truth – that he followed nature. Man was never intended to be a solitary animal. Perhaps, Bruce thought, if there were a woman he could share that joy with, there would be no such sense of shame. It was so useless, so wasteful of something inestimably precious. The seed had no place to go. He wished there were a girl he could love, and marry, and live with. There had been a girl once. He had loved her with a love such as he had never thought possible; but she had gone away. His erotic fantasies and adventures had never included her. She had been on a pedestal apart, to be adored, but never to be possessed or related in any way to the filthy business of sex. There was no woman now, or perhaps there was. Not his mother, nor his mother's ashes, but something other. Some creature that would come along the beach, scenting the air, and scoop up the guilty spots where they lay hidden mingled with the sand. She would put them in a flask and bear them away to some foul-smelling abode, and there implant them in the belly of a female sea-demon – to raise another brood of monsters in the deep.

Stephen settled down to some steady writing in the living-room as soon as breakfast was over, continuing a powerful wave of creativity that had taken possession of him as soon as they had finished supper the evening before. Bruce had no energy or interest to continue with the creosoting. He began to realize that all his physical energy and mental vitality depended on the promise of erotic joy after long restraint. Without that promise, life had no delight. Sometimes, it was true, after such a physical release he felt a new burst of creative energy and on such occasions had often written some of his best work; but now he was not in a writing vein, not engaged in any literary project. It was a barren period, perhaps because of the presence of his friend. He wandered about the house from room to room, without any sense of purpose. He went outside; the view from the house was flat like a poorly executed watercolour. Two butterflies idled by, their bodies joined end to end in an erotic embrace. Even they were partners. Bruce felt a ridiculous pang of envy and resentment. Life for him could never be simple and open like that. He went to the window of the living-room and stared inside. Stephen's pen was moving rapidly across the paper. There was no posing now, the writing was more important than the writer. Bruce tapped on the glass. Stephen looked up and smiled, and then went on writing. Bruce watched him with distaste. How virtuous his friend looked, sitting there and writing with such ease! Bruce tapped again; again Stephen looked up but this time he didn't smile. A slight frown flickered across his face. Bruce went back into the house.

'How are you getting on?'

'Very well. Very well indeed.'

'Would you like some coffee?'

'No, thank you.'

'How about a cigarette?'

'I've got some.'

Bruce felt annoyed. They were his cigarettes.

'Won't you have a break?'

'Later. It's too early. I'm just into a good bit. I must get nearer to the top of the wave before I stop.' He smiled up at Bruce and went on writing. Bruce came round the table and stood behind

Stephen, looking down over his shoulder. He read a few of the newly written sentences.

'Not bad.'

'Would you mind not standing there? I can't concentrate.'

'I'm going out in a moment.'

He picked up one of the sheets covered with Stephen's thick script.

'You won't be able to understand anything from that page. You'll have to read it from the beginning.'

'I'm just looking.'

'I wish you wouldn't.'

Bruce went out, whistling tunelessly. He stood on the lawn looking at the sea. Only lonely people whistle, it seemed to him; or foolish people, or foolishly happy people. He couldn't even whistle in tune, couldn't develop it into a melody. He sat down on the grass, and then lowered himself onto his back, staring at the sky. The empty sky. He fell asleep.

For the first time since he had started writing seriously at Bruce's injunction three years before, Stephen was enjoying the pleasure of setting pen to paper. Always before he had felt himself in an ill-fitting role. Now that he had cast away the artificial mantle laid so heavily upon his shoulders by his friend, he felt free to create. There was no struggle now. It had all fallen away into the past. He began to feel a kind of serenity, such as one must feel, he thought, on reaching the summit of a mountain. He felt a sudden warmth towards his friend. Bruce had bullied him, cudgelled him almost, towards this form of expression, and now he felt an unfamiliar sense of gratitude. Bringing him to this place. The sea outside calmed him, had taught him a new slow regularity of life. Perhaps Bruce's own regularity had helped – his morning dip, breakfast, work, coffee break, work, lunch, going for the milk, walks, work, supper, more work or talking in the evening. It was true that their few days at Harlieg so far had not followed this pattern with such perfect regularity, but the pattern was unquestionably there – a structure laid down to follow; and so it was easy to follow. In order to fight successfully, one had to stop fighting. It was not a matter of passionate erratic onslaughts, thoughtless tactics. Strategy, long-term thinking, were essential. Stephen's life had never had a strategy, an ordered fluency such as it had now. Somehow he had become organized, peaceful. In this peace lay all the power for future war, but the battles were over for the time being. Now it was time to reinforce, to line up the armaments, train the battalions. His writing was unbelievably lucid now. He knew it was good. There was nothing laboured here, except perhaps for the rather awkward beginnings, which could be tidied up later; yet neither was it facile. It had clarity, strength, economy – the jumble of images falling into place one by one. Each was a clear pool, limpid, unique; others were smooth rocks draped with seaweed. All were part of the shore, and the endless background of the sea welded them all together. His novel had an unshakable foundation. A wisdom was rising out of the chaotic mass of Stephen's past experiences. The events had retreated to a distance, somehow because of the creation of the slob city the day before, for that too with its miniature scale had created a kind of distance between recent events and himself. He had a broader, more objective view now. There was a kind of shape, a meaning to it all. The happiness he could feel now was real, tangible. He filled page after page.

Bruce woke up and looked at his watch. He had been asleep for two hours and it was almost midday. He felt uncomfortably hot and somehow deflated and dehydrated. All sorts of tiny pains which he normally would not have noticed were now apparent – faint rheumatism in his right knee, a scratch on his arm. He felt vulnerable. He sat up. Stephen was still at work in the living-room. Damn the man. Why was he so complacent? There he sat, in his friend's house, smoking his friend's cigarettes, eating at his friend's expense. And never any thanks, never any real gratitude. Stephen owed his life to him. If it had not been for Bruce, Stephen would not be there now, calmly writing at the table. He would be somewhere in some slum district, at the beck and call of some depraved middle-aged man in a raincoat. Or he might even be dead. Bruce was hurt by his friend's impassive manner. It never occurred to him that it was not Bruce but his father that was providing

Stephen with these comforts and that he himself was entirely lacking in gratitude to his parent. He went into the house.

'Still at it?'

'Yes, all the time, while you were sleeping.'

It was not meant as an accusation, but that was how Bruce took it.

'Why shouldn't I sleep?'

'I don't mind at all. You must be tired after all your exertions.'

What did Stephen know? Bruce gazed sharply at his friend's face for clues as to what he might have guessed.

'If you don't mind, why did you mention it?'

'It's not important. Unless you feel guilty.'

'Why should I feel guilty?'

'I wouldn't know. Do you feel guilty?'

'Of course not.' Bruce thought of the early morning by the rocks. 'Would you mind clearing the table?'

'Aren't we having lunch outside?'

'I feel cold. Can't you work in your room? You've spread yourself out all over the place down here.'

'It was your idea. I can easily go upstairs.'

Damn that impassive face.

'What's your novel all about?'

'I'll tell you when I've finished.'

'Why can't you tell me now?'

'It might interrupt the flow of thought to talk about it.'

'What a lot of pages! Is it good? It can't be. You're writing too much, too quickly.'

'That's what you suggested I do. You were right. It works.'

Bruce wondered how to sabotage the novel.

'I don't think anyone can write a really good novel until they're at least forty. We don't know enough about human nature.'

'Why are you so nervous?'

'I'm not. I just think you're wasting your time, working at that speed.'

'Thank you for the encouragement.'

'There's no need to be sarcastic. Shall we have lunch?'

'If you can spare the time to help prepare it.'

'Of course. I wasn't going to suggest you do it by yourself.'

'Oh.' Stephen began to gather up his papers. He took them across to the side table under the front window. He could not understand why Bruce was so irritable and negative. Was it possible that he was jealous? Stephen felt a little disappointed. He wanted Bruce to encourage him, even to praise him a little, now that he was doing what his friend had advocated for so long.

'Is there anything the matter?'

'No, nothing. Let's get lunch.'

They went into the kitchen.

*

After lunch, Stephen continued writing. They planned to go for a walk later on, but Stephen wanted to reach a certain point in his narrative first, and Bruce, still in an irritable frame of mind, went outside.

It was one of the quietest hours of the day. Everything seemed to be sleeping. The beach was deserted. People in the town were digesting their lunches perhaps. The old holiday-makers in the hotel were sleeping in the lounge, newspapers rumpled on their laps. Shopkeepers were shuffling round getting ready to open up for the afternoon. Even the sea seemed quieter than usual. The mountains in the distance were pale, faded and old and still.

Bruce walked to the top of a sandhill not far from the house. The sun was shining on the roofs of cars about a mile away in the Golf Club car-park. That part of the Traeth below the town shimmered in the heat-haze. There was almost no movement anywhere, but everything around him was tremblingly alive, as if the world were in a coma, drugged, trying to contain some unnameable pain. He thought of his mother. She too had in her last days shown the same held tremor, not wanting to cry out, keeping immense courage. There was courage now, in the bones of this landscape – superb control, as if tremendous powers, dormant now, were being held in, stored for some future catastrophe. No screams shattered the afternoon. A grasshopper whirred uncertainly in the grass.

And then Bruce heard a strange and wonderful sound. It was like the voice of a tenor singing a high note, a note held impossibly beyond the limits of human breath. It went on, seeming to rise in the heated air of the afternoon. It was joined by another identical voice, and another, and yet more and more, until a chorus seemed to occupy the entire region of the sand dunes, still holding that one incredibly plangent note, which was then joined by a real tenor voice singing louder than the rest, singing real words in a strange language, unbearably sad and enchanting words, like a heartbroken bard singing at the edge of the sea for his lost lord, or like mermen mourning the death of a queen of the ocean, or raising a dirge at the slow death of the sea itself, as it evaporated away, leaving an endless wilderness, a parched ocean of sand, whose waves were gentle undulations of dunes. Bruce longed for the sound to go on forever, it was so heartrendingly beautiful, so full of nostalgia for loved things lost; and it seemed to be coming from everywhere around him, and yet from nowhere he could place. It grew fainter, and it seemed to have changed into a flock of seagulls that were not white or grey, but shining and golden, as they rose up, becoming smaller and smaller and fading into the blue sky, as the sound itself diminished and left him alone there on a sandhill in the Traeth.

He looked towards the castle. How was it always seemed to him so benevolent, so wise, settled there serenely on its rock? What was the element that made it seem almost human? The castle was a friend. It had stood there, unchanging, ever since he could remember, and six hundred years before that. It was part of the happiness of his childhood. It was a sign of the stability and safety of former days, days that for him would never come again; and somehow now Bruce felt that it was his castle. No matter who had built it, or who now owned or visited it, it was his.

The image, the likeness of which would not emerge clear into his mind, now came to him. The castle had always reminded him of something, and now he realized what it was. It looked like an elephant. People rarely look at elephants, it seemed to him. Once or twice in their lifetimes, at a circus or a zoo, they might see one;

but they never realized until they suddenly saw one much later in their lives, what an amazing beast an elephant is. Bruce had discovered this on a recent visit to Ceylon with his father. The elephants he had seen there really taught him of the antiquity of the earth, far more than any ancient temple or monument could. These grey wrinkled monsters, with their ponderous steps, were an anachronism: they should have become extinct thousands of years before. This was one of the reasons for the analogy with the castle. But it was not only that: the walls and thick round towers reminded him of the big-boned head of an elephant or mastodon. The colour and texture were almost, from that distance at least, the same, as well as the well-spaced simplicity of the whole. The huge black windows in the walls reminded him of an elephant's eyes, deeply sunken and somehow sad and tired – dark-ringed sockets with a gleam of great experience and wisdom within them. The castle had the same wicked, friendly smile as an elephant's mouth – not malignant, yet reminiscent of past crimes witnessed if not committed, some hint of carnal knowledge, a kind of knowing humour, such as Chaucer, or Rabelais or Shakespeare might have had in their faces, as if they knew there had been better days in the past. A couple of flies were creeping along the elephant's huge brow – people walking along the castle wall. Bruce smiled, and returned to the house.

The living-room was empty. Bruce called upstairs but there was no answer. He called again, louder. The house was silent. Bruce looked at the beach. Stephen was standing there near the sea. Angrily, Bruce ran down the path. Stephen should have waited; they were going to walk together. Bruce reached the top of the rock line. A quick glance told him there were no signs of that morning's shame. The sand was dry and white. All footsteps and other disturbances had melted into gentle undulations.

Stephen was writing something on the beach near the water. As Bruce approached, his friend quickly erased the words with his foot. At the same time, an errant wave of the ebbing tide covered the marks. Stephen stepped back quickly and just escaped from getting his shoes wet.

'Why didn't you wait for me?'

'I thought you'd already gone down. I couldn't find you.'

'I was just over there on a sandhill.'

'I didn't see you.'

'What were you writing in the sand?'

'I'm not going to tell you.'

'Was it a poem?'

'No.'

'What was it then?'

Bruce very much wanted to know what it was Stephen had been writing. At first his curiosity about the words themselves had been aroused, but as soon as Stephen refused to tell him, Bruce's motives changed. He wanted to know because Stephen did not want to tell him. He did not want Stephen to have any secret he could not share. The hidden words were a source of power for Stephen, and Stephen must not be allowed to hold any power.

'Why is it such a secret?'

'It's not a secret. It simply isn't important.'

'If it's not important, why can't you tell me?'

'Why should I?'

'Only because...well, we always share, don't we?'

'Do we? Do we go to the toilet together like little girls? Do we eat off the same plate? Do we share the same bed? I think there are many things we don't share.'

Stephen thought he would be treading on dangerous ground to say any more. He thought of the many occasions when Bruce had not shared – cigarettes, the Shakespeare works...there were too many things to enumerate. Bruce was mean. It did not occur to Stephen that Bruce was generous in asking his friend to stay in that house by the sea, in giving him this marvellous opportunity, and inspiration, such as had never occurred before in his life, to write, to enjoy his new-found stability and happiness. It was not Bruce who was paying for everything, it was his father. He had not forgotten the offhand way Bruce had charged items to his father's account in the grocery shop. In other ways, Bruce was merely using him. He was someone Bruce could show off to. When Bruce was irritable like this, and petty minded, Stephen forgot his hypnotic eyes, because at such times they lost their piercing brightness and shining depths. There was a hint of a whine in his friend's voice, a note of sustained resentment. At such times, Stephen could not respect, admire or be inspired by Bruce. He turned away along the shore towards the mountains.

'Let's go the other way this time. We've never been that way.' Bruce pointed to the low green headland to the south, and the railway embankment below it flanked by the huge boulders. 'There are some wonderful pools there, like underwater gardens.'

Bruce had no special desire to go that way. There was scarcely half a mile to walk before the beach ended, and the tide somehow avoided that corner of the shore, so there was rarely anything of interest washed up there. But he needed to counteract; he needed to re-establish his hold – to force his will once more upon Stephen, to prevent him drifting too far out of his reach.

'Very well.'

Stephen turned round abruptly, and the two walked side by side along the edge of the sea. Bruce tried to walk close to Stephen, but Stephen sometimes stopped without warning to look at something on the sand, or suddenly walked faster. Bruce felt out of step, the same as when Stephen played the piano too quickly during their duets. He felt out of step in two senses; for he could not fathom the pace of Stephen's mind.

'What's that?'

Stephen stopped and pointed. Something dark and spider-like was flapping about in the water about a hundred yards ahead of them. The shallow waves turned it about from time to time. A faint sound – like a thin intermittent croaking – came to their ears. Slowly, with some trepidation, they moved closer, their little differences forgotten.

It was a sea-bird, but in such a condition that it could scarcely be termed a bird. Its entire body was smoothly coated with thick tar-like oil. There were few signs of feathers. Its wings were more like the feeble flippers of a small sea-lion, or like the wings of a chicken roasted black and then dipped in glycerine. They stood over it, and it cowered down, terrified. It opened its beak and emitted a voiceless cry. Only its head was free of the ghastly black straitjacket. There the short downy feathers, saturated with water, stood up crest-like from its skull, bedraggled and dirty. Stephen had never seen such an evil-looking yet such a miserable creature. There was nothing here of the sinewy strength and beauty of a flying seagull. The long grey bill seemed to continue right into its head, including the staring, agonized, black-ringed yellow eyes. A black pointed tongue projected from its throat like a piece of dry leather. The head was not white, as he expected of sea-birds, but of a greasy yellow colour. It was a bird, it seemed to him, possessed by a skinny yet gluttonous sea-demon, a goblin that normally writhed in the brains of old sharks. The bird, suddenly aware of the new human danger, flapped croaking away from them out of the sea. One of its legs trailed limply under its body, marking the wet sand with erratic grooves. It levered itself along on its black, crippled wings, frantically trying to escape. Stephen was almost sick.

'Christ! How awful!'

'It's got oil on it from one of the big ocean ships.'

'What is it?'

'It's a common sea-bird. It's a gannet.'

The bird, hearing their voices, squawked in panic and renewed its demented flapping efforts towards the rocks. It was something both less and more than animal: it was humanly wretched, but it was also a manifestation of the vilest malignance of the sea as contaminated by man.

'What shall we do with it?'

Bruce had often seen sea-birds in this pitiful condition, but they had always been dead. This was the first time he had encountered an oil-bound bird alive. He had often read of such cases in the newspapers – how people had caught the birds, bathed them in cleansing fluids and detergents, coated them with butter. Such acts of kindly mercy always inspired sentimental accounts in the tabloid newspapers, sometimes occupying a centre spread of photographs and exclamations of over-righteous indignation. What the papers always omitted was that the vast majority of these rescued birds died shortly afterwards of shock, largely the shock of being photographed, being handled by too many solicitous bird-lovers and stared at and deafened by hordes of noisy journalists. Bruce knew that whatever he tried to do this bird was doomed. There was only one thing to be done.

'We'll have to kill it.'

Stephen stared at Bruce in disbelief.

'Can't we save it?'

'How?'

'Can't we clean it somehow, or take it to the R.S.P.C.A. or something?' Stephen had also seen newspaper accounts and was speaking without thinking. Sometimes he was curiously conventional; there were areas of knowledge which he had not explored, quite commonplace things. His sentiments now were exactly as the newspapers intended: be kind to animals.

'You can if you like. I'm not going to try anything like that. The nearest R.S.P.C.A. office is in Dolgelly, that's over twenty miles from here. Anyway, they always die.'

'Surely there's something we can do?'

'The kindest thing is to put it out of its misery as soon as possible.'

Stephen looked at his friend's eyes. They were blazing again. But this was not the Bruce he knew. Bruce was always preaching kindness, consideration, but this did not seem to Stephen to be one of Bruce's moments of kindness. There was something grotesque in his expression; he had the same gluttonous look as the gannet had, or would have had had it been in a normal condition. Some sort of secret enjoyment, anticipation, was lurking there. It was a look Stephen had never seen before on his friend's face. There was nothing godlike there, nothing noble, creative, optimistic, and nothing of compassion. All Stephen could see was an intensity of purpose, and that purpose, he now knew, was one of cold destruction.

Stephen was not by nature violent. There had been numerous occasions in the past, it was true, when he had lost his temper; and at such times he had lashed out in blind fury without the slightest regard for person or thing. Doctors, his parents, vases, cutlery, anything he could lay his hands on, had been the victims or tools of his onslaughts. Stephen, in the tears and calm which always followed, had often been surprised at the amount of damage done. Since puberty, such tantrums had become rare, but when they occurred they were more than usually destructive. Stephen had not yet lost control in the presence of Bruce, whom he had wanted to impress by his dignity and self-mastery, although at times he had been precariously near to doing so. He had never, however, committed an act of violence as the result of rational thought, except perhaps to kill a wasp or two, and even that was a kind of emergency. He had never been knowingly cruel, and though he could see the sense in his friend's opinion, he was appalled by the idea of simply killing a wounded bird. The fact that it was so handicapped filled him with even more revulsion when he thought of the manner of its death. He would rather have thrown a singing canary in its cage into the sea if its death had been necessary. It was this same tenderness for the wretched – and the sentiment now seemed extraordinary to him, not having expected to find anything of the kind in his nature – that had rendered the idea of his suicide ultimately unrealistic. Self-pity would have prevented self-destruction, just as pity now for this bird wanted to prevent its deliberate murder.

Bruce, on the other hand, knew what cruelty meant. His father had exercised it often enough. Not only whippings during which he relished his son's agony in the pauses between each stroke, but mental pressuring – threats to withhold pocket-money, to disown Bruce even, if he did not learn obedience, to divorce his mother if she did not stop complaining – he had suffered it all. Bruce was not a masochist; he by no means enjoyed his father's cold, deliberate acts of harshness. Rather they inspired in Bruce feelings of revenge. But the revenge was not of the reciprocating kind: there was nothing he could do to touch his father. Bruce had to find other victims. He had sometimes bullied boys smaller than him at school, bending back their fingers till they almost broke. He mocked those weaker than himself. Fear of his father was parallelled by a kind of fear of those he tortured. His schoolmates laughed at him because of his social differences. Also he was afraid of frogs. He remembered one day collecting three small frogs from a half filled-up soakaway at the bottom of the garden at home. He had taken them into the workshop at the side of the house, nailed their hands and feet to the wooden bench, and then burned them with an old cigarette lighter. The frogs had literally screamed until they had died. Deliberate though the deed seemed, it was in fact a reflex action. At the time, Bruce could not have explained himself. His cruelty was irrational. He never knew it as revenge.

The gannet had reached the rocks. The two friends followed the marks it had made in the sand – wild arcs made by the wings and deep indentations where its bill had tried to support the weight of its head and upper body. Now it sank down on one side, and turned its head, beak open, and looked at them, terror gleaming in its eyes, as they approached. This was its last defence.

The sea had not been unduly unkind. The sea had brought it safely to land. The sea had returned the gannet to those who had perpetrated the agony. Man had drawn up the oil from the Arab sands; man had extracted metal from rocks and forged steel. The oil and the tanker were no creations of the sea. But the sea was there. Man had emerged from it – animals had crept dumb from the ocean and some had returned. Man had remained on land. But he was still fascinated by the sea; and in his quest to dominate all he encountered, he had tried to master the sea. He had discovered those things which floated and those which sank. His ships had drawn the drifting continents together again. The gannet was a victim in this blind warfare of evolution and invention. And the sea was there. The sea was to blame.

Bruce picked up a heavy waterlogged piece of driftwood and approached the bird. The bird seemed to understand what was about to happen and cowered down between two rocks. Bruce raised the wood above his head and suddenly brought it down hard. The end of it struck a rock and missed the bird. He tried again. The wood again struck a rock but glanced off and hit the gannet on the side of the head. Croaking softly, it lay there stunned. Stephen's face was pale.

'Is it dead?'

'No.'

Bruce's voice seemed to have a tremor in it. He felt suddenly afraid. He felt he had no right to exercise judgement of this kind. Perhaps they could save the bird after all. But one glance at the black oil-coated body told him again that the case was hopeless. Was this a mercy-killing? How could it be kindness and murder when both the very words were contradictory? The bird moaned and tried to lift its head.

'We can't leave it like that. It must be in terrible pain.'

Bruce knew it was true. He was appalled by what he was doing; but so much was done: there was no going back. He was terrified by the discovery of this third state of existence between life and death. A horrifying sense of timelessness overwhelmed him. He saw an image of himself, the helpless divine judge – bent on destruction, bent on salvation, and neither had succeeded. The bird was not dead, but nor was it any longer really alive.

The decision was made for him. Without realizing what he was doing he had picked up a stone the size of a human skull. He felt its cool, damp underside, coarse sand adhering to it. He raised it to the level of his eyes; he took aim. The stone took a thousand years to fall. A crack as it hit its fellows, a spark, and the final soft crackle and thud as the gannet's head was crushed.

There was no sound except their harsh breathing and the constant turning of the waves behind them. Bruce carefully lifted the stone. Brains and blood oozed from the sides of the gannet's beak. Its body whirred in a tremor of death – yet another stage of existence, between killing and death. The spasms lasted some three minutes, while they watched, speechless with horror. Then it lay still. Somewhere in the distance a seagull was crying its yelping cry, which was joined by another, the sounds stopping suddenly.

Bruce laid the wood across the body and stepped heavily on it. The gannet croaked. A fourth stage: even in death it had a voice.

'Why did you do that?'

'Just to make sure. We'd better bury it. Let's have a funeral ceremony.' Bruce smiled.

Stephen was unable to share the grim humour of his friend; yet the acts of violence had fascinated him. He wanted to laugh out loud, and the laughter he knew was gathered there in his chest he knew was not the laughter of a child. He kept silent.

Bruce levered the wood under the gannet's body and lifted the carcase slowly across the rocks to the edge of the sand dunes. That morning he had sprinkled the sand with the grey-white spots of his own poured-out spate of life. Now he was burying this tarred, bedraggled creature, bludgeoned to death, not far from the same spot. The sand would do the rest, and the wind. Here was yet another form of existence, neither life nor death. There was no name for it. Only two things were certain about it: whatever it was it moved; and there was a force that made it move. Raising his head from the little burial mound, Bruce gazed across the bay. The same movement was there all about him – mindlessly alive, wakefully dead. The godhead was the sea.

17. ROYAL DRAGON HOTEL

'YOU ENJOYED killing that bird.'
    'What makes you think so?'
    'You murdered it. You like destroying things.'
    'Why do I write poetry then?'
    'That's just sentimental excess. We could have saved that bird.'
    'That's being sentimental.'
    'Don't be ridiculous.'
    'What would you have done?'
    'Telephoned the R.S.P.C.A.'
    'I didn't think you were so righteous.'

They were both bristling with anger. Perhaps it was a kind of reaction to the shock of their experience with the gannet. It had somehow changed things, as if their relationship had shifted on its foundations, almost as if they were beginning to exchange roles. They had now been together for four days. They had never spent so long in each other's company without a break, and it was beginning to tell on them. Bruce, probably because of a kind of guilt or depression caused by his physical release that morning, seemed in quite a destructive, negative vein. Stephen on the other hand seemed full of energy and drive. He cleared his throat.

'I want a beer.'

'Well, there isn't any in the house.'

'Let's go and get some.'

'You can if you want to. I'm not going.'

Bruce regretted the words as soon as he had uttered them. Although to remain together was rapidly becoming unbearable in its intensity, to let Stephen out of his sight and therefore out of his control was even worse. Stephen got up from the table, where they had just finished supper.

'All right, I'll go. I can manage without you.'

He also regretted his words, but his reasons were quite different. He had hardly enough to buy himself a single drink, let alone enough to pay his fare home. This was something he hadn't mentioned to Bruce yet; he was going to ask him for a loan, but that would come later. Now he needed Bruce to come with him, yet to continue in his company was something he would rather have avoided. He felt a new urge to be free of Bruce. It was all very well to walk out grandly, but what would he do after that? He had enough sense not to cut his supply lines.

Like the identical poles of two magnets they repelled one another, but like the opposite poles of one magnet they could not exist apart, at least not happily, not effectively. Bruce stood up.

'What about the washing up? It's your turn.'

These 'turns' were a further source of irritation to Stephen. Bruce always required his friend to share all duties equally. If one cooked, the other had to wash up. Bruce kept a careful check on this and was quick to reprimand Stephen whenever he lapsed. Stephen did not mind doing such things but he hated the regimentation, the cold calculated mathematics of it all.

'I'll do it when I come back. Or you can do it for me if you like, and I'll bring some beer back for you too.'

There was a pause. Stephen seemed in no hurry to leave the house and Bruce in no way urged him. It was he who was the weaker of the two.

'O.K., let's both go. We can get some beer at the Royal Dragon.'

Stephen smiled. Peace was restored, but as always it was little more than an uneasy truce. Stephen started to clear up the supper things, and Bruce with a sudden glow of generosity helped him. Stephen had always been difficult and Bruce wanted nothing more in the world than to keep on good terms with his friend. In a few minutes the work was done.

It was dark outside. Clouds obliterated the stars. The sea was noisier than usual. Although the tide was not yet full the waves seemed strangely near, almost, it seemed to Bruce, as if he could touch them with his hand if he reached out a little way into the darkness. He imagined them lapping at his heels, as if they had suddenly risen over the sand dunes in the shadow of the evening, the house behind them a floating island miles out at sea.

The hotel, seated like a throne set in the sloping cliffside, was ablaze with lights. It was more like a liner in the night, perhaps, anchored close to a black shore. The sandhills to their left and ahead of them appeared like huge breakers, not frozen into silence like ridges of black ice, but stunned into immobility like a night seascape in heavy oils – huge rounded humps of unbroken breakers, a swell transfixed within the ornate gold frame of the masterpiece of a forgotten nineteenth-century genius. Again Bruce suddenly sensed the hopeless proximity of his mother's ashes scattered in the dunes. Who walked there now in the darkness? Once there had been a rumour of a wandering lunatic, a strange man from the mountains who sang endless Welsh dirges and knelt under gorse-bushes surrounded by spellbound rabbits, grass-snakes and adders. That was years ago, but at times like this such rumours seemed to rise anew like horrible possibilities or even nodding actualities. The sand dunes were full of weeping. A crushed gannet rose shrieking in Bruce's mind, flapping its tar-smeared wings. Mermaids, landlocked, languished in the dry sand, their beautiful tails a mass of peeling scales and putrefaction; yet still they sang, the beauty intensified by their terror at having been abandoned by the sea. Their youthful faces withered and aged in a matter of hours, like delicate yellow poppies cut and lying in the sun. They became grotesque hags, their long locks, sea-green gold, faded to lank grey, their round firm breasts shrunken like dried figs; and soon their voices turned into the croaking of the tortured gannet. The filthy smell of rotting fish invaded the night. One of the last trains of the evening clattered along the line, a dragon glow-worm with its insides lighted with pain. The passengers were all crones on their way to join a hillside coven, or the aged servants of Neptune off duty, and the train itself had just come steaming up from out of the sea. There was no youth left by the sea: all was aged and shrivelled. Nothing lived there, and nothing, it seemed, died there either. Bruce felt that he and Stephen were themselves rapidly aging; they would arrive, bent, white-haired and exhausted at the hotel, telling the story in quavering voices of their hundred-year journey from the house across the dunes.

The lights of the hotel were now immediately above them. Stephen, who had been following Bruce with difficulty in the darkness along the narrow path beside the railway line, almost believed that this great edifice glittering in the night was a true castle, lighted and peopled. The other, real castle beyond was a dead, ruined shell. In the night, the huge building had all the mystery and splendour of a medieval fortified mansion, and they were travellers from a far country nearing their destination at last. Knights and ladies walked gracefully within from room to room, keeping their love-trysts. There would be music in the gallery, stately pavanes and sarabandes in the great hall. Mead would be drunk, ballads recited, to the sound of harps, hautboys and timbrels. It was a world that Stephen, even if he had lived in such an age, knew he could never enter. He was the uncouth swain listening in the darkness, the gardener's boy, for whom a single glimpse of the multicoloured magnificence through a window was inexpressible joy and heart-wringing pain. They had taken the beach path up to the hotel garden; now they skirted round the south edge of the building. The front entrance, like that of the castle, was at the 'back'. They strolled into the warm-smelling softly illuminated foyer.

Bruce rarely drank, and even less frequently went into a bar. He 'disapproved' of any form of induced intoxication, often scornfully denouncing to Stephen all those who were addicts or who attempted by means of alcohol or drugs to escape from reality. Stephen, who had no fixed principles in this area, had soon become aware of discrepancies in Bruce's attitude. Smoking, surely, was a form of addiction, no less virulent than drinking or taking drugs; and Stephen had had a few mild experiences with the latter. Furthermore, Bruce's entire concept of art, his bardic posturings and his hazy romanticism, were all forms of escapism, and all of them were self-induced. Where was the difference? They had argued long, but nothing could shift Bruce from his dogmatic and illogical standpoint. His practices, he argued, were not harmful to the health or to society; drinking and drugs were. Stephen, keeping his mind open, could not agree. Real experience, no matter how it was achieved, was all that mattered to him.

The opulence of the interior of the Royal Dragon Hotel took both of them by surprise — the thick crimson carpeting, the polished copper-brown panelling, the many dim lamps on wall-brackets, the waiters and attendants in formal dress gliding past with quiet footsteps; all these belonged to an unfamiliar world. They were reminded of their first meeting in the coffee lounge of the Chesterton Hotel in Birmingham. Somehow the atmosphere there in the heart of the city did not seem so alien to the environment. Stephen, always aware of being conspicuous, now felt doubly so. His face, tanned by the sun and sea breezes, felt red and sensitive; his collar chafed against his neck; his arms and legs, roughened by the sand and salty air, rebelled against his clothes. For the first time in his life, he felt the absurdity of dress in any form. His shoes, filled with sand, restricted his feet, and there was sand like powdered glass between his toes. He felt coarse and raw like a rabbit with myxomatosis. He hardly realized that the sensations he was now experiencing were in fact the benefits of good health. Good health was something he had never known, and his body took it hard. New delights are not always appreciated immediately. It takes time.

Immediately beyond the foyer was a corridor running the length of the hotel parallel with the line of the cliff. A fairly long section of this corridor opened directly through two pairs of heavily framed glass doors into a spacious lounge the far windows of which overlooked the sea, now invisible in the darkness outside. The dozen or so residents there, almost fused with the easy chairs in which they reclined, were all middle-aged or elderly. The men were immobile, except for the slow coils of pipe or cigar smoke which wound round and above their heads, or for the occasional tapping off of ash or shuffle of newspaper. The women, especially a group of four or five on a half-circle of sofas, were more animated, talking with that artificial familiarity they always seem to assume in such places and at such times. Bruce wrinkled his nose in contempt. These were not people, they were less than human. They knew nothing of the simple pleasures of dwelling by the sea. The waves meant nothing to them, they never touched the sand; the wind to them was an irritant. The concept of a 'change of air' which had brought them to Harlieg was a travesty. The mountains they gazed at and enthused over were nothing but yet another charming picture, and gave more pleasure to relatives who saw them only as very distant and poorly-coloured photographs on postcards. The wealth of these people cut them off from real contact with the elements. They were a mere barely stimulated audience, decaying voyeurs who hardly bothered to look at anything. He wanted to round them up with a whip of dried seaweed, salty and rough with sand, lashing at their bare legs, forcing them to tear off their shoes and run along the beach into a rainswept gale, then dragging off all their clothes, their flabby flesh white and blue and quivering, goad them into the ruthless sea to battle with body-crushing breakers. Nothing less would cure them of their clinging heart-conditions, their chronic rheumatism, their pathetic dependence on the soothing, nerve-deadening accoutrements of luxury. Bruce, who had only once or twice ever visited the hotel in his entire life, swallowed down a wave of nausea. Contradictory as it now seemed to him, remembering his thoughts on the way to the hotel, age had no place here by the sea. These mindless invaders, with their blue hair, their painted mouths, their suave clipped moustaches and gleaming bald heads, their obsessive scrutiny of newspapers full of stocks, shares and minor disasters, their cheerfully glib exchanges and their creeping moribundity, were an insult to the pristine vitality of the sea and mountains. One day, Bruce hoped, tumultuous seas would come bounding across the golf links to erode the foundations of the hotel and consume with fingers dripping of acid salt drops the crumbling sections of fallen masonry. One day the sea, now receding, would come back. Twice before the waves had topped the Cambrian mountains. And the sea had patience. It would wait, but doomsday would come.

As they turned left along the corridor and made their way to the non-residents' bar, an elderly couple descending the main staircase nearby looked at them with ill-concealed disapproval, complaining loudly.

'They shouldn't allow them in here.'

'Indecent. I'll have a word with the manager.'

'I wish you would, dear.'

Bruce was not one to allow such to pass without comment. He too raised his voice and turned to Stephen.

'Why do people who stay in hotels never learn good manners? They're so rude. Think they're lords of creation. It shouldn't be allowed.'

'It doesn't surprise me. They've got too much money.' Stephen looked at Bruce. This was a kind of game with them. 'You are earnestly requested to exercise special care in the wetting of your pants.'

The elderly couple, red and trembling with indignation, walked into the lounge arm in arm. Bruce laughed and Stephen stooped slightly as if to break wind.

'Do you think they heard?'

'I intended that they should. Why are you standing like that?'

Stephen stood up straight.

'I've just failed to add my parting shot.'

184

Laughing they went into the bar. It was empty save for the red-waistcoated barman, obviously a local man for his weather-beaten face and sparse grey hair betrayed long hours spent in the open air. He looked like a small farmer forced into early retirement by the barrenness of the land. His hands were large and had difficulty polishing a brandy glass. He looked at the two friends with an air of hostility and suspicion – foreigners. Bruce, however, felt relieved. There was no danger here. He and Stephen could talk together without fear of interruption or distraction. Bruce quite sincerely at this time did not wish to exercise control over his friend, he had no relish for power. It was rather his fear of losing the companionship of Stephen that usually emphasized his possessiveness. Whenever there were other people present, Bruce always felt at a disadvantage, left out; Stephen neglected him at such times. Bruce needed undivided attention, his friendship with Stephen had to be exclusive. In the presence of others, Stephen changed, became almost cold to Bruce, but now in the clientless bar Bruce felt relaxed. Their common dislike of the hotel residents and personnel had done much to ease the tension between them. Out of habit Bruce took the initiative.

'What will you have?'

'I think I'll have a lager and lime.'

Bruce was so ignorant he had only a vague idea what a lager was, but he was not going to let Stephen know.

'I'll have the same.' He went to the bar to give the order.

'Ask him to put the lime in first, it mixes better.'

The barman, taking the order with a brief nod, prepared the drinks using mainly his thumbs and second fingers. He looked up at Bruce, his frown fading into the beginnings of a smile.

'You one of the Dinwiddys?'

'Yes.'

'Thought so. Your father wrote a letter to my brother. Bob Evans, see. Wants him to go down to check the fire precautions down there at Tremarfon. How long will you be staying now?'

Once again Stephen was delighted by the quaint tones. The man had the Welsh way of tightening the consonants which gave his words that unique lilt. Bruce, though he hesitated to enter into too familiar a conversation with the barman lest it disturb his time with Stephen, was delighted. It gave him a warm spread of confidence and wellbeing to have been recognized in the presence of his friend. If only that could happen in connection with his writing! If only someone would come up to him in the street and say in a nervous awe-struck voice, 'Excuse me, but are you Bruce Dinwiddy the poet?' – with his friend looking on, that adoring look in his eyes! This recognition in Harlieg, though it gave Bruce a sense of belonging to that part of the world where Stephen had none, was merely the legacy of his mother's good name or his father's shop accounts.

'We'll be quite a while. When would your brother like to come down?'

'In a day or two maybe. We'll phone down. Been a lot of fires on the rail lately.'

'We've been lucky so far. Nothing's come near the house.'

'Well, you never know, do you? Trains here are devils when the weather's dry like this.'

Bruce wondered if this seemingly simple-minded man had any feelings about Welsh dragons. At the same time it suddenly struck him that the hotel's name had a dragon in it and he had never asked anyone why. He did not want to prolong conversation with the barman but his friendly tone made him wish to reciprocate in some way.

'By the way, I've never understood why this hotel is called The Royal Dragon? Do you know why?'

'Well, now, I wouldn't know that. Haven't been working here long and I'm only here evenings.'

'The Welsh flag has a dragon on it, doesn't it?'

'That's right. I suppose that's how this place got its name.'

'But why Royal Dragon, I wonder.'

'There used to be kings and queens in Wales once.' His 'kings' sounded to Stephen like 'kinks' and his 'queens' like 'queence', and the word 'Wales' was also shortened into 'Wailce'. It was such a friendly, warm dialect. Stephen wished he could speak it. The barman scratched his head. 'Perhaps that has something to do with it.'

'I didn't see any dragon in the foyer.'

'Well, we don't see many dragons around these days, do we now?' The barman laughed loudly at his own joke, and Bruce and Stephen joined in.

'I meant some signboard or decoration. Most hotels have something of the kind.'

'Well, there's nothing like a dragon in this place as far as I know. Maybe the name's a new one. Funny now, never thought of it before.'

Stephen came over to the bar.

'Some of the guests look a bit like dragons — red and discontented.'

Again the barman gave a burst of laughter.

'Shouldn't say so myself, but...well, true enough. Some of the people who come in here are like dragons after they've had a whisky or two. You could strike a match to their breath.' Laughing the barman went back to his polishing of brandy glasses. The two friends took their drinks to a round glass-topped table in the corner, sat down and examined the beer mats. Bruce noticed that under the glass the varnished brown table top was stained grey in various places, like rainclouds in a brown sky. He wondered how the marks had got there. Perhaps the glass tops had been added later. He felt wholly at ease and looked with interest at his drink. So lager was just another name for beer. Trust Stephen to use the grander word. But he felt no ill will towards his friend. He had no enemy in the world.

'Cheers!' They clinked glasses. The taste was good — bitter-sweet. Bruce held up his glass and watched the oily swirl of lime juice near the bottom. The barman hadn't mixed it so well after all; but then he wasn't a professional, just a part-timer taking on the extra work to make ends meet. Stephen placed his glass carefully on a beer mat.

'Do you believe in dragons?'

'Oh, yes. Wales is full of them. In the mountains behind the town there are lots of twisted pines in one place I know. That's the dragons in them trying to get out.'

Stephen stared into his glass.

'In a place like this I think there must be dragons in the sea.'

This was a new idea to Bruce and he liked it.

'Yes, sea-dragons. Sea-horses look like baby dragons. And when it's windy we can see white horses on the surface. Not horses, they're dragons.'

'I'm not talking about that kind of dragon. Something much bigger, invisible.'

Bruce looked at his friend. Had Stephen felt it too? That huge living force under and behind the waves? What was it there? Bruce thought of the sea out there now in the darkness, turning endlessly, black and cold. It seemed very far away now. Could it really be there, doing that, as they sat in this bar drinking beer? There was such a difference of worlds all round them. Somehow the sea seemed irrelevant now.

'I know what you mean.' He drank an inch of his lager, beginning to feel its effects already. 'Now here's a question. Is that dragon in the sea male or female?'

'Both. Neither.' He smiled, looking at Bruce.

'I think it's female. I always think of the sea as a mother.'

'That's just romantic twaddle. The sea is quite heartless, not human at all. Just water.'

'But it has voices.' Bruce's eyes were shining bright again. 'The sea is water, yes, and it's full of fishes, monsters and seaweed and rocks deep down. That's just science. Everybody knows that. But that's not all. There's something else. I know.' Bruce drank again. 'I know.'

Stephen gazed at the table top and shifted some beer mats into a molecular pattern. He knew too, but his logical mind would not allow him to admit the existence of that other presence he had felt on the shore. He had not yet had time to analyze it properly; he had made some attempts in the novel he was writing, but he hadn't yet worked it out in detail. There was something there he couldn't explain, and until he could he didn't want to commit himself in words to Bruce.

'Wait. I'm writing about it.'

The sound of voices came from the corridor and four men in business suits marched into the bar, laughing gaily. Three of them were in their late twenties or early thirties, the fourth in his mid fifties. Bruce was instantly on his guard. He was also annoyed. He and Stephen had hardly had time to get into what promised to be an absorbing conversation, on a theme dear to Bruce's heart – the kind of conversation they used to have so often in the early days of their friendship. He made an effort to ignore the intrusion, but in doing so shifted entirely to another subject.

'Have you ever noticed that buildings sometimes seem alive?'

'You mean because of the people in them?'

'No, alive in themselves, like the sea. The castle here, for example, seems almost human. I sometimes feel it could even talk.'

'What a preposterous idea!'

'And this hotel...Royal Dragon's not a good name for it. It's got a kind of personality, like the manager of a cement factory or an art nouveau designer. And sometimes our house down there—.' He stopped. Stephen was not listening. He was staring at the backs of the four men now at the bar. The older man was second from the right, and had both his arms across the shoulders of two of the others. One of them made a smutty remark. The fourth, on the left, was turned in profile and occasionally cast a furtive glance at the two friends in their corner. 'What's the matter?'

'I think I know one of those people.'

'What do you mean?'

'The older one. I think I've seen him in Birmingham.'

The four men moved in a noisy group from the bar and took their drinks to another corner table. They sat in such a way as to be able to see Stephen and Bruce without turning in their chairs.

'Who are they?'

'Travelling salesmen, I think.'

Bruce was suddenly dismayed by a wave of helplessness. What he had feared most was happening. Stephen was being distracted, drawn away from him. A rising spasm of fury produced a scowl on his face.

'They're disturbing us.'

Stephen continued to stare at the newcomers. What was it that was so familiar about them? His first impression, he now realized, was erroneous. He knew none of them; they did not speak with the Birmingham accent he so much detested. But there was something he did recognize, especially in the older man, and it came with an unpleasant shock, seeing such people in these alien surroundings, to discover what it was. With a kind of dull despair he began to feel he could never get away from it. Wherever he went such people hovered round him, like flies round a jar of jam. There was no mistaking it – the way they looked at each other in the eyes, the longer-than-necessary touching of hands as they lit cigarettes, the occasional predatory glances across the bar, the subsequent unhealthy laughter. They were all four of them homosexuals.

It seemed to Stephen that he was suspended in mid-air between two mountains. Not long before he would have had no difficulty in melting into the group and participating in their facetious camaraderie; with such people he could always find sympathy and understanding, at least for a while. But now there was something different. His days by the sea had wrought a change in him. He could observe these people from the outside, as from a vantage point. The sea-air had given him a new strength, a new awareness of robustness and masculinity. Somehow here in Harlieg he had become healthy in body and in spirit, and these four invaders seemed therefore so much the more insipid, soiled and only half alive. Stephen rejoiced in the confidence of a new self strongly alive within him. He could easily free himself of these people if so he chose to. He was suddenly aware of Bruce's eyes very near him – pained, so tragically pained, full of a kind of godlike anger, condemning, commanding, begging. But it was not the eyes he saw. Within them, behind them, formed of the innumerable liquid flickers of light there, he could see the entire sweep of Tremadog bay – the sand dunes, the beach, the distant mountains, the endlessly quietly turning waves. Cities of sand were there, vast cities, cities afire and sinking in swirling waters. Shining, black, featherless birds shrieked in the background. The sky was full of them, soft lights glided across low hills, and behind all these, a huge visage slowly arose and came into focus. There were two full moons, black orbs revolving before them not concentrically, the whole sky was grey waving clouds, like wild locks of hair, a woman's hair but grey as of someone old; a mouth opened darkly in silence, voiceless with catastrophe like a Greek mask, and the dunes rearranged themselves and became slowly undulating outstretched arms. It was human yet vast beyond humanity, composed of all the elements, which as he looked returned to their natural state of water, earth, fire and air, and again melded into that slowly mouthing, infinitely sad face of the sea. Then the image faded, and it was only Bruce there. One of the men called across the room.

'Won't you come and sit with us?'

Bruce's helplessness and anger turned to grey despair. His kingdom was crumbling. He had tried to save Stephen, he had failed, and now he was even failing to destroy. Stephen lit a cigarette, his hand trembling.

'Where are you from?'

'Chester. We're here for a day of golf.'

The other men sniggered. One of them said something in an undertone. Bruce caught only the words 'night' and 'billiards'. Stephen did not move from his seat. He glanced at Bruce. His friend was almost imperceptibly shaking his head, or, Stephen was not sure, trembling with suppressed emotion.

'Are you staying in this hotel?'

'It's the only one in this town with hot water in every room.'

Another of the men laughed and nudged the first.

'What do you want hot water for?'

They all laughed, far more than the question justified. Stephen felt a sudden surge of revulsion. These people were wholly out of place. They reminded him of the sordidness of his past. Here by the sea he had found something pristine, an endless source of energy. His novel, art itself, suddenly seemed more real and urgent. These people were utterly destructive, entirely unnecessary. No doubt they had recognized, as they always could, a kindred spirit in Stephen. Bruce had attracted them too. Although he knew his friend despised such people, he knew that Bruce was attractive to older homosexuals. Stephen himself had been told how charming, how pretty, his friend was. But somehow Bruce had never been aware of the emotions he inspired, or if he had he had coldly laid them aside and remained untouched, unsoiled, pure, incorruptible. Stephen felt his old fascination for Bruce rekindle itself and sensed a strong wish to protect his friend. It struck him as strange that these four men should have an interest in golf; surely that was a game for people of more conventional inclinations? Or perhaps not. What about those pairs or groups of thickset spinsters in tweed suits one often saw on golf courses? What kind of private lives did they lead? And those hearty red-faced colonel types, what did they think of, what did they do at night?

'Anyway, come over here and have a chat with us. We're getting browned off in each other's company.'

'I'm with my friend.'

'Well, come on over, both of you.'

'We're talking.'

'So are we. It's our favourite pastime when we are not otherwise occupied.'

Another roar of laughter or rather a chorus of titters.

'We're having an extremely serious conversation, and, if you don't mind, we wish to conclude it without interruption.'

The older man looked surly, then smiled sourly.

'There's no need to be so pompous, young fellow. I know what you two are up to. Don't pretend.'

'I merely wished you to understand.'

One of the younger men sneered.

'Aren't we in grand company now?'

'Leave them be, Bertie. They aren't what you think.'

'You give up easily.' He indicated Bruce with a toss of his head and addressed Stephen. 'What about your dainty friend?'

Stephen stood up, his chair scraping on the floor and hitting the dull panelling of the wall. He walked over to the bar.

'Could I have a packet of Embassy, Mr. Evans? Twenty, please.'

'Twenty Embassy.' The barman, a faint smile on his face, laid the packet of cigarettes on the counter. Bruce, understanding his friend's intentions, joined him at the bar.

'We'll pay for the drinks now too.' He gave some silver to the barman. He couldn't let Stephen suffer the shame of not being able to pay in front of these people. 'Let me know if you find out anything about the dragon we were talking about.' By re-establishing this friendly link with the barman, Bruce felt on safe ground. The barman shifted his eyes to the four men at their corner table and spoke with a slight sideways nod of the head.

'All sorts of dragons in this world, it seems.' He smiled at the two friends. 'I'll tell my brother about checking the fire precautions. He'll phone down.'

'Thanks. We'll be off now.' Bruce glanced back at their table with its two half-empty glasses. 'We'll come up another night.'

'Right you are then. Better weather next time.' The barman winked. The three understood each other, something warm and Welsh binding them together. The four men in their corner had been silenced. Stephen looked directly into Bruce's eyes, speaking firmly and with authority.

'Let's go.'

Bruce smiled at his friend, saying nothing. They took leave of the barman and went out. The four men stared at them as they passed their table. Bruce felt their eyes exploring the lines of his body. As they walked down the beach path to the level of the flat below the hotel, they could hear the dragon in the sea whispering in the distance.

*

Back at the house they sat at the piano. Bruce had never felt so elated in the company of his friend. Once again Stephen had amazed him. Both of them had undergone mercurial change. Bruce's depression had left him; his former sense of control had returned. This was like the old days. Bruce felt he was exerting a truly beneficial influence on his friend. Stephen had renounced suicide, had rejected quite decisively now the kind of company which sapped his moral strength. He was writing a novel, he was writing. This was the path Bruce had long hoped his friend would walk. And Stephen himself felt unfamiliarly virtuous, but this was only secondary to his sense of triumph. He was pleasing his friend. Now it seemed to him nothing was more pleasurable than being able to please his friend. He had taken a bold initiative in the hotel bar, had put behind him a world he wanted to be free forever from, wanted to forget. And now he was writing a novel, he was actually writing. It felt good. He himself for the first time in his life felt he was good, being good, doing good, not as an opposite of evil, but good as a positive, non-relative force, creative, strong, pure. There was nothing amiss.

They hammered out a splendid fugue, in canon. Rhythmic conflict merged into harmonic unison. It was a magnificent procession and arrival. Rarely could they reach this perfect accord. And then they moved into a cathedral under the sea, slow chords in D minor, subterranean bells tolling, harmonies deep down, green, blue, purple. For the first time an atmosphere that was not musical entered Stephen's concept and execution of music, and for the first time Bruce grasped a fusion of the mathematics and the falling water of melody. They were both inspired in new ways. Both of them knew that in this moment they were near the frontiers of genius. It was a time of immense exhilaration, two minds touching, four hands keeping a synchronized ripple of time. The strong chimes faded away and the sun shone down through the water. They sat in silence at the keyboard.

They stood up, too moved for words. They went outside to look at the stars. They looked at the stars. They stood there, and still there were no words to utter.

At the foot of the stairs, before going up to bed, Bruce touched Stephen's arm.

'It'll be another fine day tomorrow.'

Stephen nodded, his eyes shining. Bruce suddenly leaned forwards, placed his right hand on his friend's left shoulder, and brought his face near to Stephen's, then withdrew abruptly.

'What's the matter?'

'Nothing.'

They stared at each other.

'Nothing, Stephen. Only...I almost kissed you.'

18. SANDHILLS

THE TWO WAYFARERS struggled through the wilderness. On every side were mountains, inaccessible crags jagged against the blue sky, and all around them were plains, arid wastes of snow where nothing grew. Everywhere they looked were immense massed armies, impenetrable forests of lances, spears, bows and pennants, all angled in squadrons according to the lie of the land. The only sound was the soft thud of the travellers' feet. The sea was a distant whispering of memory.

Bruce was enjoying the game, and Stephen too found the novelty of it stimulating. It needed little imagination to transform the surrounding dunes into a vast Siberian landscape. The higher slopes of sand, some of them carved into strange shapes by now absent gales, were the mountains; the sandy flats were the snowy plains, the irregular clumps of coarse sharp marram grass the armies. They were the lone wayfarers. Bruce, with a rough branch of birch from the beach for his staff, led the way. They were roped together. When they faced the precipices of sand they became mountaineers. Especially in the lower hollows of the dunes, when all the cliff and town of Harlieg were out of sight, the loneliness became almost too realistic. It was at times genuinely awesome; the scale of the hills was lost, the dimensions stretched out to huge proportions. It was a game that Bruce had often enjoyed with his sister in former years, but there were times when it passed beyond the boundaries of a game and became the great world itself, terrifying and elemental.

The morning had passed happily. Stephen had worked solidly at his novel, gaining strength upon strength as he completed page after page and progressed from chapter to chapter. He had never known such fluency and power. Bruce had completed the creosoting, his filial obligation resolved. They both felt in these different ways a triumph of accomplishment. Lunch had been their most cheerful meal yet, Bruce at his most scintillatingly witty, Stephen at his most unbuttoned and earthy. They had laughed until almost blind with tears. Afterwards, Stephen had willingly accepted Bruce's suggestion that they walk to the end of the Traeth.

The landscape was not entirely of unrelieved barrenness. Occasionally they had glimpses of the sea, or of the real mountains ahead of them to the north. Once they saw the castle on its rock, standing – isolated and far away – between two sandhills, almost as if it were quite small and very near them. Sometimes they saw the town, hanging on the edge of Wales, and these views of the real world beyond the desert of their imagination dissipated the faint but distinct stirrings of terror and panic that threatened to overwhelm them when the terrain of the dunes expanded into the utter solitude of steppes and made them lose their bearings.

They skirted the south-west corner of the golf course. In spite of Stephen's strength of mind the previous evening in the hotel bar, Bruce sensed this was a danger point, but there was no sign of the four men. As they crossed the fairway near the fifth green, a golf ball landed near them. To Stephen, who was marvelling at the artificial smoothness of the grass, it came like a thunderbolt out of the blue.

'Where did that come from?'

'One of God's droppings, a dragon's egg.' With a sudden urge to be mischievous, Bruce looked about him and caught sight of some empty lemonade bottles in a wire litter basket. He selected one and stood it in the centre of the fairway. There was still no one in sight but themselves, as the teeing green was hidden behind low hills. Bruce picked up the ball and balanced it on top of the bottle. Stephen felt in his pockets.

'Have you got something to write with?'

'What for?'

'Let's leave a message. "You are earnestly requested to exercise special care in the handling of your balls".'

'It might be a lady golfer.'

'Well, change it to "my balls".'

'I've got a pencil here but no paper.'

Stephen looked in the litter basket but there was nothing in it that could be written on. Bruce began to look anxious.

'Hurry up. Someone may see us.'

'Playing with other people's balls.'

Laughing like two children they ran into the shelter of the sand dunes on the far side of the fairway. Although Stephen rather wanted to, they did not stay to witness the discovery. Bruce feared the player, or players, might be the four men from the hotel. They tramped on, careworn travellers once again, crossing the last of the lost continents.

Their target was a huge sandhill almost two miles from the house, more with all the ups and downs they had to traverse. It stood out above the rest, a wild broken-down Matterhorn amid a gathering of lower hills, and they reached it about half an hour later. Below its broad bare face the wind had hollowed out a vast bowl of sand so deep that the bottom of it was lower than the level of the sea and dark with moisture. As they crossed it, they imagined themselves in one of the craters of the moon. Or it was like, Stephen said, a gigantic socket without an eye, the sun having long ago scorched it away. It was utterly desolate. At the lowest point a common panic took hold of them and they started running up the opposite slope breathing noisily. Stephen was surprised how easy it was to exert himself; his asthma seemed to have disappeared. He now felt entirely comfortable in the old cut-off trousers Bruce had forced on him only a few days before, and he felt the old pair of pumps Bruce had also supplied were his own possessions. He had lost his city stiffness; he was wholly a child of the shore.

They scaled the final cliff-face with difficulty. The sand repeatedly gave way under their weight and rolled down the slope in hundreds of miniature avalanches. The bony yellow roots of the long grasses near the crest of the almost vertical incline, exposed by the wind, came away in their hands as they clutched at them for support. Bruce dug his staff into the sand like an ice-pick and carved out footholds with his bare hands. With a sudden effort he clawed his way to the top, sat down, dug his heels into the ground and hauled his friend up on the rope. Twice Stephen collapsed face down against the cliff of sand and roots, and the sand stuck to his mouth and got in his eyes; but now there was no sense of dignity lost. He simply spluttered and laughed and tried again. Soon they sat side by side on the summit.

The view was Himalayan. They were on the roof of the world they had mastered. They could see the red tiles of the house, a tiny diamond to the south, and the long line of the cliff to the left — the scattering of houses, the hotel, the college and castle, widely spaced out now and strangely flat against their steep background; they could see the entire straggling layout of the town. To their right the sea glittered in the sun. They looked towards the corner of the golf course nearest the sea where they had planted the bottle. Two women, one of them in bright yellow slacks, were bending like dwarfs on the fairway near the distant fifth green. They had found the miraculous golf ball. They stood up straight and looked about them. Bruce wondered if the women could see them on top of their sandhill and pulled Stephen down flat and lay beside him. He saw one of the women pick up the ball and drop it back over her shoulder; the other woman took the bottle to the litter basket. He tried to picture the expressions on the women's faces. Were they angry or amused? He reflected that it was one of the things in the world that he would never know. For a split second the two golfers suddenly became giantesses towering above the sandhill where they lay watching. They raised their clubs to strike at them but they changed into fire-extinguishers spraying sand which turned into a green and yellow blizzard, then the image faded. Stephen chuckled beside him. They were safe and Bruce was relieved it was not the four men there.

They stood up, turned for the first time upon their eyrie and looked north. Stephen was filled instantly with inexplicable terror and even Bruce, who knew what to expect, was struck with awe now that he saw the landscape for the first time with adult eyes. Almost immediately below them the sandhills faded away and a frightful desert lay beyond, stretching as far as they could see until in the far distance it merged into the silver line of the estuary and the blue of the mountains, which now seemed much nearer and yet less realistic, like painted scenery. The panorama was desolate beyond words. In the near distance rows of stakes linked by walls of rotting brown corrugated iron lay exposed — attempts by man to protect the outer flanks of the golf course by trying to induce the wind to create artificial sandhills, attempts which had been only partially successful. The scarcely relieved flatness prevailed. It was like a petrified ocean. There were motionless waves of sand, serried and rippled. It was a sea infinitely more dead than the Dead Sea. It was vividly the abode of death. Nothing moved there.

'That's where you can hear them, if you go far enough.'

Stephen questioned with round unstill eyes.

'The mermaids. I told you before. Listen.'

They listened. At first there was no sound. Stephen tried hard to hear something other than the silence. The music when it came seemed to rise from somewhere beyond the back of his skull, but not behind him. It was like the siren of an ambulance played on a tape-recorder at a slow speed — a rising and falling note hideously drawn out, a blood-chilling ululation, insanely tuneless, something quite other than human, animal or instrumental utterance. It was not indeed sound of any kind, nothing that could be measured or understood by any of the five senses. It was rather a disturbance in one's sense of balance, an instinct that had lost its bearings, a demented swerving of electrical waves in the brain. It was not mermaids: it was a sun-maddened ghoul that wound its way across the brilliance of sand and found a hold at the edges of their minds that somehow had become shallow basins like the upturned bowl antennae of radio telescopes.

The initial terror Stephen experienced almost instantaneously evaporated. He felt that his whole being was being cleansed through and through, not softly, not with the burning adze of acid, but with something so fine, cold and blazing that each cell in his brain, every notion of colour and image, was bleached into absolute purity. Memory was eradicated. The only sensation was that of a stone pencil shrieking endlessly across a child's slate, scoring a dead straight white line through the dark grey sky. Neither the sound nor the line was predominant, but something other, that seared away all knowledge acquired or potential and yet left no vacuum, but brought in its wake an age-old wisdom of iron, something older than the granite of the Cambrian hills, something like the epitome of an ice-age, yet permanent, unmeltable, unbreakable, the rock bottom of existence. And with it came the absolute certainty of human power.

Bruce was witnessing the end of the world. Here was where all ashes gathered, to be ground down into something finer than dust. Here was the origin of all gales that sweep the surface of the world. Here was the dehydration of the soul, the convocation of forces before the beginning of the sea, the forge-house of the elements. Fire, water, earth, air all died here, and in dying all were engendered. All past met here; all future flew out from this wilderness. Here was the beginning that was the end. Time was not known in this country. Life and death met here in mutual assassination. When all hope, all joy, pain and all despair were exhausted, this was the last place to come but one was already there.

They sat there at the edge of the world, white-haired children, trembling titans, exhausted with abandon, holding in their finger-tips and eyelashes, unreined, raging, inexhaustible and utterly serene power. They sat there in the sandhills, together. Together, and alone.

*

'Do you mind very much if I make my way back to the house on my own?'

They had decided not to go any further. Somehow they both understood, though it was Bruce who had actually said so, that to step down into the great waste of sand before them would amount to kind of invasion into forbidden territory. Bruce was also afraid there might be quicksands, and the marsh somewhere to the right of the stretch of forsaken desert filled him with foreboding. He didn't know where it began or ended. It would be like trying to find their way through a minefield. But it was not only that: another force, a presence, was somehow holding them back. It seemed that the terrain below was peopled, though there was not a single being in sight. If they ventured out unguided into that uncharted world they might never return, they might wander there lost and insane, whining like the wind through the sand, and after a thousand years they might at last find their way out of that white maze without walls, like catacombs in the open air, all the rock and earth above them sliced away leaving an immeasurable shallow barren labyrinth unbearably bright in the sunshine. They imagined being captured, bound and interrogated by a serene, coldhearted tyrant as cruel as the Snow Queen or swept away in a huge cloud of white shrieking dust. It was no man's land, but not as an uninhabited strip between two fronts; there was nothing beyond, or if there was it was a land of total madness as brainless as a mound of dead skulls. This was a Golgotha, levelled flat and ground down into a wilderness of powdered bones. There was nothing there but danger, horror and eventual death. Such images as these rose up and hovered in their minds like shadows of preying kestrels. It was Bruce who suggested they turn back, and then Stephen had expressed the desire to return by himself.

'You want to think?'

Stephen nodded. A flicker of discontent passed like the shadow of a fluttering bat across Bruce's eyes. Whenever his friend suggested they separate, Bruce always felt it was some reflection on himself, that there was something about him Stephen did not like. It never occurred to him that Stephen might really wish to take advantage of solitude, might really wish for a time to think in. But danger lurked in the sand dunes, people there that Bruce wanted Stephen to avoid. It was as if he knew he could never trust his friend. He tried to think of a way of conceding to Stephen's request while at the same time maintaining some form of control.

'I tell you what. You see that big sandhill over there.' He pointed towards the house. Just to the left of it but actually about a quarter of a mile nearer to them than the house itself was another prominent sand dune, mostly grassed over. The top of it, however, was sandy and hollowed slightly like the cone of an extinct volcano. 'Let's separate and see who can get to the top first without being seen. If either of us sees the other before getting there, we must call out.'

This was another game Bruce had often played in his childhood. It had never failed to thrill — the cautious creeping, crawling along on his stomach, the hope of seeing one of the others, the fear of being seen, of hearing a voice cry out 'I can see you!', the frantic dash to the summit. It all came back to him now. Somehow he could not abandon those adventurous times or leave them decaying behind him. To keep the freshness of youth, this was purity itself.

'I'm no good at that sort of thing.'

'Well, let's have a try. I'll take the left side. You go that way along by the beach.' Bruce thought that if he himself kept on the golf-course side there was less likelihood of Stephen meeting anyone. Stephen, seeing that he could be alone at least for a while, had no objections. They parted.

Bruce knew the sand dunes by heart. He knew every path and every change made by the winds when they came. It was his own kingdom. He imagined himself in a land-rover driving through uninhabited terrain, choosing only those paths and slopes a motor car – reduced in scale, of course – could have negotiated. On the steeper slopes he walked in miniature zig-zags as if the road too was designed like that. The engine in low gear snarled in his mind, the cogs of the gearbox grinding as they engaged and trembled with throbbing power. He knew he would reach their destination first. He caught sight of four men in the distance to his left. They were teeing off. One of them swung his club. It hit the ground with a shower of turf fragments and a faint cloud of sand visible even from where Bruce was standing. The player sank to his knees, beating the ground with his club. The others were doubled up or leaning back with laughter. The second player took his stance and struck. The ball rose high in a swift clean arc. Bruce lost sight of it in the sky then saw it again bouncing off one side of the fairway, losing itself in the rough grass and thorns. Without a doubt they were the four men from the hotel. Bruce looked about for Stephen, but he was nowhere to be seen. The sand dunes towards the sea were deserted.

*

Stephen was only mildly interested in the game Bruce had suggested. Bruce's childishness sometimes irritated him. He had even at first been unwilling to be roped to his friend for their long trek from the house into the Traeth, only a burst of good nature and well-being saving him from making objections. The same feeling of goodwill filled him with a kind of comfort now. He thought the simplest thing to do would be to go directly to the beach and walk along close under the sand dunes until he came parallel to the sandhill where they were to meet. What he would do then he would decide later.

He stepped out onto the beach. There were no rocks here and the tide never came close to the place where he was standing now. The sand was soft and dry and scattered with all sorts of objects which looked as if they had been there a long time – an oil drum, dented and discoloured, a few ribs of a boat jutting up out of the sand like the skeleton of some prehistoric creature abandoned in the desert, mounds of dried black seaweed mostly covered by sand, a few battered crates stained with salt of the sea. He noticed more plants here, a low green succulent weed spread out in patches and an occasional clump of pale green sea-holly; at least, that was the name he gave it.

The sea was miles away or so it seemed to Stephen. He could hardly even hear it, and he was the only person on the beach. He walked along in the sand, his head bowed, his hands clasped behind his back.

Stephen did not believe in God. For years he had made a point of rejecting all forms of existence which could not be explained in concrete logical terms. In any case organized religion disgusted him; it represented the kind of unyielding, unimaginative authority which he had consistently opposed for as long as he could remember. If he could worship a god, he sometimes thought, it would have to take the form of idolatry. There would have to be something tangible, a totem, a golden image, of Baal or Moloch for example. There would have to be rituals which involved deliberate human action and were meaningful – obsessive washing five times a day, bloodletting, group masturbation, collecting the sperm in a silver basin and drinking from it one by one, or the sacrifice of lambs which afterwards could be eaten perhaps raw. There would have to be a voice he could listen to and understand, like the priestess in the hollow column at Delphi. There was some sense in that. It could be analyzed, believed in, even if it were fundamentally dishonest as the Oracle was. Anything that could not be seen or heard or touched was not credible. Faith was a sentiment he could not understand. Now here by the sea at Harlieg he found himself perplexed. He was aware that some change had come over him. It was not so much related to physical things which could be explained. That his health had improved was natural and understandable. His new-found ability to write fluently had also nothing mystical about it. The regularity of life, the coming in and going out of the tide, the rising and setting of the sun – things he had not been aware of consciously before – had much to do with this. The tranquillity of the place had now done so much to settle his mind. Hardly a week ago he could not have imagined himself dressed in this informal way and enjoying the sense of freedom it gave him; this was also natural. All these changes were perfectly in order, there was nothing in them to bewilder. It was this other thing that perplexed him. He felt as if one whole side of his mind had been cut away, letting in the light and permitting the morbid thoughts that had plagued him so long to tumble out – like hordes of grey-faced goblins dropping out of a barrage balloon. The goblins were falling but they were not killed as they struck the ground. Somehow they acquired wings and floated down like dandelion seeds in the breeze. They landed like maggots that suddenly sprouted agile limbs, ran about and jumped and exercised themselves in a jocular sport. Colour came into their faces, their eyes shone. And when they were regenerated thus they leapt up into the air and scrambled back into his mind, some of them going into a benign form of hibernation. Others laughed or sang together; some talked in low voices for hours on end. It was if they had seen someone or something in their adventure out of doors in the big world. They imagined that when they had been frolicking in the sand in the sunshine someone as a tall as a mountain had been watching them, standing there not very far away. The figure had been so huge, so much part of the landscape, they could not comprehend it in its entirety. There had been a voice too. A long slow voice had been talking high above them — wonderful wise words they had been, in a language they had so wanted to remember, and asked each other what it was they had heard, who it was they had seen standing there. Stephen could hear them now, murmuring in his mind. The goblins had become little rosy-faced men, some of them with beards and brightly coloured suits. He could catch fragments of their conversation about the big world outside and — what was it? — a tall kindly lady was it? And he felt that he too had been there with them, one of them perhaps, and he also had seen and heard that gigantic figure on the sand. It was something to do with the sea, and yet it was also something to do with Bruce. The movement of the waves and the shining of Bruce's eyes — what was it that was common to both of them? Whatever it was, Stephen knew it was something beyond his understanding and it filled him with an unfamiliar sense of wonder. Here was something he could feel, something which could affect him, yet which no matter how hard he tried he could not grasp. He knew too that whatever it was now a constant inspiration to him. It was immensely powerful, but the power was not the kind that emperors wield, it was the kind of power that those who held it shared with all that came into their presence. It was like a gift but not one that one received and expressed thanks for. The gift was never wholly received, yet the giving never ceased, and the anticipation of receiving never waned. It was like a marvellous skein of cloth being fed out from two hands as smoothly as the thread from a spider's belly and piled into his arms. There were wonderful patterns on the cloth — embroidered flowers, painted abstract designs and jewelled embossments. Each as it appeared was unique and each carried within it a promise of the next. Stephen for the first time in his life began to believe in something he could not believe. Perhaps, he thought, this was what God was, God freed of all the crippling trappings of churches and temples and priests, God unadorned, raw, untrammelled by the feeble minds of men who are so inept at understanding things greater than themselves. Man demeaned everything, he reduced everything to a human and, now Stephen realized, pathetically miserable size. Man tried to explain everything, to squeeze all miracles into books and pictures, to count and measure and assess everything with numbers and petty maxims. If only he would not try to manage and categorize experience, man might really begin to experience the marvels, the realities he is offered. God did not need to be cut and dried and catalogued. Stephen walked along the shore, rejoicing in the discovery that the mysterious was no less tangible than the billions of grains of sand beneath his feet.

He stopped suddenly. Something was sticking out of the sand a yard in front of him, something horribly pink which gleamed unnaturally in the warm light. It was a doll. Stephen had a horror of dolls. They had always unaccountably filled him with fear the origin of which was no doubt buried in lost memories of his childhood. Whenever he saw a doll he recoiled, his eyes glittering. There was something so irretrievably dead about dolls, as if they mocked life. A corpse he could bear. Even his grandmother in her coffin four days dead, her face veiled with a misty web of inchoate putrefaction, was preferable to the glossy fixed lifeless smile of a doll. The starry blue heavily-lashed eyes, intended to express and attract childlike innocence, were to Stephen more depraved than those of a woman who had spent a lifetime of dissipation. The absence of genitals, too, was terrifying − a race that could never beget offspring, a child that could never be raped. And worst of all was when the face got broken or crushed in. Stephen had once seen a doll with its china face smashed. The black hole next to the glassy smile seemed to contain the entire universe. Stephen had been afraid of falling into that hole, of being drawn helplessly in to a hideously wakeful oblivion. The hole was the essence of nightmare, and his nightmares were always filled with the shattered faces of dolls. The doll at his feet was not a very big one. It had rigid plastic arms and legs; one arm, one leg and half its body were buried in the sand. Stephen knelt down, his heart beating strongly with a kind of horrified fascination, to examine it more closely. It had silky blonde nylon hair. Its blue eyes were the kind that opened and closed. One of them was missing and the socket was full of sand instead. Petrified yet half thrilled with curiosity, Stephen touched the doll, unable to keep his hands away from it. He pulled at its arm and then sat back with a sudden shock of new terror. The doll was not buried in the sand; it was only half a doll split from the groin to the neck. Only the head, except for the missing eye, was whole. The other half was lost somewhere at the bottom of the sea or lying exposed to the glare of the sun in the desert of sand behind him. A wave of pity struck him. This doll had once been a comfort to a child. A little girl had talked to it, lovingly dressed and undressed its stiff body. Where was that child now? And what floods of tears had she shed at the loss of her precious baby? Even that was sorrow. Children have to grow old. It is not time that ages us, makes our hair go grey and deepens the lines in our faces. It is sorrow that after sorrow that does that, sorrow and excess of joy. Stephen firmly believed that the intense joy of orgasm repeated again and again was one of the greatest causes of senescence. Here was the wreckage of a toy and somehow the experience of finding it like this was more gruesome than Bruce's murder of the gannet the previous day.

Something to his left caught his attention. There was a break in the sand dunes at that point and a small gully about as big as two double-decker buses had been gouged out by the wind. There was something red there, something yellow and pink. It was moving. Stephen stood up and tried to make out what it was. With a new leaping up of horror he thought it was another doll come alive, a much bigger life-sized doll. It seemed to be crouching down in the sand in a kind of cage; the movements were small and quick. It was human. It was a boy.

He was wearing red shorts and a yellow shirt. His hair was blonde and came down over his ears and neck but it was not excessively long. Stephen's homosexual experiences usually involved men older than himself but they did not exclude young boys, especially those as attractive as this one appeared to be; and Bruce's own fascinations had heightened Stephen's interest in this direction also. A boy alone in the sand dunes, and no one but Stephen with him. How envious Bruce would be when he told him! Or perhaps he would not tell him. This was his own special discovery, better kept to himself perhaps. It might lead to something remarkable. The boy was humming softly and busily working with his hands. Whatever was he doing? He was so deeply absorbed in his business that he had not yet noticed Stephen. Stephen took a few paces nearer. The boy looked up, smiled and stood up. One glance at his figure told Stephen he had been mistaken. It was not a boy after all. It was a girl.

19. WIND CAGE

STEPHEN HAD NEVER been in love with a girl. Indeed, he had had very little to do with girls all his life. An encounter at the age of eleven had left him with an ingrained fear of the opposite sex. One day after school a girl two years older than himself had insisted on showing him her genitals in a deserted classroom. As with dolls in a sense, he had been afraid of falling into that dark, moist orifice between her thighs. The insidious movement there and a strange sickly odour had filled him with terror, disgust and finally violent anger. She had been so confident and overbearing, her laughter unforgettably wicked and scornful. She had then thrown herself at Stephen and kissed him roughly, wetly on the mouth. He had been so surprised that he fell over, and the girl had tried to open his flybuttons and pull his trousers off. He had suddenly struggled to his feet and with the full strength of his arm hit her with a backhanded slap across the face. Then he had run away. There was another cause for his anger. Nature, Stephen had come to realize, had not endowed him well. Boys had mocked him in the school changing room, gleefully calling out 'Little-Prick Pee-wit!' ruthlessly and time and time again. This is why he hated the idea of swimming in public, he was afraid of betraying the miserable outlines of his anatomy. Some his aging pederast bedfellows had also sometimes expressed initial disappointment. Stephen felt resentment against the world that had treated him so unjustly. In addition to this, his mother had not wanted a son. When he was a child she had always dressed him as a girl and let his hair grow long and curly. Stephen had felt himself to be somehow unnatural from an early age. Early discovery of self-gratification led to a nightly habit that rarely changed. His erotic fantasies never included girls.

Yet here was something different. His first disappointment at finding that this boy was after all a girl did not last long. There was something in the simple frankness of her smile, in the boyishness of her figure, that immediately attracted him. She must have been about seventeen. Her arms and legs were sturdy, as if earlier puppy fat had hardened rather than entirely disappeared. Her hips were narrow, not broad and rounded like a woman's; her buttocks too were quite prominent and not flat and sagging in her shorts. Shorts suited her, and her yellow shirt, hanging free, made her small firm breasts seem infinitely touchable. Stephen was instantly fascinated. He smiled back.

'What are you making?'

The girl knelt down again and continued her strange work. The contraption at the sandy bottom of the gully was something the like of which Stephen had never seen before in his life. There was a roughly circular framework, not unlike an inverted lobster pot with its bottom ripped off. To this the girl had tied irregular lengths of driftwood, white curving sticks, smooth boards, forked branches with gleaming brown bark still on them. They stood up like the remnants of a petrified forest. She had driven stakes into the sand at each side of the gully, about half a dozen of them, and these were linked together with fine white string, which was also stretched across the gully and connected with the upper extremities of the central basket-like arrangement – something like the combination of a kite, an early flying machine and a primitive radio aerial. The girl was 'inside' the structure tying things to the lengths of string at intervals – pieces of tinsel, strands of dried black seaweed, shrivelled sea-slugs with their headless four-legged bodies, bits of sea holly, even a few razor shells and fragments of cuttlefish bone. Empty bottles and cans dangled like orchestral bell-chimes inside the basket. 'Sails' made of paper were fastened to thin slivers of cane also stuck in the sand. There was a toy plastic windmill, its stick broken in half and its sea-battered vanes motionless in the absence of a breeze. The curious assemblage was something a child might have constructed, yet it had too greatly developed a form to be an infantile product. The overall design and the balance of its disparate parts made it almost insanely beautiful. It was a work of art.

'This is my wind cage. Do you like it?'

'What's it for?'

'To capture the wind. I want to listen to the voices of the wind, but there isn't any.' She licked her finger and held it up above her head. Her fresh-complexioned face seemed suddenly serious, possessed of an age-old wisdom and depth. 'I can't feel any. Can you?'

Stephen licked his finger in the same way and held it up. It was very faintly cool on its seaward side. He had never done such a thing before and he was surprised to find how readily he had obeyed the girl and how natural the action seemed. The girl stood up again and climbed out of her wind cage.

'Shall we whistle for the wind?' She emitted a low tuneless whistle, and for a moment Stephen shivered. It was like something the wind itself might engender from the vast sandy wastes beyond the dunes. 'Please help me. If two of us do it, we might encourage a breeze to come up. I feel sure there's one hanging about somewhere waiting to be invited.'

Stephen whistled, following her example. The twin notes formed a weird discord. The girl suddenly burst out laughing.

'How funny! I don't even know who you are.'

'My name's Stephen.' He felt as if he had betrayed a secret.

'Stephen. I'm Vera. I've seen you on the beach before. Do you live here?'

'No, I'm staying in the house along there. The one with the red roof.'

'I like that house. Can I come and see it? How lovely to stay there so close to the sea! Can you hear it when you're lying in bed?'

'Yes.' Stephen had heard it, almost every night. It was like a person breathing softly somewhere high up under the sloping ceiling walls of his room. He paused, wondering how to continue. He felt that this girl had disarmed him, with her open, guileless words had somehow entered the privacy of his room. 'You're from the College, aren't you?'

'Yes, I'm doing art. Well, I have to do other things too. French, Maths, such silly things. I like art best. I'm going to be an artist.'

'Do you paint pictures?'

'Sometimes. But I like making things like this better. Painting's not real art. I want to use natural things, like the wind or the sea, and stones and sand. I once collected lots of shining things and made a sun cage. Have you ever seen the sunlight?'

'How do you mean?'

'Trapped sunlight. It's like animals made of glass. They scream to get out.' She spoke with such childlike enthusiasm, yet Stephen had the impression he was listening to the words of a genius.

'What a delightful idea!'

'What do you do?'

'I'm a writer.' Stephen wondered how true this was. He was divided between doubt and pride, a kind of guilt filled his mind.

'What do you write? Are you a poet?' The girl looked at him accusingly.

'No, I write novels.' Again Stephen hesitated. What would Bruce say if he heard him speaking like this? He sounded almost established, but the truth was he had not even half finished one novel. What did it mean to be a novelist? Could one be a writer without finishing anything? Stephen felt sure he was a writer, but he was not yet an author. Perhaps it didn't matter anyway. He modified his statement a little. 'I'm writing a novel now.'

'Is it good? Do you write real novels? I know a lot of novelists, or so they say. They don't know anything; they don't feel anything. And they can't write for nuts. What are yours like?'

'You can read some if you like.' 'Some' sounded good. It actually meant 'some of my novel' but it could mean 'some of my novels'.

'I don't mind, as long as you don't insist on reading them out aloud yourself. That's what most people do. They like the sound of their own voices better than anything else. It's a terrible bore.'

'I don't read mine.' Stephen did not know why he lied to this girl. He had often read parts of his earlier writings to Bruce. He had enjoyed the sound of his own voice, too.

'Oh, that's good. I'd like to build a novel.'

'A cage for words?'

'That's right. I'd like to build it out of stones. A castle for ideas.'

'How would you set about it?'

'There are lots of ways, and plenty of stones along there.' She pointed south. 'But of course I wouldn't use real stones. I'd use the shadows of stone walls, the reflections of mountains in lonely lakes.'

Stephen was enchanted. Her cheerful confidence was amazingly infectious. All sorts of possibilities opened out before him. Mere words and sentences on the white page seemed almost lifeless in comparison to this new concept – a word cage.

'Shall we go for a swim? I'm wearing swimming things underneath.' She lifted the bottom of her shirt, exposing black cloth close against her skin. 'I want to build a dam by the sea.'

Stephen was aware that he had begun to blush.

'I don't have any...I haven't got time. I have to meet my friend.' He wondered where Bruce was at that very moment. Would he suddenly appear at the top of the sand gully and accuse him of dilly-dallying with stupid girls? Would he stand there in his bardic robes and pronounce a terrible judgement?

'How long are you staying here?'

'I'm not sure. Quite a few days, I expect.' How long was he going to stay? And how was he going to get home? The problem of money reared up again like the head of an oily black snake from a marsh.

'You must help me make a dam. I want to collect foam from the edge of the sea. I like the patterns it makes on the sand.'

'Will you be here tomorrow?'

'I often come here. This is my special place. The others don't know about it. They'd laugh at me.'

'The others?' Stephen felt a pang of envy. He was not one of the others.

'Yes, from the College. We often come down to the beach. We made a fire a few days ago. We were burning the darkness. Did you see it?'

'Yes. Were you really one of that group? I don't remember seeing you.' What he did remember was that one of the boys in the group had said they were going to swim naked. This girl naked? The idea excited him.

'Perhaps I was wearing different clothes. I sometimes wear a hat.' Stephen pictured Vera in a hat and nothing else. He smiled slightly.

'Did you see the marsh gas?'

'No. Was there some? What was it like?'

'We saw it from the house. Will o' the wisp. Strange lights floating out to sea.'

'I wish I'd seen them. How marvellous! I want to put some in bottles and make an avenue of lanterns right across the beach and down under the waves. Does it happen often?'

'I don't think so. We've only seen it once.'

'I saw you on the beach that evening. Philip asked you to join us, didn't he? I was collecting sticks for the fire.'

'I had to get back to the house. My friend was waiting.'

'Who is this friend of yours? Is he nice?'

'His name's Bruce. His father owns the house there.'

'Is he a writer too?'

'Yes, he writes poems.'

'Oh.'

Once again Stephen felt like a kind of traitor. Merely to mention Bruce's poetry to this strange girl seemed to him like an act of extreme disloyalty. And yet he enjoyed it. Vera's lack of enthusiasm somehow pleased him.

'I've got to get back now.'

'Must you? I like talking to you. You're different.'

Stephen was not sure how to take this. He had always been different. It had always been a pain to him that it was so, but now this girl seemed to welcome it. There was nothing scornful in her voice.

'You're not like other girls I've met either.' Stephen was amazed when he realized what he had said. It sounded like a line from a film. Boy meets girl. Stephen had never imagined he could find himself in such a situation as this. It was almost a classic beginning. Vera was staring at him.

'I know. I'm not like other girls.' She blew at the vanes of the windmill. 'I wish there was some wind.' The vanes turned two or three times with a whirring sound and stopped. 'Perhaps it'll be windy tomorrow. The others want to make a sand yacht. I love this beach.'

'So do I. I've never been here before.'

'This is my second term. I came here in April.'

'How long will you be here?'

'At least another year. The course is for two years, but I missed the first part. You must come up and see the College.'

'Perhaps I could study there.'

'We're a queer lot up there. We've all had trouble, you know. It's like a madhouse sometimes. You'll have to qualify. Have you ever had any trouble?'

Stephen almost laughed, but he thought it better not to say too much at this stage.

'I expect I could qualify. But I couldn't afford it.'

'The government pays.'

'It wouldn't pay for me.' Stephen hated the idea of state aid for the unfortunate, but he kept silent. He was beginning to worry about Bruce. He had no wish to leave this delightful girl, but he was sure he could meet her again. 'I'll try and come here tomorrow. What are you going to do with your wind cage?'

'I'll smash it if there's no wind tomorrow. But I'll photograph it first. I've got lots of pictures. I'll show you.'

Once again Stephen was aware of a kind of professional authority in the girl. There was no doubt in his mind that Vera was a dedicated artist, a real artist. She was obviously sincere, yet at the same time she had the wonderful clarity and innocence of a child.

'I'll meet you tomorrow.'

'Bye, Stephen.'

They smiled at each other. Stephen climbed up the edge of the sandhills, trying not to stumble, and made his way inland.

*

Bruce had found a dead rabbit. He had almost stepped on it. There had once been a huge population of rabbits in the sand dunes; they even used to play on the grass in front of the house. But the worldwide scourge of myxomatosis some ten years previously had almost completely wiped them out. There had been dead rabbits everywhere, their heads and eyes hideously swollen, their fur coarsened by the disease. And then, a few years later, a new generation had appeared. A few of the strongest had survived and had engendered a scarcer, tougher, perhaps larger, breed. They no longer played with careless abandon. They seemed to have become a bitter, wiser species. The rabbit at Bruce's feet was lying in the middle of the path on its side. The most unpleasant stages of putrefaction had passed, leaving mostly fur and bones. Two curving incisors jutted bravely but somehow delicately from its upper jaw, and behind them two from the lower jaw appeared to have penetrated the roof of the rabbit's mouth. Perhaps they had grown too long and pierced the brain; that sometimes happened. It was strange, Bruce thought, that there were not more corpses like this. The sand dunes must be full of them, but they had found quieter places to die, mostly underground. This one perhaps had died more suddenly or had been too brain-tortured to follow its own instincts. There was evidence of rabbits everywhere. Most of the smaller footpaths in the sandhills had been made by them; there were scatterings of small round dry droppings in numerous grassy hollows and on the paths; their burrows dotted the slopes. Bruce had often wished he was small enough to go down into the warrens and explore their labyrinthine depths. Whole dunes were riddled with tunnels. There would be rooms and chambers, some of them with windows perhaps, or even furnished with wooden tables and chairs; deep, cool places, some of them full of gleaming mounds of treasure. The rabbits were the mild dragons of the Traeth.

But there was another dragon in the Traeth. Most dragons were red or green and spouted flames and smoke, but one here by the sea, dwelling perhaps in that vast stretch of sand they had just gazed down at, was white, white with blind grey eyes. There was no fire in its nostrils, no smoke. It breathed sand; it wandered from hill to hill, circling the hollows insanely, blasting and carving out strange forms. It was a dragon of the wind. For days on end when the weather was calm as now, it lurked along the edge of the sea sniffing the air. It was tethered to the dunes. It skirted the marsh to the north-east, it mourned silently, creeping through the still grasses. In the evenings it rose and spread its body over the Traeth — the low mists that crept there waist high, and in the morning it sidled away. It was waiting for messages from the sea, commands which came and whipped it into madness. Then, unleashed, it went yelling across the flats, burning the legs of those who ventured to walk there on windswept days, shrieking without mind, without ears to hear its own demented howls. Now it was pacing out of sight, like a puma in a cage at night, but seen in reverse as in the negative of a photograph, white against white; and no eyes gleamed. The whole Traeth was a cage for the wind, till someone from the sea sometimes opened the gate and let it out.

Bruce approached the chosen sandhill, skirting round to the east side of it. It was easy to get there without being seen by Stephen, much harder when there was someone keeping guard from the top. That was how it used to be, but now the summit was deserted. Crouching low he climbed up the steepening slope. He wondered if Stephen would already be there, in the hollow at the top, waiting to pounce on him as he came up over the edge. But even as he dismissed the idea as impossible — Stephen was much too slow. Another more terrible idea grew in his mind. His mother would be there, kneeling in the sand in a white cotton night-dress, his mother emaciated and pale, her grey hair hanging straight down either side of her face and her eyes full of frenzied light like the last survivor of a concentration camp or the inmate of some forgotten asylum. She would be crying out 'My eyes! My eyes! There's sand in my eyes!' Then she would point accusingly at Bruce and cry: 'You killed me.' And at that moment Bruce would become his father, mirrored in her stricken eyes. He reached the top and snaked over the rim into the hollow. It was empty. He crossed the few yards to the other side and carefully parting the grasses peered down in the direction of the beach. The sea gleamed in the distance; the dunes below were deserted. Stephen was nowhere in sight. Bruce had got there first. He worked his way round the hollow and looked towards the golf course. There was no one there either, neither the two women nor the four men, nor on the east side where he had just come up. To the south the house stood quietly in the sun. That too had a deserted air. Bruce was alone in the dunes. Or was he? Had Stephen somehow met the four men from the hotel and were they even now wallowing naked together somewhere in the sandhills? Had the two women golfers captured him and beaten him to death with their clubs? Or had some invisible force drawn Stephen back into the sandy waste beyond the big sandhill to the north and was he now wandering there or sinking unheard into the swaying gurgling depths of the marsh? Or worst of all, had he walked into the sea and drowned himself, all his resolution and progress forgotten?

Bruce looked again towards the sea. There was no one in sight anywhere in the great sweep of the bay, and no dark object rolling in the shallow waves. He was sure that if Stephen were coming it would be from that direction. He prowled round the hollow peering out now and again, checking each side. He did not want to be taken by surprise. He returned to the west side; and there was Stephen walking quite openly across the dunes, making not the least attempt to conceal himself. Bruce stood up.

'I can see you!'

Stephen waved, and Bruce caught the white flash of his teeth as he smiled. He sat down on the rim of the hollow and waited for his friend to come nearer.

'Why didn't you hide?'

'I did, but the last part's impossible.'

'You could have come round the south side, between here and the house. There are lots of places to hide that way.'

'I don't know this area as well as you do. Anyway, it would have taken too long. I thought you'd get tired waiting for me.'

'Anyway, I got here first.'

'It was a foregone conclusion.' Stephen's face was flushed. There was a strange brightness about his eyes. Bruce looked at him closely.

'What have you been doing?'

'Nothing. Why?'

'You look funny. Did you meet anyone?'

'There's no one on the beach. Did you see those male golfing ladies?'

'No.'

'I found a broken doll. You know how I feel about dolls.'

'I found a dead rabbit.'

'Do you think we'll get any wind tomorrow?'

'If we eat enough onions for supper tonight.' They both laughed, but Stephen wanted an answer.

'This place must be quite different when the wind blows. Do you think we'll get any?'

'I don't know. We've been having a wonderful spell of weather. It doesn't often stay as fine as this so long. We've been lucky. Do you like it when the wind blows?'

'I wouldn't mind a change.'

Bruce examined the sky.

'We might get a change. Look over there.'

A line of clouds was forming to the south-west over the sea.

20. RAIN

STEPHEN WALKED ALONE along the beach. The sea to his left was sullen grey, the wind, from the south, cool behind his bare legs. The sky was slowly moving clouds, low over the bay. Occasionally he glanced behind him to see if he was being followed. Bruce had announced his intention of digging a hole for the rubbish somewhere behind the house, a chore which had to be attended to at least once a year. Stephen was unable to settle down again to his writing. Images of the girl in the red shorts and yellow shirt constantly filled his mind. He had promised to meet her again and yet he had no wish to tell Bruce about her. Bruce would disapprove, Bruce would warn him off, would even perhaps forbid Stephen to meet her again. He sensed that in this new encounter lay a path towards liberation from the clinging bonds his friend imposed upon him. Better to keep it secret. He felt extraordinarily invigorated and alert. A strange warmness turned within him as if tears, many years of them unshed, had passed from a larva to pupa stage and were now emerging not actually as tears but as a miracle creature of new hope – an imago straining to dry out and stretch its brilliant wings wide into the light of day. This was his own private discovery, to be shared with no one, his own boy-girl by the sea. He had worried at first when he had told Bruce there was no one on the beach. It was a lie of course, but Stephen allowed himself to stretch the truth a little. Vera had not actually been on the beach; she had not come out of the gully while he had been there. She was in the sandhills, and when Bruce had asked him whether he had met anyone, Stephen hadn't answered directly. He felt justified in not telling his friend about the girl, he even enjoyed the sense of power it gave him, and all that evening and the next morning he had been thinking about her. It was impossible to write. He had intended to wait until the afternoon, when going out for a walk would have been more natural and also perhaps there would be more certainty that Vera would be there. He had hoped to conclude at least one more chapter of his novel, as a kind of sop to his conscience, but as he sat at the table in his room having moved his work up there from downstairs, he found himself gazing out of the window and staring at the endlessly turning waves. Making an effort and reading over what he had already written, he felt there was something cheap about it all, something artificial, unreal, irrelevant. He flung down his pen and stood up. From the window, facing south, he could see Bruce busy at work cutting out squares of turf and laying them face down around the square patch intended for the hole. Even then he was able to marvel at his friend's immense energy. Bruce never seemed to get tired. He was always, with very few exceptions, almost obsessively active, a clockwork engine that never needed to be wound up. Stephen tidied up his papers and stepped carefully down the creaking stairs. He opened the front door, closed it quietly behind him, and running down the path escaped to the beach.

This morning the line of the sand dunes seemed to be different. The wind made them almost like the sea itself, the long grasses constantly waving. But it wasn't only that: there seemed to be more gaps between them, more indentations where pathways came out onto the beach, more little gullies like the one where he had met Vera, and all of them were empty. He hadn't remembered it being like that. Yesterday there had been one unbroken line with only one inlet – the wind-cage gully where Vera, magician and genius, crouched over her fascinating machine. Perhaps it was only magic. Perhaps it had all been a kind of dream, a daylight ghost – a child of the shore, divinely mad and never to be met again. There had been something unreal about the entire encounter, something as vividly surrealistic as a yellow grand piano at the edge of the sea with a red lobster at the keyboard picking up the keys like mah-jongg tiles in its claws and eating them one by one. Her smile, her voice, her strangely dual-sexed body, were somehow of another world altogether. A small hook of fear gnawed at Stephen's stomach. She wouldn't be there. Instead it would be a hideous grimalkin, grey-haired and withered there, stooping, one finger stroking a huge lower lip, and spinning twine from mixed strands of seaweed and sea-grasses.

Then he heard the wind cage. The sounds were only faint, for the wind was hardly strong enough to move the dangling objects. There was no clinking of bottles or cans, only the soft whirring of the windmill and fluttering of tinsel and paper, the faint knocking of hanging pieces of wood and shells; but it was there. He had found it.

He reached the entrance of the gully. Vera was not there. Half of the structure had collapsed, as if someone had half-heartedly destroyed it. It appeared utterly derelict, a forgotten masterpiece, as if the wind it had tried to master had objected to such confinement and had in a flurry of spite kicked at it with invisible hoofs. The windmill was hanging upside down; the bottles and cans lay on the ground. It was the carcase of a bird which had crash-landed in the desert, its flesh rapidly consumed by hyenas of the wind, only a wreckage of delicate bones and white feathers left to be scattered in the sand.

Stephen felt all his old resentment against the world welling up again, as if his brain was vomiting within his skull without the relief of being voided and cleansed. A dull familiar headache throbbed behind his forehead. This was the old story. People could not be depended on. There was no one who cared, no one after all who cared for him. The wave of anger crashed down and melted in a foaming spread of tragic thoughts, self-pity and destruction. He kicked at the wind cage and savagely stamped on what remained of the structure. She had not come, and she had promised to be there. She was just like other girls — fickle and scornful. Yet. Stephen could not forget those small firm breasts beneath the loosely hanging shirt. Supposing she should come now with her camera and see what he had done? Stephen knelt down and tried to reconstruct the wind cage, but his hands were trembling and he had no patience or ability. It was all useless. The quivering wings of the butterfly collapsed into a dull worm of self-contempt. He suddenly lay face down in the sand and wept, feeling the tears running through the fingers pressed to his eyes and dripping into the sand. And supposing she were to come now? He wanted her to caress his brow gently, to put a childlike arm round his shoulder and utter soothing words. But it would never be like that: she would stand there, hands on her hips, laughing at him in his misery. What was this misery? He could not understand what it was that had actually prompted his tears, why he should be so deeply moved because she had broken her promise, which after all was only a casual understanding. Surely, there were countless reasons for her not being there. But someone had been there, the wind alone could not have caused such damage to the wind cage. Perhaps she never came there in the morning, perhaps she was even now attending a class, perhaps she was ill. Perhaps...reasons and excuses piled up in Stephen's mind, but he was in no condition to be reasonable.

He sat up. Someone seemed to be laughing, a low hissing chuckle. He stood up, climbed up the side of the gully and looked inland over the dunes. There was no one in sight. He turned and faced the sea. The beach was also deserted. But the waves, in their repetitive sameness, were open-eyed and alive. It was they who were laughing. The sea was mocking him. The sea was mocking all human predicament, Stephen included. Man was such a pathetic creature. His sorrows and loves, his endeavours in society and art, all so soon evaporated in futility and despair; and the sea was always there – impassive, benignly weeping while at the same time ironically smiling. The chuckles were the waves. It began to rain, softly, finely. Stephen turned his hot face into the cool wind.

Until coming to Harlieg, Stephen had always shunned the open air. Rain for him, snow or bright sunlight, were always inconveniences he tried to avoid. He had possessed a succession of hats and umbrellas, many of which he had mislaid in coffee shops, bars and other people's houses, and walking in the rain was always an event of extreme discomfort – saturated trouser legs and cuffs, soggy shoes; rain was always the harbinger of depression and misery. Now, as he sensed the fine skein of sea-rain on his face, he felt that it came as a kind of blessing, as an unadorned baptism, free of all the trappings of religion and ritual. He tilted his face up to catch more of the refreshing anointment. He closed his eyes and felt the coolness of the moisture on his eyelids. He opened his eyes. The air was a dazzling whiteness above him and surprisingly close to his eyes, and the sun was trying to reach him through the vapour. It was like, he thought, being inside a painting by Turner. He rolled his head from side to side, drops ran down his neck into his shirt. He raised his arms, palms upturned, and stood there like a martyr, feeling that crucifixion, if it were to come now, would come like an ever-nearing promise of paradise. All his discomfiture melted away, self-pity and hatred melted with it. If it were so destined that he was always to be rejected, then so be it. He would be heroic, a stoic saint, trained and ready to endure anything and everything that came his way; he would have the courage of a Spartan warrior braving enemies and elements alike; he would be a hero. More tears came. They mingled with the rain on his face, but they were tears of gentleness and joy, and even as he shed them he smiled and turned his face almost lovingly towards the sea. He found himself speaking, curiously poetic and sentimental, like a poor imitation of the things Bruce wrote.

'Therefore, ocean, let me stand here with you. Since there is no longer anyone who cares, why should I care either? How easy it would be now to walk in a straight line into your waves and disappear smiling into the comfort of the soft voices you endlessly utter!'

He half jumped, half slid down the side of the gully onto the beach, and his hands stretched out before him like a blind man, walked towards the sea.

*

Bruce stood in the square hole, his face level with the ground. He felt the satisfaction of having completed a troublesome task. The hole was about two yards square at the top but almost half the size at his feet, and it would be difficult to continue deeper as there was hardly enough space to manoeuvre the shovel, and it was getting hard to lift the sand so high. The sand smelt good, fresh and damp, somehow virgin. Black and yellow roots of the thorns and grasses projected from the sides of the hole like severed worms or empty veins and arteries. He would have liked to carve out a huge chamber underground, but he knew there was danger of a cave-in. Several children had been suffocated to death some ten years before while digging tunnels in the sandhills. His mother had often warned him; such warnings were now pure instinct and common sense, but how fascinating it would be to have a palace underground lighted with candles, with oak furniture and tapestries, a four-poster bed with damask curtains – not small and rabbit-sized as he had imagined the previous day, but full-scale, a real subterranean mansion with open fireplaces, halls filled with paintings, music rooms, galleries lined with statues.

He smiled as he thought that if he dug any deeper he might not be able to get out of the hole. It was going to be difficult enough as it was. He leaned the shovel against one of the sides and lifted one foot onto the handle. Clutching at the tough clumps of grass at the top of the hole he hauled himself up. The blade of the shovel sank deep under his weight but he managed to crawl out and lay on the grass and thorns, feeling them sharp against his body. The unevenness of the ground pressed pleasantly against his genital area and he lay there a while his eyes closed, like a child experiencing the first faint stirrings of sexuality without realizing what it was. The ground smelt so pure and clean! Bruce opened his eyes and was startled to see a faded green grasshopper staring at him close to his face. He waited for it to spring suddenly but it did not move, then he saw that it was dead. Levering himself to one side a little and reaching one arm down into the hole, he lifted out the shovel and stood up, brushing the sand from his shirt and shorts.

For the first time he noticed it was raining. The weather had broken after all. He went round to the front of the house and felt the strand of seaweed hanging from the verandah roof, and as he expected it was moist and leathery. Maybe it really did work as a kind of sea-barometer, at least as a measure of humidity. The rain could not reach it where it hung and yet it was damp. He glanced into the living room and saw that it was empty. Of course, Stephen was working up in his room. He went into the house and called up the stairs.

'Stephen!'

There was no answer.

'Stephen! Are you up there?'

The house was silent. He went outside and looked towards the beach, but mist had come in from the sea and only the foreground was visible, the beach and sandhills fading away into the fallen sky. He looked towards the cliff. The hotel and college could just be seen but with a shock Bruce saw that the castle had entirely disappeared. Being much further from the house than the other two buildings it was hidden in the mist. Its absence was striking. Bruce had seen the phenomenon countless times before in his childhood but it always took him by surprise. With the castle missing, something vital and central was removed from the scenery, from the spirit of the place; the coast must have been magnificently bleak a thousand years before. The top of the cliff above the house was also invisible and there were drifting sheets of rain-mist scudding along above the railway line. Somewhere above him he could feel the sun teasingly trying to poke holes through the thin roof of cloud.

Bruce frowned. Stephen had been strangely thoughtful and noncommunicative the evening before and also at breakfast this morning, as if there had been something, not necessarily unpleasant, on his mind. He had smiled a little from time to time as if he possessed some secret, but no questioning from Bruce could penetrate his friend's mind. Bruce knew well enough not to probe too far. On previous occasions he had angered Stephen with his excessive curiosity. But then Bruce's father was like that – always asking directly intimate questions. How did he spend his pocket money? Who was that girl he had spoken to at the theatre? How many times had he kissed a girl? Horrible questions, and his father had always been angry when Bruce refused to answer or gave only vague replies. It was only in recent years that Bruce had found that he himself sometimes attempted the same morbid probing into Stephen's privacy. But now, once again, he felt that slight weakening of his hold over his friend.

The telephone rang inside the house. The sound of the telephone in Tremarfon always filled Bruce with strange feelings of desolation. The house became remote, a solitary dwelling in the wilderness with this single slender link with the outside world. It was especially so on days like this when sea-mist emphasized the isolation, and there was something melancholy, forlorn, in the actual sound of the bell ringing insistently in the wooden house. He remembered evenings with all the family there, the loud conversation, the sudden ringing, the hush as his father picked up the receiver, the bad line, the repeated 'Hullo, hullo', the news from far away in the Midlands, his grandmother's last, fatal, stroke. There were other occasions too, on stormy days, when gusts of sea-wind made the telephone lines outside touch occasionally causing faint clinks of the bell in the living room.

He went into the house and picked up the receiver. It was Bob Evans, the brother of the hotel barman.

'I was wondering if it would be all right to come down today and check the fire precautions.'

'Yes, I think it'll be all right. What time about?'

'Well, sometime after tea, I think. Will you be in then?'

'Yes. Do you need the level-crossing key?'

'No, I'll walk down from the top, thanks. And one more thing. Your father wants me to do a general check – all the house over, to check for leaks, you know. The winter'll be on us before we know. Will that be all right?'

Bruce said it would be all right and presently replaced the receiver. He went outside again. The rain was increasing and the cliff was now almost entirely invisible even from the house which was barely two hundred yards away from it. The hotel and the college had gone. The wind, however, was no stronger.

Bruce wondered what to do. Without his friend there, safely writing in his room upstairs, he felt unsettled. In any case, he himself was still not in a writing mood, had not written any poetry for weeks. He needed calm for that, and living with Stephen was anything but calm, though he knew a time would come later. He felt slightly envious now that Stephen was writing so fluently and yet faintly irritated when he did not as now stick to it. He must have gone for a walk, but checking the hall he found his friend's macintosh hanging there as usual. Surely Stephen would never venture out in the rain without a coat? But perhaps it hadn't been raining when he went out. Where was Stephen? Perhaps he was sleeping; or worse, and it came to Bruce as a sudden thrill of anticipation, perhaps he was dead. He went upstairs to Stephen's room and opened the door.

The bed was an untidy jumble of blankets and sheets. Books and clothes were scattered on the other bed and also on the floor. Stephen's writing materials lay on the table by the window arranged tidily but looking somehow neglected. The air smelt of body; obviously Stephen had not opened the window once since he had been at Tremarfon. Another smell came to Bruce's nostrils – from the waste-paper basket. He glanced into it, both fascinated and disgusted. A sense of his own chasteness filled him with a glow of moral superiority. At the same time, he felt the futility of so much human life wasted – rejected with its aftermath of disgust as so much rubbish. Life was no more than this – a combination in darkness of strong-smelling fluids. All spirit, all soul, inspiration, art, love, depended on this slippery issue from the body of man. It was disgusting, humiliating, ridiculous. Once again Bruce found himself loathing his own body, all human bodies. Animals. But animals were far more fortunate, having no minds to know of their own sordid beginnings, of their miserable ends. Depressed and full of pessimism, Bruce left the room and went downstairs. He made no attempt to read Stephen's novel on the table. He knew that if he did so he would never be able to act naturally with his friend should they ever discuss it. Sooner or later he would betray the fact that he had pried. Even the discovery he had just made up in Stephen's room would be difficult enough to hide. In the living room, Bruce picked up an old Argosy magazine left by some tenant years before, chose a story he almost knew by heart from having read it so often – in vacant times such as this – and half sat, half reclined in the window seat. Outside, the rain fell silently on the grass, on the sand beyond it, and further out upon the sea itself.

*

Stephen had taken no more than a few paces when he heard voices. Opening his eyes and looking to his right he saw four men, the same four from the hotel and the day before on the golf course, emerge from the sand dunes onto the beach about a hundred yards away. He quickly withdrew to the opening of the wind-cage gully and keeping out of sight watched them. They were about to go swimming. Stephen was surprised. They had said in the hotel bar that they were only going to stay for a day. They must have changed their plans. Typical, he thought, unconsciously disassociating himself from the kind of people he had spent so much time with in the past. With bursts of high-pitched laughter they started to undress. The older man seemed to have difficulty getting his trousers off while one of the others held an umbrella over him. He showed signs of unhealthy obesity and could hardly keep his balance. The others laughed at him as he stood awkwardly in his fawn flannel vest and large underpants. He lowered the pants exposing white flabby buttocks and as he bent down to remove them from his feet Stephen caught sight of dangling, exhausted genitals which even the cool breeze from behind him could do nothing to tighten. The man pulled on white swimming trunks and removed his vest. The others had changed more discreetly, and now Stephen stared with disgust at their white bodies, just beginning to show signs of overweight at the stomach; one of them had acne-like spots all over his back. They covered their clothes with towels and the umbrella to protect them from the rain and ran giggling and shrieking towards the sea. Seeing the umbrella there on the sand, like a black witch crouching down over some carrion, Stephen again had a sense of the surreal. This beach was no place for an umbrella, especially one like this, smart and black from the city. He pictured the beach covered with a thousand such umbrellas – that would be more interesting, especially if they turned into large periwinkles each with a bespectacled hermit crab inside it murmuring psalms. Hearing more cries from the sea as the coldness of the water caught the men above the thighs, Stephen wondered how he could have found such people attractive in the past. There was no dignity, nothing in any way pleasant or charming about them. They really seemed to him now to belong to the dregs of humankind. Here by the sea he had become aware of his own body, its softness and ugliness; yet he knew that in the week he had been staying there something had changed. He found new strength in his legs and arms, an unbelievable toughness, which now, seeing these four pallid bathers, he rejoiced at. Breathing full breaths now delighted him; even self-gratification had taken on a new urgency and all the functions of his body had rejuvenated themselves. His misery of a few minutes earlier had left him and this too filled him with a sense of wonder. Human emotions were so fickle, the mind could sink and revive as quickly as the movements of water on the surface of the sea. He stood in the rain, enjoying his sense of wellbeing.

The mist, he noticed, had come lower. The swimmers, if that is what they could be called, were hardly visible. He decided to return to the house, but he would go via the sandhills so as not to be seen by the four men. Vera might come later. He would visit the gully again in the afternoon. He worked his way into the dunes, enjoying the isolation they offered. The cliff was invisible and the higher sandhills seemed to reach up into the mist like huge mountains. The desolation had vanished. Now everything was close and somehow friendly. The aloneness was manageable.

He reached the top of a slope and stopped suddenly, sinking down to his knees. Something was moving in the sandy hollow before him. Two people were there, both of them naked. Red shorts and yellow shirt thrown aside in the sand told Stephen the identity of one of them. They were copulating vigorously. Stephen watched, fascinated. The sight was quite new to him, even more so in such a place and time, and he crouched low behind the long grasses and stared. The couple emitted little grunts of pleasure; their bodies worked rhythmically, the undulating movements gradually gaining momentum. Hands and feet scrabbled in the sand. They rolled a little from side to side, forcing themselves together in a frenzy of erotic fervour. Stephen who a moment ago had observed the sagging bodies of the four bathers, was amazed at the clean, virile energy he was now a witness to. There was nothing loose here; both were bristling with raw vitality, hot and pink in the cool rain. Stephen felt his own body involuntarily beginning to awaken, but mental anguish prevented further physical sensation. Vera was under the boy, one of the college students, he supposed. His Vera. He wanted to rush down into the hollow and wrench them apart, but he was afraid of being hurt, as by wild animals disturbed. He would never have guessed, seeing her yesterday so innocently at work on her wind cage, that Vera was this kind of girl. That she was a willing partner could not be doubted now; he wondered how often she had enjoyed activity of this nature. Perhaps this was the first time. Somehow she had seemed to Stephen to be above all bodily concerns, yet here she was in the throes of sexual ecstasy.

The couple were reaching the peak of their physical encounter, their grunts turning into rapid gasps and thin cries. The movements became intense, almost violent, and then suddenly reached a zenith with four or five slower heaving billows of fusion; but even then they both seemed unsatisfied and continued their efforts until, suddenly exhausted, the boy broke away and rolled over onto his back, both of them panting like dogs and Vera giggling at the same time. Stephen ducked back down behind the slope. His own body now demanded his attention, and he ran crouching low through the sandhills till he found a small overhanging bank hidden by a grassy ridge. Dragging off his cut-off shorts he masturbated with almost brutal speed into his handkerchief. For a moment he too was blinded with ecstasy, but the instant it was over he was overwhelmed by a misery and a loneliness more intense than he had ever known. He got up, all exhilaration gone, and walking slowly in the finely falling, soaking rain, left both scenes of shame and degradation behind him.

Twenty minutes later, as he toiled uncomfortably up the path to the house, he began to think more rationally. Jealousy, hatred and revenge were after all real almost tangible emotions. So often, Stephen thought, such sentiments were scorned as mere extremes of melodrama, not to be accepted either in fact or in fiction. Now he could see them as knots of mental agony, almost like cancers in the flesh, things that filled the whole mind and body with sustained pain, and he wished he could cut them out with a knife. Vera was nothing less than, what? – A tart. She had, Stephen was now quite decided, behaved with utter, libidinous abandon in the hollow. But yet...she was also a fascinating and original personality. Could it really have been the same girl? Perhaps the red shorts and yellow shirt were a kind of college uniform. Wishful thinking. No, there was no doubt that it had been Vera. He remembered her laugh. He could not forget the wind cage and their conversation the day before. That was no fiction either. What he had seen in the hollow was another side to her nature, another – now he realized with a shock of anticipation – marvellous possibility. Perhaps what he wanted from Vera or with Vera was that very same. He found himself unable to censure her for her behaviour. Rather he felt anger against the boy for using her with such apparent ease for his own pleasure and satisfaction. That was what rankled most. A new determination to meet Vera again, somewhere, somehow, established itself in Stephen's mind.

The rain was no longer refreshing to him and he was cold. His clothes were saturated with water and as the rain ran down his face and touched his lips it tasted faintly of salt. It was as if the sea had sent up clouds of cold clinging anger to enclose him to the skin as punishment. Punishment for what? What had he ever done to deserve such persecution? Not only people, the elements too constantly made living a torture to him. Everything was set up against him. He was tired, hungry; all he wanted was to lie down in front of a warm fire and sleep and not talk with anyone, not listen to anyone. He had lost all interest in his novel, that too would be a failure. After all, only people counted and people too had failed. The recent events had swept him off his feet, as if, he remembered, he was standing at the edge of the sea, his feet sinking into the sand under the shallow swirling waves.

The house emerged from the mist above him. He stepped silently onto the concrete base of the verandah and peered in through the living-room window. At first he thought there was no one inside, but then he saw Bruce in the window seat asleep, his head resting on a book. Stephen opened the front door quietly and made his way upstairs. He took off his clothes and dried himself with a towel, eyeing the wet garments with distaste. As he dressed himself in dry clothes he noticed a cigarette on the floor. Stephen had not brought any cigarettes upstairs for the last day or two and he at once knew that Bruce had been in his room. He went downstairs, carrying his wet clothes in a bundle.

Bruce was standing in the living room staring out of the window at the rain. Stephen handed him the cigarette.

'You dropped this in my room.'

'Did I? How do you know it isn't one of yours?'

'I haven't got any up there.'

'Oh.'

'What were you doing in my room?'

'Is it your room—? I was checking to see if anything needed to be done. There's a man coming down this afternoon.'

'Did you read my novel?'

'No.'

Their eyes met. Guilt clouded the faces of both of them, but neither knew the real reason for the other's discomfiture.

'Where've you been?'

'For a walk.'

'You never told me.'

'Do I have to?'

'No, but it's better if we know where each other is. Why didn't you take your coat?'

'It wasn't raining when I went out.'

'You must have got very wet. Do you want to dry those clothes by the fire?'

'Yes.' Stephen began to hang them one by one on the fender. Remembering the soiled handkerchief in the pocket of his shorts he took it out with distaste and threw it into the fire. He turned to Bruce, smiling slightly. 'How's your hole?'

Normally such a question would have inspired a spate of wordplay and laughter, but Bruce made no reaction and Stephen's smile faded. They both seemed to have retired into private worlds. Communication between them had almost ceased. They sat at the table but neither spoke. The only sound was the crackling and spitting of the fire which Bruce had made up before Stephen came down from his room.

'Don't you want to write now? We can't do much outside.'

'I'm not in the mood.'

'You can't wait for the mood. You have to make it.'

'The rain gets on my nerves. I haven't got used to the sudden change in the weather.'

Bruce could understand him. The house was like a cage in which they paced like lions almost blind. The mist outside and the rain hung like a heavy veil over them. It was almost difficult to breathe, claustrophobic. The sea seemed to be breathing inland and its breath took away all human energy. The two friends were exhausted. There was nothing to do, nothing they wanted to do. Like two male lions growing old in captivity they watched the endless rain through the bars of their cage.

21. FACES

AFTER AN ALMOST SILENT lunch Stephen, while Bruce went to fetch the milk, took another walk along the beach. He somehow knew he would not find Vera at work on her wind cage and he was not mistaken. The smashed structure lay as he had last seen it. Though the mist had lifted considerably, the rain and wind had increased, but Stephen had hardly noticed this on his way to the gully for they came from behind him. The sea was a distant thunder of grey and white, a long line of endlessly crying breakers – far away, and yet they seemed to be turning with the same interminable roar inside his skull. The beach was deserted and shining with the excess of moisture on its surface. He turned round and walked back towards the house, feeling the full force of the wind in his face and against his body. His grimy shorts had dried and he was now wearing them again but this time his upper body was protected by his macintosh; he also wore his hat. It would be no use looking for Vera in the sandhills. He was not even sure if he could have found the place where he had last seen her. In any case she would not be there now; moreover, he did not want her to know that he had seen her that morning. He wondered where she was now – comfortably in a warm college room, perhaps, eating hot buttered toast and listening to jazz. She might even be climbing on the roof of the college or cutting down one of the pine trees beside the railway line, anything was possible with her. And Stephen was here alone on the beach with only the indifferent sea for companion. Self-pity eventually takes away all that is romantic, destroys all that is heroic. Self-pity breeds utter mediocrity, and Stephen knew that of all the things he feared most it was of being mediocre, becoming a middle-aged nonentity in a raincoat; one of those lonely men who stand in public parks staring not longingly but fixedly at children and sometimes exposing themselves, or who sit near those soul-destroying mainly-forgotten monuments in city centres muttering at the pigeons. There was one such man in Birmingham who haunted his memory, a man in bedraggled brown corduroy trousers and a blackened raincoat shiny with age. He suffered from a grotesque persecution mania or some such aberration, for as he daily came out of the Art Gallery at the end of the afternoon, having spent the morning wandering round the huge gloomy rooms and sitting in the restaurant afterwards, he would take a few paces along the street and then stop and look behind him, then retrace a few steps as if he had forgotten something, then once again continue his forward progress, repeating the same forwards-and-back-a-few-steps motion with painful slowness, gradually moving further and further away towards whatever place he spent the night at. Sometimes when he turned back he shook a fist and shouted some unintelligible words at an invisible enemy, standing there in bewilderment when there was no response. It was always a distressing sight to Stephen, yet when he was with friends and they saw the man they sometimes laughed (Bruce always did), for there was indeed a funny side to it. But Stephen knew only too well how easy it would be to become a man like that, and as if to escape the reality of something like that beginning to happen now, he suddenly began to run. He ran directly into the wind and rain, gasping as they almost took his breath away. His hat almost blew off and he pulled it down hard over his ears. His face became distorted with the effort and his eyes were almost closed tight against the stinging water and initial gusts of a gale. He swerved left and stumbled up over the rocks, slipping and almost spraining his ankle, and waving his arms erratically. He ran, almost choking, up the path to the house and once on the lawn stopped abruptly. Then with slow deliberate steps he paced towards the verandah. He could see Bruce in the living room looking out at him in amazement. He continued his slow steps until his face was a few inches from the window-pane. Then with a slight involuntary twist of his head and squinting hideously he pressed his mouth and nose against the glass.

Inside the room, Bruce had seen Stephen rushing up the path. His hat rammed down on his head gave him a mad appearance, matching the eccentric combination of a formal raincoat, soaking wet, and bare legs below it. It seemed as if he were running from something he had seen down there on the shore, something which had come crawling out of the sea and was pursuing him inland. When he had stopped, walked slowly to the window and pressed his face against the glass, he stayed like that for almost a minute, until it had passed from being a joke into something much nearer to insanity. The skin of his distorted nose and lips was a mass of white, pink, red, purple and yellow contours; it looked like the face of a man terribly disfigured in a fire or accident, a face which had healed leaving a legacy of shocking scars, like a face in one of Francis Bacon's paintings, only with more yellow in it, or even, Bruce thought, like a piece of cold cooked bacon congealed on a plate. It was with something approaching panic that Bruce banged on the glass and called out to his friend.

'Stop it! It looks awful! Come inside.'

Stephen continued to twist and press his almost unrecognizable face slowly against the glass. Half laughing and half terrified, and fearing that Stephen's pressure would crack the pane and perhaps cut his face, Bruce banged again and started to open the window. Stephen took his face away, smiled, and came into the house.

'I thought you'd gone mad.'

'I do sometimes.' Stephen opened his eyes very wide. Bruce laughed, a trifle nervously.

'You mustn't shock me like that.'

'Ah, but I like to shock people; the trouble is I usually only make them snigger.'

'Do you know what you reminded me of just now?'

'The rear end of a female camel on heat, I should think.'

'No, you looked like—'

'A cunt in a chastity belt without the chastity, or—'

'No, Stephen. Listen. This is serious.'

Stephen stared at Bruce. His friend's face suddenly appeared serious, almost sad.

'What then?'

'You looked like my mother.'

'My God!' Stephen whinnied with laughter, dancing a little jig.

'My mother used to make a face like that. She used to squeeze her nose, like this, with her fingers' – Bruce's voice assumed a nasal tone as he tried to demonstrate – 'and then breathe in hard so that her nostrils stuck together. I can't do it, I don't know anybody else who can. Then she bared her teeth and squinted, like you did just now. We used to have fancy-dress parties here when I was a child, and she would come round from her annexe into the verandah with her face like that, her grey hair all ruffled up and hanging over her eyes, with seaweed round her shoulders. When we asked her who she was supposed to be, she used to moan in a strange sing-song voice, "I am the Old Woman of the Sea". I'd forgotten all about it. Your doing that just now brought it all back. It was just here in the verandah where we're standing now.'

It brought back another image too, but he did not tell Stephen. A few hours after his mother had died, he and his family had gone to the hospital. Each of them in turn had kissed her on the forehead, still unnaturally warm. It had been Bruce's first and only encounter with death at first hand, and his mother's face had been the same then too – the teeth slightly bared, the nose pinched and narrow; only this time her eyes had been closed. But the mad smile of the Old Woman of the Sea had been there, and it had not faded. And that was the last Bruce had seen of his mother. She had been cremated and now she was dust in the sandhills, an old woman returned at last to her real homeland, and Bruce was constantly aware of her presence.

The sky had lifted even higher, but it was growing darker with clouds of greater weight than before. The wind had much increased, but the rain seemed to have lessened a little. They stood in the living room looking out of the window at the wild desolation of the shore.

'I wrote a poem once called "The Old Woman of the Sea". It was one of my first. It was published in my school magazine. My first time in print. It was terribly bad.'
'I expect it was. Like everything else you've written since.' Stephen let out a spasm of laughter and look at Bruce who was also laughing. 'The sea's magnificent now, isn't it?'

Bruce nodded. A new warmth was developing between them, as if the rising violence of the weather was also a harbinger of human peace. The sea was always magnificent. More than ever now

Bruce knew it was unchangeably a part of his own being. Even if he were to lock himself in some castle dungeon deep in the mountains in the heart of Asia, or drink cocktails in a city lounge, the sea, he knew, would always be with him — a dull, wonderful, inspiring thunder at the back of his mind.

'This kind of weather always makes me want to start writing.'

'Me too. I'm going to go upstairs now and have a good go at my novel. That's why I came back early.'

'I'll make you a pot of tea.'

'Thanks.' They smiled at each other, but in their minds a kind of joy was welling up and bounding with energy like the shouting waves out in the bay.

A tapping at the at the north window made them both turn sharply. A figure was standing there, his face close to the glass staring in, a long tanned face under an old cloth cap.

'Christ! It's Bob Evans!' Bruce beckoned the man round to the verandah and went to open the front door.

'Made you jump I did. I'm a bit early.' Mr. Evans grinned and after wiping his feet on the mat came into the house, taking off his cap. His hair was thin and wispy but he was younger than his brother the barman. They went into the living room.

'Yes, we thought you were coming after tea. But it doesn't matter. We're not busy now.' Bruce glanced at Stephen with a kind of apologetic shrug in his eyes.

'Weather's turned nasty now, hasn't it? Pity, that.'

'Well, we've had a good week, so we can't complain.' Bruce winced slightly as he found himself making such conventional remarks in the presence of his friend. 'By the way, this is my friend, Stephen Pewit.'

'Pleased to meet you.' He shook hands with Stephen, giving him a single sharp look and then smiling. 'You from these parts?'

'No, I'm from Birmingham.'

'Ah, so you're from the Midlands too, like the Dinwiddys. Well now.'

Stephen yet again marvelled at the accent. The 'f' of the 'from' seemed to have been tripled in strength, the 'o' shortened drastically. 'Midlands' was something like 'Mitlants' and 'Dinwiddys' came out at as 'Dinwittys'.

'Would you like to check the house immediately, or will you have a cup of tea first? I was just going to put the kettle on.'

'Yes, well now, I'd better have a look round first.'

'There's a fire extinguisher on the stairs.'

'I saw that one. Have to test it later. Do you have the keys? Have to go round all the outside places, too.'

Bruce fetched the bunch of keys from the hall.

'Do you want me to come round with you?'

'No, I can manage, thanks. I know my way about.' Bob Evans smiled brilliantly, displaying one gold tooth in the flash of white. Bruce nodded, also smiling.

'I'll put the kettle on and we'll have a cup of tea when you're finished.'

'That'll be fine.'

Bob Evans went out. They heard him walking about the house, opening doors and knocking things.

'Is it normal to let him go everywhere like that?'

'He's a sort of caretaker. He's always in and out, especially when we're not here. His father was gardener's boy in my mother's family up at Crown Grange before she was born, or something like that.'

'Everybody in Harlieg's got some connection with your family, it seems.'

Bruce laughed shortly.

'There are lots of people who have nothing to do with us.'

'I wish I could speak like he does.'

'You'll haff to come and liff in theess partss then. Lasst Muntay moorning Clarissa Grayffs fell tdown in chapp-ell and hadt a fitt. Pit-ty tooo.'

It was Stephen's turn to laugh.

'How did you pick it up?'

'I've been here at least twice every year of my life. Many long summer holidays. And I spent the first three years of my life here too. I acquired it quite by accident. I'm quite surprised I can do it, really.'

238

A sudden squall outside blasted a sheet of rain into the verandah. More followed, and soon the wooden seat and table were shining and dark with the salty moisture. Some of the rain even blew against the window panes, sheltered as they were in the alcove of the verandah. Bruce went into the kitchen to put the kettle on. When he came back Stephen was peering through window into the wild murk outside. He turned to Bruce.

'Who's that outside?'

Bruce looked down towards the beach path. Four figures were coming slowly up it towards the house. As soon as they reached the lawn they stood uncertainly trying to peer into the house. There were no lights on in the living room so they had difficulty seeing if anyone was in. At the same time there came a lull in the wind and rain, and Bruce went out into the verandah, to find that what he had feared was true: they were the four men from the hotel. They were drenched to the skin, except for the older man, who was wearing a black plastic macintosh and a yellow sou' wester. One of the others was holding the umbrella now twisted out of shape and pathetic looking. The older man started to undo the strap of his sou' wester.

'Is this a café?'

'No, it's not. And you're trespassing.'

'It's one of those boys we saw in the hotel.'

'You're on private property. Didn't you see the notice at the bottom of the path? The path to the cliff's over there.' Bruce pointed to the boundary fence of his father's land about eighty yards to the north. One of the younger men spoke in a plaintive voice.

'We're wet through. The rain's trickling right down my leg inside.'

The older man spoke again.

'Could we come in for a while and get dry? We went for a walk along the beach and we've got terribly wet, as you can see. We'd like to get dry a bit before we go back to the hotel. I can see you've got a nice fire in there.'

'This is my father's house, and I've been instructed not to admit strangers.'

'Well, you know us. We saw you at the hotel. Anyway, you're not a child, are you? Your father wouldn't mind.'

'My father would mind very much. If you don't get off this property I'll call the police.'

The older man frowned.

'I wouldn't advise that. Anyway, there's only one policeman in Harlieg and before he got down here, if he bothered to come at all, we'd be miles away.'

'I know where you're staying.'

'We're leaving tomorrow.'

'That wouldn't make any difference.'

'My God! Don't you have any humanity?' It was the man who had been addressed as Bertie in the hotel. 'Here we are, shivering and miserable, dying of pneumonia. You make me feel like King Lear.'

'I'm sorry, but—'

'You're not sorry at all. Don't be a hypocrite.'

'The hotel's only a couple of minutes away.'

'We can't go in there like this. We look like tramps.'

'That's your responsibility.'

'You heartless bitch.'

'I don't see why they shouldn't come in for a few minutes. It won't do any harm.'

It was Stephen who spoke. Standing in the doorway behind Bruce, he had seen and heard everything with increasing anger at his friend's unfeeling and autocratic tones and at the same time feeling some real compassion for the miserable travellers. It never occurred to him that they had come to the house deliberately. Stephen had forgotten the feelings he had had that morning when he had seen them changing on the beach, and also the episode in the hotel; or rather he was now more concerned with Bruce's cold attitude. The older man smiled at Bruce.

'That's just what I thought. We won't do any harm.'

'Look, Stephen, this isn't my house and it isn't yours either.'

'I know that very well. You never think of anyone else, do you?'

Bruce knew there was nothing he could do now to prevent this invasion. His prejudices were too strong to admit these men as forlorn strangers: they were enemies and he knew they had come intentionally; he also knew that their target was Stephen. Why did this kind of thing have to happen just when his friend was settling down again? With bitter thoughts he could see how easy it was for Stephen, after all Bruce's efforts, to fall so readily into this trap. He made one more effort to put them off, but he knew that it was doomed to failure.

'The rain doesn't look so strong now, does it?'

At that moment Bob Evans appeared at the door carrying a large old-fashioned fire extinguisher. He clicked his tongue.

'What a day! We're in for a long wet, I should say.' He saw the four men and looked at Bruce. 'Got visitors now, have you? Well, excuse me, please.'

Passing Bruce and Stephen and the four men, he carried the red cylinder out onto the sodden lawn and set it down on its side. The four men came closer into the protection of the overhanging roof of the verandah. The older man took off his rainwear and the umbrella was shaken and closed. They all watched Bob Evans, who did not seem to mind the rain at all.

'Got to test this one now. See if it still works. Been there nearly forty years, I would say.' He gestured into the house.

It looked older than that. It was labelled MINIMAX, with the first and last letters the largest, the others getting smaller so that the middle 'i' was the shortest. Below were four photographic illustrations stencilled onto the red-painted metal. Each picture was of a young woman in a white long-sleeved blouse and a dark skirt down to her ankles; her hair was long and tied back by a large ribbon. The first picture showed her removing the extinguisher from its wall-bracket; in the second she was kneeling slightly with the extinguisher raised vertically in her right hand; the third illustration showed her striking the base of the cylinder on the ground, and in the last she was aiming it at the flames and smoke of a fire. Appropriate instructions accompanied each graceful picture. It seemed as if a fire in those days was something rather gentle and discreet, and putting one out was a dignified activity for charming young ladies.

Bob Evans, keeping his body as far from the device as possible, picked it up and struck the hammer at its base on the wet turf. Nothing happened. He brought the extinguisher to the edge of the concrete round the house and tried again. This time there was a crack and a long thin stream of misty-looking water shot out in a wide arc from the nozzle at the top of the cylinder. The sometimes uncertain and definitely irregular jet lasted for a full minute and a half, during which Bob Evans began to look somewhat embarrassed. One of the four men, the smallest, who had straw-coloured hair, bright blue eyes and a weak chin, began to titter and pointed at the jet.

'I couldn't do it for as long as that!'

Everybody laughed loudly. Even Bruce could not prevent himself. Bob Evans's embarrassment faded into a sheepish smile.

'Well, really now, I wouldn't have thought of it quite like that.' The jet of water had now declined to a miserable trickle which finally stopped. He took the extinguisher round to the back of the house. Stephen wanted to say, 'You are most sincerely entreated to keep your nozzle under perfect control', but he was not sure of Bruce. The blue-eyed boy giggled.

'I've never seen one of those things working before. Rather disappointing, wasn't it?' Bertie laughed.

'It's a bit old, I suppose. Things get weaker with age.' He looked significantly at the older man, who smiled thinly.

The atmosphere had changed. The hostility in the air seemed to have evaporated. Bruce felt relieved in a way, and went into the kitchen to turn the shrieking kettle off. To hell with the lot of them! If they wanted to come in and get dry, let them! He wouldn't say yes and he would no longer refuse. Let Stephen take care of them, queers or not! Besides, things might not be as bad as he feared. When he returned to the living room, the four intruders were settled round the fire; Stephen was draping the plastic mac over the back of a chair. It began to drip onto the floor. They were still talking about the extinguisher.

'Well, it wouldn't put much of a fire out, would it?'

'I wish an orgasm would last as long as that. It was beautiful.'

'That poor man out there didn't know where to look.'

'Well, he wasn't looking at you, if that's what you were hoping.' The oldest of the four turned to Bruce and made polite but rather cold introductions. He could afford to be polite, Bruce thought, now that he had wormed himself inside the house.

'I'm Larry Garner. That's Bertie.' He was pointing to a tall thin youngish man with a scholarly face and black-rimmed glasses, which he was now wiping with his handkerchief. The glasses and his rather hooked nose made him appear to be looking inwards, as if at some defenceless, furless small animal in his brain, rather than out at the world. His mouth was small and cherubic. Larry indicated the smaller straw-haired boy. 'This is Dolly.'

'That's not my real name.' He scowled. 'Why can't you have more dignity, Larry?' He turned to Bruce rather wistfully. 'I'm Edward White.'

The fourth man, whom neither Bruce nor Stephen had yet heard speak, was called Fred O' Gorman. He was full-lipped and his black hair was gleaming and oiled back over his head. His eyes were brown and bland and he had a thin black moustache. He began to murmur something as he was introduced but it was obvious that he had a pronounced stammer and he relapsed into silence. Bruce turned to Larry Garner.

'I thought you said you were only staying for a day.'

'That was our original plan, but we like it here so much. We're not in any hurry to move on. It all comes out of our expenses.' He laughed. Edward spoke next.

'We were planning to play golf again today, but the weather turned nasty, so we—' He was cut off by Larry.

'Nice place you've got here. Do you live here?'

'No, my father lives in Birmingham.'

'What does he do with this place all the year then? Does he let it?'

'Sometimes. To certain people.' Larry ignored the guarded coolness of Bruce's reply.

'Good place for a party, eh, Bertie? We could have a real orgy down here, bring a whole lot of the boys over.' There were some knowing sniggers. 'How many does this place sleep?'

'Quite a few.'

Bruce's disquiet returned. Not only was he sullenly angry with everyone in the room including himself for his own weakness, he was also quite seriously alarmed. Things were getting out of control. He had no idea how he could end this invasion nor how it would end. Stephen was talking pleasantly with Bertie and Fred, while Larry watched, and Bruce realized there was nothing he could do to prevent their communication. Edward was gazing out at the weather, his blue eyes shining with the beginnings of fear. The wind was gathering momentum again, as if it had paused for the comic relief of the extinguisher episode and was now returning to act out the tragic denouement. It whistled through the long grasses, bending them low to the ground, lashing them with insane gusts from the sea. The rain was again blasted in splattering sheets into the verandah and against the window-panes. None of the visitors showed any sign of leaving. Larry lit a cigarette. This started off the others, and Bruce felt a kind of helpless sickness in the pit of his stomach as Bertie, who was the second eldest of the four, touched Stephen's hand a shade too long as he lighted his cigarette for him. Stephen, without looking directly at Bruce, then suggested tea. He and Bruce went into the kitchen.

'You shouldn't have suggested they come in. They'll stay for ages.'

'There's nothing wrong in that.'

'I don't like them.'

'Nor do I particularly, but they're not as bad as all that. That Edward chap looks quite interesting. He's been to university.'

'How are we going to get rid of them?'

'We don't need to. They won't stay long anyway.'

'Whose bloody house is this?'

'Well, it's not yours.'

'You're my guest—'

'You know perfectly well your father wouldn't mind. Judging from what you tell me about him, he'd probably be most interested if he were here. To see what happened. You just used his name as an excuse. Fight your own battles.'

Bruce fell silent. They made the tea and carried it through. Larry smiled indulgently.

'Who's going to be mother?'

The others smiled. Bruce, a victim of his upbringing, felt himself called upon to perform the functions of pouring the tea. His hands trembled as he did so. Stephen handed the cups round. Nobody spoke as spoons and china clinked. The wind grew louder outside, not gradually, but in sudden blasts, each stronger than the one before it. Occasionally the telephone bell went 'ting' as the wires touched outside. With each paroxysm of wind the whole house shook. They heard the back door slam and after a while Bob Evans came in, wiping his face with a handkerchief. His clothes were extremely wet, so a place was made for him near the fire, where he sat, steam rising from the legs of his trousers. Stephen handed him a cup of tea. Bob Evans looked serious.

'Got bad news for your father, I'm afraid.'

'What's wrong? Fire precautions inadequate?'

The memory of the geriatric fire extinguisher raised a few titters.

'No, it's a good deal worse than that. The house, you see, is riddled with woodworm. Some in every room. Right through the wood. Terrible under the stairs and in that back room. Loft too. It's got a real hold.'

'Can't anything be done about it?'

'Couldn't say that now. Needs looking into. Best thing would be to paint all the walls.'

'Rentokil?'

'No, none of that stuff. Does no good that. I mean house paint; the thick stuff, not emulsion or water paint, you know. Seal off the air. Woodworm can't live without air.'

Bruce heard Edward give a low chuckle.

'I like that one. Woodworm can't live without air.'

'Well, it's true now. No joking. House'll fall down, it will. And that's not the only thing. Your father's got a lot of expense coming.'

'Is there something else wrong?'

'South wall there. Rotten through and through. 'Twas cemented over once, that end, but straight onto the wood boards, it was. Rain's soaked through. The whole end's rotten soft, even the main pillars. That's the trouble with wooden houses in Wales. Can't keep the rain out, and all that salt in it, too. Eats right in.'

Bruce thought of all the labour he and other members of the family had put into creosoting year after year.

'Doesn't the creosote do any good then?'

'Not on that end. It's all cemented over, see.'

'Do you think I'd better phone my father?'

'Could do. It's urgent now. Might have the whole end fall down in a gale like this; and that wouldn't do any good, would it now?'

Stephen looked, somewhat accusingly, at Bruce.

'I'm sleeping in that end of the house. Upstairs.'

The visitors all looked at him with interest. Bruce could sense them appraising the sleeping arrangements of the two friends. Larry looked at Bruce.

'What about you? Do you sleep in a safe place?'

Bruce did not deign to answer him. He continued his questioning of Bob Evans.

'How much do you think it'll cost?'

'Over a thousand, I expect. At least nine hundred pounds.'

Stephen loved the 'huntret pounts'.

Fred emitted a long whistle. It was the most articulate communication he had so far made since their arrival.

'Thing is, I could get the carpenter to come down in the morning and have a look. He'd be able to give you a better opinion.'

'Is it dangerous now?'

'Could be if this weather continues. Big gale coming up on the radio.'

They listened to the wind outside. It came in savage intermittent flurries so that sheets of rain swept hard against even the north windows, those of the bay window, though they were usually quite sheltered from the fury of the weather from the south-west. Some kind of backlash swirled the wind and rain right round the house. Bruce could visualize the wind as an almost human spiralling of clouds and mist with a face like those sometimes etched in the corners of old maps. The gutter above the verandah was overflowing. Sometimes there was a lull, and then they could hear the wind further away yelling through the grasses to the south of the house. There was something demented in that irregular continuous shrieking. A monster was advancing out of the sea. It seemed to have singled out the solitary red-roofed house for its onslaught and was trying to shake it from its foundations. They could hear the sea, too. It seemed to be just outside the door, a churning thundering mass just below the level of the lawn, roaring and crying to come inland, trying to retrieve lost territories. Bruce glanced up at the picture of the house above the fireplace. Now it looked terrifying, somehow far too well painted to be a joke. There was the house with its red roof standing not in the safety of the sand hills but right down on a shining windswept beach; and close behind it, where the cliff should have been, huge breakers were crashing down, breakers as high as the house itself and threatening to submerge it. Bruce felt the painting was a prophecy about to be fulfilled. The sea did not always recede; sometimes it changed its mind, was unpredictable. Now, outside, the sea seemed to be thundering right over the roof above them, in a great deluge of roaring surf and dashing spray. He felt as if the sea were trying to reach him personally, to punish him for the meanness in his nature. And Bob Evans sat there smoking a cigarette. He had come down like a man from the mountains and was now proclaiming the doom of the house. It would come crashing and splintering down over their heads. And the four men from the hotel were ghouls in mild disguises, crow-like bearers of evil omens. There was a hideous grin lurking behind all their polite conversation, virulent schemes coiled in the carrion of their lewd remarks. They sat hunched their round the fire, like huge half-feathered birds sheltering from a storm. They were waiting for a final visitation, and the whole house was gripped by an evil — vile strands of poisoned fluid that ran in the bloodstream of the rain and the wind.

'May I use the phone?' Larry stood up. 'I just want to ring up the hotel to tell them we may be late for dinner.'

Bruce was past caring.

'I suppose you'd better.'

'I'll pay for the call, if you like.'

'It doesn't matter. It's only local.'

Larry picked up the receiver, listened, frowned, jiggled the call button, and dialled. He waited. Then he replaced the receiver and repeated the whole procedure. Everyone stared at him.

'The line's dead.'

'The wires'll be down somewhere.' Bob Evans stood up and took the receiver from Larry. Edward's expression of fear grew more intense.

'How are we going to get back? We can't go out in this.'

Bruce's imagination began to work again. The four men staying the night. Stephen seduced. He himself attacked and raped by Fred O'Gorman. A mad carousel on the lawn in the stinging wind and rain, all of them naked. Bob Evans looking on, laughing, or trying to stop them and felled by a single blow from Bertie suddenly turned into a leering ogre. The house collapsing behind them; the sea ten times higher than the land, huge breakers hovering at an immense height but never falling. It was almost as if the weather was conspiring with the four intruders to trap the two friends and ruin their stay in the house by the sea. And they would find Stephen's novel, read it aloud in mocking voices and tear it into shreds, scattering the pages into the invisible streamers of the gale.

Stephen too was moved by the weather outside. He marvelled at the strength of the wind that could shake the entire house and at the rain lashing against the window-panes. The sounds excited him — the tense voices in the room, the savage attacks of the elements upon the house itself, beyond that the howling of the wind in the grasses, and further still, as an incessant background, the dull, brave deep-throated basso ostinato of the sea, the huge waves trying to race each other to the shore and never winning, the despair of an ocean in its endless conflict with the shore. It was all new to him. But it was exactly in extraordinary situations of this kind that he excelled. A sea-storm outside as evening approached. Strangers gathered unexpectedly in a room shaking with the onslaught of the weather. The telephone dead. Anything could happen. He wanted something to happen. He wanted the four men to stay all night just to see what would happen, just to see what Bruce would do, how he would handle this situation which had been thrust upon him and must be new for him too. He was not in the least afraid of the four men from Chester, and he was now actually enjoying Bruce's predicament. He pointed to the large corner cupboard between the two windows and looked at Bruce.

'Isn't there some whisky in there?'

'I'm not sure.'

'You know perfectly well there is. Let's have some.'

Stephen went to the cupboard and opened it. Bruce's father always kept a few almost empty bottles of whisky or sherry in the corner cupboard precisely for occasions such as this — unexpected guests or for people such as Bob Evans who came down to do odd jobs on the premises.

'I wouldn't mind a bit of whisky now.' Bob Evans flashed his white gold-tinted smile. 'Your father usually gives me a drop when I'm down here.'

Stephen took out seven glasses, all of them of different sizes and shapes, and a bottle of White Horse he found there. It was two-thirds full. He gave everyone a measure and went to fetch some water from the kitchen. Bruce said nothing. The entire situation was quite beyond his control. He felt ignored, useless. Everybody, it seemed, was against him. He refused the glass Stephen handed him but the others did not seem to notice this futile attempt at non-participation and protest. There was a clinking of the water-jug on the rims of glasses and an atmosphere of renewed cosiness and cheerfulness. The whisky was stronger than the weather. Stephen drank his quickly and emboldened by the instant confidence it gave him went to the piano. He sat down at the keyboard and the others at once crowded round him, encouraging him to play. Larry gave him some more whisky. At the same time, Bob Evans finished his and put his glass down. He nodded to Bruce.

'Thanks. Best be getting back home. Wife'll be worrying.'

'Can you walk back in this weather?'

'No trouble at all. Used to it. I'll ask the carpenter to come down in the morning. Telephone too: I'll tell the post office the line's down.'

'Thank you very much.' They went to the living-room door and the people at the piano looked at Bob Evans in surprise. Edward peered out of the window.

'Are you going out in this?'

'It's nothing to what's coming. I'll just get a wetting, that's all. Bye now.' They said goodbye but it was obvious that they were more interested in Stephen at the piano. Bruce went with Bob Evans into the hall. The Welshman put on his cap and opened the front door. A great billowing sinew of wet cold air burst into the house and wrenched the door wide open. Bruce was reminded of Titus Oates at the South Pole. The rain in the verandah was loud and splattering violently from the gutter. The darkening air seemed to be a mass of advancing spray and the thunder of surf. Bob Evans stepped out and turned, his teeth shining white in the gloom, then pulled up his jacket collar and disappeared into the semi-darkness, running slowly with his head bent down. Bruce waited for a while, trying to see if the waves really were trying to claw their way over the nearest sandhills, but he could see nothing and with an effort slammed the door. With the departure of Bob Evans he now felt isolated, alone in a den of enemies. Stephen belonged more to the group than to his friend. With a sinking heart he returned to the living room and switched the light on.

Stephen had begun to play. Larry was standing behind him, one hand on his shoulder. The other three stood either side, Fred beating time surreptitiously with a thick finger not quite accurately. Stephen was maintaining a low, growling passacaglia with his left hand near the end of the keyboard, his face only inches above the stained keys. From time to time he added a battery of harsh discords with his right hand. The extemporisation became louder and wilder — like a dance of gale-crazed trolls. The sound made everybody forget the weather outside, as if the clashing rhythms were neutralizing its power. Even Bruce, in spite of his misery, could not help feeling impressed. Stephen was surpassing himself. Somehow he had clutched the chords directly out of the frenzy of the rising gale: the wind, rain and his lashing right hand were in miraculous harmony. The insane rolling reiteration produced by his left was strangely reproducing the booming, submarine turning of the surf. The storm had come into the house.

Bruce sat down at the table, staring at the verandah window. It was almost dark outside, and because of the light in the living room he could see his own reflection on the glass. The way his head was tilted slightly to one side reminded him of his mother. He lit a cigarette, and then, with a swift almost involuntary movement, drank off the whisky Stephen had previously offered him. The music at once began to fill him with an unfamiliar sense of abandon, no doubt aided by the drink and the cigarette and the tension of his nerves. Stephen was lost. All efforts Bruce had made were now crumbling away like the city of sand under the tide. Bruce no longer cared. He was full of nostalgia and grief. He wished his mother were still alive. He wished it were her playing the piano now with one of her hilarious endless Beethoven endings and not Stephen and these leering spectators. He thought of his mother now, her ashes, lost somewhere and blowing lonely out there in the stricken dunes, the spirit trying to gather itself together but not able to overpower the bludgeoning wind. The wind shrieking in the grasses was not the wind, nor was it the voice of his mother. It was the million voices of his mother's ashes, tiny, fragmented voices full of the despair of lost children searching for one another and not being able to find their companions. And all the voices were sounding together and magnified by the sea; it was the infinitely multiplied utterance of a disintegrated soul. And as Bruce gazed out into the storm all he could see were thousands of diagonal lines of rain and streaming water, green, blue and grey, a slanting curtain of mist and waves and spray, and behind it he could see a figure walking slowly towards him. It was his mother, but her face was the pinched face of death she had worn the last time he saw her. But then the face smiled, its teeth bared and its nostrils closed slits, and the grey hair wound all about it. And it was the Old Woman of the Sea walking straight towards the house out of the storm, out of the tragic sea beyond.

Someone was looking in through the window from the verandah. A white face hovered there, with brilliant eyes, a living face hung all round with broad strands of brown seaweed streaming with rain. It did not move. Then a hand came up, a hand blackened with tar mixed with sand, bits of green seaweed and blood; it tried to wipe the glass, to make it easier to see into the room, but the claw left a smear only, then disappeared. With a violent thrust Bruce pushed his chair back, standing up and dropping his glass to the floor, where it shattered.I He pointed at the window, his eyes round with terror.

'Look! Look, she's there!'

The five at the piano turned to him in angry surprise, which turned to expressions of horror as they caught the look on Bruce's face. The music stopped abruptly, the last chord echoing and dying inside the piano, while they all became aware of the crackling of the fire, the moaning of the wind outside and the hoarse background of the sea. Then they looked to where Bruce was pointing. His voice continued, this time low, almost a croak, and hissing out the words.

'The Old Woman of the Sea! The ashes have come back!'

Seeing the apparition at the window, Edward ran whimpering into the corner behind Bruce. Stephen involuntarily kicked at the base of the piano and jerked backwards, the piano-stool falling over with a crash, spilling its contents – Victorian song books and Mrs. Curwen's Exercises for Children, mingled with other obscure piano pieces with pale green inscrolled covers and some sheets of music paper covered with the broad sloping music-hand of Bruce's mother – across the floor. Fred O'Gorman and Bertie slowly backed away from the verandah window and stood by the table holding hands. Only Larry seemed unperturbed, almost irritated. The face at the window remained motionless. Then it disappeared. They heard the front door open and swing back with a tortured rending sound and the sound of the wind was suddenly louder. A cold draught moved the living-room door slightly ajar. Someone was coming in. The door slowly opened, a slimy, stained hand came round the edge and the figure entered. It was clad from head to foot in shining, greasy robes of brown and black seaweed which dripped noisily onto the floor. Its left hand was clutching a sodden bundle. Stephen instantly recognized the red and yellow.

It was Vera.

22. CHANGING TIDE

'HALLO, STEPHEN! Sorry to come in like this.'

Bruce looked sharply at his friend. Who was this girl so familiar with Stephen? Stephen looked embarrassed. His secret was out. How would Bruce react? The four men from the hotel, nonplussed by the sudden appearance of this extraordinary female, remained silent. Disappointment and annoyance showed clearly on Larry's face. Vera smiled brightly and began to explain to Stephen.

'You see, my clothes got wet and I was cold. So I took everything off. Don't you think this is a marvellous costume? I feel like a real sea-nymph. It's ever so warm.'

Stephen was both delighted and irritated. He thought the sea-weed was wonderful, but what a pity that Vera had to blunder in here and spoil everything! Now he would have to explain to Bruce.

'This is Vera. I met her on the beach yesterday.' Bruce raised his eyebrows. 'Vera, this is my friend Bruce.'

'Hallo, Bruce.' She held out her hand for him to shake. 'Oh, look at my hand! It's bleeding. I fell down in the dark on the pebbles. I'm sorry, I can't shake hands with you. I'm longing to see your poems.'

Stephen looked at Vera in dismay. He knew Bruce would be angry at her flippant tone. Yet he stared at the girl with renewed fascination. What was she wearing under the seaweed? Was she naked? He was burning with curiosity and longed to put his hands through the slippery fronds and feel her body underneath, and at the same time he was amazed at what could only be called the normality of his feelings. Vera attracted him, without any doubt physically and, for Stephen at least, somehow healthily – the age-old fascination of man for woman; and he rejoiced at it, his anxieties about Bruce seeming to melt away. The image of Vera squirming in ecstasy with the boy in the sand dunes came back to him with a new urgency. He had a strong desire, new and demanding, to take the boy's place. He had to find a way. He came back to reality with a rush as Bruce indicated the water on the floor.

'I must say your coming in like this is rather—'

'Eccentric.' Vera smiled brightly again.

'People seem to use this place as a kind of resthouse. They just walk in and out as they please. No bloody manners anywhere.' Bruce's eyes were blazing.

'I'm awfully sorry, but I was quite lost. I saw the light.' Bruce's expression did not melt.

'Coming to the window like that and peering in. You ought to have known better.'

Edward shivered.

'You almost gave me a heart attack. I've got a weak heart, you know.'

Larry, who had been exchanging glances with Bertie and Fred, came forward.

'I think we'd better be going. We seem to have rather overstayed our welcome as it is.' Vera turned to him with interest.

'Where are you from?'

'We're staying at the Royal Dragon.'

'Wait for me then. I'm at the College. You can help me get back. I can't find the way by myself. I just want to dry my clothes.' She smiled at Bruce again. 'Do you mind?' She hung the red shorts and yellow shirt over the fender in front of the fire. Now that his unwanted guests seemed ready to depart, Bruce's fury was changing into a sense of businesslike command.

'You'd better put the seaweed outside and clean up that hand of yours. You'll find a towel in the bathroom. I'll show you.'

'I'll take her if you like.' Stephen started to move towards the door, but Bruce stopped him.

'You stay here and look after your friends.' The note of authority in his voice prevented Stephen from making any further move. He knew he had missed his chance. To say anything more would seem too unnatural and he could not very well override Bruce and just march Vera out of the room. He inwardly deplored his own weakness of spirit.

Bruce took Vera to the bathroom. She immediately dragged off the strands of seaweed and dropped them into the bath-tub, a long iron old-fashioned one with legs. Bruce saw that she was wearing a black swimming suit. She turned on the taps. Bruce went out and shut the door. He went into the kitchen and started to think about what to have for supper. He did not want to return to the living room and he found himself wondering why. Was it because he wanted to avoid the company of the men from the hotel? They would be leaving soon; it wasn't that. Did he want to show his power over Stephen, his control over the girl he had found on the beach? Did he even want to arouse Stephen's jealousy? He had sensed immediately the animal magnetism of Vera, just as Stephen had done, and it was obvious to Bruce that the girl attracted Stephen strongly. Perhaps even now Stephen was wondering why his friend was so long out of the living room. Well, let him! The girl wasn't his exclusive possession. Did Vera really interest him, Bruce wondered, or was it that he wanted merely to disturb Stephen's relationship with her? Whatever the case, Vera had added a new dimension to the state of affairs between him and Stephen. Bruce was just putting some potatoes out to peel when Vera called him from the bathroom.

'Bruce – is there anything I can put on my hand? It's cut a bit.'

'There's some iodine in the little cupboard over the bath, the one with the mirror on it.' There was a pause.

'I can't find it. Can you come and show me? You can come in.'

Bruce opened the door. Vera was standing in the bath-tub in a cloud of steam, naked and facing him. The flesh of her perfectly filled firm body was pink and gleaming. Bruce's eyes fixed themselves on the darkish pubic hair and then moved up to the small taut breasts. He had never seen a woman or girl naked before, except his sister in their childhood, and he blushed instantly and started to close the door.

'What's the matter? Don't go away. Show me where the iodine is.'

Bruce stepped into the bathroom, trying to keep his eyes off the fresh, shining figure of the girl, opened the small cupboard over the bath and took out the bottle of iodine.

'Here it is. Didn't you see it?'

'I didn't even look.' Vera stared at him almost brazenly without making any attempt to cover her body and then she laughed. 'You look so amazed! Haven't you ever seen a girl with nothing on before?'

Bruce told a kind of lie.

'Yes.... But you took me by surprise, that's all. It was rather...unexpected.' He laughed nervously. 'Can you manage now?'

'Yes, unless you'd like to help me.'

Bruce did not know what to think. His mind was confused. Too much had happened that afternoon and he was just unable to take in this unabashed exhibition of nudity. The whisky also complicated matters. What was he supposed to do? Close the bathroom door, strip off his clothes and embrace the gleaming figure in the bath? He was terrified that Stephen would find him there. Things were bad enough as they were.

'If you can't manage it yourself, I'll have a look at it in the living room. It's not light enough in here—'

'Please yourself.' Vera looked a little disappointed. 'I'll come out in a minute. Do you think my shorts are dry yet?'

'I doubt it. I'll go and check. Use that towel if you like.' Bruce pointed to a large white bath-towel on the wall-rail. Then he went out and closed the door. His face was red and he felt hot and somehow ashamed, even slightly contaminated. He washed his face with cold water in the kitchen sink then returned to the living room, where the others were drinking whisky.

'You look very hot. Is everything all right?' Stephen was staring at him with hard eyes.

'It's the whisky. You know I'm not a strong drinker.' They all looked at him, and Bruce felt himself blushing even more strongly. 'She's coming soon.'

'By herself?' Bertie smirked. 'Did you help her a bit? You've been out quite a while.' The other three men laughed, but not Stephen.

'I was in the kitchen.' Bruce was almost paralyzed with discomfort. He was naturally shy and a situation such as this was a kind of torture. 'For God's sake—' He went to the fender and checked Vera's clothes. They were dry on one side. He turned them. Larry added to his torment.

'I wouldn't be surprised if those two weren't up to something out there in the bathroom.' Bruce blazed out at him.

'I wish you'd bloody well keep your filthy insinuations to yourself!'

'All right, all right. Keep your hair on.' Larry emptied his glass and picked up the whisky bottle to refill it. The rain outside seemed to have abated a little, but the wind was as strong as before. Edward sighed and shook his shoulders.

'What an evening!'

Bertie smiled.

'It's like something out of Wuthering Heights. This must be a wonderful place to do some writing.'

'It isn't.' Stephen was not smiling. 'You don't know anything about it. The sea stops you from concentrating. It never stops moving. You can't get any peace of mind. I'm sure I'd go mad if I lived by the sea.'

At that moment Vera came back into the room, the white towel round her shoulders. She was wearing her black swimming costume again, but though it was still wet she looked warm and clean. Edward looked at her with curiosity, but Larry could hardly disguise his distaste at the proximity of this healthy feminine creature and turned away his face. Stephen looked from Vera to

Bruce and back again, trying to read their expressions. Bruce was stoking the fire.

'I left the seaweed in the bath. Will it be all right? You can eat it if you like. It's marvellous boiled, I've tried it. It makes a delicious soup. Full of iron.'

Stephen smiled. This was the Vera he knew and liked. Everything she said seemed to him so fresh and original, and also both rich and simple at the same time. She seemed to be quite unabashed in this exclusively male company, in fact was quite obviously enjoying the effect of her semi-nudity. She sat by the fire. The shirt and shorts were still steaming. She turned them over.

'Almost dry.'

'How's your hand? Is it all right?' Vera flashed a bold smile at Bruce.

'No problem. The iodine burned beautifully. It's a lovely kind of stinging feeling, isn't it? Hurting and giving you a getting-better feeling at the same time. I put the bottle back in the cupboard.'

'Thanks.' Bruce smiled, feeling more relaxed. He too was affected by the way Vera spoke. There was no doubt that she cast a kind of spell. She looked at Stephen, still smiling.

'I liked your music. It seemed to be coming out through the glass and mixing with the wind and rain. What was it?'

'Nothing in particular.' Stephen handed her a glass of whisky. 'You'd better drink this. You might catch cold.' She took the glass and held it in both hands, sniffing the contents deeply and sipping very lightly from time to time.

'Oh, I do love the smell of whisky! It's so plummy and rich, and sour at the same time.'

'Do you like it better than brandy? Brandy smells even better.'

'Oh, brandy! That's a drink for old men with cigars. I hate the way they cradle their glasses and pretend to be so knowing. You don't like brandy, do you, Stephen?'

'Well—no, not really. Only the smell.'

'I love smelling things.'

Once again Bruce began to feel left out of everything. A new weight of fatigue and disillusionment gave him a sense of being old and worn out. The threat of the presence of the four men was bad enough, but this new turn of events seemed even more disastrous. Stephen had a girlfriend. It was totally out of character, the last thing he expected of his friend. Stephen had always scorned the opposite sex. Stephen had a girlfriend, and he Bruce didn't have one. He found himself increasingly fascinated by Vera's whole personality, but she was not for him. Stephen had found her first.

Larry tried to make polite conversation with Bruce, almost as if to cut Stephen and the girl out of his range of communication, deliberately turning his back on the chatting pair, and Bruce was almost grateful for this attention.

'It looks as if your father's going to have a lot of trouble with this house. How old is it, by the way?'

'About fifty years, I think.'

'It costs a lot to have things done nowadays, and people are so slow. It took me six weeks just to get a man to put one slate on the roof of my place. It must be lot worse here in Wales. For all their smiles, they hate the English.'

'My mother was born here. It helps a lot. The people are very kind to us.'

Bruce hardly knew why he was continuing this conversation. He wished he had a machine-gun. He wanted to stand at the back of the room and mow them all down, except Edward perhaps. They had shattered his entire conception of things. Just when he and Stephen seemed to be settling down into some sort of understanding and meaningful routine, they had to come and ruin everything. Stephen and Vera were talking like old friends.

'The wind cage got blown down.'

'You can make another.' Stephen had no intention of telling Vera about the destruction he had wrought in the gully that morning, nor was he going to let her know he had seen her in the sandhills that morning, not yet anyway. Vera was now a doubly exciting prospect. Not only did she sparkle with wit and charm and originality, she was also a lovely touchable animal, and she was so open and straightforward in both respects. Now that she was here close to him in the warmth of the room, the coarsely bestial side of her nature which he had witnessed that morning seemed less offensive to him. The boy she had been with then was now not present and Vera appeared not only more vulnerable somehow but also desirable and accessible. He had wondered at first whether she and Bruce had formed some kind of private relationship while they had been out of the room. Bruce had looked so embarrassed and guilty when he came back. Stephen had never seen him like that before; but he relaxed as soon as Vera began to talk exclusively to himself. He had nothing to fear from Bruce; perhaps he was just shy to be alone in the presence of a girl, even though it was for such a short time. Stephen listened in delight as Vera continued.

'I want to make a machine for counting raindrops. I've thought of a way it could be done. Could I have some more whisky?' Stephen gave her some from the bottle and was about to add water. 'Neat, please.'

Bertie eyed her with displeasure and interrupted the conversation.

'Do you often drink? Whisky's bad for women, you know. Bad for their insides.' Vera looked him up and down and recognized him for what he was instinctively.

'It's bad for men, too. Inside and out. Some more than others.' She turned back to Stephen. 'I don't drink much actually, but I like whisky when I'm cold, but I'd rather have it in coffee. When are you coming up to the College?'

'When can I come?'

'Any time you like. I'm sorry I couldn't meet you today.'

Stephen looked at her straight in the eyes.

'What happened to you?'

'I was with a friend.' She giggled. 'It was rather funny really.'

Stephen thought of the writhing couple in the sandhills. At least, she hadn't lied; but she hadn't told everything either. There would be time for that later. He again suddenly felt the desirability of her taut body. He wanted to reach out and touch the pert breasts snug in the swimming costume. She smelt warm and animal.

'Shall we meet tomorrow?' He caught sight of Bruce's face; it was a mask of misery.

'Yes. I'll be in the same place.'

Stephen took a risk, keeping his gaze fixed to hers.

'Where do you mean? In the sand dunes?'

Vera stared at him, innocent and wide-eyed. Stephen thought he detected a faint sign of puzzlement.

'No, on the beach of course. By the wind cage, or what's left of it.'

Fred O'Gorman was mumbling something about feeling hungry. Larry stopped talking with Bruce and got up, looking at his watch.

'We really must be going. We'll miss dinner.'

Vera stood up, her legs close together.

'My clothes are almost dry. I'm going to put them on.' She went out. Edward was peering out of the window into the dark.

'The rain seems to have stopped now. How convenient! We needn't get wet going back.'

Bruce came and stood beside him. He felt sorry for the youth, that he should be tied up with these unsavoury men. He found Edward's wistful expression refreshing; a spark of warmth burned in his heart.

'In any case, the wind'll be behind you.'

Bertie sniggered.

'It usually is. At least, mine is.' Nobody laughed. Vera returned, holding her damp swimming costume in her hand. Stephen was at once conscious of her nude body inside the shirt and shorts. An erotic impulse shivered through his body. Bruce led the way to the hall and opened the front door. The wind had dropped a little; moonlight was straining to get through somewhere in the rapidly drifting restless clouds. Bruce could just see the white line of surf in the darkness below. He felt almost jovial with relief that the unwanted guests were going at last, scarcely at this moment sensing the burning pain and confusion in his mind. The four men, Larry pulling on his plastic macintosh, went out into the verandah. Vera followed them. There was an assortment of goodnights and goodbyes, a few thank-you's, and the five visitors disappeared into the darkness. Vera's voice, a stream of cheerful remarks, gradually faded into the rushes of the wind. The two friends returned to the living room. Stephen started to gather up the whisky glasses, but Bruce motioned him to sit down.

'Leave that now.'

There was a long silence, broken only by the settling of the fire and the sea and the wind outside.

'Why didn't you tell me?'

'What about?'

'Oh, don't be so stupid! About that girl.'

'I only met her yesterday.'

'That doesn't make any difference.'

'Is there anything wrong with her?'

'I don't know anything about her.' Bruce remembered the scene in the bathroom and was aware of the faint untruth of his words.

'She's an artist. She's at the College.'

'I don't mean that. What sort of person is she?'

'I believe she's a genius.'

'You're going to meet her again, aren't you? I heard you.'

'Yes, why not?'

'What about your novel?'

'Oh, that.' Stephen paused. 'I'm doing that.'

'Look, Stephen, I don't trust that girl. She's bound to have a bad influence on you.'

'Don't worry about it.'

'I do worry. I always worry about you. I've been trying to help you, Stephen.'

'I can look after myself.'

'I don't think you can.'

'Look, I'm very grateful, Bruce. But I don't need a nursemaid. No, sorry. I don't mean it like that. But surely I can choose my own friends?'

'I wish I'd never asked you here. We used to get on much better in Birmingham.'

'I don't think so. We're doing very well. We know each other much better. I've been here almost a week now.'

'What sort of week do you think it's been for me?'

'Haven't you enjoyed it?'

'First of all you didn't speak at all except in monosyllables. Then you threatened to kill yourself. Then you started messing about trying to write a novel or something; and just as you started to settle down, you go and make friends with this girl and hobnob with a bunch of queers. How do you think I feel?'

'You don't like girls, do you?'

'Nor did you. Until now, if I'm thinking right. I can't understand you.'

'I'm rather surprised myself.'

'What about me? I'm your friend, aren't I? I was planning a lot of things we could do together.'

'We can still do them.'

'With you thinking about that girl all the time? I saw the way you were looking at her.'

'Do you want me to leave this house?'

It was not a question; it was a threat.

'No, Stephen. No, no. I just want you to write your novel in peace, and to enjoy writing it. I just want to go for walks with you sometimes, to have conversations, as we used to. I don't want you to be distracted.'

'Do you think it's possible for me to work here without distraction?'

'What do you mean?'

'You never leave me alone. You're always going on at me. Write, write. Be more stable. Settle down. Then, let's go for a walk. It's your turn to wash up. Where have you been? You're always moralizing, trying to set me on the goody-goody right path. I'm not like that, Bruce. I can't follow any path someone else works out for me. It's not honest. I've got to find my own way. And you've got to let me.'

'Why did you say you couldn't write here?'

'Oh, that. I was talking to that Bertie man. I was telling him about the sea.'

There was another silence. Somehow they could both understand each other. It was as if they were standing on separate islands, with a turmoil of surf between them. The sea, far from uniting them, was constantly forcing them apart.

'You said the sea was making you go mad.'

'Yes, I did. It's making us both crazy. We can't live here together like this. Making sand castles, killing birds. It's all mad. The whole situation's hopelessly contrived and unnatural. Just romantic drivel.'

'It was such a wonderful idea.'

'Such a wonderful idea. I agree. Look, Bruce. We need other people. We're just smashing each other to bits, like this.'

Bruce knew it was true, but he could not bear the idea of Stephen having another friend on an equal footing with himself. He could not bear the idea of being isolated. He was trying to hold Stephen still – his special friend, his exclusive, brilliant companion, his disciple, his discovery, his triumph. But Stephen wouldn't heed the reins.

'What are you going to do about it?'

'Vera asked me to go up to the College sometime. It sounds interesting. Won't you come too?'

'I don't think we ought to go there. They're all peculiar people. There's something the matter with them. They're misfits. It's not safe.'

'So are we misfits. At least, I know I am.'

'I've been trying to help you, Stephen. You know how easily influenced you are.'

'By you too.'

'But can't you see I'm trying to give your life some shape, some meaning? Trying to get you to finish something, feel some sense of achievement?'

'Things don't work out like that.'

'Other people don't care about you like I do. They just use you for their pleasure.'

'What do you do?'

'I don't use you.'

'I think you do sometimes.'

'How?'

'You need someone to govern. Without me you'd have no one to set straight. You can't survive unless you're perpetual master. I can see through all your "benevolence", you know.'

'But even if I like to have power, I try to use it for your good.'

'I sometimes wonder if you do. You've been on at me for years about my being a queer, and now that I've hardly even spoken to one girl, you want me to leave her alone. If I were in your position, I'd welcome such a development. And anyway, how can I follow your example and be normal when you yourself like boys. You were rather attracted to that Edward fellow, weren't you? You're all mixed up and you mix me up. You're just playing with me. You treat me like a puppet. And another thing, Bruce, I might as well say it now. You're like a child. Nobody I know of your age makes sand castles or plays mountaineering games in the sandhills. You're just immature. It's time you grew up.'

Bruce stoked the fire. Everything Stephen was saying was true, but he could not endure to be told he was in the wrong. He sat down again.

'I think we're saying too much.'

'It's time we did sometimes. We need to clear the air. I've just about had enough. My mind's clogged up.'

'What are you going to do?'

'Well, for one thing I'm going to meet Vera tomorrow, whether you like it or not.'

'What about me?'

'You can do what you like.'

'I wish—'

He did not continue. He did not really know what he wished. He was at a loss. Stephen was now so unbearably hard and strong. Ruthless. Bruce felt near tears. After all he had done. It was true that he had tried to govern his friend, but it was also true that his efforts had been sincere, that he had really intended to help him.

'You make me feel useless. I might as well go and drown myself. You wouldn't care, would you?'

'You wouldn't dream of doing anything of the kind.'

'You don't know me. I always seem strong and stable, but I'm not like that at all. I need you, Stephen. Helping you gave me a purpose.'

'You'd better try to help yourself.'

They both relapsed into silence. They were exhausted, and they knew that further discussion would prove fruitless. It had happened like this before sometimes, but the rift had never been as wide as it was now. They cleared the table and prepared supper, keeping speech to a minimum.

Outside, unknown to either of them, the tide reached its full height, and then, without ceremony, began to recede.

23. NEW THING BREATHING

'ROUGH AND READY sea for the shoving on of ships! Tumble and rough waves. Slow, see-saw ocean. Tough, tugging bitch with vicious voice, snatching at sirens' long locks and otherwise long lost songs! Hoarse virgin, purest of all whores. Unsated dustbin of sundry lands. Spittoon. Eager coffin of sea-dogs, dogs and the dead at sea!

'Demanding nothing of us but us sometimes, and recognition. Taking willingly anything we care or care not to give – keel-weary treasure-ships, dregs of nations, or random child-thrown coins or the whistle for wind! I somehow know your welcome and endless cold-shouldering, and superficial smile in fair weather – knowing though that under that there's no loving heart, only the first cold womb constantly weaning generations.

'No man labours as you do for other dwellings to live in. No pioneer wins so much at new shores. You pass effortlessly over the highest peaks, not once only, leave bones of your bodies in the desert, and the sound of your neuroses in shipwrecked shells.

'Oh, my music maker! When can I be with you again, and become, even from the most sunless places, as a new thing breathing on the shining face of the world?'

Bruce stood at the edge of the sea crying out across the thunder of the breakers. That morning the sound of the sea and wind had resounded irresistibly in his ears, and soon he had sat down at the table under the west window of the living room and written the words he was now reciting. The whole bay was rolling and wild with the weather. There was no rain. The sky was a fast-moving canopy of low grey clouds, sweeping in towards the mountains and the north-west; the mountains were dark blue-grey, with only their lower slopes visible. The sea was a vast grey plain whipped into thousands of white horses, the under-current pulling the tide northwards, while the waves struggled and bounded towards the shore. The beach was a gleaming sheet where the spray came further than the tide, and nearer the sand dunes the surface sand was blasted into fast, white low-lying constantly changing eddies, which burned and stung his ankles and built up in white drifts against the heaps of black drying seaweed and pieces of driftwood. In his mind, the entire morning — what he could see and what he could hear — was one magnificent orchestration of elements. And he was the maestro at the centre of the world.

It was more than music; yet trying to name it, trying to explain to himself the wildness and savage ecstasy all around him, all Bruce could do was imagine himself in a huge, slowly revolving concert hall. The urgent and deafening blasts of the wind were thousands of serried strings — insane violins, crooning violas and mourning 'cellos and basses. The clouds overhead were massive bellows of brass, and the mountains echoed with endless forlorn cries of horns. Seagulls, beating their wings against the wind yet hardly moving forwards, could be heard — single woodwind phrases — mewing over and over above and within the surge of sound. And behind all was the interminable drumroll of the surf, and with it, and within it, and infinitely vaster than all of it, the sea was an immense chorus of innumerable voices, nothing heavenly about them, but laden with unnameable passions and fervour, like a worldwide Hebrew incantation, or Celtic choirs and the memories of older Celtic choirs echoing without end through the valleys and hills of Wales. Bruce stood there, as the ungraspable harmony strode over him, like mighty Brucknerian crescendoes, chords like mountains marching, chords held until the end of the world.

Then he was running along the edge of the sea against the wind, calling out to the ocean words which afterwards he had no memory of, his arms outspread, the sheets of paper clutched in his hand fluttering high in the air above him like a pennant. And he was a champion knight on a black horse rushing into battle against the gathered gales of earth, sallying out to win all wars, and never to die, never to die, never to die.

For him death was an impossibility. Somehow he felt, or rather he knew, that nothing could ever terminate his existence. The prose-poem he had composed that morning filled him with extraordinary optimism. For weeks he had felt that his creative impulses were dead, and suddenly today, like a dam collapsing, the words had come flooding into his brain. Inspiration, which he had long since ceased to believe in, had taken him by surprise, and he was full of jubilation. All pettiness and mean thoughts had been washed out of his mind. Sickened stallions had miraculously stood up, whinnied and come cantering out into fresh air. He was gripped by an almost unmanageable stirring of energy. The storm was over, and now the whole world was blowing northwards, invincibly strong, denying all mortality.

Stephen had gone out soon after breakfast and was now somewhere along the shore with Vera. Bruce had at first felt a terrible bitterness seeing his friend leaving him like that with hardly a word, and he had stared at the sea in the lowest depths of dejection and frustration. Stephen had another friend, a girl friend; they shared a world Bruce could not enter. A fresh rush of despair had gripped his entire body. What did Vera and Stephen do there along the beach in the sand dunes? What was the wind cage they were talking about the evening before? Were they going to meet together to talk or make love together? Or worse still, had they had already done that? Virgin as Bruce was, he felt helpless and lost at the idea of Stephen making love to a girl. Deep down, he knew, that was what he himself wanted. He had been thinking about it in bed the night before, disturbed and excited by the image of Vera naked in the bathroom. He had not succumbed to self-relief, but the image had aroused erotic stirrings in the dark. Now, with Stephen gone, it came to him clearly that there was, after all, nothing that he could do. He understood the limitations of human power, of his power over Stephen. Stephen was strong and he Bruce was helpless. But helplessness, he gradually began to realize, is a low-lying land. All roads from it lead eventually towards slopes, into foothills, then into mountains; and Bruce found that whichever way he went now it would lead upwards: there was no further way down. He was alone in the house by the sea, and the sea seemed to be flowing through his body, as if his bloodstream were wholly at one with the streaming of the tide. And it had always been so. The lines of poetry which had come into his head were not sudden thoughts inspired by the weather. They were laden with experience, born from a deep-down knowledge of the sea, a primeval instinct that had risen, after millions of years of submersion, to the surface of his conscious mind. He was truly now a child of the ocean. He felt a burning, a craving, a terrible longing for that first cold womb, a longing to be in that mother-darkness once again. But somehow in those moments of despair as Stephen went down the path with firm steps, Bruce had suddenly been driven by some inner force, and the words of the poem had come flooding into his mind.

Bruce reached the south end of the beach under the cliff and railway line, turned like a reined horse and ran back this time with the wind behind him. His feet seemed hardly to be touching the ground; to run now was effortless, almost as if the force of gravity had lessened, as it was on the surface of the moon. With shining eyes he turned right in a wide arc and bounded up over the rocks, up the path, into the house, snatched his swimming things from the drying rack in the kitchen, changed rapidly in the lower bedroom next to the bathroom, leaving his clothes in an untidy heap on the floor, then rushed out of the house, down the path with his towel streaming out behind him, across the rocks as nimbly as a mountain goat, dropped his towel, galloped out onto the firm beach and without looking behind him ran straight towards the sea and plunged headlong into the waves. They were so strong, rolling like huge foam-spewing logs of wood that hit him then dissolved, that the breath was knocked out of his body. He was flung over onto his back, twisted onto his side, and then rolled over and over, while he gasped and swallowed and spat out mouthfuls of the harsh salt water. He stood up, facing the wind. There was a pain in his stomach from the pressure of water of the first wave that had struck him, but he struggled forwards deeper into the sea. Another huge wave bore down upon him, but he turned his back on it and it broke with a roaring explosion over his head. Bruce stood firm. Wave after wave broke thus over his back and head, while he was regaining his breath and gathering strength for a new onslaught. Then he turned, his head down, his shoulders hunched, his fists clenched at his side. Looking upwards without raising his head as the next wave approached, Bruce looked it in the eye, aimed his right shoulder at it, and it burst over him like thousands of stacked up blue-green glasses and bottles charged at by a bison. He staggered once, but stood firm. Again and again he challenged the waves head-on. They buffeted him, they shouted in his ears, they bruised his mind, but they couldn't knock him down any more. Bruce looked far out at a line of distant breakers churned into a long white restless frontier of surf above a submerged sandbank. What a great battlefield of joyous despair the sea was on days such as this! With what tragic passion the waves thundered, thudded and smashed against his body, and with what proud and confident yet utterly useless energy they went rolling on past him towards the shore! Here was the entire embodiment and incarnation of suicide, its whole history and futility laid out like a heroic yet forlorn pageant along the world's shores. Bruce turned to look at the beach, the waves still crashing harmlessly into his back. The dunes, the red-tiled roof, the whole grey cloud-topped cliff, looked dead and forsaken, but here was he, Bruce Dinwiddy, bravely shouldering off the onslaughts of the wind and the sea! The white horses were crying behind him; there was such a deep, and such a high, sad mind-crazing fervour of emotion in the voices of the breakers. It filled him with unbearable longing, with the aching, delightful, yearning burden of a love that was doomed from the moment it was created from the sea, and he wanted to cry and cry out till his hair turned as white as the spray. A great wave smashed against his back and sent him bounding forwards, but he kept his feet, and then began to leap with the water towards the shore. He himself was a wave being driven from the sea. He felt a huge arm, a booming subterranean voice, a vast mother-petrel of the sea pushing him out of the unruly nest of the ocean, urging him to grow sea-wings and fly out into the barren world of dry land. Yes, well then, yes, he would fly; he would fly up, out, over and high above all the sorrows that plagued mankind, and he would never be hurt again. He ran faster, his feet splashing in the last shallow dying waves, and suddenly he was standing free on the glistening sand, his body tingling and red and warmly frozen with the salt and the dash of the surf, and he emerged onto the shore, purified and triumphant, as a new thing breathing on the shining face of the world.

He looked to his left. There was no sign of Stephen any-where on the beach; but to Bruce the world was now a different place, and the place of Stephen in his life was also utterly transformed. So let him go. What did it matter now if Stephen had other friends? Why should he, Bruce, demand exclusive rights to the companionship of Stephen Pewit? Why not become truly tolerant and kind? Let him go the way of his will, and even if it led him into ruin and grief, let it lead him. He had tried to persuade, but he had no right or power to command. Stephen was after all a human being and no longer a child. Bruce could feel the pangs mothers feel in letting their sons go out into the world. The first cutting of the umbilical chord is hard enough perhaps; the second, that which occurs in the mind, is infinitely more hard to bear. Bruce could feel the first lines of age actually forming at the edges of his eyes, like lines of dunes forming at the edge of the sea, the first greying of hair somewhere down under his skull.

Strangely now it seemed that he had failed even to destroy. Unable to help his friend, he had set out on a path of destruction, but Stephen had risen up under his cold hands stronger than ever, stronger now than he himself was, and the barrenness in Bruce's mind had suddenly blossomed out into a seething mass of creativity.

He walked to the rocks and picked up his towel, shaking off the drifts of sand that had accumulated in its folds. He at once felt warm, comfortable and secure, filled with new energy and wellbeing as he made his way up the path to the house. Once inside and out of the wind, he immediately became aware of his body. To his amazement he felt a vigorous hardening inside the front of his swimming trunks and looked down. It was happening again. Without an impure thought or thrill of anticipation in his mind, his body was rewarding him once more. Swaggering slightly he walked into the downstairs bedroom and stripped. Boldly he stepped out of the room and walked into the kitchen naked. Without a thought of who might see him, he walked out again along the passage into the living room, stoked up the fire and stood by the west window, intoxicated by the involuntary power of his body. Only three days since his last release, and here it was again, urgent and thrilling. He strolled to the bathroom and opened the door. Immediately, the memory of Vera naked gave him a fresh lunge of rising ecstasy. He stood by the bath-tub, transfixed with mindless anticipation. Then there was no stopping it. And this time, he instantly understood, there was no guilt, no sudden deflation of ecstasy. The pleasure was entirely unexpected, unsolicited, and it stayed with him. Having passed its peak, it spread all over his body as if ichor were running in his veins. He felt pure, innocent, elated with natural animal health. He rinsed himself down with a sponge, drying himself in the next room where he had left his clothes. Still, and this amazed and delighted him, there was no dull ache of excess. Inspired with the joy of being alive and male and young, his heart pounded with energy and confidence. There was no need for thought or analysis. This was he, this was life at the best he had known it, this was promise and hope. He was happy, and doubly so in knowing that he was happy after an event that usually left him with feelings of sin and gloom. Dry and dressed and warm he went back to the living room.

Light of heart, he busied himself with a number of practical matters. He telephoned his father in Birmingham, reporting the structural decay of the south wall and the woodworm. Not long after that, around eleven o'clock, the carpenter came down, made estimates, and immediately returned to the town to make emergency preparations, telling Bruce he would begin repairs the following morning. For the first time Bruce felt he was acting as a responsible adult, one who had no time to indulge in sentimental and romantic extravagancies. When the carpenter had gone, he wrote a long letter to his father explaining the situation in detail. He felt curious satisfaction in knowing that his father, who had usually been so critical of him in the past, would be pleased at this new show of initiative and decisiveness. Stephen did not return for lunch. Bruce made his own, then fetched the milk, posting his letter at the top of the cliff and forgetting in his enthusiasm for action to put a stamp on it. Back at the house, he got out his bulky folder of poems, long neglected, and began to sort them out, putting some of what he thought were the best ones together as a collection, planning to type them out later and send them to a publisher. The sun occasionally shone through the racing clouds, and there were patches of blue sky, but the wind was if anything stronger.

In mid-afternoon he came out of the house and stood on the lawn. On the beach, quite near the house, five youths were pushing along a strange contraption. It consisted mainly of a large board to which were attached four bicycle wheels, the front two dirigible. Fixed vertically onto this framework by means of wires was a mast – a six-foot cane, to which a crossbar and sheet for a sail were tied with cord. A little way past the house, to Bruce's left, in the corner of the bay, they stopped and turned the machine round. One of them sat on the board. Slowly, and then more quickly as the sail filled, the sand-yacht began to move. The others ran alongside shouting excitedly; their voices came to Bruce unevenly and half-shattered by the wind. The yacht raced along the sand, like a seagull trying to take off with a piece of wood tied to its feet, and soon the runners were left far behind. Suddenly, in the distance, the contraption veered out of control and fell over. The yachtsman, unhurt as far as Bruce could see, stood up and as soon as the others had caught up with him they turned the machine round again and began to push it back along the beach.

A wave of loneliness filled Bruce's mind. Always, it seemed, he was the one person left out, the one person who didn't fit into the schemes of other people, whom no one cared for, no one loved. He was alone. But, after all, did that matter so much? Even alone there were many compensations. He had a mind, and a mind that could do things with words, a mind that could heal itself after hurt, that could grow and blossom. And he had a body, lithe, young and oozing with piercingly delightful fruit. Both mind and body operated without the agency of others; they were independent, free. He needed no one other than himself to survive as a personality. Perhaps he was even greater alone. Other people held him back, pulled him down. Other people irritated him, wouldn't go his way. He had more power alone than when he tried to exercise it over others. Better then to depend on no one but himself, better not to believe in others, better to be Bruce Dinwiddy and thrive.

With a firm look at the sea, he smiled and shook his head slowly, and pressing aside his self-pity with new resolve, with deliberate steps he walked back into the house.

24. SMELLING BOTTLES

VERA NICOLSON was seventeen. She had spent her childhood in a quiet suburb of Manchester, where her father was a history teacher at a grammar school. Her mother, a rather witless woman, spent the entire day keeping their semi-detached house spotlessly and uninhabitably clean. In her early teens, Vera had started to rebel against the conventional dignity of her household. She detested her father's pipe-smoking complacency, his weekends in the garden, his onions, potatoes and tomatoes, and she grew to loathe the neat vases of flowers her mother placed in the most obvious places all over the house. The fact that her father was a schoolmaster played not a little part in her early opposition to authority. Just as doctors' children are generally more often ill than average children, so was Vera more than usually impervious to discipline, and she frequently played truant from school, which, perhaps fortunately for both of them, was not the one where her father taught. She quarrelled constantly with her father, and her mother was too vague and too much concerned with domestic symmetry to take sides. She was soon staying out late with boys and lost her virginity one day before her fourteenth birthday. At fifteen she was smoking pot regularly and had once been involved in a police case, from which, however, she escaped with a mere warning. A year later, she had her first abortion. Her parents knew about everything; she never tried to hide anything from them – and this was the one bright spark in a household that was slowly dying of lack of communication. Mr. and Mrs. Nicolson were naturally shocked and remonstrated with their daughter – their only child – often and sometimes bitterly, but with no noticeable effect. They were more concerned with preserving their respectability in the neighbourhood. In spite of Vera's so-called moral lapses, or perhaps partly because of them, she displayed undoubted talents as an artist. Art was the one subject in which she excelled at school, and it was the one activity, apart from her often-dangerous experiments with boyfriends, which she took seriously. Feeling that their daughter would go from bad to worse, the Nicolsons had decided to send Vera away from home and thus from the bad influence of her companions in the neighbourhood. They had got to know of the College at Harlieg from one of Mr. Nicolson's colleagues in education, and had applied – wondering whether Vera, who had had every opportunity for a normal education, would qualify for admission. The administrators of the College, who prided themselves on their broadmindedness, overlooked this factor, and on the strength of her school reports, in which art was the only redeeming feature, and her police record, accepted her. They promised to do their best to set Vera on the straight path; but like many idealists in the academic world, they were completely blind to what went on among the students under their own roof, and those members of the staff who had some inkling did not attempt to interfere. Unknown to parents, administrators and the students themselves, the College – by grouping together dropouts and delinquents, who thus strengthened their inclinations by sharing their experience and experiences – did more harm than good. Vera was almost instantly at home in her new surroundings and soon became even more deeply embroiled in sexual and narcotic adventures than she had been at home. The only notable difference was that at the College, removed from the stigmas of her conventional background, she had more freedom, mental and physical, to enjoy her activities and to develop her artistic talents. The College anticipated and tolerated strange behaviour to a certain degree, and as long as students turned up for classes and therapy sessions, did little else to guide them. The sand dunes beyond the golf links below the College provided an ideal playground for the students' uninhibited games and liaisons, and in addition a few students, Vera among them, had banded together and rented a small stone cottage in the hills above the town, where they sometimes went for weekend jamborees – holding wild parties and bizarre orgies. At such times, other students co-operated and covered their absences. Vera was supremely happy. Her parents received her weekly letters – full of innocent enthusiasm about the College, the castle, the mountains, the beach, and, of course, the sea – and sighed with relief.

Sitting beside Vera on the top of a sandhill, Stephen knew that his first impressions had not been false. The fascination he had felt at their first meeting had in no way diminished. Her conversation captivated him; every sentence she uttered sparkled with humour and originality, and he found himself laughing often in a light-hearted manner quite alien to him. Vera also found in Stephen someone who excited her, but she did not quite know why. She had at once detected Stephen's lack of experience with the opposite sex, his awkwardness when their eyes met sometimes, and she felt an immediate desire to introduce him to all the secrets of her own world. To corrupt him was not how she thought of it; she already sensed that he was not entirely without experience in certain forms of sexual activity. She wished somehow to educate him, to offer him new degrees of exhilaration. It was not only their childlike enthusiasm for art which attracted them to each other. Stephen, too, after talking with her for several hours, became aware of huge gaps in Vera's intellect. Of philosophy, literature, music, she knew next to nothing. He began to feel a kind of pity for this brilliant girl. What miracles she could perform if only her originality were linked to theories of logic and mathematical order! He must teach her what he knew. But it was not only this. He had not forgotten seeing Vera naked in the sandhills, and her physical presence even now excited him more than anything else about her. If only he knew how to behave, what to do. He had no idea how to set about it. He lacked the necessary vocabulary, was totally ignorant of the process and stages of intimacy. All his previous sexual exploits had been initiated by others, and by men older than him. He feared too that were they ever to get as far as undressing, Vera would laugh at what he thought of as his physical inadequacy. Even as they sat there, Vera seemed to sense Stephen's anxiety, and very gently she moved her hand towards his resting on the sand between them, touched it as if by accident, and then suddenly took hold of it, as a child might, looking at it with interest and squeezing his fingers. Stephen, almost dizzy with rapture which seemed to him not in the slightest way sexual in origin, returned the pressure. The delight was in his heart, in his mind. The normality of it, of holding hands with a girl, came to him as a tremendous relief. Nature was after all a benevolent force. Man and woman were meant for each other. Nothing, thought Stephen, was more natural than this, more simple, more beautiful, more divine even, than merely sitting there at the edge of the sea, listening to the vigorously conflicting yet miraculously harmonious buffeting of wind and waves; sitting there with a faery-minded girl and holding hands. It had a magic, a simplicity and purity that was utterly new to him, and for the moment he wanted nothing other.

'Let's go for a walk and smell bottles.'

Once again Stephen was enchanted by the novelty of her ideas. In all his walks with Bruce, it had never occurred to either of them to open shipwrecked bottles and smell their contents. Still holding hands and swinging them gently, they ran down to the beach and walked along the tideline further away from the house. From time to time they stooped and one of them would pick up a bottle. Some of the tops, rusted or encrusted with salt, were difficult to remove, and once that was achieved the smells were sometimes nauseous − tomato ketchup brown with age, slightly yellow gin, detergent. Once there was a bottle that had once contained lavender water, which delighted both of them. They kept it with them, sniffing at it in turn. The contents of others they could not recognize, and then they started guessing, making up all sorts of ghastly combinations, some of them so preposterous that they sometimes worked themselves into paroxysms of silent laughter, crouching down on the sand and then suddenly bursting out into wild yells. But Stephen also had serious thoughts. Even the sea, it seemed to him, could not swallow everything. From time to time it coughed and vomited up these old bottles and the thousand other indigestible objects that man finds with such delight along the shores. Or with disgust. He remembered Bruce telling him during one of their walks that the things washed up nowadays were lacking in variety. There was too much celluloid and polythene, he said, too much that was valueless and ugly. The tideline seemed to reflect the progress, or the lack of it, of mankind. Man less frequently used wood to make things, bottles made of glass were scarcer. Now it was all plastic, nylon, synthetic fibres and fabrics, things that wouldn't merge with the natural environment, wouldn't change their colour. Wood became smooth and underwent a gradual sea-change; glass became sand again. But the detritus of modern times wasn't flexible. It stubbornly retained its brilliant artificial greens and blues, hideous oranges and glaring yellows, like the faeces of overfed monkeys in zoos. Now Stephen saw it in yet another way. These imperishable objects were like messages from the sea, like screams of agony, the evidence of some incurable disease. The sea couldn't take any more. Man was pouring an endless stream of filth down her gullet, and she was sick with it. Many inland lakes of the world had already succumbed, were dead, and now the sea itself was dying, unable to absorb any more of the poison spewed from the guts of civilization. All she could do was regurgitate, moan, and warn mankind that the end was near. Man was committing matricide without knowing it, without knowing that when he had exhausted all the resources of earth, the only place he would have left to go to would be the sea; and the sea by then would already have been choked to death.

Vera found a very soft yellow and white beach-ball. They kicked it along, running and still holding hands, often almost both falling over as one of them swerved aside to catch the ball and send it flying along the next stage of its journey. Behind them they saw the students with the sand-yacht, but neither of them mentioned it. They sensed an empathy between the two of them, which neither wished to disturb by sharing it with others. Tired of kicking the ball at last, Vera sat on it and it burst, causing them both to laugh hysterically. Then they fell silent and looked at each other. Stephen wondered whether this was the moment he was waiting for. He opened his mouth to speak, but Vera spoke first.

'Are you coming up to the College tonight? We're having a sort of show.'

'What kind of show?'

'We have one every month. It's a kind of therapy. They're supposed to relieve us of our tensions.' Vera laughed irreverently. 'We sing songs, recite poems, make speeches, do little skits. It's quite stupid really. But anyway I want you to meet my friends.'

Stephen had no desire to meet Vera's friends. Not now. The very thought of them filled him with a kind of distant despair. He hoped Vera wouldn't suggest they join the sand-yacht group at the other end of the beach. Yet at the same time he was curious to see what sort of people they were. Bruce had called them misfits. Vera was anything but a misfit, or, if she were, it was because she was superior to the others. None of them could possibly have her brilliant wit, her sparkling energy, her original turn of mind.

'Yes, I'd love to come.'

'Oh, good!'

'What about my friend?'

Stephen could not feel any antipathy towards Bruce. He felt strangely warm towards him now, even sorry for him, and a little guilty that he had left him alone at the house. His one-time master, his former lord abandoned by his solitary retainer, alone by the sea. After all, it was Bruce who had brought him to this magnificent place. And here he had met Vera. The irony of the situation struck him: Bruce had longed to be alone with his friend, and his friend had been spellbound by a boy-witch of a girl. He looked at Vera. There was a slight gleam of humour in her eyes.

'Well, what about your friend?'

'Can he come too?'

Stephen was almost amazed by his own generosity of spirit in letting Bruce have any share at all in his new-found happiness.

'Does he want to come?'

'I'm not sure; but I can't very well leave him down there. I'm supposed to be his guest.'

Vera frowned a little. She disliked people who were proper and thought of others. Stephen sensed her disapproval.

'It doesn't matter so much. I mean, I'm sure he wouldn't mind if I was out for an evening.'

'Is he a very special friend?'

Stephen hesitated. What did Vera mean?

'Well...yes, he is.'

His own admission surprised him. But he suddenly realized that it was true. Bruce was his special friend, and now that he was away from him, even though it had been only a few hours, he began to see Bruce as a rather splendid person. Why was it that when they were together there was always so much friction and squabbling? Familiarity breeds contempt. Where had he heard that? Surely it was a contradiction. How could it apply to man and woman, boy and girl? Were all husbands and wives secretly contemptuous of each other? In spite of what he knew of various families, including his own, he could not believe in such a pessimistic view. Maybe it was because both he and Bruce were such exceptional people. And what about Vera? Suppose he got to know her better? Would he ever feel contempt for her? Never! She was far too fascinating.

'He can come if he wants to. Does he want to read his poems?'

'I don't think he'd want to do that. He's rather shy about them with strangers.'

'He wasn't very pleasant yesterday.'

'It was those people from the hotel. He doesn't like people like that.'

'Oh. I thought it was me. So he's not like that?'

'No—not really. He's a bit funny with strangers.'

'Do you want to read some of your novel? We could invite you as a special guest.'

'You said you didn't like people who read their novels out loud.'

'You're different.'

'I don't think you'd like it. It's rather philosophical.'

'I'll tell you if I get bored. Yes, that's a good idea. Both of you come. It'll liven things up a bit. Nobody's got much talent at the College. It'll make a change.'

Stephen was secretly very pleased. He liked having an audience, especially when he was asked to read, which rarely happened.

'What time shall we come?'

'Any time after supper.'

'Vera—'

'What's the matter?'

'Shall we—go into the sandhills?'

'What for?'

Stephen did not know how to continue. He had hoped Vera would understand him without words. He felt sure she had understood him, but she sat there beside the burst beach-ball, looking at him with that faintly mocking, humorous expression he had seen from time to time. Stephen's reply was understandably lame.

'I thought perhaps we might find some—bombshells there.'

Vera put back her head and let forth a stream of uncontrollable laughter. She looked at Stephen through tears of mirth, trying unsuccessfully to be serious.

'I'm sure there are lots of bombshells going on in the sandhills, Steve.' She collapsed into a shaking mass of laughter again. She wanted to add: 'I could show you a few bombshells', but instead she just laughed and threw the miserable damp shreds of the beach-ball at Stephen. 'There's a bombshell – quite squeezed out!'

Stephen was excited by the wantonness of her laughter. At the same time, he felt his fears rising again. She seemed to be laughing at him, as if she had already undressed him in her mind and knew his miserable secret. But perhaps there wasn't anything he need be ashamed of. All the sex manuals he had read were vehement in emphasizing that genital dimensions made no difference to a woman's pleasure, and that although minimum dimensions might greatly differ from person to person, maximum dimensions were very much the same. At the back of his mind, however, he felt a certain doubt. Why did everyone say women liked negroes? Sexual pleasure was surely not entirely a physical matter; there were psychological nuances and overtones. Men liked women to have big breasts, he had heard, the bigger the breasts the greater the pleasure, and the greater the anticipation of that pleasure. Looking at Vera's compact body, however, her small firm breasts, Stephen felt a sense of contradiction. Or was it that he was somehow different? What was he supposed to feel? He felt confused, at a loss. He stood up. The spell was momentarily broken. Vera also stood up.

'Why did your friend call me the Old Woman of the Sea?'

Stephen told her about Bruce's mother. They walked back along the beach in silence. Until then, neither of them had been strongly aware of the sea. They had been too wrapped up in their thoughts, of one another, of many things. And the sea was too far away. But now as they walked into the wind, the sound of the surf penetrated their conscious minds. Vera was thinking of ways she could cut up the solid undersides of waves into cubes and build a sea-palace with blocks of liquid marble, blue, white and green. Stephen was thinking of Bruce, his mother's ashes somewhere in those sandhills. He felt once more aware of the greatness, of the sadness of his friend. He saw Bruce's eyes, and remembered now that whenever he looked at them he could always see the turning of the waves. Vera interrupted his thoughts.

'What are you thinking about?'

'Mermaids.'

'How do they keep their tails clean?' She laughed.

'You shouldn't laugh, Vera. There's nothing childish or silly about mermaids. I'm not thinking of the ones you read about in fairy tales, with fishes' tails. The ones I'm thinking of are infinitely more terrible than that. They don't sing delightful songs.'

'What do they do then – tickle each other?'

'They stare. They whine and hum and moan. They stare. You see, all of them are senile and grey-haired. They're all mad. And if they stare at you too long, you go mad too.'

'Have you seen them?'

'No, but my friend knows about them.'

'Is he mad?'

'Yes. Or perhaps—not yet. I think he hears them all the time. Something to do with his mother. You can see it in his eyes. Next time you meet him look at his eyes. I think you'll understand what I mean.'

'Sounds a bit fishy to me. No, I didn't mean to make that pun. It just came out. I agree, there's definitely something—strange about him.' She bent down and picked up a bottle. 'Let's smell this one.'

Stephen was slightly irritated by Vera's lack of interest in Bruce, yet also somehow comfortable. With a quick smile he took the bottle from her. It was large and made of pale green glass. A trace of clear fluid remained inside it. With difficulty Stephen unscrewed the cap, which had rusted slightly. He put his nose to the opening. It smelt of weak ammonia without the pungency. Vera took it from him, smelt it, looked at Stephen and burst into laughter.

'Do you know what that smells like?'

'I'm not sure.'

'You ought to know better than me.'

'What do you mean?' He smelt the bottle again. Then he understood. Yes, the smell was similar. Blushing slightly, he looked at Vera. Then suddenly he threw the bottle as far as he could towards the sea.

'Why did you do that? Don't you like it?'

The smell had repelled Stephen, as something unclean, and attracted as he was to Vera he did not know how to answer. He once again sensed Vera was making fun of him. She was so strong and seemed to know everything about him, even the smell of his intimate body juices. It did not surprise him after what he had seen in the sandhills the previous day, but he now wanted to find a way to restore the balance between them. Without that equilibrium the relationship lost something of its charm. Then suddenly he knew what to say. He smiled and gestured at the bottle, giving Vera what he hoped was a knowing glance.

'That? Oh, that's nothing. I've got something better in mind.'

'In mind? In mind or body?' She giggled.

A glance of comprehension passed between them, but again Stephen lost the initiative. He knew that he could not continue this farce of double-talk. If only he had the courage to grip Vera by the arm, lead her wordless into the sandhills and there satisfy his longing. But Vera was playing the old game. She had to be conquered, and it was just this kind of cat-and-mouse sexual fencing that he detested. Vera was in this respect just like any other girl, a coquette, a little flirt. Stephen was disappointed. Why couldn't girls be simple and easy to deal with? Why did they bandy about with men's passions so? He knew this was not the moment to make the crucial advance. He didn't dare to risk rejection by Vera. He would have to wait for another chance.

'I think I'll have to be getting back.'

A sudden coldness fell between them.

'See you up at the College then. Do you want this bottle?' She held out the lavender-water bottle.

'No, you keep it.'

'I don't want it. It smells of my grandmother.' Vera flung it onto the beach where it hit a solitary stone and smashed.

'Pity.'

'Don't be sentimental.'

'I wanted you to keep it—as a souvenir.'

'In memory of what?'

'Today.'

'What's special about today?'

Stephen couldn't answer. He wanted that morning, for himself at least, to have been unforgettable, his first time with a girl, but the encounter was turning sour, fading out like a damp sparkler.

'Nothing. What are you doing this afternoon?'

'I've got some classes.' Vera sounded prim and proper. 'If you want a souvenir of today, why not keep that other bottle, the one you threw over there? Lavender water we can buy in shops, but that smell was...heavenly.' She giggled again. 'Unforgettable.'

'It might have been.' Stephen decided to play the same game.

'Not this time.'

'Perhaps next time.'

'Anyway, you keep that bottle if you want to. I can smell a smell like that whenever I want to – up at the College.'

'Or in the sandhills.'

Vera stared at Stephen.

'Yes, even in the sandhills. So can you – any time you like.'

'I'm not very fond of that particular smell.'

'I am! It's the most exciting smell in the world!'

'Would you like some, in a bottle?'

'I'd rather keep it somewhere else.'

'Let me know when it's convenient.'

'I'm not in the mood today.'

'I'll wait until you are.'

'I'll let you know.'

They had wandered close under the sandhills during this exchange, and Stephen was just about to take Vera by the hand when she suddenly pointed towards the sea. The boys with the sand-yacht were rushing along close to the tideline. They passed the point where Vera and Stephen were standing, one of them on the vehicle, the others around it shouting encouragement. Vera started to run towards them, shouting goodbye to Stephen over her shoulder. Stephen did not try to stop her, nor did he run after her. Their conversation had shaken him with alternations of excitement and frustration and he needed time to let his mind settle. He wanted to think. Vera was not going to be so easy a bird to catch, he could see that. It was useless, he realized, to force the issue. If only he could see into her mind! If only he knew how to take action and take it at the right time! Well, there was much promise in her hints, in her eyes, in her smiles and giggles. They would meet that evening at the College. Today wasn't the day, but the future was pregnant with possibility. He thought of what Vera had said about the bottle he had thrown towards the sea. Yes, and he had shocked her again with mention of the sandhills. Stephen started to walk back towards the house, keeping close to the line of dunes. Something blue and gleaming caught his eye – another bottle. He picked it up. It was squarish and the azure glass was filled with what looked like little trees of veins or internal fractures, and there were a few air bubbles also. It was a hand-made bottle, wide-mouthed and unstoppered, almost a work of art. He lifted it to his nostrils but as he did so he noticed that it contained nothing but a little dry sand. Nevertheless, he smelt it. What was it? Faintly salty, a hint of the jellyfish-like scent of geranium leaves, a fresh, clean smell, pure; but what was it? He emptied the sand out and continued walking, delighted at finding such a treasure. This would be a real souvenir of his stay at the house by the sea. And as he walked it slowly came into his mind when the smell in the bottle reminded him of. Without his being aware of it, he realized now, it had been everywhere about him since he had come to Harlieg. It hung on the air throughout the day and night. It was, simply and nothing other, the smell of the sea.

25. THE COLLEGE

BRUCE HAD NEVER been inside the College before and as soon as he entered the Great Hall he found himself wishing that he could have been its owner. The hall was illuminated by a single central chandelier equipped with ordinary bare bulbs some of which were missing and about a dozen dim wall lamps some of them with their glass shades broken. At the north end, standing like a noble, slender Gothic castle faintly silhouetted against a tall window beyond which he could see the dark blue evening sky, towered an organ and its loft, the pipes gleaming a dull mysterious grey in the soft light. Below was a raised platform, upon which at one time might have been a banqueting table; a rather peculiar arrangement, as the music 'gallery' should have been at the other, south end of the hall. The rest of the tall 'baronial' chamber was almost bare. A large threadbare crimson carpet had been laid over the centre of the stone-paved floor, and round the wall were several old leather sofas, their upholstery in a worn condition, especially on the arms, and full of splits which looked as if they had been deliberately cut with knives or razor blades. A number of dirty, bedraggled cushions were scattered around on the floor, looking like stage-prop rocks. Upon these and draped over the sofas, some thirty young people, informally attired, were lounging, some of them in small groups, or in pairs closely entwined, a few by themselves. No one stood up or showed any sign of surprise or interest as Vera led Bruce and Stephen into the hall. Bruce was at once conscious of the general air of dilapidation and ennui. He tried to imagine the hall as it would have been in his mother's day – filled with ladies and gentlemen in formal evening dress, politely conversing; resounding with the polished wooden elegant tones of a Mozart quintet, subdued applause and murmurs of approbation. If Bruce had lived there, he would have held bardic enclaves, magnificent recitations: the hall would ring with great orations and jeremiads, with echoing shouts of acclamation. Candles would burn there in brackets round the walls, the chandelier would spread a warm aureole of flickering light over heavy wooden tables loaded with wine, meat and new bread; banners would hang from the roof beams; the organ would croon with deliciously sad, forlorn voluntaries, like far-off horn-calls across the hills. It could have been, must have been, such a splendid place, with darkly-glowing oaken furnishings, huge oil paintings of mountain landscapes and Greek myths set in heavily ornate dull-gold frames, and vast tapestries of hunting scenes or the campaigns of Alexander the Great. Nothing of such splendour remained save the great silent organ frowning down on the miserable scene below. Bruce strongly regretted the building was now a college for the delinquent and deprived.

Bruce glanced at Stephen. His friend looked slightly irritated. Bruce was not sure whether it was because of Stephen's distaste at the scene before him or because of a small incident that had occurred outside the College a few minutes earlier. Just before entering the main gate from the main road, the gentler of the two hills up to the town, a boy on a bicycle had come tearing down the slope and had called out a greeting to Bruce as he sped past.
'Who was that?'
'Oh—the delivery boy from Hughes the grocer.'

'Do you know him?'

Bruce smiled, half guiltily.

'He brought the food down four or five days ago. You were out walking.' Bruce was not disturbed by Stephen's sharp enquiries. He felt strangely moved, as he had when the boy had appeared in front of the house by the sea the previous week. He felt touched that the boy had bothered to greet him, but he also felt a twinge of sadness. There had been a slight crack in the boy's voice as he called out. His voice was breaking. There had been something slightly cocky, something knowing, experienced, in the way the boy had spoken, waving his hand at Bruce, and letting the bicycle swerve dangerously into the middle of the road. The boy had turned back to look at him, for too long, Bruce thought, as if he could see right into Bruce's mind and understood the soiled thoughts that simmered there. Stephen stopped and stared at his friend for a while, then smiled a little ironically. Bruce knew what he was thinking, but he was not going to let his friend invade this little private territory of his. He smiled back at Stephen, feeling the power of having this secret – what was it? – relationship with the boy. He would keep Stephen guessing. Let him think what he would. Then they had entered the College.

Vera introduced the two friends to various other students. One of them was Philip, whom Stephen instantly recognized as the boy he had seen with Vera in the sandhills, the one who had before that invited him to join their party on the beach. Stephen found himself now loathing Philip's languid ease. Most of the students, he felt, came from well-to-do families, and he became aware once again of his own miserable background. This was a playground for wealthy dropouts, he could tell that at a mere glance. Many of the 'students' were drinking beer, and some were smoking. Stephen recognized the distinctive aroma of marijuana. He wondered if the authorities knew about it; he was surprised by the apparent absence of supervision. He hated all forms of authority, of course, but somehow there was something even worse in this easy-going atmosphere. He frowned. He had been irritated by Bruce's secretive air on the road outside, but he knew that his friend was making a pretence about the boy. He knew that Bruce would never break his code of purity, though he might like others to imagine there was something slightly unclean about such a relationship. That was Bruce all over, part of his contrived enigma. He glanced round the hall again. The students seemed to be almost exclusively in control of the building. Posters and notices were pinned up on the walls, some of them half torn off and hanging with bits of grimy selotape stuck carelessly across their corners. Stephen could see Bruce looking at the same notices. He knew his friend hated selotape like that: he had often told Stephen that it always looked better if attached vertically or horizontally but never across the corners, another of Bruce's fixations. The entrance hall of the college and the corridors had been disfigured in the same untidy way. No officials or teachers were to be seen anywhere. A general air of improvisation, flux and administrative laxity prevailed.

For a while Bruce and Stephen were left to their own devices. Nobody seemed to be doing anything. Vera melted into a group of girls reclining on one of the sofas. Stephen noticed that two of the girls were holding hands and sometimes caressing each other's faces. He began an involved conversation about existentialism with a tall, pimply youth wearing gold-rimmed glasses. Bruce, overhearing parts of their discussion, felt that neither of them was well versed in the subject. They were just exchanging high-sounding statements without any real human communication at all. He heard Stephen use the word 'pragmatic'. Stephen probably didn't know what the word meant! Bruce walked away from the stale air of what seemed to him to be nothing but self-conscious intellectual snobbery. He stood near one of the unoccupied sofas looking up at the organ loft. On the panelled wall nearby, someone had pinned a notice announcing an expedition to climb Snowdon by way of Crib Goch. Bruce wondered if any of the people involved knew how dangerous that route was. There was one signature in the space provided, in a very subdued hand, as if the writer feared to be ridiculed for showing such healthy signs of energy or as if perhaps he knew about the knife-edge properties of the ridge and feared for his life. Turning from the notice, which appeared to have been posted up some six months earlier, Bruce was aware of a tall girl with long auburn hair clad in a pale green toga-like robe, drifting about the hall, her arms raised in an angular pseudo-Greek series of poses. He supposed it was intended to be some kind of dance or ritual, but hardly anyone showed signs of interest, for there was no music. Those who did notice mostly grinned or giggled, and the girl continued her trance-like movements as if she were the only occupant of the room. The student who was talking with Stephen suddenly broke away and spreading out his arms took the dancing girl into them. They locked themselves into a passionate but motionless embrace. Someone laughed, but the couple just stood there mouth to mouth, totally oblivious of all around them. Presently they sank down onto some cushions at the edge of the carpet, staring into each other's eyes. Stephen, not at all put out at having his conversation, which he realized was leading nowhere, unceremoniously cut off, was suddenly deeply moved by the sincerity and devotion expressed in that loving encounter. He began to look at the people around him with new interest, with new respect.

Bruce found himself hating everyone in the hall. There was nothing normal about these people. As he told Stephen, they were all misfits. Or, if they were normal, and if this was how average young people spent their time, he despised them all. He was disgusted by the lack of enthusiasm, the absence of any organized activity. With a sudden surge of anger and pity, he thought of his mother, and felt resentment against the College authorities, or the government, or whoever was responsible, for permitting this miserable state of affairs in what had once been a stately home, a seat of human dignity. It was sacrilege. His mother had once played the piano in this same hall; his grandfather had held recitations here. Distinguished men and women had gathered here in the noble pursuit of art, and there had unquestionably been moments of real greatness. Now it was a mere den of broken-down teenagers, a haven of exhaustion and idleness; and worst of all was the utterly destructive air of human indifference.

A revoltingly obese boy in a black T-shirt with 'California' printed across the front in white letters climbed onto the platform and sat on a chair, the zip of his stained and straining jeans half undone and the heels of his once-white pumps trodden down and revealing hard yellow skin. He began to wheeze an obscene song, beating time with one foot. It was supposed to be humorous, but the language was so crude and the rhymes, which he read from a piece of crumpled paper, so obvious, making copious use of words matching 'front' and 'suck', that nobody laughed. Somebody halfheartedly told him to bugger off, but the boy, looking and sounding like a middle-aged stoker out of the belly of a condemned tramp steamer, ploughed on in his droning, spiritless voice. Midway through the 'song', the boy leant over and broke wind not very convincingly, but again nobody showed any signs of appreciation, although Bruce noticed that Stephen was torn between utter disgust and a powerful desire to shriek with laughter. His face had reddened a little.

Vera left her group of girls and approached Stephen.

'Would you like to read some of your novel?'

'After that?' Stephen nodded towards the platform.

'Yes, after that.' Vera burst into a volley of giggles, and Stephen let out a squeal of quickly suppressed mirth.

'Are you sure you want me to? You said you—'

'Never mind what I said before. Read some. We need something good. You've got it with you, haven't you? I told you to bring it.'

'I don't think anyone here would be interested.'

'Don't take any notice of anybody. They're always like this at first. They need stimulation.' Vera giggled again.

Bruce joined them, and Vera, looking at him full in the face, began to understand a little of what Stephen meant about his friend's eyes. They burned with such liquid fire and pain; they were like oceans covering small, entire worlds. She wished she could create some way of capturing and preserving the light of those living eyes. What a source of energy and passion was there, what sadness, what age-old joy! The artist in her was fascinated.

'I'm trying to persuade your friend to read some of his novel, but he's hesitating.'

'Read a bit, Stephen. See how they react.'

'What about your show tonight? Has it started yet?'

'That clown,' – the boy was still grinding on with his ungainly quatrains – 'is one of the items. He does the same thing every time.'

'Including the sound effect?' Bruce couldn't resist this. Vera laughed, and so did Stephen though unwillingly, Bruce thought.

'That was new. But we're absolutely fed up with the poem. He adds a few new lines now and again, but most of it we know by heart.'

Bruce gestured towards the platform.

'Don't you have any programme or anything?'

'Oh, no. It's very free. Anybody can do anything.'

'As I've just observed. O.K., Stephen. I'm sure it'll be all right for you to read some. It'll do everybody good.'

An uneasy truce subsisted between the two friends. When Bruce had returned to the house that afternoon, Bruce had not asked him any questions, and Stephen had showed no inclination to talk about his meeting with Vera. As if to avoid a subject they knew would exacerbate their relationship, they had talked of trivial matters, making strenuous efforts to be polite and pleasant. It was as if their several hours apart had given them a breathing space, enabling them to appreciate each other's point of view a little more objectively; but Bruce knew that beneath their outward calm, pain and resentment were still smouldering. Stephen sensed it too, and took great care not to arouse his friend's temper. For the same reason he had not pursued the matter of the boy on the road outside the College. Earlier that evening at about six o'clock, the telephone had suddenly chimed into their silence, giving them both a fright. It had been Vera inviting them up to the College for the evening. Bruce had been relieved that the telephone was now in working order again. It was not a pleasant sensation being cut off from the rest of civilization. But he felt some trepidation about visiting the College, curious as he was to see what it was like inside. Stephen, however, was so warm and apparently sincere in his encouragement to go with him that Bruce found it hard to refuse. They had set off together, Stephen with most of his novel under his arm. Bruce wouldn't take any of his poems, although Stephen tried hard to persuade him. Stephen asked him whether he could recite from memory, but Bruce rather grandly said he never memorized his work. The only poem he had ever learned by heart was the one he had chanted from the sandhill in his bardic robes, frightening Stephen so; but he thought it better not to mention that poem, for fear of bringing up that episode again. He decided to let Stephen have the limelight that evening.

Stephen began to finger through his papers nervously.

'Where shall I sit?'

'You can have that chair on the platform, when that fat sod's finished.'

'Who is he?'

'His father's a member of the House of Lords. That's what he says, anyway. He's probably only an usher or something, or chief lavatory attendant to the Peers.'

Stephen, who had pricked up his ears at the mention of the House of Lords, laughed. Vera said such outrageous things. The fat boy stood up and bowed.

'Thank God for that: he's finished now.'

The obese Californian looked around, hoping for at least a little show of applause. He smiled with anticipation and bowed again. Then, realizing that no one was interested, his round flabby face fell, and he looked utterly miserable. Then someone let out a mocking cheer followed by a long raspberry, and the boy's disappointment twisted into a scowl. With a mouthful of half-incomprehensible abuse, he swaggered off the platform and threw himself into a sofa, scrutinizing his bits of paper with new intensity.

Vera led Stephen to the chair. Stephen sat on it, feeling the hot greasy warmth of its previous occupant in the polished wood and in the immediately surrounding air. Vera clapped her hands several times, and everybody looked up.

'This is Stephen—Pewit.' Stephen winced at the pause before his surname, which was thus given extra emphasis. He half expected everyone to laugh, but nobody did. 'He's a new friend of mine. He's going to read us some splendid—prose, of his own composition.' A voice came from the back of the hall.

'Pro's? What kind of pro's? Is he one of those?'

'Shut up. He's writing a book.'

The announcement sounded auspicious enough, but no one applauded. They merely stared with rather ill-mannered curiosity at this strange newcomer. Stephen shuffled his papers as Vera left the platform, half stood up, and then sat down again.

'I'd like to read you one or two extracts from my latest novel. It's not finished yet.' Bruce frowned slightly at Stephen's grandiose tones: he sounded like an accomplished author! If only the audience knew the truth, how Bruce had cudgelled and threatened him to squeeze out those few pages! 'I'm still working on it, but certain parts of it are as complete as they ever will be. Before I read, I think I'd better explain a little about the background of the novel. You see, I'm experimenting with a new form. The novel has two parts. The first part is called "Low Tide" and the second part "High Tide".' Stephen thought he heard someone murmur, 'High time', but went on. 'The central character passes from the lowest depths of pessimism to the heights of optimism. I'm going to call it "The Causeway". You see, it's set in a house at the side of an estuary, and a causeway has been built from one side to the other.'

Bruce heard a low voice utter: 'Get on with it. High jinks, low jinks', but Stephen appeared not to hear, and continued unperturbed. Bruce felt compassion for his friend. His speech was intolerably pompous, and he knew that nobody present would appreciate his high-flown tone, even if they could understand what he was saying. Stephen had a way of never failing to get people's backs up. It was happening now. Those who had initially shown the most interest were already frowning in disapproval or distaste or with mere boredom.

'The central character is a man who had once been a child prodigy – as a concert pianist; but as he grew older he became disillusioned with the world he was living in. He tried to commit suicide several times, but he always failed.'

Somewhere from the centre of the hall, a girl's voice murmured, 'Pity.' Stephen looked at his audience. Few of the faces, he now noticed, were turned in his direction. Bruce and Vera were staring expectantly, but others in the hall lighted cigarettes noisily or ripped open cans of beer; one or two even changed their places and began low conversations. Stephen continued with his explanation, raising his voice, which began to harden with barely suppressed irritation and disgust.

'He goes to live by the sea and spends hours walking along the shore. One day he sees an old book floating in the sea — a book on anatomy with diagrams. This is a symbol of his life. He himself feels he is just like the book, drifting, his mind falling to pieces, his whole life falling apart at the seams. The next day he finds the same book washed up on the sand.' He changed the tone of his voice; it became a little more aggressive. 'Now, if you don't mind, I'd like to read an extract from this part.' He paused, lifted out a single sheet from his papers, and began to read.

'"He stood there, the bedraggled book in his hands, tears streaming down his face. His own life, he thought, rubbing the back of his hand across his eyes, was no more than this. And here he was, holding it in his hands. One by one, he tore off the limp pages and let them float away in the breeze. These are the days of my life, he thought, fluttering uselessly away in the wind. And how many are left? The tears welled from his eyes, salt as the sea. He turned his face to the blue, empty sky and let the book fall to the ground. It lay on the sand, its damp pages fluttering in the fresh sea air—"'

Stephen heard a subdued giggle somewhere in the audience. He looked up. Bruce was still staring at him, trying, it seemed, to encourage him. He even appeared to be moved. Vera was no longer sitting beside him. Then he saw her. She had returned to the sofa and was whispering with the same group of girls as before. The giggle had come from that direction. Stephen felt a stone of disappointment swelling heavy and cold in his heart. Of all the people he had wanted to impress, Vera was the most important. But she wasn't listening. He stood up. Bruce was struck by the coldness of his eyes, and the hard edge to his voice as he spoke.

'Of course, if you don't like it, I won't continue.' He stepped down from the platform, his face red with anger. He went straight to Bruce.

'I'm leaving. I've never been so insulted.'

'Wait a moment.'

Bruce knew he had to do something to relieve the situation, and he knew he had to do it quickly. Stephen might make an angry speech or lose his temper before marching out and slamming the door. Bruce wished he had brought some of his poems after all. If he could read something immediately after Stephen, perhaps everybody would forget about Stephen while Stephen calmed down. He knew it would be fatal to recite the 'I Dread Death' poem now. It would infuriate his friend. In fact, Bruce realized that whatever he read would infuriate Stephen, especially if he succeeded where Stephen had failed. He glanced up at the organ loft, and without thinking further made a quick decision.

'Hold on a minute, Stephen. I'm just going up there.'

'What are you going to do?'

'I'm not sure. But please don't go yet.'

Bruce walked quickly to the small door which he knew would lead to the steps up to the organ loft. It was not locked. He bounded up the narrow steps in the dark and came out onto the small balcony overlooking the hall. Several faces were staring up at him; he ignored them. He turned to the organ keyboards. There were three manuals, uncovered. He switched on the instrument. The bellows groaned somewhere behind polished wood and began to fill with a hoarse whispering sound. He pulled out a number of stops on both sides and depressed the swell pedal to a little over half of full volume. His left hand hovered over the middle keyboard.

Bruce had hardly ever played a pipe-organ before, although he had often wished to. At the age of sixteen, he had ventured shyly up to the vicar's house in his home village, to ask if he might use the church organ across the road. The vicar, after eyeing the slim teenager standing before him, had agreed, as long, he said, as he used it when no one else wanted to, and as long as he didn't play too loudly; and also he had to put some money in the collection box every time. At first Bruce had tried to master a book of simple exercises, but after a while these bored him; and he would start extemporizing. He found he could do this with a certain amount of success — at least, in a way that he found satisfying — much better in fact than he could later improvise at the piano with Stephen. The sustaining quality of the organ notes enabled him to dispense almost entirely with the melodic or rhythmic elements: he just played chord after chord, merging one into the next. The sounds he thus created delighted him, even moved him profoundly at times, caused him to meditate deeply. He sometimes came to believe that what he was playing was actually great music; he felt he was in control of a huge orchestra, almost in control at any rate. Because he himself was playing, he seemed to be inside the music itself. He was unable to listen to it objectively, and was therefore not able to form any proper critical judgements of his own playing. To him it often thus seemed sublime. Then one day, a middle-aged lady in a grey coat had come into the church to 'do the flowers'. Shyness had at once overcome Bruce. He had tried to continue: to stop would make him seem even more conspicuous, but when he caught sight of the enigmatic smile on the woman's face, his confidence was shattered. She was laughing at his futile efforts. She knew it wasn't real music. All the vast castles and minarets in the imagination of his sounds had fallen clanging dully around him, like brass bells dropped to the ground, fading away in a jangle of broken harmony. All his sense of wellbeing and power had left him. With trembling hands he had closed the lid of the keyboards and crept out of the building, hot with shame. He had never visited the church again.

Something now, however, inspired Bruce. With a sudden burst of savage energy, he struck out seven strident chords in the middle registers, held in the last one, and brought in a massive climbing bass on the pedals. Then with his right hand he added snarling fanfares of piercing brass. His anger and frustration of many days carried the whole structure of sound forwards and on. The chords echoed strongly in the dark-beamed roof and shuddered down under the flagstones of the floor. Bruce felt a tremendous building up of power, as one chord generated the next. Each new layer of sound he struck out seemed a blow aimed at the langorous people below. He felt he was cleansing the air, blasting the stifling and stifled atmosphere out of the hall, out of the entire building. His moral strength returned, and with it a new conviction that what he was doing was incontrovertibly right and good. He was doing this in the name of his mother, in the name of those who stood for human dignity and uprightness of character. He was doing it for past generations who held a nobler view of life than these insipid creatures lounging about on the floor below. He was doing it as Christ had purged the Temple. The huge waves of sound crashed down round him. He was hardly able to believe that such magnificence stemmed from his own fingertips, heels and toes. The sound was coming from another source, and then he knew instinctively that that source was the sea. What he was playing was maddened sand forced through steel pipes and then through hypodermic syringes. The wind in the organ bellows was drawn directly from the long grasses in the sand dunes, from the maelstrom generated gales that found their genesis in mid-Atlantic and howled and roared afterwards round the granite crags of the Cambrian mountains. The whole Great Hall of the College was deep down under the breakers: it was these that thundered now within those lofty walls. White horses, like those he had wrestled with that morning, were crashing and neighing and hissing across the surface of a grey-green swaying ocean. Incensed mermaids, like furies, their grey hair streaming straight back from their foreheads, were screaming and shaking their fists and glaring with wide blazing eyes at the land, their coiled blue-grey tails like those of sea-dragons, lashing the water into yellow sizzling foam. He himself rose up in their midst, supreme mogul of the sea. Every drop of it was his empire, every turn of the waves and each upflung lace-like strand of spray was created exactly as he had designed and commanded. He was the master, master of the ocean, and master as never before of the onslaught of sound from the organ; and somewhere in the background, behind the grey and the white of the confusion, beyond the armies of mermen brandishing savage whips torn from the adze-like skins of sharks, and lashing at the wind – in a vast dark blue and green and purple cavern, its walls gleaming and working like the blue-black throat of a whale – a huge human visage had arisen, in some ways resembling his mother, but more brave, more noble, more primeval and infinitely more tragic; had arisen and was smiling the heaven-like smile of one insane who for a moment has regained her senses, or as the Wandering Jew on that last day when at last he was allowed to die – smiling as one released from centuries of agony, a fleeting smile of pure sunlit joy before a final plunge into total despair. Bruce guided his thundering chariot of a hundred sea-born horses in a bold curve as broad as Tremadog Bay, and let them charge free into the final straight – galloping and gliding as those long Atlantic rollers straight into and between the mist-dazed headlands and nesses of the northern lands. He held the chord, pressed the swell pedal to maximum, and held the chord on, and then suddenly reined in all the pounding stallions of sound, and the music stopped – creating as it did so an appalling concave of silence, with a host of echoes like grey-cloaked ghosts rushing away into a rain-shrouded distance.

Bruce sat there on the organ bench, his head bowed, how long he did not know. Then, when the very last scudding distant bell-chime whisper of sound had faded away, he switched off the instrument and stood up. Trembling, he came down the steep staircase from the loft. As he emerged into the hall, nobody applauded, and nobody spoke. It seemed that everyone was staring at him with frightened eyes, and in the shadows beyond them other eyes were fixed on him, and the walls of the hall seemed to have melted away. He looked for Stephen. He was standing with Vera, and both of them were staring at Bruce's eyes. Vera moved forwards. She took Bruce's hand and led him to the most brightly illuminated part of the hall under the chandelier. Stephen followed them. He was the first to speak.

'Now I understand what you mean.'

Vera took up the words, addressing them not to Bruce but to Stephen.

'Now I understand what you mean.'

In a daze, Bruce stumbled towards one of the sofas, not quite knowing whether it was genuine emotion he felt or whether it was another example of self-dramatization. Someone handed him a lighted cigarette; he took it with shaking hands, looked at it to see if it was a real cigarette, then drew on it deeply. The air was heavily charged with feeling, but at the same time he felt faintly ridiculous. It seemed to him he was a kind of hero after a dangerous rescue, but no one, it seemed, least of all himself, could properly understand what he had done. Was it all contrived posturing or had he really set in motion some kind of gigantic catharsis? He gazed round him, almost as if he were half blind. Vera and Stephen, near Bruce on the same sofa, were deep in conversation, yet they seemed a very great distance away from him. Bruce was handed a glass of beer. He drank it down and closed his eyes. He heard Stephen's voice close beside him.

'Are you all right?'

Bruce nodded. He wanted to escape from this pseudo-romantic sense of hero-worship which seemed to be directed at him, yet he also wanted to enjoy it. He felt a kind a guilt, not in the least diminished when Stephen spoke again.

'That was the best things you've ever done. Everybody was immensely impressed, absolutely transfixed. I didn't know you could play like that.'

'Nor did I, but I don't think anybody understands. I was angry.'

Vera stood before him.

'We needed something like that. Nobody here can play the organ.'

'Nor can I.' Bruce suddenly decided to deflate the heavily charged atmosphere. 'Everybody here can play their organs — except me.' He laughed. Vera knelt down in front of the sofa.

'Don't be silly.'

Stephen laughed, but there was no bitterness in his voice.

'It certainly went down better than my novel.'

'I think what you read had superb things in it. They didn't listen because it was too good for them.'

'Don't be absurd. Why did they listen to you?'

'It was too loud for them not to.' Bruce laughed again. 'I enjoyed that.'

'I felt your enjoyment.'

Vera said nothing. She had said nothing to Stephen about his novel. It had bored her. She understood only practical things, or things made with the hands. Bruce's extemporization had thrilled her. She thought of the pipe-organ as another kind of wind cage. It made her own creations seem paltry and futile. Here was a much more splendid machine, one which could master the wind far better than she had been able to. She marvelled at Bruce's sense of control. The striding pillars of sound had filled her with admiration for this strange friend of Stephen's; and afterwards she had seen his eyes, and they had seemed like the brightest stars in the world sky.

The tall boy with gold-rimmed glasses and his green-robed companion edged near. They were both gazing at Bruce with a kind of stupefaction. The boy stammered a little.

'I say...what was that you were...playing. It was...splendid. Who composed it?'

'An old woman, with grey hair like Beethoven in his last years.'

'I don't know any woman composers. Is she living?'

'No. Yes, she lives in a huge green cavern at the bottom of the ocean.'

Bruce had not meant his words to be taken seriously. He was surprised when the tall girl suddenly intoned:

'I know that place. I've been there.'

The youth pursed his lips in suppressed annoyance. He didn't like people making fun of him.

'I only asked you the name of the composer. I like good music.'

'Thank you. I didn't know it was good.'

'Who was the composer?'

Bruce was suddenly irritated by the boy's pedantic insistence.

'You obviously don't know much about music. Haven't you ever heard of Dinwiddy? Bruce Dinwiddy.'

'I'll have to look him up.'

'He won't be in the dictionaries. He was a confirmed recluse.'

'Oh...Well, thank you anyway.' The couple drifted away, the girl crooning softly. Bruce smiled and glanced at Stephen, who did not respond.

Bruce was not so much impressed by the effect he had had on the people in the hall as by the knowledge that he had been able to master, for the first time in his life, a musical instrument, not in the sense that he could compose real music, but that the keyboards and pedals had responded so magnificently to his virtually blind manipulations. He simply could not believe that he had produced such effective sound. Always before he had been overcome by doubts as to the quality of his 'music'. This time he was sure: it had moved not only himself but all those present in the hall. Even now many of them were still looking at him, and talking together – as if something extraordinary had occurred. Bruce began to enjoy his new position of authority.

Stephen's feelings were mixed. From the musical point of view, he knew that Bruce's performance was more or less harmonic and melodic nonsense; but he had nevertheless felt its inexplicable power. Bruce had been playing with conviction, even with a certain expertise, and that alone gave the performance authenticity. Any trained musician would have scoffed, even Stephen would have scoffed at another time in another place, but there were no genuine musicians present. Even Stephen had enough humility to assert, to himself at least, that he was not now really competent to judge the true qualities of music. What was music, then? Was it organized notes on a page of lined manuscript? Or did everything depend on the performance, on the situation, on the nature of the people present at the time? Could bad music be good? Certainly, good music could be badly performed. If so, non-musical music, such as Bruce had produced, could equally be superbly performed. Bruce therefore had triumphed. At the same time, Stephen felt a burning bitterness that his own reading had been such a failure. He had meant to impress his audience, had wanted them to be moved to tears, but no one had paid the slightest attention, except Bruce. But Bruce didn't matter; it was Bruce himself who had almost created the novel, dragged it out of him. It meant nothing to have been praised by Bruce; it was almost as if his friend was praising himself. And he resented the fact that Bruce, without intending to, had in a way scored over him, and scored over him so devastatingly. And not only that. Up to now it had always been Stephen who was leader in their activities at the piano, but Bruce had scored over him there too with his organ improvisation, taken away the one thing in which he excelled his friend. It went even further back. All his life, Stephen had longed for acclaim as a public performer of music; he had craved for applause and approbation. Now Bruce had won just such recognition. Not that his audience had been a real one, an intelligent one, but Bruce had been successful. Success, quite apart from fame, was the one thing Stephen had never been able to achieve. He was also deeply pained by Vera's insulting behaviour, the way she had giggled while Stephen was reading; and he was hurt too by her enthusiasm for his friend. It was always Bruce who stole the limelight, never him, never him. He had not wanted things to be like this.

Philip ambled over to them and spoke to Vera.

'We have to close down in ten minutes. You'd better explain to your friends.'

Stephen immediately took offence at Philip's surly manner; but he was glad that after all these slovenly creatures, these wastrels, had to knuckle under to some form of authority. His reply had a slightly mocking tone.

'We're just going actually. We didn't intend to stay in this godforsaken place long. You needn't worry. We won't give your teachers any cause to scold you.'

'I was just telling you. We don't want any trouble here. Vera, come over here a minute. Sally wants you.'

Vera went off with Philip and joined the group of girls, who had now moved and were standing near the door. There was a burst of laughter from two of the girls after Vera had said something. They all turned and looked at Bruce and Stephen.

Bruce stood up and placed his empty beer glass on the arm of the sofa.

'Let's get back, Stephen.'

'Very well. I'll just have a word with Vera.' Stephen joined the group by the door; he and Vera spoke quietly for a few moments. Vera nodded, and Stephen beckoned to Bruce. Vera led the two friends towards the entrance hall. Near the door of the Great Hall, the fat boy who had sung so obscenely was standing with a rapt expression on his face. As Bruce passed him, the boy suddenly gave a brilliant smile, and Bruce was struck to the quick by its undisguised warmth and sincerity. For a moment he felt he could see right into the boy's heart and a wave of pity engulfed him. The boy should never have come to the College. There was nothing wrong with him; he was just misunderstood. Bruce wished he could have been the boy's teacher. He was sure that in a few hours he could have washed away the swirl of misery that clouded the boy's mind, a misery that life in the College was only increasing. He returned the smile and gently patted the boy's shoulder. Bruce and Stephen stepped outside into the cool night air. As they came round the south side of the building, to take a short cut to the track alongside the railway line below the College, they felt the wind on their faces, and as they stepped carefully down into the darkness, they could hear to their right the distant cry of the sea beyond the sand dunes.

26. HAMMERS

FIVE DAYS LATER Vera came to lunch at Tremarfon. At first Bruce had objected strongly, but soon found that he had no real grounds for refusing. Although he had tried to maintain his tolerant attitude towards Stephen, he found it disturbing when this idea appeared like a new cloud on the horizon. After their visit to the College, Stephen had gone out every day, staying out from morning until just before supper-time. His novel lay untouched on the dresser in the living room. In any case, he would have argued, writing was now out of the question. The house was too noisy, and though Bruce halfheartedly informed his friend that Einstein had always been able to work best surrounded by noise, especially noisy children, he could not deny that Stephen had a point. The carpenter had returned as promised, unusually for Harlieg people rather sooner than expected, bringing with him three mates and a lorry-load of timber. The sounds of hammer, chisel and saw reverberated through the wooden house. Stephen complained, said the row gave him a headache, the dust gave him asthma; and though Bruce knew this wasn't the real reason why Stephen went away into the sandhills, he could almost sympathize with his friend. He himself spent much of the day watching the men, not because he didn't trust them to get on with the job as quickly as possible – though his father had asked him to check on just this – but because he was fascinated by what they were doing. It was intensely satisfying to see them cut out the rotten timbers at the south end of the house, dark and soft with moisture, and measure, cut and fit in new joists, pillars and crossbeams. There was nothing phony about this form of creation. The real artists of the world, Bruce began to think, the real craftsmen, those whose works of art really counted for something in the world, were people like these, who had spent years in training and getting experience, and who now worked with ease and expertise so pleasing to behold. The smell of the new wood, too, was almost intoxicating to Bruce. It gave him almost erotic pleasure to breathe in the clean, resinous aroma that drifted throughout the house. He felt new energy accumulating within his healthy body, and merely to touch a newly-planed plank aroused curious associations with his own sexuality. Even the smell of the creosote, with its surprisingly deep red hue as it sank into the new wood, invigorated him, and his anxieties about Stephen seemed almost to melt away.

On the second day, Stephen had returned in an unusually buoyant mood. His clothes and hair were covered with little bits of dried grass and patches of sand. His face bore a new strange expression of jubilant satiation, though his eyes as he looked at Bruce betrayed a faint shadow of guilt, or guilty triumph; but he offered nothing to Bruce by way of explanation or apology.

And so Vera came to lunch. When he had first seen her, on the day of the gale, and then again at the College, Bruce had felt an instant dislike for Vera. He disliked the smug, bland roundness of her face. Her lips were rather full and seemed always to be pouting a little wetly with anticipation. Her nose was straight, almost classically Greek, like a somewhat stunted Burne-Jones. Her eyes were a cold pale blue and had nothing of innocence in them. They were eyes that had seen too much. Bruce feared them: they were too experienced, too knowing to be comfortable with. Especially when he had seen her naked in the bathroom, they had seemed to be mocking him, and yet at times they were also faintly admiring. To Bruce, her whole manner was too strident, too confident. There was little truly feminine, or rather purely feminine, about Vera.

At lunch, which she had helped to prepare with irritating efficiency in the kitchen, she had hardly spoken to Bruce. She made no mention of his startling performance in the College and asked him nothing about his poems. She and Stephen seemed wholly absorbed with one another, almost as if Bruce were not there at all. It was obvious to him that he was merely a tolerated presence, and this strengthened his bitterness towards Vera, who had come thus like an abrasive wedge between the two friends and had caused Stephen to change so much. This image of a wedge had been brought home to him forcefully that morning as he had watched one of the carpenter's mates split a plank using a tough segment of wood. The plank had emitted a grotesque sound, something between a wail and a groan, and he had felt it penetrate the very marrow of his bones.

And yet Bruce could not ignore the fact that Stephen now seemed much happier than he had ever seen him before. He was almost radiant, and spoke with far greater animation and enthusiasm than Bruce thought could have been possible. He and Vera seemed to inspire one another and undeniably witty repartee sparkled between them. Stephen was no longer the unruly adolescent whom Bruce had striven to control towards a happier, more creative existence. Stephen had become decisive and masterful. Even the way he sliced bread with new energy and precision seemed to have been affected by the girl; and though Bruce hated Vera for both captivating and capturing his friend, he felt glad in a way that Stephen seemed to have gained so much confidence and peace of mind. He was far less irritable, in spite of the carpenters, and once Bruce had agreed to the lunch invitation treated him with unexpected gentleness. Bruce, however, was suspicious of his somewhat ingratiating manner, which he knew stemmed from Stephen's having got his own way, and he felt that this new solicitude was rather a kind of condescension – that Bruce was a special friend, something of a genius perhaps, an eccentric at least, and therefore had to be permitted his little whims, had to be humoured; or as if he were a child standing by while adults concerned themselves with maturer things. Whenever they acknowledged his presence that lunch time, Stephen and Vera treated him with studied respect, which Bruce knew was unnatural in both of them.

He knew that his friendship with Stephen was ruined. Nothing would ever be the same again. They had come there to write, to talk, to walk together by the sea, and now this grossly independent girl had stepped in between them, forcing them apart. Everything was spoiled now. The wonderful shore that Bruce had loved so much was contaminated; the sandhills where he had spent his childhood so happily had become a playground for depraved teenagers. Perhaps it had been his own fault; perhaps he himself had initiated that uncleanness by polluting the sand with his own wet seed barely a week before. A kind of revengeful process had been set in motion. The sea, the mother in the sea, was hitting back. Even the house was decaying. The seasalt in the wind had seeped into the wood and corrupted it. But if so – no, it must have begun a long time before that. Whatever it was, it had been mistake to bring Stephen here. Everything Stephen touched, as if he were a grotesquely reversed Midas, became tarnished, green and greasy with mildew. Bruce himself had somehow become tainted by the presence of his friend. Would he have ever spurted out that white life of his upon his mother's grave if Stephen had not been there? Had he himself become as depraved as all these people around him?

Stephen had dragged him down from his splendid eyries of noble dreams. Far from saving Stephen from a world corruption and destruction, Bruce had been drawn towards it. His friend was after all the stronger of the two. They would never again be able to share those magnificent hours of former times.

After lunch, which they prolonged as much as they could in a seemingly innocent way, Vera abruptly waved goodbye to Stephen and returned to the College, somewhat surprisingly to attend a class. Bruce and Stephen stood on the lawn in front of the house, amid piles of rotting beams with rusty nails and fragments of cement coating projecting from them. Nearby were neat stacks of fresh-smelling boards. The sea was a wonderful deep blue; the wind was strong, and the sky was startlingly ablaze with full-blown mountains of white clouds. Wrapped in their private thoughts, they gazed across the bay. Bruce pointed suddenly towards the Lleyn peninsula.

'Do you remember the name of those three mountains?'

'What do you mean?'

'I find Vera rather attractive. She reminds me of a girl I once knew.'

Both statements were untrue, but Bruce felt a thrusting urge to upset his friend. He laughed coldly.

'Those three mountains are called the Rivals.'

'So bloody what?' Stephen digested Bruce's meaning. 'You won't get far, if that's what you mean.'

'That remains to be seen, doesn't it?'

Stephen was not remotely moved by his friend's bluff: he saw through it instantly. He knew Bruce would never be able, would never dare, to disrupt his relationship with Vera.

'What are you going to do about it?'

'Vera liked my organ playing.'

For a brief moment, Stephen wanted to laugh out loud. Like some maiden aunt, Bruce was completely unaware of the double entendre. Stephen had spent hours in the company of people who did little else but indulge in sexual wordplay. He looked at Bruce belligerently.

'She never said anything to me about it.'

'You thought it was good, didn't you?'

'Not really.'

'You said so.'

'It was just the timing, the effect. Musically it was rubbish.'

'You couldn't have done it. You wouldn't have dared.' Bruce paused, adding weight to the next stage of his attack. 'Vera didn't think much of your novel, did she? She was laughing while you were reading.'

Stephen said nothing. The memory still rankled. Bruce continued, aware of an advantage.

'You haven't written anything since you met her. I told you she would be a bad influence.'

'That's immaterial. Besides, her existence has given me a new sense of reality. Everything before that was just mental masturbation. I don't need to write now. Real life is far more interesting.'

'Just excuses. You see, you're too weak to stick to anything. I knew this would happen sooner or later. And as soon as you get tired of Vera—'

'Look, if you haven't anything more edifying to—'

His voice died as one of the carpenters came round the house and selected a few boards from the stack. Bruce smiled at him and Stephen at once felt a loathing for his friend's easy change of expression – so superficial, just to keep up a cheerful front, to protect his reputation in the town!

'Better weather now, isn't it?' The young carpenter grinned brightly, unaware of the clouded atmosphere between the two friends.

'Much better. Do you think it'll hold?'

'Can never tell these days.' The carpenter went off, whistling. Stephen cursed inwardly. Why on earth was Bruce so difficult to deal with? Why did they always get involved in these verbal brawls? Their entire relationship was intolerably neurotic, totally unrealistic. They had been living in an ivory tower, a putrid blackened narrow cell, like a rotting wisdom tooth. Why couldn't they live simple lives like these carpenters, openly like Vera? He returned to the attack.

'It's very easy for you to be pleasant, isn't it?'

'Why shouldn't I be pleasant? There's nothing twisted about these people. I don't feel anything against them. They're very kind, normal people.'

'What do you mean by that?'

'You're a hypocrite, Stephen. You come from just the same background as these people, yet you reject them all as inferior beings. You're a snob. You're living in the wrong world. You don't belong here. That's not normal, is it?'

'You don't know anything about my background.'

'I'm sorry, but I do. You've told me yourself.'

'You've never seen what it's like.'

'I don't need to. Anyone can see through your pose. You're so pompous – always trying to use big words. I heard you up there at the College, talking about existentialism and all that blather. You used the word "pragmatic". You don't even know what it means, do you?'

'For Christ's sake—!'

'Well, what does it mean?'

'I refuse to...'

'You see, you don't know. That's why everybody laughs at you. Like they did at the College, when you were introducing your—'

'I don't want to hear any more about that.'

'You see, you're not even honest.'

'Fuck off, will you!'

'I'm going to fetch the milk. Are you coming?'

'No!'

'Thanks for the help.'

With this parting shot, Bruce went into the kitchen to fetch the empty bottles. He dropped one of them on the floor and it smashed. The kitchen was loud with hammering. Leaving the shattered glass on the floor, Bruce slammed the back door and took the path for the zig-zag.

Stephen went into the living room and picking up the pages of his novel sat at the table. The constant hammering invaded his brain. Really, it was impossible to live in this house. He started to read through what he had written, selecting a page at random. Was it good or was it not? At the time of writing, it had seemed superb, inspired. It had taken shape so smoothly; he had even marvelled at his own lucidity of expression. Why didn't Vera like it? None of the College students had liked it. Perhaps, after all, as Bruce had then hinted, they were unable to appreciate real literature. But just now Bruce had said that he Stephen looked down on people. He meant working people, like these carpenters, but how true was it, that he looked down on people, all kinds of people? Was he looking down on the College people? That they were all social misfits he knew, but was that any reason to consider them inferior beings? As for these carpenters, people from the same class, if there were such things as classes, as his father – only just a few minutes before he had been envying them for their simpleness and uncomplicated existence. He picked up another page. Who were the real judges? Stephen was plagued by doubts. What was he, who was he, in reality? What was reality? He had struggled all his life for identity, and he was still struggling now. No sooner had he set up some framework in which to exist than someone came along and swept it all away like Vera's wind cage. Vera. Would he, as Bruce had taunted him with, tire of her? Nothing was constant. There were no firm standards to measure oneself by. People changed. Bruce had once stood as something rocklike, an almost infallible criterion, but Bruce appeared now as not only childish but also as an embittered person. The integrity of his friend, on which Stephen had almost unconsciously depended, was after all nothing but the tottering instability of a frustrated over-aged adolescent. What was that he had said about the word 'pragmatic'? Had he, in his conversation with that golden-bespectacled poltroon, used the word deliberately or unconsciously? There again – the word 'poltroon' had entered his thoughts. Looking down again. Was he himself not a 'poltroon'? What was a poltroon? He remembered looking it up once in a dictionary? Could he recall the meaning now? 'Spiritless coward.' Was he a spiritless coward? Had he any right to brand that tall youth as a spiritless coward? 'Pragmatic' again. Well, what did it mean? He'd better test himself. Could he remember? Was he using the word correctly? Was he using it naturally? 'Treating facts of history with reference to their practical lessons.' Could he have carried on that particular conversation without resorting to that word? Probably, but did it matter? If it had been correctly used in its context, was it not perfectly acceptable? It was more likely that it was Bruce who didn't know the meaning and was therefore out of his depths when he Stephen used such words. Was that it? To Stephen, Bruce was an enigma. His poetry was undoubtedly sturdy and virile. Even his organ improvisation had been undeniably impressive, possessed of − something. Exactly what, Stephen couldn't quite identify. At times, Bruce appeared immensely strong, a being infinitely, but sometimes quite disarmingly, quite humbly, superior to himself; and yet, at other times, all his strength seemed to crumble away, leaving in its wake a querulous, ageing, spinster-like child. Vera was a child, but Vera was different. Although there was something 'not there' about her, she didn't make such intellectual, such emotional demands on Stephen. She never, as Bruce did, passed judgements on him. Yet she had giggled while he was reading his precious words. Precious? Perhaps that's just what they were, precious in the other, derogatory sense. Yet that giggling didn't seem to be a moral judgement. It was just a natural reaction. Perhaps there was something laughable about what he had written, or the way he had read it. Yet again, she seemed to accept him just as he was. To be in her company was relaxing, and yet, again, at the same time she was never dull. Stephen felt that with her he could become his real self, or at least an acceptable self. All complexes and frustrations melted away when he was in her company. To live − with her eyes and ears constantly open, with all her senses on the alert, to live intensely − was what mattered most to Vera. Art for her was not a separate world, an ivory tower which only the anointed could enter. Art for her was a part of actual life, making things with her hands, looking at things as they really were, listening to actual sounds − the wind and the waves; it had little to do with the mind. Making things, doing things − making love, that was one of the things.

Stephen laid aside the novel. Would it matter now if it were never finished? Bruce had emphasized Stephen's need for achievement, had scorned his ability to stick at any one thing for long. But Bruce did not know what had occurred the previous day in the sand dunes. As in a kind of dream now he repictured it to himself as seen by someone other than himself, just as he himself had witnessed a similar scene a few days before in the rain. Stephen knew that in those marvellously ecstatic moments with Vera and in the heady hours of anticipation spread over a day or two, he had achieved far more than any novel could. But how, he wondered, could he ever explain that to Bruce? How could he even tell him, when he knew that such a revelation would gain nothing but instant and irrevocable expulsion from the house by the sea which was his lifeline to Vera?

Stephen's head ached. The hammering of the carpenters seemed only inches from his skull. They were not just single blows; at least three hammers were at work at once. Sometimes their knocking rhythms coincided, but mostly they were out of time, a rapid erratic clattering of steel thrust at steel thrust into virgin wood. The whole house seemed to him like the sounding board of a huge hollow instrument, an instrument not for music but for the application of torture by means of crazing and whitewashing the mind with a blackening cacophony of deafening hammer-blows; and Stephen was inside the instrument, with no way to escape. He closed his eyes. There were no carpenters. There was only Bruce, smiling, and nailing nails one by one into Stephen's skull. If only he could get away. Bang. But if he left the house he would have nowhere to go and wouldn't be able to carry on his daily meetings with Vera. He would have to leave Wales, go back to Birmingham. Bang, bang, bang, ba-bang. Filthy, grimy Birmingham, on that claustrophobic, steamy, asthma-inducing train. He wondered if he could enrol at the College. Surely he was deprived enough. Deprived of friends, deprived of identity, deprived of sanity almost. Bang, bang. That would solve everything, but he had no idea how to set about it. Bruce would know; that was the trouble: Bruce knew about such things so much better than Stephen did. Ba-bang, ba-bang, bang, bang, ba-bang. But Bruce would do nothing to help him, and, indeed, he had no wish to be helped by Bruce. He would ask Vera. But how, if enrolled, would he be able to pay the fees? And how would he get on with the others there? None of them liked him, that much was obvious. And would he be able to endure the regular hours of study – classes, seminars, regimentation? Even

Vera was able to do that. Bang, ba-bang. Bang, bang. Bang. One of the hammers missed and hit something soft. Stephen heard a muffled curse from somewhere outside and a burst of laughter.

He got up and went outside. He walked round to the south end of the house and watched the carpenters. The foreman was hammering in a five-inch nail. His neck was tensed, and his head jerked forwards and backwards with each regular swing of his arm. Bang, ba-bang, ba-bang. What a tedious life, Stephen thought — hammering in nails all day, sawing wood! What unrewarding work! And how impermanent it all was! That very nail the carpenter was now knocking in would in a few years go rusty; the wood would rot, and all the effort now being exerted would have been in vain. At least, if one wrote a novel, it would be there after one's death. People would read it. There was some kind of future there. These workmen had no concept of the future. Was that looking down again? For this carpenter, the business of knocking in one nail was all that mattered in the world. And in the evening he would go home, eat his supper, watch television perhaps, probably never thought much about his wife now. There would be little thought of the next day's work. That would come when it came; there was no need to worry. Stephen found himself despising this blind way of living. Even if it were looking down on others, he couldn't help his feelings; he had spent half his life trying to escape from such futile existence. People were so stupid. There were millions of men like this carpenter, all of them short-sighted and pinheaded. No, he would never allow himself to become a person like that.

He turned and looked towards the sea. There too was endless, useless repetition. Wave after wave, tide after tide — a mindless reiteration, without purpose and without consequence. Perhaps it was of no avail to look for anything permanent in the world we lived in. We must live from hour to hour, minute to minute, like these waves, like these carpenters, as Vera did, taking what comes, doing whatever is offered or demanded, but without will to create or to abide by any ossifying codes or rules. It was no good, Stephen thought, making plans. None of them ever came to anything. One wave was always eliminated by the next; the entire climax of its short life was merely to rise up, curl smoothly over, collapse, and disappear forever. We ourselves, he thought, can do no better. What was the use of trying to achieve anything? Achievement was pure chance, success a matter of luck. Stephen would make no decisions; he would wait and see what happened. Life in Tremarfon could, at worst, for the time being at least, be tolerated. The College could wait. After all, there was Vera. Vera every day. And the sand dunes always there, to hide from the rest of the world the hours they could spend together – as they had yesterday! Ah, that. Then a shadow fell across that bright memory. Bruce. The hammers. How did Bruce fit in to this world of no will that Stephen now inhabited? In spite of everything, Bruce was still there, and though just a wisp of a child at times, he was behind that always something more, what was it? Will-o'-the-Wisp? Leading strangers into fen fastnesses? Leading them or hounding them, like the huge giant in Goya's terrifying painting, to annihilation? Bruce survived. How did he achieve that? Was it because he was like the proverbial bamboo that bends before the storm? He had the same green, clean, slender strength and elegance. If so, Stephen must be the knotty oak that the winds felled. But, no, whatever he was he was not that! The whole idea was too ridiculous. Bang, ba-bang.

'Bang, bang, bang!'

Stephen turned sharply to find Bruce behind him. Bruce smiled.

'So you're round here. Fascinating, isn't it? By the way, have you noticed? The wind's dropped.'

27. EAST WIND

AS SOON AS he came out of the house the next morning for his swim before breakfast, Bruce knew there was something wrong with the sea. Something was missing from the pattern of the shore, and he knew immediately what it was: there were no waves. The sea was blue-grey to its extreme edge. Only an occasional thin white line showed, to mark the boundary between water and land. It was like the shore of a lake, and the lake was strangely flattened, marked with a few white flecks, and a strong current was running away from the land. To say there were no waves was not quite accurate. The sea, as always when the tide was not in ebb, was attempting to press forwards up the beach, but as each line of subdued swell approached the shore, it somehow lost heart and turned over with a quick dull flop, and a low ragged fringe of spray was blown back the way it had come. The wind was in the east.

The air was curiously hot. It was as if an oven door had been opened somewhere inland and a wave of unbreathable heat was being blasted out across the land towards the sea. Bruce moved out from the shadow of the house and felt the curiously dry but humid wind touch his bare back, and in spite of its warmth he shivered. There was something uncanny about this weather. It was unnatural. Here on the western shore of Wales, south-westerlies prevailed; the weather most of the year blew in from the sea. The sea constantly freshened the land, bringing cool rains, days of dark clouds, gales, or less frequently when the wind moved round to the north-west, spells of fair weather. This morning the pattern was changed, and there was something stale and death-like in that land-generated breath. It was like the used air from a vent on the deck of an ocean-going steamer – unhealthy, used up, disease-carrying, as if all the grey-aired towns of the north midlands were opening their mouths and fumes were pouring from acid stomachs pocked with ulcers past gateways of decaying teeth. It was like the breath from chronically asthmatic lungs. The morning, it seemed to Bruce, was sick.

He knew it was dangerous to swim on such days. He remembered a long day once with such a wind as this when he had been a child. Three children on the beach had pushed an oil-drum into the sea and climbing onto it had drifted far out into the bay. Two of them had drowned. There had been a khaki-coloured helicopter hovering overhead, policemen and a tall swaying ambulance on big wheels on the beach, an atmosphere of tragedy, which he could recognize as such even at the tender age of six, in the town and in their own house for days afterwards. He knew it would be foolish to venture now into the treacherous sea. He went back into the house to get dressed. Stephen was coming down the stairs.

'There's an east wind. I can't swim.'

Stephen nodded and went into the bathroom to clean his teeth. At breakfast Bruce told him about the children on the oil-drum.

'Everything gets washed straight out into the bay.' He paused, remembering another episode from his childhood. 'I say, it's a good day for putting a message in a bottle. Let's do that.'

Stephen let out a faint sigh, frowning slightly. Another of Bruce's childish whims. But the idea appealed to him nevertheless.

'What's your message going to be?'

'I'll put a poem in. Let's do it after breakfast before the wind changes.'

Stephen agreed. Each morning the two friends seemed to be trying to start the day off well. The previous afternoon, after Bruce had returned from fetching the milk, Stephen had gathered up his novel and retired to his room upstairs, announcing that he was going to 'read it through and make alterations'. Bruce had nodded, trying not to look pleased. Stephen had sat in his room, read a page or two, and then fallen asleep. After supper he had disappeared upstairs again, ostensibly to continue with his work, but had retired early. Bruce had sat alone in the living room, wanting to play the piano, but not daring to for fearing of disturbing his friend. He had worked for a while on some of his poems, but he kept thinking of Stephen and Vera. Hand in hand, and smiling secretly to each other, they wandered through his thoughts, and he was unable to concentrate. He tried to romanticize the situation, tried to express what had happened in verse, but it was too painful, too near, too real. He needed time, time to fit these new developments into his mental framework, trying to adjust. Emotion recollected in tranquillity, but there was no tranquillity yet. He wished he could make his poetry more immediate, more relevant. There was something stale, second-hand, old-fashioned, he began to realize, about most of his poems, as if they were hidden by mist or a kind of purple haze. Stephen's writing seemed much more modern, so much clearer and fresher. His own poems had the faint sickly odour of that faded lilac perfume that steeped the pages of some of his grandmother's books.

After they had cleared away the breakfast, Bruce went upstairs to his room and Stephen sat in the living-room. There was no harm in this idea of Bruce's. Childlike it was, but somehow, like Bruce himself, a little quaint and charming. He wondered what to write. A page of his novel, the sentences hovering incomplete at beginning and end? A letter to someone overseas? He didn't know anyone overseas. He sat there, a blank sheet of paper in front of him. He began to write.

> Two friends lived at the edge of the sea. One hovered on the borders of genius. The other went mad. They built a city of sand that was burned and drowned. They killed a bird without cause. A beautiful witch cast a spell over one of them. Mermaids with wrinkled faces claimed the other.

He added the place and date and signed his name and folded the paper into a thin roll. Bruce came into the room with an empty lemonade bottle.

'I've written a letter to the Old Woman of the Sea. What about you?'

'I've told the truth.'

'Can I read it?'

'No.'

'You can read mine.'

'I don't want to.'

Bruce read through his own piece, nodded, folded the paper and put it into the bottle, handing it to Stephen. Stephen pushed in his own slim roll. Bruce screwed the black rubber top tightly onto the bottle, and Stephen felt himself half admiring, half despising the suppleness and power of Bruce's tensed fingers and the lines of concentration and effort around his mouth. They went outside and down the path to the beach. Bruce looked at Stephen.

'Who's going to throw the bottle?'

'It was your idea.'

'You can if you like.'

'I don't want to. Anyway, your arm's probably stronger than mine.'

Bruce stood back and swung his arm behind his head. Then, swivelling his body powerfully, he flung the bottle, glittering as it turned over and over in the air, far out into the sea. It made only a small splash, righted itself for an instant, then lay down and bobbed up an down, drifting slowly like a dead, aerated jelly-fish into the distance. They stood there, watching it in silence. There had been no real joy in it for either of them. It was as if a child were dying in the room where their friendship dwelled.

A little while later, without words and without returning to the house, Stephen moved off towards the sandhills to meet Vera. He came back just before lunch-time. After an almost silent meal, they sat in the verandah. The carpenters were not there because it was Sunday. Bruce was surprised when he realized that. The days of the week had all but disappeared into the timeless confusion and wayward freedom of the recent events.

'Bruce?'

'Yes?'

'Would you mind if I brought Vera here to stay the night?'

Bruce bent forward, sighing deeply like an old man, and buried his face in his hands. He suddenly sat up, and when he spoke it was almost a cry of despair, long and drawn out like a single cry of a seagull.

'Why?'

'It'd be so much more convenient.'

'For what?' He did not allow Stephen to answer. He was afraid to hear the actual words. 'My father wouldn't allow it.'

'He needn't know about it, need he? She can sleep in my room. There are two beds. Or, if you prefer, we could sleep in one the outhouses.'

Bruce, though he had feared it, had not dared to imagine Stephen's relationship with Vera had progressed so far. He was totally opposed to premarital sex. The idea warred against all his instincts. It had been bad enough to know that Stephen was spending so much time with Vera, but this was too much to bear. Now Stephen wanted that girl to invade the house at night too, to occupy his very bedroom. One of the outhouses – perhaps his father's 'fornicatorium', as a family friend had once called it. Bruce laughed inwardly, bitterly. What would his father think of that?

'Have you made love to her?'

'Of course.'

'When?'

'You want to know – exactly?'

'Yes.'

'Two days ago. I thought you had guessed.'

'Where?'

'Over there.' Stephen waved towards the sandhills.

'I thought you had some kind of—' Bruce was going to mention Stephen's complex about his physical make-up, but Stephen interrupted.

'There's no problem. It was all in the mind.'

'Do you love her?'

'Love her?' This was a new thought to Stephen. 'I don't know what that means.'

There was a pause. Bruce sighed again, watching a thin repressed line of waves straining towards the shore.

'You haven't got any control, Stephen. You've no self-discipline at all.' His mind was in a turmoil. Stephen had broken the last link. 'I feared this.'

'What's wrong? It's quite natural. What is there to be afraid of?'

Bruce could not name the fear. It wasn't so much Stephen's renunciation of Bruce's moral precepts, of all he stood for in the name of purity. It was that Stephen had entered a world that Bruce himself longed to enter, but had never known how, had never had the chance; and that Stephen had taken such a step before he himself had. A terrible wave of envy gripped him once again, the fear of being left behind, the fear of being lost in a desert, the fear of knowing there was happiness, achievement, companionship elsewhere, which he could have no part in, the burning pain of being abandoned, a derelict human being, to be laughed at, scorned as unnatural, unfulfilled, failed and growing old. Always it was he who had to be the one alone. No friend ever stayed; people came near, smiled, admired, understood, lost their smiles, and drifted away again, but none ever stayed to take him by the hand, to look into his eyes, to make him feel loved, by someone, to let him feel that a long journey had come to an end with a promise of beautiful new journeys to be undertaken together after that. He heard Stephen's voice coming to him, it seemed, from far away, like a radio at low volume close to his ears.

'You think there's something wrong about it. Everybody does it nowadays.'

'No, not everybody, and anyway that doesn't make it right. It's people like you—like her, that make the world the way it is. She's ruining you.'

'I don't think so at all. She's done more than anyone I know to make me feel a normal human being.'

'Normal? What is normal? Are you normal?' Bruce let out a short bitter laugh.

'More than you are. I don't hanker after little boys.'

'That's nothing. That's beautiful.'

'Don't lie. It looks lovely, yes, but what's in your thoughts? What do you actually think of when you think of things like that? What do you really actually want to do?'

'I don't think you understand. You've never been pure. All those filthy old men. Look, Stephen: haven't I done anything to help you feel normal?'

'You didn't succeed.'

'Well, I tried.' Bruce was near tears. Stephen could sense that but ignored it.

'Anyway, can she come?'

'No.'

'Why not?'

'I said no.'

'But why not?'

'What do you think I feel, Stephen?'

'You could be generous, but it's not one of your best points.'

'What have I been, up to now?'

'We wouldn't get in your way.'

'I don't like her.'

'You said you found her attractive.'

'I don't like her greedy, cold eyes. She's nothing but a prostitute.'

Stephen stood up.

'I'm going.'

'Stephen—' Bruce was also on his feet.

'If you're going to speak like that about my friends, I'm not going to stay here. You try to make out that you're always concerned for my wellbeing, my happiness, but as soon as I begin to feel, perhaps for the first time in my life, anything like real happiness, you try to destroy it. All you want is to exert power over everybody, over me especially, not power for good, but power just to destroy. I've had enough of it. I'm going.'

Bruce's pain suddenly transformed an angel in his mind into a demon. His brain burned red with anger, which glittered out of his eyes.

'Oh, yes, go, go on then, go, go, get out! Go and copulate in the sandhills! That's all they're good for. They're made for people like you.' The two friends stood face to face in the verandah. 'You disappoint me, Stephen. Not for the first time either. No one's ever disappointed me as much as you have. Oh, go away! Get out!'

Stephen, though taken aback by this outburst, still wanted to get his way, tried to avoid a total breakdown.

'Look, let's be more reasonable. We can be. Remember our first conversation in that hotel.' He forced a smile and put one hand on Bruce's shoulder.

'Don't touch me. Keep your clammy hands for that girl. You're as soiled as she is. And don't think that because you've had sex with her you're any better as a person. You're a confirmed queer and you always will be. You just follow the filthy desires of your disgusting body. You're like an animal. You make me sick, not just physically sick, but totally sick in spirit. You've poisoned me in body and mind, right down to the depths of my guts, spread a disease into every pure thought I ever had in my head. You don't even love her. The only thing you find attractive about her is that she looks like a boy. You're all twisted inside the mind. You've brought all your filthy slime to this marvellous place, and now everything's diseased and rotten. Because of you, because of you, and only you! The biggest mistake I ever made in my life was to call you my friend, to treat you as a friend, to try to help you in your misery! If my mother were here now, she'd thrash you out of the house!'

'Your mother isn't here.'

'Yes, she is, Stephen. What's left of her. Out there. And little do you care about it. You've defiled her grave. You go out there with that slut of yours and fuck her on my mother's ashes!'

Bruce suddenly began to cry. He rushed into the house and half blindly in the kitchen swept up the empty milk bottles. The one he had smashed the day before still lay scattered on the floor. He kicked the fragments aside, opened the back door, and made his way running towards the railway line.

*

Half an hour later he was back in the kitchen, sweeping up the broken glass. Somewhat calmer of mind now, he resigned himself to the inevitable, reluctantly deciding, for the sake of their friendship, for the sake of his own sense of worth, to give meaning to his earlier intentions and words relative to Stephen's happiness – to let Stephen have his way, however strongly it stood against his beliefs, however hard it might be for he himself to bear. The house was silent. The living room was empty. He thought he heard a sound upstairs and went up to Stephen's room. That too was empty, entirely empty of Stephen's possessions. The bedclothes were on the floor, the wastepaper-basket on its side, its contents spilled out. A few sheets of paper, pen and ink lay on the table next to the red lamp from his mother's annexe. Bruce hurried downstairs and went through all the rooms. Stephen had gone. His pork-pie hat, hanging in the hall, was the only thing he had left behind. Bruce went outside and stared round wildly. A figure stood on the beach, close to the edge of the sea. Bruce ran down the path, Stephen's hat clutched in his hand.

Stephen was standing in the water, his shoes and socks submerged and his trousers soaked dark to the knees. He held the pages of his novel in his left hand. With slow deliberate movements, he was taking the pages one by one and letting them float down on the oily, faintly breeze-roughened sea. His typewriter case and carrier bag, like objects in a surrealistic painting, stood primly on the beach a few yards behind him. The surface of the water was dotted with the white sheets, more than fifty of them, some of them slightly curled, like little boats, like resting seagulls, drifting like some crazy child-admiral's fleet out into the bay. Bruce splashed into the water and grabbed Stephen's coat.

'What are you doing this for?'

'I like destroying things. Like you. Only I do it more beautifully.'

'Oh, don't, you fool!' Bruce snatched up some of the sheets from the water. 'You mustn't throw it away. You're mad. It's great.'

'I can do what I like with my own things.' He let another sheet fall.

No, it's not yours, Bruce's mind screamed. It's mine! I made it. I made you write it. You're destroying my work, my creation. Without me, without this place, you'd never have written it. He floundered in the water, wildly reaching out for the scattered sheets.

'You won't be able to save them, Bruce. Some of them are already too far out. Look. Anyway, the ink's all smudged.' Stephen dropped a bunch of sheets into the water.

Something like a cold stone suddenly weighed Bruce down in the pit of his stomach. He looked at his friend. Stephen stood there in his suit and raincoat, its lower edges also dark and wet, his feet close together. Calm of voice, calm of hand, he continued to drop the pages, sometimes singly, sometimes several at a time. Then with a sudden jerk of his arm he threw what remained in his hands as far as he could out over the steely water. The pages flew all ways in the air and settled down like a descending flock of small white birds. Stephen turned and gazed steadily into Bruce's eyes.

'Let your old woman of the sea read them. It'll give her something to laugh about.'

He turned from the water, picked up his luggage, and started walking north along the beach. Bruce, knee-deep in the sea, tried to run after him. The water dragged at his ankles. He stepped into an unexpected depression carved out by the sea in its unaccustomed struggle with the east wind, and fell over onto his hands and face. Struggling to his feet, he splattered out of the water and caught up with Stephen, clutching at his sleeve.

'Where are you going?'

'Away from you.' He shook off Bruce's hand and continued walking.

'Don't, Stephen. I didn't mean—'

'I've already decided.'

'Vera can come. I've reconsidered.'

'I don't want Vera to stay in that house. Not if you're there.'

'Where will you go?'

'That's none of your business.'

'Tell me, Stephen.'

Stephen stopped walking. His face was set with a new strength and confidence.

'If you want to know, they've got a cottage up in the mountains. I'm going there. And don't try to find it. I won't speak to you.'

'You can't do this, Stephen.'

'I can, you know. I'm doing it.' He started walking again.

'Look, Stephen, I'm sorry.'

'I'm not.'

'Stephen...please.'

'It's no good saying anything now. It's too late. I know exactly how you feel.'

'When will you come back?'

'I'm not coming back.'

'Will you write to me?'

'No.'

'Can I write to you then? Let me have the address.'

'No.'

'I want to explain everything.'

'There's nothing to explain.' Stephen was still walking, Bruce, half-turned, pacing frantically beside him. 'I know all I want to know about you. I've had enough.'

'You can't run away from it.'

'I'm not running away. Not like you did just now up at the house. I made a rational decision.'

'You are running away. That is exactly what you are doing. You're like a stupid child. That's just what they do.'

'Am I the only stupid child?'

They looked at each other, but there was no communication in their exchange of glances. Bruce read nothing in Stephen's eyes but blank grey wordless pages. Stephen saw only blindly turning fire, like phosphorescence under the sea. Bruce held out his right hand.

'Shake hands, anyway.'

'No.'

'Just one shake. Then I'll let you go.'

'No, Bruce. If I do that, you'll never let me go. Never, never. You're malevolent. You're like a spider, like that old man of the sea who locked his legs round Sinbad's neck.'

Bruce made one last desperate effort. He held out Stephen's pork-pie hat, heavy and dripping with water.

'Here's your hat.'

Stephen looked at it, then raised his eyes and gazed at Bruce's face. For a full minute they stood there, Bruce once or twice twitching the beginnings of a smile, the brightness in his eyes rising and falling and fermenting like the northern lights as hope and despair constantly stirred and exchanged strengths. Stephen's mask-like expression never broke, but something ancient moved behind it, like a face formed by imagination in the features of a granite cliff or a rainswept window. There were no signs of a smile, or anything like a smile, but something lurked there that was not totally unfriendly. Stephen gestured with one hand laden with the carrier bag towards the hat. He spoke in a very quiet voice.

'Keep it. It belongs to the past.'

He turned and walked rapidly away, not once looking behind him. Bruce slowly lowered his outstretched arm, and stood there, the few rescued pages of his friend's novel clutched damply in one hand and the sodden hat in the other.

*

The wind had dropped. The sun was hovering, round and huge just above the long pale line of Lleyn, reflected like polished brass as a broad, undiminishing roadway in the sea. Bruce stood on a grass-covered sandhill between the house and the beach, listening to the quiet movement of the gentle waves below.

Nothing now troubled his mind. The blight of the previous two weeks had lifted, like a swarm of flies leaving a carcase where there was nothing more to be consumed, nothing more left to decay, only clean white bones gleaming and indestructible in the golden light. It seemed to Bruce that all the while Stephen had been at the house, flocks of jackdaws had been clattering and screaming in the sky above them; as if the shore had become littered with evil-smelling corpses, the sand dunes filled with sweating, writhing bodies. Now nothing remained but silence and the peaceful sighing of the sea. Stephen had brought with him generations of corruption gathered from life in the city, and had brought a kind of madness with him too. It was this that had done so much to excite and fascinate Bruce whenever the two friends met. But like the scent of poppies on a sweltering summer's day, it had at first charmed and then poisoned his mind. To think of being with Stephen was like looking forward to going to a series of new films by such old masters of classics like Eisenstein or Bergman or Fellini or Kurosawa, or more appropriately, a new joint creation by Buñuel and Hitchcock; to be with him was like lurking outside an abandoned lunatic asylum, peering in at the windows and seeing a brilliantly illuminated paradise of wild forests and gothic buildings within. His personality, once encountered, was, at a distance, full of promise; at close quarters and over a prolonged period, Bruce now realized, it was a mass of contradictions, fragments of violence, impulsive, irrational decisions, burning disappointments. Bruce was glad his friend had gone.

At first he had dreaded it. He would have to explain to his father; he himself would have to live with the humiliation of having failed to rescue one on whom he had expended so much solicitude and energy from a world ruthlessly spiralling down towards annihilation. He would have to accept that as a teacher, guardian, leader, and also as a critic, he had been utterly defeated, that as a friend he had been found wanting. The entire moral edifice he had built up over the years lay shattered like a magnificent castle made of glass and coral shaken to its roots by a devastating ten-second earthquake. The courageous patterns of his mind had fallen into chaos like a smashed kaleidoscope. All that he had held sacred from his childhood up had been subjected to ridicule and scorn, derisively exposed like lighted birthday-cake candles flickering feebly under glaring arc-lights. The delicate haunts of his younger days – the winding pathways in the sandhills, the gleaming stretches of beach, the wooden echoing floors of the house – all of them had been trodden over by heavy, soiled hobnailed boots, boots which had been worn for days on end in a slaughterhouse for diseased cattle. His mind lay exposed like a festering wound. Chasteness, virtue, common decency – things he had been brought up to respect and believe in – lay like stained and threadbare sheets spread over the grass. As Stephen had walked away across the beach, Bruce had felt like a child standing in the ruins of the nursery it knew and loved so well, with the best and the most loved toys torn apart and flung to the floor or taken away forever.

Yet now, as Bruce stood there in the sunset, it seemed that the east wind, with its final tainted breaths, had blown everything foul into the sea. All the hard words, the fragments of broken playthings, the traces of animal decay, had fluttered and glided past his feet, and like the unsaved pages of Stephen's novel, had floated out of sight on the strangely flattened sea and sunk down into the all-engulfing maw of the ocean. And then the wind had dropped. Anything that came now would come out of the sea, but it would come fresh, transformed, cleansed. What the sea washed up on the shore was only what it could not or would not digest. Millions of plastic bottles, wood which could still be of use to mankind, living creatures which still had hope of life on land, or corpses to feed the living – all these came back, rejected or redelivered by the ocean. Fragments of toys would again litter the shoreline, but hard words spoken on land would never re-emerge with the supremely beautiful choruses of waves. Human conflict was always resolved in the sea. The sea healed all.

Bruce stood there between the sea and the land. The land was where he had to live. He knew he could never live in constant companionship with the sea. There was something demented there – too much love, too much intensity of passion. No one, Bruce thought, could remain by the sea long and keep tranquillity of mind. The Seafarer yearned to travel to far places; the Wanderer sought for a new lord. They didn't seek for companionship with the bitter-cold, cruel waves. The sea was only a place to come to for a while, like a visit to one's birthplace, if that had been a place of happy memories, to gain new strength, to stand and listen to for a few hours, to watch quietly for a few days. That's why, Bruce realized, the Harlieg people so rarely if ever came down to the beach from the town. The sea was too abrasive, too brutal, perhaps, too astringently salt for the freshwater palate of man. Fishermen, mariners, far-voyagers, they must be the most courageous, the most hardy breed of men, and Bruce knew he was not of that race. But he knew that wherever he went, no matter how far inland he might have to spend the greater part of his life, he could always come back, not only here at Harlieg, but anywhere where the long waves came gliding in like reaching hands up the slopes of beaches;

he could come back and speak to the ocean-mother whose voice he constantly heard in his ears.

The sun had almost disappeared behind the western peninsula. Bruce knew that no matter what friend he might find in the future, or what love he might feel for woman or child or man, no love could be greater than the love he felt now, here, standing in the curve of Tremadog Bay, for the endlessly crying music of the sea.

And therefore, he knew now too, that even if no friend ever came, even if there was no one to love, or to love him, he could never be wholly alone again. Here he was with no one, but here too he was with someone part of but more than himself, as if his hands and mind and organs of generation could reach out towards and embrace and become one with the turning and moaning of the surf.

As the sun began its last headlong plunge behind the horizon, he turned and stepped down back from the sandhill, where three years before, the exact place unknown to him, his mother's ashes had been scattered; and with the slow steps of an adult, he walked back to the silent house.

28. LETTER

MY DEAR, MAGNIFICENT friend,
I begin with a poem about you, Bruce, which I wrote a few weeks ago after I came out of hospital.

> I was a child when the hero came
> into my life, like a secret
> folding me inside himself. He named
> my laughter, and my name rang about me
> dark years long. Those eyes
> raved at me in the bleak room
> where I touched his hand. I became

blind from loving him, and somehow, blind
I borrowed his vision. The dark world
contained only one man, and no sound
but the sound of the sea, and his feet
on the sand. There was nothing
that could engulf him.
We have seen the sun
go down into the sea so many times.
We have gone down to the sea and walked
far out into the waves by now. I would
abandon the hero if I could, but somehow
his eyes are at the back of my head
wherever I go. All I can do is take them
where they have not seen before, and wish
that one day something they see would close them.

Is it any good? It's a new thing for me to write poems, and I don't know how to arrange lines properly. Tell me how to. Do anything you like with this one. Throw it into the sea if you like, if you ever go there. The last line is not intended as a death curse, only an expression of freedom concerning me. But I don't want to analyze too much. You'll understand.

I have a great many things to tell you. You can see that I'm back at home now. I'll tell you how and why.

The cottage the College students rented above Harlieg is a delightful place. To get there you have to climb up a winding precipitous road with ivy-covered walls. It's impossible to believe that cars can get up there, but they do. The gradient is steeper than 1 in 5. Perhaps you know the place I mean. The cottage is built of stone, but the outside is painted white. There's a little garden. As soon as I settled down there, I began to cultivate it. I planted some potatoes and sprouts. The neighbours, in a twin cottage higher up, are wonderful people – Mr. and Mrs. Williams. Mrs. Williams used to talk to me over her wall, and I listened for hours on end to her enchanting voice. I still wish I could speak like that. I haven't been able to pick it up at all, not like you have. It sounds like the sea running back over the rocks. She might be a kind of good witch.

The sea was up there, too. You won't believe it, but I could feel its presence everywhere. I went for long walks every day. I never liked walking until I came to Harlieg. I often went along a narrow lane between very high stone walls. There are pale green lichens on the stones and rocks like dried seaweeds or shrivelled sea-anemones, and in the crevices and damp places rich mounds of green moss. And you should see the trees. They seem to be incredibly old, as if they've been there for centuries, but none of them is very big. They've been twisted by the wind into grotesque shapes, just like sea-goblins with skinny hands bound by spells. The trunks of some of them are doubled right over in S-shapes. I felt as if that old woman of the sea had reached her hands right up into the mountains, trying to petrify everything. There was a lot of mist there too, especially in the mornings, but sometimes all day long, as if she were breathing inland. It made my asthma come back. It had almost disappeared before that. You know, I think trees are nothing but overgrown fungi. Clumps of moss are just like miniature forests if you look closely. And the copses up there, damp with clinging lichens, are just the same, magnified hundreds of times. You probably know what I mean.

I have to tell you about Vera. She used to come up at the weekends. We had wonderful parties. She used to bake fresh loaves of bread in the oven of the old cast-iron range in the kitchen. They were delicious. But she left the kitchen in a terrible state – the walls smeared with dough, and doughy plates, dishes, bowls, rolling pins and wooden spoons everywhere. She also introduced me to macrobiotic food. There's a little shop in the town that specializes in that kind of thing. I eat very little now. I've lost my roll of fat! You can't pinch it now – impossible to get a purchase on the skin with your fingers! I eat miso soup, oat-cake omelettes and dried raisins. I drink ginseng in hot water. You must try them.

I smoked a lot of pot. It's wonderful what it does to you. You can learn everything about yourself. The whole world is transformed, and it's something you can remember. It's not like drinking. It doesn't seem futile afterwards. It's one of the best friends I ever had, but I think my mother's my best friend now. Vera's friends brought acid, too. I had one or two terrifying experiences with that. I was sometimes sick.

Vera behaved very strangely at times. When we were in bed, she would suddenly get out and get into bed with one of the girls sleeping in the same room. The noises they made there, incredibly loud sucking and slapping noises, were, even for me, horribly embarrassing. I didn't know where to look next morning, but Vera just smiled and things went on as usual. She built a wonderful mill in the stream behind the house, and took me out by the hand to show me. She's such a child really. But after a while, I began to notice that she preferred the company of girls. They used to sit together on a pile of cushions in the corner, clawing at each other in a heap. Sometimes they collapsed in laughter, giggling and whispering for hours and looking at me with eyes round and wet with tears of mirth, and then laughing again as if they could never stop.

Sometimes I tried to teach her about philosophy and literature. She listened very seriously and even tried to read the books I gave her. But she could never stick at it for long. She would toss them aside, and go into the kitchen and bake bread and rock buns, or sit in the garden watching, she said, the plants growing. I can understand you better now, Bruce. I can understand how you felt about me, when you tried to help me. I tried to help her in the same way. But you can't change anyone, especially a girl like that, especially a person like me. She has absolutely no sense of responsibility. We never had regular meals, unless I cooked them, and I got good at that. I began to feel that she was just using me for her own amusement, trying to initiate me into most peculiar ways of living and doing things. I began to feel like a sort of rare animal kept in a cage, which she and her friends would sometimes prod and stare at, to see what it would do next.

Once we went to the castle. I showed her the well and told her about the girl you told me about who drowned there. She behaved even more strangely after that. I think that was perhaps the real beginning of the madness that gripped everyone soon afterwards. She insisted that we walk over the hills to the Lily Lake. It took us hours to find it. It's a terrifying place, isn't it? So quiet and cold and still, and those lilies on it, their stalks reaching right down into the black water. You told me it was haunted. I can well believe it. Vera was convinced of it. While we there a white dog, some kind of mongrel sheep-dog, not a very big one, ran past us. Suddenly it stopped, looking at the water of the lake. Then it began to growl, and the hairs rose on the back of its neck. We couldn't understand why it was behaving like that. But Vera was enchanted, and from that moment she literally became the Drowned Girl of the Lily Lake, and walked about moaning her name. She seemed to change completely, and sometimes sat in the front window seat of the cottage, gazing out at the rain and weeping silently for hours and hours. She used to tie strands of ivy round her forehead. They made her look astonishingly evil.

One Saturday night, we all decided to do some table-tapping. We wrote out the alphabet and spread the lettered bits of paper in a circle on the table and each placed a finger on the tumbler in the centre. There were six of us altogether, all girls except me. At once the tumbler began to move strongly and calmly, and we were all afraid. Then Vera said she could feel a curious tingling in her hands, and we all joined hands. We could feel a force running round our linked hands from person to person, growing stronger until one of the girls couldn't stand it any longer and broke the circle. Immediately all the current seemed to pile up in my shoulders. I went into a trance. My head became a shark's head, my voice a deep growl between bared teeth. I said I was a man with shark's blood running in my black veins and a lord with many servants who could answer many important questions. And yet at the same time I knew it wasn't me who was speaking. The voice said it had come to join us all and to answer questions we needed answering. Vera asked me who I was, and the voice inside me said she was the Old Woman of the Sea, and we were to put our fingers back on the tumbler again. We did so, and the tumbler immediately moved sharply three times and spelt out three letters – P.Y.M. I suddenly remembered that this was your mother's maiden name. Then I went mad.

It was after midnight, but I rushed outside. I can't remember what happened exactly, but hours later I found myself in that great stretch of sand at the far end of the dunes. We saw it once, you remember, when we went for that 'mountain-climbing' walk. It was getting light, and it was raining. It wasn't heavy rain but I was soaked through. The voice inside my head was wailing incessantly. I couldn't get rid of it. Then I realized it was my own voice. I ran about in the sand, in circles which seemed to get smaller and smaller. I fell down and tried to force my head under the sand. (It sounds funny now!) I began to eat sand. I remember how delightful it was to feel the grains of sand, tiny fragments of shells really, crunching and grinding between my teeth, and the dry salty taste. I remember picking up a jagged rusty piece of corrugated iron and deliberately cutting the soles of my feet with it. I've got terrible scars. And then I found a small corroded unexploded shell left over from the war or something, and tried to thrust it up my rectum. I realized I was screaming, but although I was quite conscious of the sound coming out of my throat I didn't know how to stop it.

Later I found myself on the shore. The sea was pure and white and the entire long line of surf was thousands of pale grey seaslugs about three feet tall, all of them foaming at the mouth and dancing fantastically. It was just like something out of The Ancient Mariner. A long dark shape lay on the wet sand in front of me. It was a dead seal. Its mouth was all eaten away and its teeth were exposed in a permanent hideous grin. When I rolled it over, large very pale yellow maggots fell writhing out of a hole in its side. The stench was terrible, but I remember thinking it was delightful to my nostrils. I lay down by the seal. I embraced it. I kissed its grinning teeth. Then I got up and with all my clothes on rushed into the sea till it was almost up to my neck. Waves knocked at my skull and ribs with extraordinary violence.

Later still, I was walking along the sand. There were people on either side of me. I think they were people from the College — boys and girls. I glanced round many times, and someone was crawling along the beach behind me, whimpering and trying to catch me by the ankles. It was Vera. I somehow knew the soles of her feet were bleeding, much worse than mine were, though I had no sensation of pain. I must have cut hers too. I remember beating her face somewhere with a spray of that pale green sea-holly. She was crawling along on her hands and knees, and when she stood up I saw her knees and the tops of her feet were raw and bleeding where the salt and sand had burned the skin away. It was fascinating, I remember, to see the blood soaking into the sand of the beach.

I don't remember much after that. There was a long train journey, with many changes and hours of waiting on remote grey platforms in anonymous stations. And later I was in a sort of hospital ward with people sitting round in old leather armchairs. They were mostly old men, and menopausal women whose husbands had left them. There was one middle-aged spinster who was a history lecturer and whose face looked as if it been punched violently and often. There was also a parrot which flapped its wings in a cage in one corner of the room and screamed all day long. It seemed as if all the madness in the brains of the people there was drawn out and concentrated in that poor demented bird. It was a kind of Hebrew goat, burdened with all the problems and complexes of the inmates (detestable word!), like a vile brown hanging fly-paper cluttered with masses of little black legs and bodies and veined wings. Then I went home and began to write poems. My mother was very understanding, and now I think, as I said, she's the best friend I have in the world — except you, of course.

I haven't seen Vera since. I think there was a scandal about the College shortly after I left Harlieg. It was in the newspapers.

You probably read about it. The College is closed now, isn't it? It's a pity about Vera. She could have been such a wonderful companion if she'd been with the right kind of people, if things had been different. One's background does such awful things to one. Vera's a genius, a kind of blighted enchantress. I don't know where she is now. I hope she prospers. Perhaps we'll hear something about her one day. She might become famous.

How are you getting on teaching? That's what you're doing now, isn't it? And that's what I know you can do best. What are you writing nowadays? Write and tell me about the interesting people you've been meeting.

Dear Bruce, I think we travel the same paths, and it is never so apparent as when we are apart. I am not mad, but I am unlike any other thing in the world. I am alone most of the time and my life is very rich now. I am in love with the world, and I am delirious with joy and under it all very peaceful. You were not wrong and I was not right. I should very much like to see you again.

You must not think our staying together in that house was all in vain. I am a much happier person now, much more stable (another horrid word!). I'm studying every day. I'm going to enter university next year, to read philosophy. So after all I'm doing what you've always advocated for so long.

The other day I had a wonderful dream – about the castle at Harlieg. I was standing somewhere high up but far out at sea. When I looked at the castle it suddenly began to unfold like a roll of film on edge, like a thick grey screen jointed with vertical cylinders. It began to spread out and glide like a snake down from its rock. It looked like Great Wall of China on casters, but with round towers at intervals instead of square ones. It came right down to sea level and stretched wide across the Traeth (is that the right spelling?) below the mountains. The walls facing me became film again and on each section were four or five brilliantly coloured panels – pictures of things we saw or did when we were there together, like a picture gallery of fascinating scenes, not still ones –

things in them moved and the pictures kept changing. Sometimes there were seascapes with beautiful fresh waves turning, sometimes close-ups of shells, starfishes and fern-like seaweeds under crystal clear water. Sometimes you and I appeared, laughing sometimes and sometimes crying in gentle golden light. There were sunsets, gorse bushes, wild flowers on the zig-zag, you playing the organ in the College in brilliant sunshine or reciting from a sandhill in bardic robes, me walking on the beach and (would you believe it?) singing wonderful Welsh airs, with thousands of women in Welsh national dress playing harps in serried rows behind me. There were no grotesque scenes. Everything was enchanting, bathed in sunshine, beautiful. The long jointed screen drifted right out over a bright green sea and then lay back and melted into separate panels floating on the surface of the water, the colours still fresh and brilliant. I turned and close beside me a great benign giantess, clad in every shade of blue you can think of, tinged with purple and pastel greys, was standing there waist-deep in the sea. She was taking up the pictures one by one, like a person looking at photographs, examining each carefully and smiling with delight and real pleasure at the scenes she saw there, and looking at me and smiling at me with such gentle, such deep and sincere sympathy that I wanted to weep with sheer joy and rush into her arms. And then I saw you, in your bardic robes again, but not made of cloth. They were woven from very strands of the sea, satin-like threads of water, so closely meshed that you couldn't see the threads but knew the whole thing was woven water, miraculously held together like liquid silk against all the rules of probability and science. You were smiling at the edge of the sea, facing that huge swaying smiling priestess of the ocean and smiling at me too and stretching out your arms to me, and the tears in your eyes were tears of both joy and sorrow. And then all round me the sea began to rise up, gradually closing over you and that golden-hearted sea-woman and up over me too, so that soon I was sinking down and looking up through clear green-blue water, as they said Shelley looked up as he drowned, but I was not drowning. I was delightfully alive and utterly free of fear and pain, and felt so clean, as if my brain was being held in a sieve and washed again and again in warm, newly distilled sea-water, and all the foul things in it being filtered away. When I woke up, I was so happy that I went and told my mother about it, which is why I can remember the details so clearly now; and she laughed with relief because I was so happy, and we hugged each other and wept, and felt something new in the world.

That dream tells you more than anything about what coming to Harlieg really meant to me, means to me now. I'll never forget the best times we had there by the sea, and in other places before that too. Don't worry about the last five lines of the poem. I wrote them when I was not quite clear in my mind about how I felt about you. Now I am more certain, so you can cut them out if you like, or make a new ending. You know better than I what to do. I'm at home now. I expect you'll come home from Berkshire for the Christmas holidays. Then we can meet.

From your happy, your mad and your loving,

Stephen.

29. REPLY

YOUR LETTER, DEAR STEPHEN, came like a seagull bringing messages inland from the ocean. I too begin with a poem. The strange thing is, it was written just two days before your letter came, perhaps at the very same time that you were writing to me. It's called 'Crying Distance'.

> If I lived by the sea, I would go serenely
> mad in a matter of days: to hear its crass dirge always
> would turn my hair and my mind as white and grey
> as waves are on those horn-haunted winter days
> when the long sea fascinates stricken minds.
>
> Genius in the surf astounds me: in blue summer
> the sea is a dragon sleeping, and its fire is the iron
> sinew that at other times bends hulls and carves stone
> dead titans along the edges of the world.

Never live by the sea: there is too much love,
not there, but along the wind-blown curtained
corridors and polished staircase corners of my mind;
and there would come nightmare days when the gales
that pull fair weather from paradise would unhinge
all comforting songs, and the diamond-cutting sun would
adze down my tender and necessary dreams with salt;
and the rains, which are after all only gentle
ice in dereliction of duty, would somehow
find a way into the slate-blue castles I dwell in.

Along the sounding-boards of the ocean.
There is no love there, but mine when I am there.
To go there, to be there, to know those things would
awaken the dormant thunder that never ends
behind the stone walls of my half-dark mind, and would
drive out the splintered white light from my eyes,
fasten my fingertips like coral to black shipwrecked stones,
and turn my voice into the sea-cat cries of lunatic gulls.

Never ask me to live, never let me
live by the sea: it is enough for a stillborn hero
to listen, uncertain miles inland, and grow old
not within crying distance of the breakers,
in a landlocked city where men can despair
without showing it in the whites of their eyes.

Too long, of course, but don't be depressed by it. It's not as elegiac
as it seems. It's just that I understand the sea better than I did. So
do you. I was, I should say am, deeply moved by your excellent
poem. I'm not going to touch it. It's perfect. If your others are as
good, send me more, all of them. They are surely the best things
you've done. Don't you think I've got a new voice, too? Not so
hazy, not such romantic drivel as I used to pour out. I seem older.
Tell me what you think.

Yes, I read about the College. I wasn't really surprised. But
I'm not going to fill this letter with moral pronouncements. I don't

do that anymore. I don't regard myself as a divinely inspired leader of the world any longer. I've stepped down from my bardic pedestal. You were right: it was all a pose. And I feel immensely relieved to have cast it all off from my shoulders.

You'd hardly know me now. I don't carp these days as I used to. It doesn't work. My pupils don't like it. You know, I really love my pupils here, not in a physical way – can I hear you laughing? – but as people I can legitimately teach and guide. They're all so naive and clueless. But maybe that's too critical. Anyway, not like you, my friend, who always champed and strained with brilliant, fascinating energy. Most of them are foreigners. We have twelve different nationalities here at the moment. It was tough-going at first. They couldn't understand anything I said, and if they could they couldn't catch the meaning. There's nothing like reality for teaching teachers what to teach. I've had to change my ideas, and my ways of expressing them, but it's wonderful now to be respected as a normal human being.

I've bought a car. Second-hand. It's a terribly old dull blue Ford Prefect, very thin and high off the ground with enormous wheels. I passed my driving test last week. I'll take you for a spin. (I don't like that phrase. You'll find I've become horribly conventional. You'll probably loathe me now – more than ever!!)

Like you, I don't feel any regrets about all those things that happened while we were staying at the house. It was somehow inevitable. It's strange, isn't it, how we never seem to get on well if we spend too long together. Whenever I think of you now, it is with great longing, a warm fondness, Stephen, which I've never felt for anyone but you.

I've got bits of your novel with me now. What a pity you did that! But here I am, carping again! (It's hard to change one's habits.) But, you know, the odd pages I have are all amazingly self-contained. They're like fragments of a lost epic, yet each is a separate poem. You ought to get them published as a collection. You could call it Shipwrecked Pages or something like that. I'll type them out and send them to you. The parts that are lost are now part of the sea. Perhaps they'll be redelivered one day like the book washed up on the beach you wrote about. That idea was so beautiful.

I had a fantastic dream too not long ago. I think I told you about Crib Goch, that craggy knife-edge ridge that forms one of the shoulders of Snowdon. It's the most dangerous in the British Isles, they say. Fiddlesticks! I walked along it when I was six. We did it in a family party, about fifteen of us one afternoon. But perhaps being as young as that I had no fear of great heights, no sense of the danger. Anyway, in my dream, I was going along inside the ridge, near the top. It was like a series of attics, each one a different shape and height, all joined together at crazy angles, with all kinds of little passages and quaint flights of steps. It was so unforgettably exciting. Each attic was filled with forgotten treasures − trunks full of old stage clothes, brightly coloured and jewelled and sequined; old dusty gilt-framed portraits of heroes, Alexander, Frederick the Great, Marcus Aurelius, Nelson and hundreds of others. One of them was of you as an old man, laughing from the frame in a seventeenth-century wig. There were so many delightful things in those attics − old wooden clocks, some of them still working and chiming as I went through; oil lamps made of brass, grotesque masks, spinning-wheels, huge green glass bottles, heavily bound books full of coloured illustrations, old ones originally engraved on steel, smiling bronze Buddhas and Persian tables inlaid with mother-of-pearl, Turkish carpets, flasks made of beaten gold and ivory caskets full of jewels − oh, too much and too many to put down here; but I can never forget the sheer joy of anticipation as I scrambled through to each new attic. Then I heard organ music − superb brilliantly executed toccatas, rumbling passacaglias, mournful chorales; and then, and this was extraordinarily fascinating, I was inside the workings of the organ. There were grey tin pipes of all sizes all around me at all angles, jointed not in smooth curves but with straight-edged sections, four of five to one right angle − so quaint; and there were all sorts of wooden boxes, bunched together like honeycombs, and lots of thin levers and pistons and tappets, some of them moving up and down very close to my face −

and the music went on and on and seemed to be inside me. I came to a huge set of bellows in a varnished wooden frame, wheezing and breathing and gasping like a great trapped whale in a cage without water; and then it was a whale which opened its mouth and sucked me in and I went sliding down a long very dark green tunnel, highly polished and slippery but not unpleasant at all. And I came down into a huge cavern, like one of those in the slate mines near Ffestiniog that I told you about (did I?), with stalactites and stalagmites and lanterns – they were short squat candles burning inside jelly-fishes that seemed to be hovering in the dark damp air. There was the sound of dripping water all around me, and I knew, I knew it so clearly that I almost awoke, that I was under the sea. The walls of the cavern glinted with copper hues and greeny-blue tinted squares and diamonds of light, and one passage glowed brighter than the rest and led to an immense hall with a throne in it made of huge smooth pink bones, and over it a canopy, hung with the most beautiful seaweeds I've ever seen, lace-like, like the foam on the surface of the water just behind a wave at the edge of the sea, constantly moving and changing shape as they hung there. There was no one on the throne but near it I saw, of all people, Vera, imprisoned in a cage of coral busily at work making – oh, it was so fantastic! – an extraordinary machine out of shells and conches and huge mermaid's pencils, to record, she said, the language of dolphins. And she looked so happy, Stephen, so contented, so fulfilled. I was very happy to see that, I don't quite know why. Then I went further on beyond the throne, and by and by I felt someone holding my hand, and I looked and saw a little old lady there, with neat grey hair dressed in a long gown made of fish scales but soft as velvet. She smiled occasionally but most of the time was quite serious, and seemed to be leading me somewhere important, but she wouldn't tell me where we were going. Sometimes, she became my mother, sometimes she had your face or what I thought was your mother's face, and sometimes she was very stern. She led me up endless flights of steps and we came to a window in the rock wall, and she made me look out. I looked out and down below me lay the whole of Tremadog Bay glorious in morning sunlight. I saw all the mountains and valleys, I saw the shore, the Traeth (yes, your spelling was right), and the sand dunes;

I saw the castle, the College, the hotel, the whole town laid out like a medieval painting, and I saw our own house by the sea, but it was standing in the sea, like that painting we have in the living room there, and there were thundering waves behind it, and behind those – I was gliding down now with wings like a seagull's – a vast chorus of mermaids singing wildly, insanely with their eyes closed, with delicious sad joy, so beautifully! And somehow I was conducting them, my baton a piece of dry white driftwood. And I stood there, as the sound very gradually faded, and I drifted into sleep, and then into a most lovely world somewhere between sleeping and waking, and then I awakened and the morning sun was shining on my face.

That was my dream, but as you know, as soon as you try to write down a dream you do things to it, so I don't know how much of it was real dream or imagination afterwards. Real dream? What is that? I do know, though, that I've forgotten or missed out a thousand other details. As soon as I try to think of them they dissolve instantly. You surely know what I mean.

The sea, Stephen! The sound of it never leaves my ears. I hear it all day long, crying and moaning, a constant background to all my thoughts and actions, even here a hundred miles inland. I know that all my life I'll never be able to move away from that sound. And yet, though it haunts me with a kind of never-ending dull pain, I don't ever want to escape from it. This sounds almost puerile, I know, but I love it more than anything else in the world. I love it with a wonderful warm feeling of sadness and despair, because I know perhaps that it will never love me in return.

There is no doubt, is there, that the Old Woman of the Sea exists, at least in the sphere of our lives, yours and mine. We both know about it, it must be so if she figures so strongly in our dreams, but neither of us must try to analyze it any further. I'm not talking about ghosts or mermaids or anything like that. It hasn't really got anything to do with my mother, either, although she too knew about it. It's something much vaster than that, something much more intangible, and no matter what we say, or write, or think even, we'll never be able to get close to it; and yet it is near us, within us, part of us, all the time. And not only us, but all living things. And we know, too, that the most terrible thing about it is its terrible fascination. All this sounds quite futile and prosaic, I know, and it seems somehow sacrilegious even to mention it in human language like this, but I can't help it.

We must go there again, Stephen. We must. We must go there again and together watch the sun go down behind the land beyond the sea. But whatever happens, we must not stay there long. We know what happens, and we must not allow what has happened ever to happen again.

A man is always splendidly alone, Stephen. No matter who comes, who stays, no matter who goes away, no one has ever come close enough to me for me to feel other than that a man is always bravely, magnificently alone. And you too. And I am your friend. A great rock shooting sheer out of the exploding grey muscles and green-white bursting flesh of the sea. I am there. I am here. And sometime soon we shall be there together. After all, you are, you are still, you are always, my friend.

Perhaps I need a girlfriend. That perhaps would solve everything, and make me less 'romantic', and stop me writing all this nonsense like this. But there isn't anybody yet. Do you think there ever will be anyone – for me, I mean? Tell me what you think.

Whatever, keep writing. Keep doing whatever you are doing. And do whatever you think is best. Never listen to me again. I have no right in the world to utter to you any word of guidance. I have no wisdom. I am a simple, ordinary person, now really beginning to feel the beginnings of growing old. I have inherited your roll of fat, you loveable Yahoo, you neckless, back-of-head-less, walking bottom, thighed in pink dungaroons! How long wilt thou shalt?

Send me some more poems. I want those poems. Oh, God, I need those poems. I wanna get them grand poems. I wanna godda get dose gem pomes. Oh Jeez, I gotta hab dem pomes! Put 'em in a bag right now and send them over the blue, blue land to my mansion in the green wood. And remember, never touch a shitting dog.

Happiness is a weeping princess and a frog singing with a youth's voice and a promise in his pouch on the rim of the well of the world's end. There's no magic left on earth to change things into what they could be. A toad is always a toad, a Houyhnhnm always a Houyhnhnm, a Yahoo always a, ha! – you! Who's who?

And you are always my friend, through thick and thin, through thong and thing, in field, fen, marsh, bog or dung, under every dig and dug, and I am still what I never should have been but always longing to be what I never can.

Your friend,
Bruce.

30. DINNER TABLE

THEY MET ON NEW YEAR'S Day. Bruce had spent Christmas at Tremarfon with his father and sister, who had both returned to Birmingham that morning. Bruce now stood once again on the station platform waiting for Stephen's train. This time his friend had started out in the early morning and his train was due in at noon.

While he was waiting, an episode occurred which at first seemed likely to disturb Bruce's peace of mind. The delivery boy from Hughes the grocer had suddenly appeared on the platform. He was now much taller, quite a lanky youth, even though he could hardly have been fifteen. His figure had acquired a new dignity, however, or retained perhaps the dignity of the best days of his boyhood. His complexion was clear, except for two or three clearly defined spots, and his eyes shone with something Bruce could only identify as a sense of decency or responsibility. All this he took in as the boy walked past him and uttered a surprisingly deep 'Hallo' with a quick smile but with little depth of expression; and then disappeared through a door marked 'Private' into what seemed to be the station master's residence — for the main station building included a two-storey whitewashed 'house'. For a moment Bruce had an almost overwhelming desire to follow the boy through that door and somehow share with him the life he led there; but he knew instantly that that was forbidden territory. He knew that a world existed there that he would never be able to enter. Nevertheless, he longed to know more. Was the boy the station-master's son? Was he a relative, or a friend of the family? More awful to think — did he have a girlfriend in there? Bruce was suddenly wracked with an inexplicable longing, and closed his eyes in pain. When he opened them again he found he was staring at a ground-floor window next to the door. A lace curtain was attached to the lower half of the window, but above that Bruce could see the boy's face, grinning broadly, looking out at him on the platform. The boy raised his hand in a quick friendly salute and disappeared again, into the fascinating darkness of the room within. Bruce smiled in return, his gloom instantly evaporating. His smile did not fade as he turned away from the window. It had been enough. There was a kind of understanding between them, enough to quieten down Bruce's sense of unrest. His smile gradually transformed itself into a long gentle sigh of resignation, and he felt he had aged something like ten years in a matter of minutes. But, he thought, it didn't matter now. The boy who had delivered the groceries to the shore house back then no longer lived in that elfin world; and the youth that he himself had been at that time was now a man with a better sense of reality and a stronger self-command. He could even marvel now at the way he could rationalize and control his emotions. He smiled again, and in that smile something looked longingly far back and something else gazed far forward with a kind of confidence and wisdom that he had not before been aware of. He took a deep breath of the crisp cold air of the station, feeling its almost singeing touch on his hot forehead, and even on that fresh winter's day he could smell the sea, invisible far beyond the station but unquestionably there, audible now as a rushing, ringing sound in his ears.

The cry of a jackdaw made him glance up at the castle. The first day of the year was a holiday only in Wales then, and two flags were flying – the red dragon of Wales on its background of white above green, and the Union Jack. They fluttered brilliantly against the clear winter sky. A kind of guilt at the recent episode made him look again. For a moment he had thought the flags were waving in opposite directions, the British one seeming to point almost accusingly straight at him, the Welsh one rippling bravely towards the south-east. The station bell clanked.

The train, a blue two-coach diesel, arrived at the platform, its motors drumming urgently as if it wanted to hurry on to the next station like an express, which it decidedly wasn't. Stephen alighted.

He seemed, to Bruce, much taller than he had remembered, but this was partly because his face was much thinner. He was clad in a long black coat, of imitation astrakhan wool-fur, tight and curly. On his head was a black hat – a plain high dome for the crown, a perfectly flat brim five inches wide all the way round. He was wearing purple trousers with rather widely flared bottoms, and broad-toed brown leather shoes. Most noticeable were his huge eyes; they burned with intense brightness and seemed to be straining wide whichever way they looked. His fingers trembled as they shook hands, as usual, briefly.

Bruce himself was also wearing a long coat, an old one, of shapeless brown herring-bone tweed, which came down to his ankles. He was wearing a moth-eaten green tam o'-shanter, flecked with red and yellow. Stephen noticed that his friend was fatter in the face and looked around with an air of confidence, almost of complacency. But there was something the matter with his eyes, Stephen thought, and he looked somehow too healthy – not realizing that both these observations were the result of Bruce's recent encounter with the grocer's boy. Bruce also seemed taller.

Bruce took Stephen's luggage, a small black Greek shoulder bag, embroidered with simple but bold horizontal stripes. Stephen was holding a bottle wrapped in brown paper.
'I've brought some wine. Happy New Year.'

'Same to you. Red or white?'

'Rosé.'

They exchanged glances sharply, then smiled. They knew how easy it would be to disturb their mutual equanimity. The merest indication of difference of opinion or superiority of knowledge was enough to shatter the fragile edifice of their reconciliation.

As they were crossing the line at the end of the platform, a flock of jackdaws rose up noisily from inside the castle, as if something had alarmed them. The two friends glanced at one another again but said nothing. The castle slept with its old tired elephant eyes wide open, firmly saddled on its broad rock above them.

Bruce opened the door of his blue Ford and Stephen got in. Bruce rather self-consciously started the engine; it needed two or three tries of stertorous electrical sniffings before it fired. Its note was noisy, and the car rattled as it began to move forwards, its clutch shuddering.

Stephen glanced up at the College, lifeless and silent, as they drove along beneath it in the shadow of the pine trees, but again neither of them spoke. As the car emerged from the line of trees, Stephen gave a sudden exclamation.

'Hey! What's happened to the hotel?' Bruce stopped the car.

'It went bankrupt. It's been vandalized. I meant to tell you in my letter.'

They both got out and stared up at the huge, deserted edifice. Nearly all the windowpanes had been smashed, and some of the frames shattered or knocked right out. One or two hung precariously from one corner. From one of the upper, dormer windows, a pink bedraggled nightdress fluttered limply like an abandoned distress signal. The inside of the hotel was dark and cavernous. The vandals, exhausted by their own excesses, had gone away to recuperate and then to look for further targets for their wanton destruction.

Stephen remembered the decrepit guests sunk in their armchairs in the lounge overlooking the sea.

'What happened to all those moribund old people? Were they murdered?'

'No. I don't think there was any sudden onslaught. I think the place just fell into decay bit by bit.' Bruce chuckled. 'Maybe they're still there.'

'Maybe they don't know.' They got back into the car, and once again fell silent. The stark reality of that grotesque image of lost splendour was both frightening and saddening. With the College closed and the hotel in ruins, Harlieg would never be the same again. And then suddenly Bruce had the extraordinary feeling that the castle was now somehow younger than these two much later buildings, and far more durable. It was a truly noble ruin, while the College and hotel were just like part of a ghost town and would soon fall down of their own accord. After the car had crossed the railway line, Bruce stopped again and looked back at the three great buildings, and to him it seemed – yes, he thought, it really did seem – that the castle was quietly smiling, like an old elephant, remembering.

The car bumped and bounded over the grassy track along the edge of the golf course, and soon was crawling, its engine snarling and whining in low gear between the yellow-grassed winter sandhills. The house was directly ahead of them, its black triangular silhouette jutting up against the sky. Smoke drifted from the chimney. Bruce turned to his friend.

'We're getting old.'

'Where?'

'We're both wearing old coats.'

'It's the newest thing.'

'I see you what you mean. This was my grandfather's. Yours looks as if it once belonged to an old woman.'

As Bruce uttered the last two words, the eyes of both of them widened momentarily, then Stephen smiled.

'It did. I bought it from a second-hand shop. Like this motor-car of yours.'

Stephen's use of the word 'motor-car' reminded Bruce of many things about his friend, but more strongly he noticed a dullness in Stephen's voice, as if he had been under some form of sedation, but he made no comment. The car came to a standstill in front of the house. Stephen got out. Bruce backed the car and parked to the left of the bay window on the north side. He joined Stephen in the verandah. They both stared at the sea. For some minutes neither spoke. Neither of them could find anything significant enough for the occasion. The tide was a long way out. They could hardly hear the waves.

'Am I in the same room?'

'Yes, if that's all right. I'm in the downstairs room this time. You're directly above me.' Bruce looked to see if this last statement had any effect, though none had been intended. There was a ghost of a smile on Stephen's face.

When Stephen went into the house, followed by Bruce, he immediately noticed that it was much brighter inside, and he realized why. The walls, which had previously been stained dark green, were now painted in bright yellows and creams, with blue and green and red trimmings. The woodworm had been arrested.

Bruce went into the kitchen to put the kettle on. Stephen took his bag upstairs, but came down again a few minutes later.

'I've brought you a present.'

He handed Bruce a small brown-paper parcel. Bruce was taken by surprise and with a pang of regret wished he had thought of doing the same. It had never occurred to him to give Stephen a present. Then he remembered something and relaxed. That would have to do.

'Oh, that's kind. May I open it now?'

Stephen nodded, smiling. Bruce stripped off the paper. It was a book, the cover of old faded green leather, the pages edged with gold. He opened it, started slightly, and then smiled. All the leaves were blank. Stephen had written something inside the cover in his strong vertical handwriting. 'Bruce Dinwiddy, my friend and fellow traveller. From Stephen Pewit.'

'Just what I need for my poems. It'll make a marvellous notebook. Or perhaps it's too good for that. I could copy out your poems in it. Yes, that's a good idea. Thanks, Stephen.'

'I thought you'd like it.'

'I wish I'd got something to give you. I never thought of it. But—'

He hesitated. Stephen smiled. Bruce knew from the serenity of his friend's silence that there was nothing in the whole world that he could give Stephen which would please him more than the fact that they were together there again in that house by the sea.

'Have you had lunch?'
'I had something on the train.'
'What do you eat now?'
'Nothing special. Same as you. Only less of it.'
They both laughed, but very briefly. Bruce unwrapped the bottle Stephen had brought with him.
'We'll have this wine at dinner.'
'What are you planning to serve?'
Bruce knew this was the right moment for what he had in mind.
'Wait a minute, I'll show you.' He went from the living room into the hall, and returned almost immediately, holding something behind his back.
'You wanted to know what we're having for dinner. I've got it behind my back. Guess.'
'Broiled kumquats wrapped in laver strips and garnished with snail sauce.' Stephen's face reddened as he remembered the list they had made before going up to the town for shopping and to visit the castle.
'No, you idiot. Something much more simple.'
'Steak and kidney pie, beans and chips.'
'No.'
'I give up. Tell me.'
'Pork pie.'
Bruce took his hand from behind his back and held out Stephen's former grey hat, a dry-cleaning label still attached to it. Stephen stared at it, with Bruce watching him anxiously. Perhaps he had done the wrong thing, committed a gross blunder. Then Stephen suddenly laughed, for the first time wholeheartedly since

they had met that day. It was a wonderful laugh, full throated but still with that long whistling wheeze at the end of every breath. He took the hat and stopped laughing, his eyes bright with merry tears.

'Just what we need. A tangible link with the past. We'll serve it steeped in fresh brine.'

They both laughed again and shook hands, and kept their hands clasped, and each felt a different kind of tears rising beneath their eyes; but they brushed their emotion aside quickly, as if ashamed of unwonted sentimentality, went outside, and drank tea in the verandah.

Bruce brought out some photographs to show Stephen.

'Do you remember these? That man took them, the one with his wife and daughter.'

'I remember the dog.' Stephen looked through the half dozen pictures. They had been well taken. By carefully angling the camera, the man had excluded all other features such as the rocks and sandhills, and their city of sand had assumed the proportions of a real one. Although there was only one basic colour, the pale coffee hue of the sand, the strong shadows cast by the sun brought out the contrasts clearly, and the roofs and towers with their strange turrets and minarets were powerfully realistic. Bruce leaned nearer his friend.

'You can almost see the people, can't you?'

'It's a lot more impressive than I remember.' Stephen picked up the last photograph – he in his cut-off shorts and Bruce, slim and willowy, standing behind their afternoon's creation. He let out a short burst of laughter. 'How ridiculously young we look! Do you remember what they said?'

'They were very impressed. I know that.'

'They said "You two might be famous one day".' Stephen laughed again, but there was no derision or bitterness in his voice.

'So we might. World Famous Slob Artists!'

'Slob.' Again Stephen laughed. 'I like that word. It's very evocative. You ought to use it in a poem. Have you?'

'Not yet. I think the work itself was better than anything I could write about it.'

Stephen looked at Bruce.

'We made it together.'

'Yes. And then the sea came and washéd it away.'

'We could make another.'

'We could. But it wouldn't be the same as that one.' He paused. 'It was very kind of those people to send the photographs, wasn't it? I didn't think they would bother.'

Stephen handed back the pictures to his friend. He looked serious.

'They were nice people, those.'

He smiled, and to Bruce it seemed that the warmth of Stephen's smile, like that of a very tired but happy old woman, was spreading out all round them into the sunlit winter air. Hundreds of images of their two summer-end weeks together at the house flooded through his mind. How long ago had it been? It seemed to Bruce that at least ten years had passed, but it was much less than that. He let the memories spin round till they slowed down and glided away over the peaceful sea before he answered. He touched his friend's arm.

'I know what you mean.'

*

Later they walked along the beach. The wind had dropped completely, and the bay seemed enormous, much bigger than Stephen remembered. There were patches of snow on the mountains, but the air was surprisingly warm now. They walked for more than an hour towards the point, where the sand dunes were hardly higher than the beach. They looked across towards the cliff or rather the long continuation of the mountains, almost a mile distant in the east. The grey houses of the town, with the square block of the castle in their midst, lay like an ancient sleeping fossilized dragon on the side of the long sad hill of Wales. Smoke from a hundred chimneys rose, almost motionless, vertically into the windless air.

They hardly spoke. Their minds were filled with the slow turning of the distant surf behind them. There were voices enough to listen to without either of them needing to speak. No language, no music could make meaningful what came to their ears, but both of them could understand the fading cries, the sobbing laughter which echoed across the stretches of sand. In deep silence, their hands in the pockets of their long coats, their heads bowed, they walked slowly back to the house.

*

On a sudden impulse they decided to have dinner outside, down on the beach. It was Bruce's idea, but Stephen loved the dottiness of it. Bruce had already explained that it rarely got really cold on that temperate western coast, and even though there was now a slight nip in the air they thought that by wearing hats and coats at the table and covering the hot dishes before taking them down they wouldn't have any problems. With a minimum of words, they carried the heavy oak gate-legged table down to the beach, and two high-backed wooden chairs.

Dusk was just beginning. It had been one of those rare Harlieg 'Japanese' days, as Bruce's grandfather had called them. The air was absolutely still. The mountains to the north and west, the highest white tipped, were like porcelain, a pale ultramarine blue and totally devoid of shadows, emerging from a delicate band of mist that hid the point where land met sea; and the sun, a great glowing blood-orange disk, hovered seemingly motionless above the horizon. The sea was unexpectedly darker than the sky and perfectly calm, of that unique shade of blue that can be found only in Japanese woodcut prints, a blue the pigmentary composition of which was such a profound secret that artists in that part of the world somehow lost it, so that now it can no longer be produced. There were no hard edges anywhere in the landscape, yet there was nothing vague or insipid about it. It was a perfectly clear, clean, oriental end of day.

Bruce was busy in the kitchen, cheerfully coping with bubbling saucepans and the sweltering oven. With great amusement he revealed to Stephen that they were having pork after all, roast. Stephen opened the bottle of wine, pleased that his choice agreed with the menu, and stood it near the fire in the living room to let it breathe, not sure actually whether that was the correct thing to do with that breed of wine. He came back into the kitchen.

'Shall I lay the table?'

'If you would. I'm almost ready.' Bruce licked a finger.

Stephen got a tray and loaded it with cutlery, glasses and cruet. He added some side plates, white linen table-napkins, a basket of rolls and the wine bottle, and took down three brass candlesticks from the mantelpiece in the kitchen; the candles had never been used and were slightly bent, and their slight craziness made Stephen smile. He carried the tray down to the beach and laid the table. He lighted the candles, walked a few yards from the table, then turned, looking at it with satisfaction. The roseate wine and the brass gleamed warmly in the candlelight. It was perfect. After a while he returned to the house.

Carrying two more trays laden with dishes and tureens cosily smothered in towels, they walked together, treading carefully on the soft sand and over the rocks, down to the shore. Bruce stopped suddenly and froze.

'You've laid the table for three!'

His eyes were wide and startled, almost accusing, bright in the light of the setting sun. The flames of the candles fluttered slightly.

'Don't worry. There are only two chairs.'

Bruce stared at the third place laid at the side of the table facing the sea. He thought of the letter he had put in the bottle on the day of the east wind. Then he smiled, and nodded slowly with understanding, then faster with approval.

'Thanks, Stephen. I'd forgotten the guest.'

'No, you've still got it wrong.' Stephen paused and chuckled softly. 'We are the guests.'

They arranged the dishes between them and sat down at the table. The sea murmured, drawing closer.

Other works by GAVIN BANTOCK:

Christ, an Epic Poem in Twenty-Six Parts (Donald Parsons, Oxford, 1965)
Juggernaut (Anvil Press Poetry, 1968)
A New Thing Breathing, poems (Anvil Press Poetry, London, 1969)
Anhaga, Translations from Anglo-Saxon verse (Anvil, 1972)
Eirenikon (Anvil Press Poetry, 1972)
Gleeman, poems (Second Aeon, 1972)
Isles, Excerpts from *Christ* (Quarto Press, 1974)
Dragons, poems (Anvil, 1980)
Pioneers of English Poetry (Kinseido, Tokyo, 1980)
Nanny, E. M. Slaughter (Privately produced, 1986)
Journey of the Wind by Tomihiro Hoshino (Translation from Japanese, with Kyoko Bantock) (Rippu Shobo, Tokyo, 1988)
Road of the Tinkling Bell by Tomihiro Hoshino (Translation from Japanese, with Kyoko Bantock) (Kaiseisha, Tokyo, 1990)
Just Think Of It, poems (Anvil, 2002)
Floating World, poems (Redbeck Press, 2002)
SeaManShip, Nine Configurations (Anvil, 2003)
Hail, Salubrious Spot! (How's Your Rupture?) – Memories of a Worcestershire Village (Machinami Tsushinsha, Japan, 2011, Second Edition, First Servant Books, 2020)
The Old Woman of the Sea, a novel (Machinami Tsushinsha, Japan, 2011, Second Edition: First Servant Books, 2020)
Third Form at St. Claire's, an Enid Blyton spoof (Machinami Tsushinsha, Japan, 2011) (Second Edition: First Servant Books, 2020)
Sonnets to Ganymede (Brimstone Press, 2015)
White, poems (Brimstone Press, 2015)
Bagatelles, concrete poems (Brimstone Press, 2015)
Christos, an Epic Poem in Twenty-Six Parts (Revised) (Brimstone Press, 2016)(Second Edition: First Servant Books, 2020)
Leo Sirota, The Pianist Who Loved Japan by Takashi Yamamoto (Translation into English from the Japanese by Gavin Bantock & Takao Inukai) First Servant Books, 2019 & Second Edition, 2020
Katharsis, A Trilogy – Hiroshima, Person & Ichor (First Servant Books, 2020)
Thys Felyship, Oxford Days Around 1960, A Memoir (First Servant Books, 2021)
First Servant Shakespeare Edition,
Shakespeare for Student Actors,
38 Shakespeare Plays adapted, in 35 vols. (First Servant Books, 2022)
Playhouse, A Theatrical Cavalcade, Sixty New Poems (First Servant Books, 2022)

Note: All Anvil Press editions in print are now available from Carcanet.

GAVIN BANTOCK

Born in England in 1939, Gavin Bantock, poet, novelist, dramatist and director of drama, majored in English Language & Literature at New College, Oxford, where he also wrote his prize-winning long poem *Christ*. He has lived in Japan since 1969. He won major UK poetry awards in 1964 (Richard Hillary Award), 1966 (Alice Hunt-Bartlett [Poetry Society] Prize), 1969 (Eric Gregory Award), 1997 (Cardiff International) and 1998 (Arvon International). He has seven publications with Anvil Press Poetry (now Carcanet), and several more with First Servant Books, the most noteworthy being the revision of his epic poem, republished as *Christos* in 2016 (2nd Ed. First Servant Books, 2020). More recently he has published a 1960s Oxford memoir, *Thys Felyship*, and sixty new poems under the title of *Playhouse, A Theatrical Cavalcade*.

A professor of Reitaku University for twenty-five years, Gavin Bantock, now a professor emeritus and retired but still active with drama, has directed all 38 of Shakespeare's plays in English in Japan, many of them several times, as well as numerous other Greek & European classics and modern dramas, mainly with university students and members of the community. He has also written and directed a number of original plays, notably *East, West, Home's Best, John Manjiro in America* (2013), and *Excalibur* (2017). Most of these can be viewed on YouTube, as well as the poet himself reciting his own major works.

Together with his wife Kyoko, he published two highly-esteemed translations of the best-selling poems & essays of Tomihiro Hoshino, the well-known paraplegic artist & author – *Journey of the Wind* (Rippu Shobo, Tokyo, 1988) and *Road of the Tinkling Bell* (Kaiseisha, Tokyo, 1990). He read extracts from the former in the Carnegie Hall, New York, in September, 1994.

Gavin Bantock, grandson of the British composer Sir Granville Bantock (1868-1946), supervised the English translation of the Japanese biography of a Russian-Jewish pianist famous in Japan between the two World Wars – *Leo Sirota, The Pianist Who Loved Japan* by Takashi Yamamoto (First Servant Books, 2019 & 2020).

Printed in Great Britain
by Amazon

44708918R00205